NONE STOOD TALLER

The Price of Freedom

From the bestselling author of None Stood Taller

NONE STOOD TALLER

The Price of Freedom

Peter Turnham

An SOE field agent.
Audacious, charismatic, flirtatious, a ruthless assassin

Also a woman

A CIP catalogue record of this book is available from the British Library

Cover design and interior formatting by JD Smith Design

ISBN No: 978-1-7399941-0-5 (e-book)
978-1-7399941-1-2 (paperback)
978-1-7399941-2-9 (hardback)

Publisher: P&C Turnham
www.peterturnhamauthor.com

Also by Peter Turnham

None Stood Taller
From the ashes of the Blitz to the D-Day landings.
One woman's remarkable story.

None Stood Taller - The Final Year
From the D-Day landings to the VE-Day celebrations.
The final year of one woman's remarkable story.

Autumn Daffodils – Charlie's Story
We are all the product of the past, but the future is ours.

Autumn Daffodils – Joanna's Story
Joanna will break your heart, but you will forgive her.

www.peterturnhamauthor.com
peterturnham.author@gmail.com

Acknowledgements

My wonderful band of beta readers.

Cover design by Jane Dixon-Smith.

My wife Carol, my spell- and grammar-check, my editor and IT consultant, my indispensable other half.

A huge thank you to you all.

Dedication

This book is dedicated to the memory of the 39 female agents who served in Occupied France during World War Two, as members of the Special Operations Executive

Agazarian, Francine
Aisner, Julienne
Baseden, Yvonne
Beekman, Yolande *
Bloch, Denise *
Borrell, Andrée *
Butt, Sonia
Byck, Muriel *
Charlet, Blanche
Cormeau, Yvonne
Damerment, Madeleine *
De Baissac, Lise
Deveraux Rochester, Elizabeth
Fontaine, Yvonne
Granville, Christine
Hall, Virginia
Herbert, Mary
Jullian, Ginette
Khan, Noor Inayat *
Knight, Marguerite
Latour, Phyllis
Lavigne, Madeleine
Le Chene, Marie-Therese
Lefort, Cicely *
Leigh, Vera *
Nearne, Eileen
Nearne, Jacqueline
Olschanezky, Sonia *
O'Sullivan, Patricia
Plewman, Eliane *
Rolfe, Lilian *
Rowden, Diana *
Rudellat, Yvonne *
Sansom, Odette
Szabo, Violette *
Wake, Nancy
Walters, Anne-Marie
Wilen, Odette
Witherington, Pearl

*Agents who did not survive the war

Table of contents

Dear Reader

I didn't dream as a self-published author that "None Stood Taller" would become a bestseller. It has enjoyed success beyond my wildest imagination. And then, in order to bring the story to its natural conclusion on VE-Day, and to allow the characters to properly develop, a three-part series has resulted. I thank everyone who helped to make that possible, and of course I thank you, the reader. It all started with a simple idea: take a woman from the East End of London, leave her with nothing when her home is destroyed during the Blitz in 1941, and then send her out to find her way in war-torn Britain. That was when I realised it wasn't my character Lily who had to find her way in war-torn Britain - it was me!

During my research I found many extraordinary people who did extraordinary things. People such as Vera Atkins, who contributed so much towards setting up and running Section F of the SOE. Or Joan Bright who ran the secret intelligence centre in the Cabinet War Rooms under Winston Churchill. I can't take the credit for my character Lily Heywood; she already existed in those women. Lily owes more to Vera Atkins than she does to me.

The same can be said for my character Dotty. Thirty-nine women served in Occupied France as SOE field agents. Dotty owes more to those thirty-nine than anything in my imagination. Her SOE operations in Occupied France and Germany that appear in the third book may be fictitious, but the details of those operations, like everything else in this series, are grounded in reality.

If there is a single reason for the success of these books, it is that readers connect with the characters. I effectively lived the lives of these people; in many ways I feel I was there with them! These books are the result of that shared experience. I can't begin to tell you how gratifying it is when readers tell me they have shared that same experience. Over ninety percent of people who read the first book go on to read the next in the series. This is what makes it all worthwhile.

Writing would be nothing without you, dear reader; I couldn't continue without your support. Your comments and reviews are my lifeblood. Now I must move on and find another Lily, or Dotty, another historical context, another story. This is an immensely hard act to follow. I hope you will join me on that journey.Best wishes.

Peter Turnham
September 2022

https://www.peterturnhamauthor.com
peterturnham.author@gmail.com

Introduction

Following the enormous success of the "None Stood Taller" two-part series, the character of Dorothy Archer has remained the untold story. In every respect this book completes the circle. As the third and final part of the trilogy it is probably better that Dotty answers your questions rather than poses them. However, her fresh perspective of the events and characters will also offer the new reader an introduction to the "None Stood Taller" series.

Chapter One
The Train To Middlebourne

The life we live is not always ours to choose. If you think your life is defined by your place of birth and upbringing, you would be wrong. Those things define what you are, not who you are. None of us truly understands what lies within until the moment comes when everything you hold dear is threatened and your country asks a question of you. When the time comes, your answer to that question is what defines you as a person. Are you prepared to sacrifice everything in the defence of your country? I answered 'yes' without hesitation.

I'm Dorothy Bartlett, I was Archer in those days, everyone calls me Dotty. I'm no-one really, I was just a woman from the East end of London. I stepped forward like so many others, and like so many others, I didn't recognise that person. War defines us like no other event can. In its wake, when all else has been stripped away, only one thing remains. We are left with memories steeped in sorrow. Ours is knowledge that everyone should carry in their hearts. Humankind's greatest tragedy is that the collective wisdom of the ages dies with each generation. Until the next time.

It's a strange irony that the clearer those memories are, the less I choose to revisit them. The time before has been consigned to the past; it's not lost, it's eclipsed behind the shadow of war. All that remains is who I am today. My son has been told his father and I are so-called war heroes. Charlie says he is imbued with a sense of pride. How can he possibly understand? There is only one crowning achievement in my life, one enormous sense of pride, and now he wants to understand our part in the war.

I understand his desire to know the truth about us, I also know it is not within my gift. If I must, then I can only reluctantly tell him what happened. That's wholly different from understanding the truth of our wartime involvement. How can he understand that memories lie in wait behind every shadow? If I invite those memories back, they will consume me. The echoes of the past are all there, waiting patiently for me to step through the portal back into World War Two. I only have to close my eyes, and in an instant I am back to where it all began, sitting in a train carriage travelling towards Tunbridge Wells in Kent.

My rooms in East Ham are gone; a single raid in January 1941 destroyed the entire road. I emerged from the Tube station in the early hours of the morning to be confronted with a scene of total devastation. I didn't even recognise where I used to live. With only the clothes I stood in and nowhere to go except for the rest centre, what was I to do? I didn't even consider going back to my parents; they represented the last place on earth I wanted to be.

The government wanted us women to work in the factories or the Land Army, and so what better time could there be? I signed up for the Land Army because they said I would be given board and lodging with a nice family in the country. I remember the recruitment woman used those very words, 'a room with a nice family'. Her words were my motivation. I didn't understand the concept of a nice family, but it sounded inviting.

I sat in the train carriage watching the countryside move past me. With only the East End of London to compare it to, something completely alien flashed before my eyes. The rows of terraced houses were replaced with a patchwork of green, lined with trees. Cows grazed where I expected to see people, and sheep wandered like gangs of street urchins. I knew nothing about the countryside and even less about the Land Army. It all looked like a remote foreign country, but that's why it appealed to me. Whatever the countryside may be, it was a long way from East Ham!

Even the people I shared the carriage with seemed alien to me. I grew up as one of those street urchins. I might have amounted to little more than an East End "toe-rag", but everyone treated me like their best friend.

It didn't matter if I knew them or not; we were all East Enders. I didn't have the sense to realise but sitting in that carriage, I was the outsider. Tunbridge Wells is close enough to London that people commute to work; despite that, it might as well be a million miles away. One smartly dressed man in a pinstripe suit and bowler hat looked at me as if I was something he'd trodden in. Only one person spoke to me, a Londoner, a cheerful bloke.

As the train slowed, I pulled the window down and gazed out towards the rapidly approaching station. I caught sight of a clock tower before a cloud of smoke and steam obscured my view. There were complaints from my fellow passengers; I didn't understand - a whiff of smoke from the engine hardly compared to an East End smog. I wondered if all country people were so sensitive. The conductor announced Tunbridge Wells West, the end of my journey.

We gently came to a halt with a final screech of brakes and a cloud of steam. The previously sedate and polite passengers burst into life. They grabbed their overhead luggage and spilled onto the platform like sand running out of an hourglass. I momentarily joined the throng of passengers, some leaving, some waiting on the platform to board. One moment there were people everywhere, carriage doors were slamming shut, and the next moment I was the last person walking towards the exit.

"How do I get to Middlebourne?" I asked the railway porter.

"Follow that lad with the flat cap, he works at the manor," he replied.

A quick sprint and I caught up with the flat cap; a teenage boy stood beneath it. I found a likeable lad, cheeky as hell, but he met his match in me. Middlebourne village is a good half hour walk from the station, and by the time the village came into view, I had heard his entire life story. Alfie came from neighbouring Sussex. By all accounts, he really dropped on his feet when he secured himself a job as a trainee gardener at Middlebourne Manor. Change his country accent and he could have been an East End barrow boy. He seemed to know everyone, and if he couldn't get it, he knew someone who could. I wasn't sure if it was the bravado of youth, or perhaps he really was the local Mr Fix-It.

"Handy, you working in Middlebourne, Dotty," he said. "I'll be able to take you out one night."

"How old are you, Alfie?"

"I'm old enough to take you out."

"You're a cheeky bugger, you really are, just concentrate on getting me to Mrs Taylor's."

"We walked past it a couple of minutes ago, it's that thatched cottage back there."

I gave him a clip round the ear for his cheek, to which he responded with a huge grin. He walked on a few paces, then turned around.

"Don't forget, you owe me one, Dotty."

"Don't you worry, young Alfie, I've got your card marked."

Alfie proved to be quite a distraction; only when I stood outside Mrs Taylor's cottage did I realise my new adventure was about to begin. A completely new life waited for me on the other side of the door. I had no idea what that life would be or where it would take me, but I clung to the fact that here I could be whoever I wanted to be. Nobody knew me and East Ham might as well have been a million miles away. Dorothy Archer still resided somewhere among all those horrible childhood memories, but here I could just be Dotty.

I stood in wonder, looking at the rose-covered thatched cottage. The lattice windows glinted in the sun with each little pane giving a slightly different reflection. Thatch carried over the little windows in the roof, making them look for all the world like eyebrows smiling down at me. The scene before me combined with the unfamiliar fragrance of flowers and the surrounding farmland; together it conjured a magical experience. I expected Mrs Tiggy-Winkle to answer the door. Perhaps Peter Rabbit hid behind the wheelbarrow. At the very least, there must be a Tom Kitten.

I banged the heavy lionhead door knocker and waited. A little old lady appeared. She opened the door wide and raised her head to look up at me as if it was all an effort. Beneath the silver hair was a furrowed brow and a weathered face, but the sparkling eyes and warm smile seemed to belong to a younger person. By the look of her pinny, she had been doing some baking.

"Hello," I said, "I'm Dotty, I was told to come here."

I don't know what I expected, but a Cockney accent was definitely not one of them.

"Hello, luv, I've been expecting you. You must be gasping for a cup of tea, come in," she said.

I took one step inside the door when this bloody great labrador came bounding towards me, almost knocking me over.

"Spencer," she shouted, "get down, you bad dog!"

I'd always wanted a dog; he didn't frighten me in the slightest. I grabbed him by his collar and twisted it a bit, just enough to make him realise he was in trouble. As soon as he calmed down, I made a fuss of him.

"Why do you call him Spencer?"

"His full name is Spencer Tracy," she said, "well, you can guess why, can't you?"

"Yes, I get it. Well then, Spencer Tracy, I reckon you and me are going to be best mates. What do you think?"

"You'll do," she said. "Let's have that cup of tea."

I sat down in her kitchen as she pottered around, making a pot of tea. I had never seen a kitchen anything like it. You could sit at the table and still leave room to walk around it. There were copper pots and pans hanging from wooden beams, blackened by generations of smoke. Beneath them, she placed the kettle on top of a great big cast iron range. The lustrous black shine boasted a lifetime of proud polishing. She tapped the door open and dropped in a log, and for a moment, the smell of wood smoke filled the room. I sat in the warmest and most welcoming kitchen I could have imagined.

"Tell me about yourself, luv, where are you from?" she said.

"I'm a Londoner, East Ham. Well, I was; it's gone now, the bastards bombed the whole road."

"We don't use words like that in my kitchen, Dotty."

"Oh, sorry. Can I swear in the other rooms, then?"

The old girl gave me a clip round the ear! I couldn't believe it.

"No, I don't have that kind of language anywhere; besides my other girl Fiona would be mortified."

"Who's Fiona then? Is she family?"

"Of course not, she's another Land Girl. You're sharing a room with her."

"Will she mind sharing?"

"Fiona's a lovely girl, you'll like her, she's very polite."

She poured the tea into bone china cups with saucers. Then she produced a cake tin and gave me a plate, especially for putting it on. I think the look on my face answered her question without her asking me. Well, I'll tell you what, that was the finest cake I had ever eaten. We chatted away like a couple of East Enders because Margaret, it turned out, originally came from Millwall. That might have been an extraordinary seventy-odd years ago when she last lived there, but there was no doubt about her East End roots. She confirmed the old adage that you can take the woman out of the East End, but you can't take the East End out of the woman. I made my mind up there and then. I finally realised what a nice family looked like, and for once in my life, I had landed on my feet.

Lovely is the only word to describe Margaret, there's no other word for it. She might have been really old and a bit doddery, but her mind remained as "sharp as a drawer of cutlery". I'd received a clip round the ear for swearing; she told me off for leaving crumbs on the table, and you would have thought using the wrong tea towel amounted to a cardinal sin. But all the while, she smiled; she liked me, I could tell. We just seemed to connect in a way that I had never connected with an older person before. My grandmother died while I was very young and I never experienced that relationship with my parents. You don't realise something is missing from your life if you've never had it. But the opposite is also true; you realise something must have been missing when someone steps into that empty space.

As we sat laughing about something, I heard the front door open and Spencer leapt to his feet. Fiona appeared, struggling to keep the dog under control. Dressed in her Land Army overalls, she tried to undo her headscarf, if only Spencer would allow her. She removed it with her one free hand and a mass of wonderful blonde wavy hair fell out of it. I expected her to be another East Ender like me, so her reply when I introduced myself came as a surprise.

"Hello, Fiona, I'm Dotty, Dotty by name, dotty by nature."

"Oh, hello," she replied, sounding like the Queen. "Margaret told me you were coming. I'm delighted to meet you."

"I'm told we're sharing a room, is that all right?"

"Actually, I've never shared a small room before. I've shared a dormitory, but I understand from the other Land Girls that this is quite normal," she said.

"It's fine with me, I'm just grateful for a bed. Hope I don't fart in my sleep."

"Oh, good heavens! I do hope not, that wouldn't do at all."

It was all a bit of a surprise; I didn't expect a room-mate, especially one so obviously from the other side of town. I didn't see how we were going to get along at all; we were poles apart. Fiona was proper posh, she was tall and elegant, and seemed to do and say all the right things. While me on the other hand, well, I was just a "toe-rag" from East Ham. There was nothing elegant about me. Margaret was quite right though; Fiona was terribly polite. She seemed to make a virtue of being nice to me. Bloody fool that I am, it took me a while to realise. Fiona didn't pretend to be nice; she *was* nice!

They both showed me to our room, where I stood with wide eyes. To my amazement, we had a bed each! I thought sharing meant sharing top and tail. It might have been inferior for Fiona, but I had never enjoyed such luxury before. I even had my own chest of drawers, and a clothes rail, you know, like in a clothes shop. I hardly had anything to put in the drawers, and even less to put on the rail, but if I did, I had my own hanging space. Fiona smiled at my reaction; or maybe she was just being nice again.

I soon realised that we would have to do the cooking and cleaning. I didn't really know how to cook, but I could make up for that with energy and enthusiasm. I had lots of that. As I set about scrubbing spuds, Fiona disappeared into the scullery to have a bath. When Margaret told me she had a bath every night, I couldn't believe it.

"You mean she has a proper hot bath every night? You've got a bathtub?"

"It's only the old tin bath," Margaret replied, "but farm work is a filthy business, especially working with the animals. You will be the same, you'll need a bath." She noticed my expression. "You're not used to having a bath, are you, Dotty?"

"No, it's been a stand-up wash for me."

"You've had a rough time, haven't you, luv? It's nothing to be ashamed of, you know, life does that to you sometimes."

"Does it show that much?"

"No one else would notice."

"But you did, didn't you?"

"The more you live, the more you see, and the more you see, the more you understand about life. Don't you worry, luv, you're safe here."

I can't explain what came over me. I hardly knew the old girl, but I put my arms around her. Fiona stepped out of the scullery wrapped in a towel and enveloped in a cloud of steam. I felt a bit embarrassed standing with my arms around Margaret, but somehow it didn't matter. She breezed past us in her elegant fashion.

“Margaret has a way of getting to you, doesn’t she?” she said with a smile.

Well, she certainly got to me, Margaret read me like a book. Nobody ever cared much for me. It took a stranger to show me I might be worth caring about. The moment passed without further mention. I didn’t realise it then, but that lovely old lady would become really important to me. I continued scrubbing the spuds. Fiona returned looking like a different woman, even more elegant and sophisticated. For all that she acted like Lady Muck, she wasn’t afraid to get on with the chores.

They amazed me with how much we had to eat. Being used to rationing in London, to me this amounted to something entirely different. It was rationing, but not rationing as I remembered it. Apparently, the black market in the countryside is not so much black, more a kind of fresh sausage colour. They told me it could even be a Sunday roast colour on special occasions. It was a revelation I can tell you. I hadn’t eaten so well since I couldn’t remember when. Fiona agreed, life in the country had its advantages.

“You don’t get bombed either,” I said. “I keep expecting to hear the siren.”

“We had it bad in Chelsea, but I think you had it far worse in the East End. Was it awful, Dotty?”

“I can’t tell you how awful. I went down the Tube every night, that was bad enough. When I came out in the mornings, I saw some terrible things, I mean things that keep me awake at night.”

“We’re so lucky living here. I can’t imagine how horrible it must be,” said Margaret.

“You don’t want to imagine it, believe me. I’ve seen people so traumatised they couldn’t even speak. I didn’t know what genuine pain was until I saw a mother who’d lost her child.”

“How did you cope with it?” Fiona asked.

“It never ceases to amaze me how strong the people of the East End are. They call it the spirit of the Blitz and believe me, it’s real. You can feel it everywhere you go. I don’t know what Hitler hopes to achieve by killing thousands of us, but it’s not going to work. The worse it gets, the stronger that spirit seems to be. He’ll never break us.”

“Well said, Dotty,” replied Margaret, “and you can do your bit here on the land. The nation needs feeding.”

“I would rather put a knife to that bastard’s throat, but I suppose growing spuds is important.”

"What did I tell you, Dotty, about language in my kitchen?"

"Sorry, Margaret, but it really pisses me off…oh, sorry."

"Actually, Dotty, I quite agree with you," said Fiona. "I wouldn't normally express it in those terms myself, but it pisses me off as well. Sorry, Margaret! I wish we could do more but growing food for the nation is important. Reg desperately needs help with all the men in the army."

"Who's Reg?"

"He's the farmer you will work for."

"What's he like?"

"He's a grumpy old devil, but I suspect beneath it all he's got a heart of gold. I just haven't seen it yet."

"He will have to teach me everything, I haven't got a clue about farming."

"Don't worry, neither have I. It's ninety percent hard work, and trust me, Reg will work you until you drop."

"I'll have a surprise for Reg, then. He won't make me drop."

"You sound very confident."

"I used to run a lot as a young girl, I had so much anger, I just ran until I could run no more. Someone told me about an organisation called the Women's Amateur Athletics Association, the WAAA, and I ended up joining an athletics club. Well, the long and short of it was that it proved to be the only thing I'm any good at."

"Why were you angry?"

"I didn't get on at home, everything seemed to make me angry. I don't talk about it. What did you do, Fiona, before you joined the Land Army?"

"That's the problem, I did nothing. I went to finishing school, you can imagine how well that prepared me for the Land Army!"

"Crickey, I've never met anyone who went to finishing school."

"Your athletics club is far more useful, believe me. Did you win any competitions?"

"I competed once at the White City Stadium. It was three years ago, a national women's competition. I came third in the quarter mile race."

"You mean you came third in a national event? That's amazing."

"Well, I suppose I did. There wasn't much competition, if you ask me, and I didn't take it seriously, not like most of the other girls."

"Reg is really going to love you!"

Chapter Two
Reg's Farm

Sharing a bedroom with a stranger felt a bit awkward at first for Fiona. It was not something she had ever experienced. It didn't bother me. I never had a proper bedroom to myself until I left home, and even then I shared it with the bugs and the roaches. Fiona spent a long time brushing her hair and putting on face cream. A quick wash in the scullery and I wished Margaret good night. I made my way up the "apples and pears", quickly followed by Spencer.

"I don't allow him in the bedrooms, Dotty," Margaret shouted.

"Well, I should think not, he's a boy dog, isn't he? Let a boy in your room and you can't get rid of them."

"Dotty, really!"

"Sorry, Margaret." Pointing at Spencer, I gave him one of my looks. "Goodnight you soppy dog, I'll see you in the morning."

A tired voice came out of the bedroom. "What did he say, Dotty?"

"He said he can't help being soppy, he's just a dog, but he's going to guard our virtue all night."

"Go to bed, Dotty."

"Sorry, Margaret, I'm going."

It had been a very long day. I was "cream-crackered", but I quickly realised that farming was even more exhausting. When I went into the bedroom Fiona tried to make conversation, but the ongoing battle with her eyelids had already been lost. Despite my tiredness, I lay awake for a while, my mind racing in all directions. Fiona was so nice to me, and

Margaret welcomed me so warmly, I had never eaten so well, and I even had my own bed with no bugs in it.

For once in my life, despite everything I left behind, I had come up smelling of roses. This was definitely what they called a nice family. The Dotty part of me just wanted to embrace it, but the Dorothy Archer part from East Ham, well, she was wary. Nothing is ever what it seems, I told myself, nothing lasts. The following morning, I happily made up for the hours I laid awake, until Fiona gave me a shake.

"It's six o'clock, Dotty, come along."

"It's still dark, I'm asleep."

"Not any longer, it's time to get up."

I struggled up, grateful for the recently installed electric light. Desperate for a wee, I made my way down the stairs only to be accosted by Spencer. He had one particularly annoying activity. He would stick his head between your legs with great enthusiasm.

"Not now, Spencer; I'm in a hurry. Oh, for Christ's sake, piss off, you silly dog."

"I heard that, Dotty."

"Sorry, Margaret, he seems to like me."

When I returned from the outside privy I was absolutely frozen. They were both fully dressed, and I realised immediately how comical I must have looked going outside in my nightdress. There were so many lessons for me to learn about life in the country, the privy at the bottom of the garden being among the first. Margaret's kitchen welcomed me back like a hot water bottle. The smell of bacon cooking in the frying pan, the kettle whistling on the range. I could hardly wait to put on my Land Army uniform and get back down those stairs. As I approached the breakfast table, I took a deep breath, almost afraid I might wake up and find myself back in East Ham. I cut through the egg and the yolk ran out over the fried bread. I suddenly became aware that both of them were looking at me, smiling.

"What?" I asked.

"Nothing, luv," replied Margaret. "I've just never seen anyone so happy at the sight of an egg before."

"Well, this might be normal for you, but it's a real treat for me."

"You enjoy it, Dotty," said Fiona, "I'll start on our sandwiches."

They had a routine worked out for breakfast, which I tried to fit into. The routine left no time to relax; the next thing I knew, we were marching down the road with the sound of Spencer wishing us farewell receding into the distance behind us. With spring beginning to make its presence known, sunrise wouldn't be far behind. I'm not sure how my senses would have reacted to Reg's farm in the dark. We certainly had our share of nasty smells in East Ham, but nothing could prepare you for the overpowering stink of cow shit. Reg, Fiona told me, had a dairy herd, and they came into the yard twice a day.

"I think I might have guessed that," I said.

"It's awful isn't it, but you get used to it," Fiona replied. "Reg can't even smell it. He's already milked them this morning, he will be just finishing his breakfast."

"What time does he start, then?"

"Four o'clock."

"Oh, my goodness, that's a long day."

Just at that moment, the door to the house opened, and Reg appeared. Us city folk have our own idea of how a farmer should look, you know, a flat cap with a bit of straw sticking out the side. Well, Reg appeared wearing exactly that. He wore a blue bib and brace tucked inside his wellies, and an ancient threadbare jacket. His flat cap actually had a piece of straw sticking out of it. Reg might have been the archetypal farmer, but I also fitted his exact image of a towney dressed in my brand-new Land Army outfit. He looked at me as if in complete despair.

"I'm Dotty," I said, apprehensively.

"Yes, I can see you are. First time in the country, I suppose." His expression said a lot.

"That's right, I've never stood ankle deep in cow shit before. But I bet you've never been forced to sleep at night in a Tube station."

"Why would I want to do that?"

"Same reason I'm standing in cow shit. We do what we have to do."

I don't know why I felt the need to demonstrate that he couldn't intimidate me, but he wasn't. Fiona probably knew from past experience not to dwell on such matters.

"What do you want us to do today then, Reg?" asked Fiona.

He stood silent for a moment, looking me up and down. "You can carry on cleaning out the milking parlour, Fiona. I'm going to show Dotty how to dig post holes."

We followed him towards one of the sheds. Me and Fiona walked several steps behind him.

"He's testing you," Fiona whispered. "He did this to me; he likes us to realise how useless we are."

"What do you mean?"

"Digging post holes is really hard work. He doesn't expect you to dig many."

"We'll see about that."

Fiona made her way into the milking parlour, where I suspected the stink became even worse. I followed Reg into a field where a line of wooden posts lay on the ground. He produced a ball of string and a post-digging spade.

"Right," he said, "stretch this string from the end of this fence down the side of the field and tie it onto that tree in the corner there. That stick leaning on the fence is six feet long. You use that as a measure between post holes. You use the string to keep your posts in line. I want each post to be two feet into the ground, got it?"

"Got it. What about that great big mallet? Can I bang them in with that?"

"If you can lift it, you can use that for the final fixing."

"I can do that, Reg, leave it with me."

As he walked off, he left me with an expression that said, you won't get far doing this. Not having any other attributes to call upon, I remained determined to prove him wrong. I marched down the field with the ball of string and quickly set up my line. Digging the holes wasn't that difficult at first. The trick is keeping the soil on the narrow spade, so the deeper the hole is, the harder it becomes. The big wooden mallet took some lifting, but I managed to thump it down onto the post. I missed the post once or twice and nearly did myself a mischief, but I gradually got the hang of it. By lunch time, I reached the halfway point. I looked up to see Fiona in the distance beckoning me with a wave.

If the truth be told, my body ached all over; in fact, I would have been hard pressed to find a bit of my body that didn't hurt. I admitted it to Fiona, but I wasn't about to let Reg know. Fiona produced our sandwiches and a cup of tea from our thermos flask; I never realised cheese and pickles could taste so good. We were both covered in muck and I had no doubt my face must have been just as rosy as Fiona's, but we both sat there smiling.

"How are you getting on with the fence posts?" Fiona asked.

"I think I'm doing well; I've done about half of them. If my body doesn't seize up, I hope I can finish it today."

"Reg is really going to love you. When you get to know him, he's actually not so bad. He has a really hard life; it must have been difficult for him when he lost his farm labourers. Then to be faced with women like us who understand nothing about it - I don't wonder that he's a bit miserable at times."

"You almost make me feel sorry for him, Fi. But I can see what you mean, starting at four o'clock every morning, that's hard."

"Then he has to milk the cows again this evening, his day isn't finished until about seven o'clock."

"You're right, Fi, I do feel sorry for him, that's a long hard day."

"Finding it hard going, are you, Dotty?" asked Reg, who appeared as if out of nowhere.

"No, Reg. I was talking about your day; you work bloody hard."

"That's not hard, that's just farming."

"Well, you've got us now, and don't think we can't be helpful. I can work as hard as any man."

"We'll see about that, but don't think I'm not grateful."

"That's a big admission for you, Reg," said Fiona.

"I watched you this morning digging those post holes. Do you think I don't know how your back aches, Dotty? Or how your arms hurt swinging that mallet. I've never seen a woman swing a post hammer like that. Credit to you."

"I'll have that fence finished this afternoon."

"I think you just might," he replied.

I have no idea how I kept going that afternoon, but I let nothing beat me, including that last fence post. When we walked home that evening, I struggled to put one foot in front of the other. The only thing that kept me going was the smile on my face. We were both as tired as each other. Fiona didn't do as much physical work as me, but neither was she as physically capable. The moment we set foot indoors, I realised why Fi needed a bath every night. The expression on Margaret's face as she stood looking at the pair of us said it all. We were filthy!

"Which of you is going first, then?" asked Margaret.

"What do you mean, Margaret?" Fi replied.

"Who's having the first bathwater?"

A sudden silence descended upon Fiona as she realised we would have to share the bathwater. The last time I had a bath was when I could fit into the kitchen sink! Sharing the water didn't sound like a problem to me, but for someone posh like Fiona, it must have been a bit of a nightmare.

"You go first, Fi, I'm filthier than you."

"Oh, thank you, Dotty. Are you sure?"

"You go ahead, but don't take too long."

When my turn came, I can't tell you how much I enjoyed it. I put an extra bucket of hot water from the copper into the tub. It didn't bother me in the slightest that Fiona had sat in it. This was my first experience of a proper bath, and I'll never forget it. I would have happily shared the water with the entire village. The fire in the grate under the copper kept the scullery really warm; I couldn't see how a bath might have been any better. I just lay there, feeling like the Queen must feel on bath nights. Without my aches and pains, I suspect I might have fallen asleep.

Fiona filled the bath, so I had to empty it, a bucket at a time. I wouldn't normally have noticed the weight of those buckets, but that evening I struggled to lift them half full. Eventually, clean and dressed and feeling human again, I joined them in the kitchen. I did my bit towards the evening meal, and I have to say I had never felt hungrier. Margaret asked lots of questions and was terribly concerned that Reg shouldn't work me too hard. Fiona sang my praises; she said she had never seen a woman do such heavy work without complaint.

"Don't you let Reg take advantage of you, Dotty, because he will, you know."

"Don't worry about me, Margaret. I used to do a bit of bartending in the evenings. I'm well used to men trying to take advantage of me."

"Oh no, Reg wouldn't do that! No, I mean working you too hard."

"It's all the same to me, Margaret. I can deal with Reg."

"I noticed that today," said Fiona, "you twisted him around your little finger. I wish I could do that."

"Where did you learn to fix that water pump, Fi?"

"Mechanical things interest me; I surprise myself really. I'm not as clever as Reg thinks I am; I cheat, you see. Margaret's nephew Jim is an engineer, and he lives two doors along. When I need to understand how anything works, I ask Jim, he's a treasure."

There was so much more to Fiona than I first realised. I didn't know any posh women; I didn't dream that we would get on so well together. We are almost complete opposites. She is well educated, clever, and absolutely charming, all the things I'm not. I assumed at first that she just politely tolerated me, but I soon realised how genuine her friendship was. If you told me when I arrived we would be friends for life, I would have been amazed.

I got on like a house on fire with Fi and Margaret. I even had Reg convinced he couldn't do without me. Fi was right about him; he did have a heart of gold. And so my life in Middlebourne progressed, we worked hard and had little time off, but never once did we stop smiling. After the war, of the thousands of women who worked in the WLA, nearly all agreed. They had never worked harder and never enjoyed themselves so much.

In April 1941, Margaret told us her granddaughter would be coming to stay with us. She often mentioned Lily, they were obviously very close. The prospect of Lily staying with us filled her with joy, Margaret literally counted down the days. Apparently she had been bombed out of her home in Stepney and needed to get away from London for a bit. I could empathise with that, all right.

Fi and I didn't think about it very much, it just sounded like a family visit. Lily would have to share our room, which meant Fi and I would have to double up. Fi's reaction to that caused a bit of a laugh, but it wasn't really going to be a problem. Life progresses in incremental steps marked by events. Sometimes the big events are all too obvious. It can be great joy or desperate sadness that defines the moment, but usually we know when we reach a fork in the road. Neither Fiona nor I realised Lily's arrival would change our lives so profoundly.

Chapter Three
Lily Arrives

I arrived back from a day mucking out the pigs, so naturally I would be second in the bath. Fiona went immediately into the scullery to have the first bath while I went straight upstairs. Imagine my surprise when I walked into the bedroom to find a complete stranger standing there.

"Oh shit, I didn't realise you were here yet! You're the old girl's granddaughter. I should've tidied up a bit."

"Hello, I'm Lily."

"I'm Dotty. Dotty by name, dotty by nature. Bloody 'ell, look at you. How do you keep your hair looking like that?"

"Well, I try to make a bit of an effort."

"Bloody 'ell, what must you think of me, then?"

Lily was something, I can tell you; talk about first impressions. She wore a simple pleated skirt and a woollen top, nice but nothing special. Something else about her stopped me in my tracks; she seemed to fill the room. Not as tall as me, and about three years older in her late twenties. The woman who stood in front me was certainly attractive, but not one of those drop-dead gorgeous women we all secretly envy. It wasn't even her great shock of red hair that so impressed me. It was the way she looked at me. Her eyes are more green than hazel, but they progressively become a golden brown towards the pupil. When Lily looks at you, she appears to be staring, even though she isn't.

I couldn't believe that a posh-looking woman like that came from the East End. The moment Lily spoke to me, well, I couldn't "Adam and Eve" it! Lily is an East Ender, exactly like me. There's no doubting it. Lily is way more clever than me, and whatever sophistication is, she has it in spades. But make no mistake, beneath all that refinement, we came out of the same mould. She's had all the rough edges removed, that's all.

"What *is* that stuff you're covered in? It smells awful!" she asked.

"Oh, this? This is pig shit; you soon get used to it." Lily graciously smiled at me, even though I must have looked awful. "You're from the East End, which part?"

"Stepney," she replied.

"You never are! I'm from East Ham, just down the road."

The moment we started talking, we had so much in common. I couldn't stop asking her questions. She might come from the East End, but I quickly realised Lily was way above my league. She said she managed her uncle's shipping agency at the Victoria Dock. I didn't even understand what that meant, but I knew if Lily did it, then it must have been important. When I told her I served in a shop, she was interested in what I did.

"We'll get on fine, you and me, Dotty," Lily said, "but there's just one thing."

"I know, but you get used to it, trust me," I laughed as I stepped out of my overalls.

"Do you want a bath tonight, Lily? I reckon you better go next if you want one. We have a system, you see, cleanest goes first. Fi's been repairing the stables today, so she's okay. We can guess who's going to be last!"

What a stupid thing to ask, of course someone like Lily didn't want to share the bath water with the likes of me. She looked horrified at the prospect, but somehow my silly question didn't matter. I stood there in my underwear with pig shit on my arms and face, but none of it mattered. We were both from the East End of London. We were poles apart in many respects, but so close where it really mattered. I had not the slightest doubt about it; we were going to get on really well together. We went downstairs and as soon as Fi came out of the scullery, I introduced her to Lily. Just as it surprised me to find that Lily really did come from the East End, I think she was equally surprised to find that Fiona didn't.

"This is going to be a nightmare for you, Fi," I said, "you've got two of us Cockney girls to contend with now."

"I'm sure that's not true, Fiona. I'm delighted to meet you."

"We have heard so much about you from your grandmother, Lily. I'm sorry we have commandeered your bedroom."

"We'll have to share, I hope you don't mind," Lily replied.

"You're lucky to have a bedroom to share," said Margaret. "The country's full of homeless people, far worse off than you."

"Thank you for reminding us, Gran, you're quite right."

"Yes, thank you, Margaret, but at least the homeless don't have to share a bed with Dotty," laughed Fiona.

I was heading for the bath, so I gave Fiona a big hug as I walked past. She recoiled in horror, as she always did.

"Nothing wrong with a bit of pig shit, Fi."

"*Dotty,* I've told you about that language in my kitchen."

"Sorry, Margaret."

"Quite right, Margaret," Fiona said, "you might even make a lady out of her."

"Not much chance of that, is there, Gran?" I replied.

"I'm not your grandmother, Dorothy."

"I lost my Gran years ago, in fact I can't really remember her, so now that we've got Lily here, I'm going to adopt you as my Gran instead."

"That's a great idea," replied Fi, "you've got three granddaughters now, Margaret."

I could tell that Margaret was happy at the prospect of us all calling her Gran, so I gave her a big hug as well.

"Get away," she shouted, "get in that bath!"

Spencer decided the time had arrived to come and pester me. To everyone's amusement, I struggled towards the scullery with Spencer in hot pursuit.

"Piss off, Spencer, find yourself a proper girlfriend."

"*Dotty.*"

I knew Gran intended the usual reprimand, but she couldn't say it for laughter. When I finished my bath, I made an effort to dress up a bit; Lily had that effect on me. I made a grand entrance at the kitchen door.

"Ta-da, see! Do I clean up well or what?"

"You certainly do," replied Lily.

"It's an illusion," said Fi, "she's still Dotty."

"I'm not going to do or say the wrong thing for at least ten minutes,"

I said, putting my arm around Lily. "You're outnumbered now, Fi."

"I suppose you're right, Dorothy," she said. "I'll just have to make the best of it, I suppose; but don't expect me to talk like you!"

The entire kitchen filled with the aroma of roast lamb, which for me was such a distant memory, I wasn't sure if it was a memory at all. Obviously Gran intended laying on something special for Lily. We were treated to roast potatoes and Brussels sprouts; I had never eaten a meal like it. Lily appeared equally surprised; she was used to rationing the same as me. Gran assured us it was all home produce. When Lily remarked that we didn't have a flock of sheep, Gran gave her one of her looks.

"You tell me off, Gran, for the odd swear word, but here you are supporting the black market."

"This isn't black market, Dotty!" Gran replied, looking terribly indignant. "This was from Reg. I didn't pay for it."

"So what did Reg get in return?" asked Lily.

"He didn't pay to have Jim service his tractor."

"So if money doesn't change hands," I said, "it's not black market."

"Of course not," Gran said.

We all sat smiling. Black market or not, I've never forgotten the meal we shared that night. Thank heaven for the country's barter system. What an evening we had, Lily fitted straight in, we chatted away endlessly. Fi and Lily were about the same age. As soon as we realised Lily was married, I looked at Fi, who looked back with a resigned expression. She only felt left on the shelf when someone her age reminded her of it. I knew Fi wanted to be married, she just hadn't met the right man. As for me, well, I didn't do relationships, not permanent ones. There was only room for one on my shelf.

It soon became clear that Lily had been through a bad time. When she told us about how she had been bombed and buried alive, I really felt for her. The events she described were nothing new to me; I'm afraid people like her neighbour, together with their children, were being killed every day during the Blitz. Fiona and Gran were horrified, while Lily and I shared an understanding expression. The East End spirit of the Blitz was alive and well in Middlebourne. When it came time for bed, Lily kissed Gran goodnight, and without thinking I did the same, as did Fiona.

"What's all this, you silly girls? Be off with you!" Gran said, her smile illuminating the room as she hastened us up the stairs.

We sat on our beds, desperately tired but wanting to continue our conversations. Suddenly it dawned on Fi that she was about to share with me.

"Oh, God! I've just realised I'm sharing with you, Dotty," Fiona said, half serious and half smiling.

"Could be worse, Fi, it could be that randy bastard Spencer."

I struggled to get my nightclothes on for laughing. We sat in bed and looked at each other, and in an instant we burst into laughter again. At the end of a long day working on the farm, there is no finer feeling than easing your aching back by lying down in bed. We each struggled to stay awake, there was so much more to ask Lily about.

"Tell us about this husband of yours," Fi asked, "do you hope to have children?"

Lily's frank reply surprised me. She admitted that they only married because she found herself "in the club"! Then, just weeks after the wedding, she lost the baby. Gerry was serving on HMS Hood, so he was unable to support her at all after their house had been bombed. She wouldn't see him for many weeks and didn't even know when he would be due shore leave. Fiona didn't admit it, but I knew she would be quietly mortified that Lily had been forced to get married. Fi is nothing if not a prude. We must have talked for half an hour, but all the while we were battling to stay awake. As soon as I realised mine was the only voice left in the room, my eyes closed as well. At breakfast the following morning we resumed our conversation, Fi asked Lily what her plans were, and her reply came as a surprise.

"Well, I've thought about it; I think I'll join you girls - I'll join the Land Army."

"I'll talk to Reg," I said, "he's always complaining that he doesn't have enough farm labour. You have a word with Jim - he knows about getting you signed up."

"What are you smiling at, Dotty?" Lily asked.

"I can't wait to see you covered in pig shit, Lily! You really will be Lady Muck then!"

It proved to be a fateful decision for Lily. I'm not sure if she came to Middlebourne intending to stay or not, I suspect not. Joining the Land Army proved to be the first step of a long journey for each of us. We didn't realise it then, but we each embarked upon a journey which always returned us to Middlebourne. Lily joined the WLA, and one evening when Fi and I returned home after another long day, we found her showing off her new uniform.

"You're supposed to look like a farm worker, not a bloody fashion model," I said with a wry smile.

"At least that's something you'll never be accused of Dotty; I've never seen a fashion model covered in pig shit!" Fiona said.

"*Fiona*, did I hear you say *shit?"* Lily laughed.

"Oh, my goodness, I did! What a dreadful effect you're having on me, Dotty."

"No, that can't be me, I wouldn't say a thing like that, it must be Lily."

Needless to say, Lily didn't stay looking like a fashion model. Reg, true to form, had her clearing ditches on her first day! We warned Lily about Reg's version of an initiation ceremony, but for her it proved to be a baptism of fire. That evening Lily returned home absolutely shattered. So exhausted, in fact, she didn't even complain about sharing the bath water. I smiled at Fi as Lily walked towards the scullery, carrying her towel beneath her arm. Every step required a monumental effort, while her unfocused gaze appeared oblivious to the surroundings.

I did Lily's share towards the evening meal, and this became the pattern of our daily life. Neither Fi nor Lily was really cut out to be a farm labourer. Whenever anything extra needed to be done, or whenever the work became particularly hard, it was always me they looked towards. I didn't mind; the three of us became such close friends, I would have done anything for them. It didn't really come as a surprise when Fiona showed interest in an advert in the local paper. There was a job vacancy at Middlebourne Manor, some kind of administrative position. Of us three, Fi was the least suited to farm work, so we both encouraged her to apply for the job.

As soon as she agreed, we all became very enthusiastic about it. When the letter arrived from the manor inviting her to attend for an interview, I'm not sure who was the more excited. Someone needed to cover for Fi at the farm, and of course, that would be me. She marched off towards the interview, looking absolutely lovely and full of confidence. With all of her private education and finishing school, I was in no doubt she would be offered the job. The moment she returned to the farm, Lily and I pounced on her, wanting to hear every detail.

Fi didn't stop talking about it. His Lordship conducted the interview personally. When she wasn't talking about the job or the manor, she talked about His Lordship.

"What's the old boy like, Fi?" I asked.

"Well, that's the thing," she replied, "he isn't an elderly gentleman, he's in his early thirties, and terribly charming."

We prised every detail out of her. He sounded wonderful, and the job sounded ideal, so we simply assumed Fiona would be offered the position. It came as something of a surprise, therefore, when the letter arrived politely informing her that on this occasion she had been unsuccessful. If Fi felt upset, she hid it well. We laughed it off, saying it was probably a lousy job anyway and no doubt beneath her.

It seemed likely, however, that the truth might be the exact opposite; the job sounded really demanding. He made it clear to Fiona that he required some very special qualities in the applicant. Someone with a sharp analytical mind, the ability to make quick decisions and to act upon them. Above all, he wanted someone who would inspire others in a leadership role. The more Fiona recounted her conversation, the more it became obvious he was describing Lily.

I'd met Elsie Morgan on a couple of occasions. She worked as the housekeeper at the manor, so I took matters into my own hands. One evening after work, I ran across the fields to the manor and knocked on the servants' entrance. Elsie's a good sort, she offered me a cup of tea and a piece of cake.

"What brings you here, Dotty?" she asked.

"It's about the job that His Lordship advertised in the local paper, the administrative job."

"Are you going to apply, then?"

"Don't be silly, of course not. My friend Fiona applied, but she was turned down. The thing is, Elsie, I know someone who would be ideal for the position, and I'm wondering if you would be able to arrange an interview for her?"

"It's not for me to arrange such things, but I could mention it to His Lordship. Who is this person? Why do you say she would be suitable?"

"She's Margaret Taylor's granddaughter, Lily Heywood. Lily's the smartest woman I've ever met. She used to run a big multinational shipping company. Whatever His Lordship is looking for, Lily can do it."

"You're very confident about her, Dotty."

"I am! Lily's…well, I've not met anyone like her before. She's a bit special, and she's my friend."

"With a recommendation like that, I will have to mention her to His Lordship."

"I owe you one, Elsie; by the way, this is a lovely cake."

True to her word, Elsie mentioned it, and she even sent young Alfie, the trainee gardener, to tell me. Fiona answered the door, escorted by Spencer Tracy. She came back with an enormous grin on her face.

"You've got an admirer at the door, Dotty. A very young admirer!"

"What? Who is it?"

"He says he's Alfie, a friend of yours."

I went to the front door to find him standing there, as cheeky as ever.

"I've been sent with a message, but first I need to know when I'm taking you out?"

"You really are a cheeky little sod, Alfie, just give me the message."

"Mrs Morgan says your friend can come tomorrow at nine o'clock in the morning."

"Thank you, Alfie. I'll make you a promise. When you've grown into a nice young man, I'll have a drink with you."

"I'll keep you to that," he said, leaving with a mischievous grin on his face.

"Don't forget," I shouted after him, "I said a nice young man, not the cheeky little bugger who just called."

I chose my moment that evening to tell Lily. At first she didn't believe me, then she became really cross with me. When I said she needed to be there at nine o'clock the following morning, she went into a right old strop. She looked at me with those staring eyes of hers and for the first time I worried that I might have stepped over the line. Certain she would be thrown out, she blamed me for what she said would be a terrible humiliation. I suppose I didn't really give her much of an option, but I was sure she would get the job.

I covered for her the next morning, and she left home dressed in her WLA overalls because she needed to return directly to the farm. I was far more nervous than Lily, I really would be in trouble if it all went "pear-shaped". The moment Lily returned to the farm it became obvious that it did not go well. My heart sank. I'd never seen Lily so annoyed, more like incandescent. She was hopping mad with His Lordship, and equally as mad with me for arranging it. I felt terrible.

"What went wrong?" Fiona asked.

"Everything! He is the most arrogant, insufferable man I have ever met."

"That doesn't sound like the man I met."

"Oh, believe me, Fi, I've never been treated with such contempt. And it's all your fault, Dotty."

"I'm sorry, I did it with good intentions, Lily. I thought you were bound to get the job. I told Elsie Morgan you were the smartest person I know, which is true. And I told her you ran a big multinational shipping agency."

"What! No wonder he didn't believe me. Oh, Dotty, you idiot. I ran the business for Uncle George, but we only had one office and a handful of staff."

"So what happened, Lily?" Fi asked. "He didn't actually throw you out, did he?"

"He did. I've never been so humiliated or treated with such utter disdain."

We discussed it all that evening until she calmed down a little. It seems the interview resulted in a series of confusions, and none of them was favourable to Lily. His Lordship took one look at her dressed in her WLA uniform and assumed she was applying for a farm job. One thing led to another and Lily lost her temper. She ended up telling him just what she thought of him. I wish I had been there to see it. I could just imagine Lily with her flashing eyes giving him what-for. We did eventually laugh about it.

"Am I forgiven, Lily? I meant well."

"Yes, I suppose so."

"Well, some good has come of it. I've learned some great new words. He was arrogant as well as insufferable. Best of all, he treated you with utter disdain; I really like that word. I've made a note of that."

"I've got no option, have I, Dotty. How could I not forgive you?"

Chapter Four
Meeting His Lordship

As it turned out, that wasn't the end of it, fate had another destiny for Lily. I've come to realise that life is like that. You rarely see it coming; an event can drop out of the blue and change your life forever. This was one of those events, and it changed not only Lily's life; it changed all of our lives. It started when Lily received a letter from His Lordship, requesting that she re-attend at the manor. It was all a bit of a mystery; we assumed she had overstepped the mark to such an extent that His Lordship wanted to put her in her place.

Lily made more of an effort with her appearance this time. I think she went with the full intention of giving him another salvo of East End rhetoric. Well, you should have seen her face when she came back. One moment, His Lordship had been the most insufferable man on the planet, the next moment he had become utterly adorable. He offered Lily the job of managing his estate!

At that stage, none of us knew exactly what Lily's new job really entailed, and that included Lily. One thing remained obvious to me, if Lily could manage a shipping agency, then she could manage His Lordship's estate. Of course, she had no idea that the job as described amounted to that one-eighth of an iceberg that sits above the water level. What Lily certainly didn't know, what none of us knew, was that her new job wasn't just about to change her life forever. Fate had something else in store for all three of us.

Our only thought was to go to the pub and celebrate. We had

Saturday afternoons off and no sooner had we washed and changed than we were walking towards the pub. The Forge Pub was charming in every respect. It had obviously been the local blacksmith's forge at one time and remained a lovely old building, still with the original blacksmith's canopy over the fireplace. The blackened oak beams spoke of a time when smoke from the forge was a constant companion. We stepped through the door and were met by a crowd of smiling faces, including a bunch of airmen. They caught my eye, so I acted without thinking, immediately walking over to them.

"I know what you boys want," I said, flashing my big brown eyes.

In those days, I did that kind of thing all the time. The fact that I could have them eating out of the palm of my hand within ten seconds meant I had a sort of power over them. I think if the truth be told, I enjoyed the fact that I could manipulate them; it empowered me.

"And what do you think we want, then?" one of them answered.

"You want to buy me and my friends a drink? I knew the second I saw you."

They looked over towards Lily and Fiona and obviously thought Christmas had come early. We quickly found ourselves sitting at a table with them, and sure enough, they bought us a pint each. Fiona, especially, pretended to be mortified at my cheek, while Lily couldn't help smiling at me. To be honest, they were a lovely bunch of flyers, not your average pub rowdies. We just seemed to hit it off together, Lily and I had great fun with them.

One of them, a handsome pilot called Johnny, couldn't take his eyes off Fiona. Fi got that all the time; we often wondered if people mistook her for Ingrid Bergman, she's really lovely. You might think it would give her confidence but Fi was always very reserved as far as men were concerned. So, you can imagine my surprise when she appeared to be drowning in Johnny's eyes. The pair of them couldn't take their eyes off each other.

When the lads had to leave, me and Lily kissed them all, but Fi wouldn't let Johnny out of her arms. The boys had to prise them apart, and when they finally drove off, Fi looked as if she had lost a pound and found a shilling. If you'd told me then that Johnny was to be her future husband, do you know, I don't think it would have surprised me. Needless to say, she was full of it; the reserved and terribly polite Fiona had thrown caution to the wind. We'd already drunk far too much, but when I suggested we go back into the pub and have another, they foolishly agreed.

What happened next is the incident that Lily and Fi love to remind me about. Much to their amusement, I made a complete and utter fool of myself. I'd drunk so much, I even had trouble walking to the Ladies. How could I have known it was Lord Middlebourne? I'd never seen the bloke. All I could see was this really dishy looking fella sat at one of the tables. Well, apparently I did my usual, I told him I knew what he wanted. Except it didn't work, did it! I must have said a lot of things that I wish I hadn't, because His Lordship soon had enough of me. This is when he came out with that immortal line that they keep quoting back at me.

"You have made a serious misjudgement, Madam. I can assure you I would rather have Hitler as my father-in-law than be acquainted with you."

I'll never live it down, will I? They helped me home, where I promptly threw up in the garden. It's true what they say, it wasn't my finest moment. The next morning they had great fun at my expense. It was May 24th, 1941, just another day on the calendar until we heard the terrible news that, after a brief encounter with the German battleship Bismarck during the Battle of the Denmark Strait, HMS Hood had been sunk. I'd seen so much death and suffering during the Blitz, you just had to distance yourself from other people's pain. When that pain belongs to your dearest friend, well, that's altogether different. Poor Lily, there were 1418 men on board the Hood, and only three survived; Gerry was not one of them.

She screamed as if death had taken her as well. The sobbing woman in our arms wasn't Lily! She was all that remains when every vestige of hope has gone. She had no body, no funeral, nothing to commemorate Gerry's departure from this life. There is always a point when the past ends and the future begins, but Lily had her own way of dealing with death. She firmly believed the grim reaper had one hand on her shoulder. Her way of dealing with it was to fight back, and if the cold hand of death has ever met its match, then it must surely be Lily. Towards the end of the week, she returned to the farm, insisting Reg gave her the hardest job he could find.

Fi and I watched her all day while she loaded heavy tree branches onto a trailer until she literally dropped. When I saw Fi struggling to help her walk across the field, something just came over me. I ran towards them so fast my feet barely left an impression on the freshly tilled earth. I grabbed Lily round the waist and put her arm over my shoulder. We had her home in no time. I would have carried her myself if I had to. There's nothing I wouldn't do for Lily, but despite both of our efforts, we couldn't dissuade her from starting her new job. She really needed time to recover, both physically and mentally, but Monday was only two days away.

Having learned those big words about His Lordship, it concerned me he might be really uncaring. In her current state, Lily would struggle to cope. On Saturday afternoon I went straight from Reg's to the manor, only to find a military guard at the entrance. I knew the soldier on duty, which was handy. Me and Brian Harris had shared a drink in The Forge. He was a nice bloke, Brian, he made me laugh, but he hadn't told me he was guarding the manor.

"Hello, Brian, what are you doing here?"

"Hello, Dotty. I'm standing here waiting for a pretty girl to go past, and here you are."

"No, really, why are you here?"

"Don't ask me, it must be something top secret, though. I can't let you go past."

"But you know me."

"I don't know you that well; you know, really well."

"You cheeky bugger. You never will know me really well if I don't get to the manor."

"I think in that case I might have to turn a blind eye."

I flashed my eyes and blew him a kiss. Like all men, Brian had that one fatal weakness. I was grateful, though, and I didn't want to get him into trouble. Moments later, I had another admirer making himself a nuisance. Young Alfie, who had "more front than Selfridges".

"When are you coming out with me then, Dotty?"

"I'm too good for you, Alfie. I don't set my sights on anyone below management level. What was your position? Trainee, wasn't it?"

"It's your chance to catch me on the way up, isn't it?"

"I'm not sure you are going up, Alfie," I said, as I walked on, "but I'll keep my eye on you, just in case."

When I knocked on the servants' entrance, the most impressive bloke I had ever seen opened the door. He wore a black tailcoat with a white waistcoat and striped trousers. His white bow tie seemed to prevent him from looking down at me. He just stood there with his chin in the air. I thought this must be another Lord or something. It really took me by surprise, I didn't know what to do or say.

"I'm sorry to trouble you, My Lord," I said, like an idiot, "but do you think I could see Mrs Morgan?"

He finally lowered his chin slightly, and the hint of a smile appeared on his face.

"I am not His Lordship," he said, really sternly, "I am His Lordship's butler. And who might you be?"

"I'm Dotty, Elsie knows me."

"Wait here," was all he said, as he walked away. I was relieved when Elsie appeared.

"Who was that?" I asked.

"That was Mr Jennings. Best not get on the wrong side of him. And what can I do for you, Dotty?"

"I need to see His Lordship, only for a moment."

"He won't see you without an appointment."

"I'm not leaving without seeing him, Elsie. Would you tell him it's about Lily?"

"Well, I can send a footman with the message, but he's really busy."

"I have to see him; did you know Lily's husband has been killed?"

"Oh my God, oh no. I'll go myself; come in, Dotty."

It all seemed to happen so quickly. One moment I was standing there like an idiot, and the next moment I was being shown into a room the likes of which I had never seen in my life before. His Lordship stood up to greet me. He must have recognised me from my disaster at the pub, but he offered me his hand. He was really polite.

"Do come in, Miss Archer. What is this terrible news about Mrs Heywood's husband?"

"That's right, My Lord, he served on HMS Hood, and well, he's been killed."

"Oh no, this is awful, my heart goes out to Mrs Heywood. Thank you for telling me, Miss Archer. I assume she will not be starting here on Monday."

"This is the thing, My Lord; she's adamant that she will be here Monday morning."

"In that case, I shall insist that Mrs Heywood take as much time as is required. I will send a message immediately to that effect."

"You don't know her, My Lord; if all of Hitler's bombs couldn't stop her, I'm afraid your message hasn't got a cat in hell's chance. Oh, I'm sorry, I didn't mean to say it like that."

"Not at all, Miss Archer, I appreciate your frankness."

"There's another thing, My Lord, I wanted to tell you about her husband, but I'm also here to ask you to treat her gently. Lily's really fragile at the moment, and I don't want you or anyone else upsetting her. I know you're a Lord and everything, but Lily's my friend, she's a really special friend. I look out for her, you see. Anyone who upsets her at this difficult time, well, they'll have me to contend with."

"You're very forthright, Miss Archer. When I met you in The Forge the other night, Mrs Heywood commented that you shine a light in her life; I understand now. May I assure you that Mrs Heywood's fragility is completely safe in my hands."

"Thank you, My Lord, I just needed to be reassured. About the other night, I need to apologise."

"No need, Miss Archer, no need at all. Mrs Heywood's endorsement of you is more than sufficient for me to dismiss the matter immediately."

"That's very gracious of you, I'm not sure I deserve it."

"Well, actually, I think you do, so we need not mention it again."

I don't know why, but I went in there really angry. Going by what Lily had said the first time she met him, I felt sure he was a cold-hearted sod who wouldn't show her a shred of compassion. The reality turned out to be the exact opposite, he was really lovely. I had been horribly rude towards him, and yet he treated me so kindly. I now knew what Lily meant when she said he knocked the wind out of her sails. He escorted me to the door, where the footman prepared to show me out. His parting words made me smile.

"Actually, Miss Archer, rest assured, I feel that your acquaintance is preferable to having Hitler as my father-in-law!"

Nothing would have stopped Lily from starting her job that Monday. That proved to be the start of it all, really. The day Lily joined Edward our future destinies were decided. I didn't immediately follow her; my destiny took a little longer to reveal itself. I thought my life as a Land Girl would continue as before, but the path ahead of me only led in one direction.

Chapter Five
Christmas 1941

The spring and summer of 1941 were especially eventful for Lily, but for Fiona and me, it remained business as usual on Reg's farm. From Reg's top field, you could see much of the manor grounds. I watched the huts being built, and I noticed an ever-increasing number of new people arriving. It seemed obvious that Middlebourne Manor had become some kind of secret military establishment. As the summer progressed, Lily came home less frequently, until she hardly came home at all. We only got together with her at weekends but all the while Lily would never speak a word of it.

Fiona became absolutely besotted with Johnny, and anyone would have realised that Lily was gooey eyed about His Lordship. I didn't see any future for her there, but it constantly reminded me I didn't have anyone in my life. I didn't actually want anyone in my life but stranger still, I missed not having something that I didn't want. It sounds daft, doesn't it? But that was me! The next event to change our lives completely happened towards the autumn of that year. Fiona informed me that Lily had offered her a job at the manor, as her assistant. I didn't need to be told what this meant to Fi. She came back from a meeting at the manor with the face of a child who had just met Father Christmas. Part bewilderment, part pride, Fi's excitement was boundless.

"What's going on at the manor then, Fi?" I asked.

"I can't say. I had to sign the Official Secrets Act. I can't say anything."

"So it is all top secret then."

"If I were able to tell anyone, Dotty, I would tell you. All I can say is that it's really important."

"Will you be staying at the manor, like Lily?"

"Oh no, they treat Lily quite differently. I'm just a member of staff. I wish I could talk about it, Dotty, I really do."

"I'm not surprised about Lily. I think we realised when she applied for the job, she's got something special, hasn't she?"

"You should see her at work, Dotty, no wonder Edward turned me down. I couldn't do what she does."

"What's all this, 'Edward', business?"

"Everyone in the circle is on Christian name terms, including Edward."

"And you're in this circle?"

"I'm Lily's personal assistant, so yes, I'm in the circle."

"And what's His Lordship like, then?"

"He's not what I thought at all. He's amazingly clever, and to be honest, he's lovely. Lily's crazy about him, but that's not going to work, is it?"

Fiona went on and on about how wonderful it all was. She never once let slip exactly what they did, but she painted a picture of something that I felt decidedly left out of. This is the story of my life. Ever since my school days, it always seemed that I was the one left out. I knew I wouldn't be able to do what Fiona did, and I certainly couldn't do whatever it was that Lily did. This only added to my sense of failure. I didn't show it, of course, I just worked even harder at Reg's. The more life gets on top of you, the more you have to push back.

I got on surprisingly well with Reg. He appreciated how capable I was on the farm and he respected me for it. I had respect for him as well; his life could not have been harder, but he never once complained. With both Lily and Fiona gone, we really needed more help. And so when Reg said we had another Land Army girl coming, I found myself looking forward to a bit of company. The prospect of the new girl coming lifted my spirits. With autumn well underway, the days were getting increasingly shorter. Fair play to the new girl, she turned up on a bicycle before first light.

"Hello," I said, "you're the new Land Army girl?"

"Yes, that's right, I'm Ruth. I take it I'm in the right place."

"Yes, welcome to Upper Farm. I'm Dotty, Dotty by name, dotty by nature. Where are you from, Ruth?"

"I'm staying in Upton Village, it's not far on the bike. London's my home, though."

"Yes, I'm from London, East Ham. What about you?"

"Wandsworth, not far from the bridge."

She might have been a year or two younger than me, but full of confidence and quite a looker.

"I'll warn you now, Reg likes to put his girls in their place on your first day. He'll have you doing some really hard work. My tip is to not overdo it, pace yourself, and never complain, not to Reg anyway."

As the sun rose, Ruth looked around her at the dilapidated state of the farm and the sea of cow muck we were standing in. Her expression was priceless. Reg appeared dead on the dot of half past seven, and as he walked towards us, Ruth's expression changed to one of apprehension. I understood him well by then, I could play him like a fiddle. When he reached us looking his usual stern self, I put my arm around him and gave him a hug. He always complained when I did that, but never quite managed to conceal the hint of a smile. This was my way of presenting Ruth with a slightly more friendly Reg.

The three of us got off to a good start. I gave Ruth plenty of support, and I wasn't past buttering up Reg whenever I thought it necessary. We settled into a good routine. Apart from rationing, the war rarely affected us in Middlebourne, our only constant reminder being the planes regularly flying over us. The Lancasters passed overhead with a thunderous roar, and when the fighters soared into the sky, they lifted our spirits with them. They flew so low on occasions that I used to wave to the pilots.

The newspapers were full of the war, but I rarely read them. Things weren't the same without Lily and Fiona. When we got together on the weekends, they spoke about little else but the war. This became especially true after December the 7th when the Japanese bombed Pearl Harbour. I'd never heard of the place, but according to Lily, this would change everything. A week or two after that, I noticed two cars and a couple of lorries pull up outside the manor.

Being naturally curious I moved closer. They were about a hundred yards away; I blinked and looked twice because I could hardly believe my eyes. There was no doubt about what I saw. It was only the Prime Minister, Winston Churchill! I realised immediately that whatever was going on at the manor, it really must be important. Sat in The Forge having a drink the following Saturday evening, Lily and Fi seemed different somehow; they were both on edge. Anyone sensible would have known not to mention it, but I've never been sensible. I simply had to ask them about what I'd seen.

"You have to tell me what's going on. I saw who arrived at the manor the other day."

You should have seen the look on Lily's face. I realised I'd said the wrong thing.

"*Dotty!* Whatever you think you saw, forget it. You must never repeat that again to anyone."

"But I saw him."

"Okay, you saw him. Now I want you to swear to me you will not mention a single word of this to *anyone*." Lily always spoke with great authority, but never more so than on that occasion.

"You know me, Lily, you know I would never let you down. I won't breathe a word of it, but you have to tell me, what's he like?"

"You're incorrigible, Dotty, you really are."

"That's a good word, I've made a note of that, but what's he like?"

"He's amazing! I've met no one remotely like him, and I never will. If he walked in here tonight, I think you would feel his presence even before he entered the room."

"Wow, fancy that. You two must really be important. It sort of makes me proud."

"We're not allowed to say anything, Dotty, but what goes on at the manor is vital for the war effort."

"I wish we could tell you, Dotty," said Fiona, "I feel proud as well. I'm proud to be a part of it."

"All right, I get the picture, I won't mention it again. But what's all this I hear about you and Greg Norton, the Estate Manager, Lily?"

"Can't I have any secrets?"

"Not between us three, no."

"I'm very fond of him, okay?"

"I thought you were gooey eyed over His Lordship."

"Admit it, Lily," said Fi, "you're gooey eyed over him as well."

"Only my two best friends could say something like that." Lily replied. "I'll get it sorted out."

"Are you going to bring Greg to the Christmas party?" I asked.

"It looks like it, especially because Fi has invited him!"

"What about Johnny, is he coming, Fi?"

"I asked him, but no, he can't. What about you, Dotty, are you inviting anyone?"

"Me! No, of course not, I don't have anyone."

That was the story of my life, really. I always had boyfriends galore; they swarmed around me like bees round a honeypot, but I never allowed them to get close, not to my heart, anyway. With Christmas rapidly approaching, I found myself looking forward to it more and more. This would be a novel experience for me. I would take part in what they called a family get-together. For the first time in my life, I was part of a family. It might not have been mine, not really, but for me Gran had become my family. She taught me everything; I made biscuits and scones. Imagine it, *me*, making cakes! We glued strips of paper together with flour and water paste to make paper chains. When the big day came, the first people I met were Lily's Mum and Dad.

"Hello, Lily's Mum and Dad," I said, "what should I call you, Pam and Jack, or shall I call you Mum and Dad?"

"Oh, that makes us feel old, Dotty, it's Pam and Jack."

"Give me a hug then, Pam, you'll get your turn, Jack, don't worry."

I might have got a bit carried away hugging Jack. In my excitement, I left lipstick all over his face. Later in the day Greg Norton appeared, helping Jim to carry in Aunt Mavis' upright piano. Well, he made something of an entrance, I can tell you.

"He's lovely!" I said, "you work with him all the time, and you're telling me you haven't ... you know?"

"We're work colleagues, Dotty, I told you," Lily replied.

"Well, in that case, he's fair game, then."

"Please don't, Dotty, I know you could, but please don't. It would spoil everything."

"Not for me, it wouldn't, he's too good to waste."

"I agree, Dotty," said Fi, "he's lovely, and I know you find him irresistible, but Lily's right. Please don't, would you promise me?"

They were being perfectly serious. "What's going on here ... oh I see ... I suppose I'll have to not notice him ... oh shit!"

"How many times have I told you about that language, Dotty!" shouted Gran, from across the kitchen.

I didn't want a single thing to change. This was what a proper family Christmas should be like, and I loved it. We put Aunt Mildred's kitchen table next to Gran's and covered it all with table cloths. Forget the rationing, I had never seen so much food. We had chicken, as well as the pheasants Greg brought us. There were roast potatoes and parsnips, we had everything. How I found room for Christmas pudding, I don't know, but I did. I sat there looking around, listening to Lily's family. It was truly wonderful and best of all, I was a part of it. They were my family now! Eventually we had to find the strength to do the washing up, and I seemed to be the only one with a reserve of energy.

"Come along, galley slaves, the washing up calls," I said. "Not you, Gran, you sit down and make eyes at Greg."

Then the time came for the giving of presents. I had made and bought a couple of things for Gran and the girls, but I expected nothing myself. When they said that several of the presents were for me, it completely overwhelmed me. Really nice presents were not available during the war, it had to be mainly little things, and a lot of knitted items. It didn't matter what my presents were; they were the best presents I'd ever been given. My eyes welled up, and I made a bit of a fool of myself, I wasn't used to being given things.

The next tradition started with Gran playing the piano, and then Lily sang for us. I didn't realise Lily could sing; I thought it would just be a bit of fun. Well, it might have started out as a bit of fun, but when Lily started singing, I couldn't believe my ears. She had the most amazing voice. I wasn't able to do or say a thing, I just listened, mesmerised. Everything remained fine until she sang Gran's favourite operatic aria.

Lily said it was 'Un Bel di Vedremo' from Madame Butterfly. Needless to say, I'd never heard of it, I had no idea what to expect. The moment Lily started to sing, the hairs on the back of my neck stood up. I didn't understand what the words meant, but I realised well enough that the words were telling a tragic story. As the aria neared the end, Lily's voice suddenly rose ever higher, and it lifted me up with it. Something happened to me, I burst into uncontrollable tears, and started shaking like a leaf.

"What's wrong, Dotty, what is it?" asked Lily.

"I've never heard anything like that before! I can't even understand the words, but it was wonderful… and all this… and you… and Gran! It's all too much for me, I'm sorry."

"Let's go upstairs, Dotty, come along," Lily said.

"I'm sorry, I really don't understand what came over me. I didn't know you could sing like that, Lily. *Bloody 'ell*, I didn't know anyone could sing like that!"

"Gran always cries. It makes it difficult for me to sing. If I look at her, my voice cracks."

"It's not just me, then?" I said, trying to smile.

"No, that's the whole point of opera," Lily explained, "it's telling a story through the emotion of music."

"What is it really, Dotty? We're your best friends; can you tell us?" Fiona said, trying to reassure me.

"I didn't expect that voice. It really affected me, Lily, it did something to me. And it's all this family thing, seeing everyone so happy, I've never had that. They treated me so badly as a child, but I just thought that was normal. Then, when I see your family, Lily, I realise it wasn't normal at all, so it makes it all seem much worse."

"What happened to you, Dotty?" Lily asked.

"I can't talk about it. I'll never talk about it."

"Well, you don't have to," Fiona said, "you've got us, and we're your family now."

They were both wonderful to me. I dried my eyes and summoned up the other Dotty that I usually hid behind. When I looked reasonable again, we went back downstairs. The lovely thing is that no one mentioned it. I made an absolute fool of myself and nobody embarrassed me about it. I realised this is what proper families do. This was what my new family did.

Chapter Six

The Road To Wanborough

1942 became a time of uncertainty. I had little idea about the progress of the war, but at least the Germans no longer bombed us all the time. Ruth and I got on just fine, but I wouldn't have called us close mates, not like with Fi and Lily, but we were friends. During the winter, the daily grind on the farm became harder. The wet and cold often made it miserable. The short days didn't help. I went to work in the dark and came home in the dark. It all felt worse because Fi would come home looking really smart, while I looked like... well, you can imagine, can't you. Fi always came home full of some news or another, while mine wasn't news at all!

All of that abruptly changed when another of those life-changing events occurred. It happened during the spring of 1942. While working in the top field, I noticed a group of people near the newest of the huts in the grounds of the manor. They were obviously training and doing physical exercises. I could do that, I thought to myself. A little later they went on a run around the perimeter. The runners came quite close to where I crouched in hiding, while noticing how much they were puffing and blowing.

I knew I could do that, and I wouldn't be out of breath. Then they started some kind of close combat exercises. They were too far away for me to see clearly, so I climbed over the wire fence and crawled closer in the tall, dead grass, getting as close as possible; I found it fascinating.

A person posed as a German sentry, and another person crept up and dispatched him with a knife. I could do that, I thought.

I got a bit carried away, trying to get even closer, and they spotted me. Where the military guards were hiding I don't know, but suddenly two soldiers came running towards me, armed with rifles. I didn't panic or anything. I had a fifty yard start on them, and there wasn't a snowball's chance in hell that they would catch up with me. I knew those fields like the back of my hand. There was already a hundred yards between us when I jumped over the wire fence.

The soldiers struggled over the barbed wire. My hundred yards quickly became two hundred yards. I headed for a gully on Reg's farm; the cattle didn't like it, and so the scrub grew taller there. The soldiers must have thought I'd vanished into thin air. Twenty minutes later, I strolled into the pig shed as if nothing had happened. That was the end of it as far as I was concerned, but not a bit of it. A short time later I heard an almighty screech as an army vehicle slid to a halt in the yard. I prepared to leg it again, but Lily stepped out of the car, accompanied by Corporal Harris. Lily looked as if she had steam coming out of her ears. I thought better of legging it, deciding instead to face the music.

"I'm in trouble, aren't I, Lily?"

"Do you realise how close you were to being shot, Dotty? So yes, you bloody fool, you *are* in trouble, big trouble."

"Oh shit! I thought I was. I've been watching them for a day or two, and they fascinated me. I know what's going on, Lily. They're spies, aren't they, and this is a training camp?"

"You didn't hear that, Corporal Harris, did you?" Lily said.

"Hear what, Mrs Heywood?"

"How do you know that?" Lily asked.

"I've overheard them, and all the physical training stuff, I'd be so good at that."

"This really is a problem, Dotty." I had never seen Lily looking so serious. "You must come with me to the office."

"I'll do better than that," I said, "I'm going to join you! I want to do what they're doing. I just know I'd be good at it. You can organise it for me, Lily, can't you?"

Lily turned towards Brian Harris. "I find myself in a difficult position, Corporal. This woman has been incredibly stupid. I have no option but to take the matter further. The trouble is, she also happens to be my dearest friend. Do you see my problem?"

"I'm not sure that I do, Mrs Heywood. We interviewed this witness, and she says she's seen nothing. Bit of a wasted trip if you ask me."

"I'm looking forward to our next New Year's kiss, Corporal," Lily said with a smile.

"No need to wait that long, Mrs Heywood."

"Watch it, Corporal!"

I realised what was going on. Thanks to Brian, it sounded like I might get away with it.

"Thanks, mate, you're a bloody star, that's what you are, Brian!"

They drove me back to the manor, and then marched me into Lily's office.

"*Dotty*, what are you doing here?" asked an incredibly surprised Fiona.

"The intruder - you're looking at her," Lily said.

"Oh, my goodness! You *are* in trouble, Dotty."

"Get me the Official Secrets Act, will you, Fi?" asked Lily. "At least that's a start."

It all happened so quickly my head spun in every direction. Lily's office was like no office I had ever seen. The far end of the room seemed to be a mile away, and wow, talk about posh. Fi put the Official Secrets Act in front of me and Lily gave me a really serious lecture about it. If I spoke a word about what I had seen, I would go to prison. If I did anything considered treasonous, then I really was for the high jump. Well, not so much the high jump, more the long drop! They both looked at me with expressions I had never seen before. They were not larking about; this really was deadly serious. I signed it with a shaking hand. I took it seriously all right.

"I know I've done the wrong thing, Lily, but I really want to do what I've seen those people doing. You know I would be good at it. There's a woman amongst them. You have women doing this. Please, Lily, I'd be so good at this."

"It's out of the question, Dotty."

"No, it's not. You can make it happen. I know you can. If you won't do this for me, I'll apply anyway."

Lily looked at Fi, and they spoke behind my back. I meant every word I said - if Lily wouldn't help me, I'd somehow find a way in. She understood how determined I was.

"All right, Dotty, I'll arrange it, but it's against my better judgement. The people you saw training are SOE field agents. We are a part of the

Special Operations Executive; Middlebourne Manor is an SOE station. We're Station M and you will never repeat that outside of these walls."

I didn't realise it then, but Lily only agreed because she was sure they would reject me with my lack of language skills. Had I known that it would have dented my confidence. As it turned out, I had to wait for several weeks, but somehow Lily got me enrolled without needing an interview. I received a very anonymous looking letter inviting me to a job interview at Wanborough Manor in Surrey. It felt like a mistake, no mention of special training, but I guessed this was it, and then Lily confirmed it. Finally, I had to break the news to Reg. I was sure he would be able to find a replacement, so I wasn't too worried about it. When I told him, his reaction took me completely by surprise. He asked where I was going.

"I'm sort of joining the army, Reg."

"You mean the Auxiliary Territorial Service?"

"Yes, it's a bit like the ATS. I've got to go for training in a place near Guilford."

Reg looked as if I had pulled the rug out from beneath him. "I don't know how I'll manage without you, Dotty."

"Ruth is coming on well, and you'll soon get a replacement."

"Not like you, I won't. It's not going to be the same without you, Dotty."

"Is this praise, Reg?"

"Yes, of course it is! You've been a shining light around this place. I'm really going to miss you."

"Oh, Reg! I'm going to miss you too, you old bugger."

I put my arms around him and we stood there ankle deep in cow muck, holding each other.

"If I get thrown out, Reg, I'll come straight back, I promise."

"Will you still be at Margaret's; will I see you now and again?"

"I don't think I'll ever want to leave Middlebourne. Besides, you owe me a pint, Reg. I won't forget."

We parted on such good terms; it wasn't what I expected at all. Fiona always said Reg had a heart of gold, and she was right. It's not that far to Wanborough, so I persuaded Jim to drive me there. He dropped me off outside but I had to be careful not to tell him anything about the place. I stood there in complete amazement. Nothing spoke of a military training establishment.

I stood before the most wonderful country manor house; it was built out of red bricks with so many elevations and roof lines, I couldn't keep track. All the while, a part of me worried I might be in the wrong place. This didn't look remotely like a training school. Then I thought about Middlebourne Manor, which didn't look like a secret establishment either; perhaps that was the point. I looked along a garden wall with a central gate hanging between two brick pillars. An enormous tree stood in the garden to the left of the entrance. The front of the house had a covering of ivy all neatly trimmed at the level of the first floor.

As I walked towards the ivy-covered entrance porch, it still worried me I might be in the wrong place. There were no guards on duty, I just marched up to the door and knocked. A man in military uniform opened the door and quickly invited me in. I stood in front of a desk, a bit like a provincial hotel reception. He sat down and spent an age looking for paperwork before finally acknowledging me.

"Miss Archer?" he asked in a crisp voice.

"Yes, that's me. I was told to report today." I showed him my letter.

"I don't understand, Archer, your file is blank."

"Don't ask me, I was just told to come here."

"Something is wrong, we only receive trainees who have passed through their first interview and aptitude tests."

"Perhaps you've made a mistake, check your paperwork."

He walked off, leaving me standing there like I was some kind of reject. Five minutes later, another officer came in holding more paperwork. He stood looking at me as if I was from an alien planet.

"This is most irregular, Miss Archer. I have instructions from General Gubbins' office to admit you without an interview or aptitude test. This is a request from SOE Station M but I have never heard of Station M, Miss Archer!"

"Well, I've never heard of General Gubbins, so I suppose that puts us on an equal footing. But you're correct about Station M, though."

"It says you have signed the Official Secrets Act, and I am to admit you. You must have contacts in high places, Miss Archer."

I couldn't help smiling; I understood exactly who to thank for this, and I also knew enough not to say who.

"Not for me to say."

"Quite right, Archer; welcome to STS 5."

As they marched me through the building, the "hotel reception" abruptly changed into a military establishment. A woman in military uniform met me, one of many I saw walking around the place. The officer handed her the same file, and that seemed to capture her full attention. After what seemed like an eternity, she looked up over her reading glasses and addressed me.

"Archer?" was all she said in her refined Home Counties accent.

"That's me."

"I don't understand, Archer, your file has nothing in it!"

"Cock-up, is it?"

"When you attended your interview in London, did you go to Horse Guards, and who interviewed you?"

"I've not had an interview at Horse Guards or anywhere else."

"Wait here, Archer, I'll be back in a moment, I need to clarify this."

I had a bad feeling about it; I knew Lily had pulled strings to get me there, but I began to think maybe she pulled the wrong ones. The woman came back within a minute or two and marched up to me, looking very intimidating.

"Come with me, Archer," she said, abruptly.

"What do I call you?" I asked.

"Lieutenant," came the reply.

She took me into a small room and closed the door. She sat behind a desk, directing me towards a chair.

"I've not heard of this Station M before," she said, "but that's not entirely surprising within SOE. Most of our female recruits come to us from the Women's Auxiliary Air Force or some other indirect route. I can't recall anyone coming here from within SOE. What's your position with M Section, I mean Station M, Archer?"

"I'm not sure I can answer that," I replied in complete innocence.

"I understand. How long have you lived in France?"

"I've never been to France."

"But you can speak French, of course."

"No."

"Oh, I see. What languages do you speak then?"

"English."

"I don't understand, all of our trainees are here because they can speak a European language. We predominantly recruit for F Section. Our agents must be able to integrate seamlessly into French society. What qualifies you to be here, Archer?"

I didn't understand what the woman was talking about, but whatever it was, I didn't like the sound of it. Without a good reason for being there, it seemed likely that I might be thrown out on my ear. My only option was to bluff my way in, but I only had two cards to play. There was Station M, that I knew nothing about, and I remembered the name of the General that so impressed the officer at the door. Like any good poker player, I played my two cards with a straight face.

"I can't really discuss my function in Station M, but languages are not the primary requirement. They want me to be proficient in what you might call physical activities. You will notice the request comes down from General Gubbins' office." I smiled as if butter wouldn't melt in my mouth.

"This is most unusual, but as you say, this request comes right from the top. This Station M, they obviously have a specific application for you; I understand why you can't discuss it. Welcome to Wanborough."

Years later, Lily admitted to me she assumed my lack of French would exclude me from the course. I walked into it without even knowing that speaking French was considered essential. So, had I been clever, or just plain lucky? Okay, well obviously just lucky, but by chance I had stumbled onto the perfect smokescreen. Station M was so secret that nobody had heard of it. It naturally followed that if a top-secret section had a specific requirement for me, then of course, I wasn't allowed to talk about it.

The Lieutenant accepted that without hesitation; I was in. Her tone changed immediately; she became much more congenial. None of that detracted from the seriousness of the lecture she gave me. With the SOE training manual open on her desk, she looked up at me over her reading glasses.

"This part of your training is probably the most important. It is in your interest that we impose very strict security rules. You will not leave the grounds of Wanborough Manor unless accompanied by a staff officer. As your House Commandant, things like recreational walks are at my discretion. Is that clear, Archer?"

"Yes, perfectly."

She nodded, as if to say so far, so good. The thick file she read from looked very intimidating, I wondered how much of it she intended to read to me. The tone of her voice was friendly, but I was in no doubt about the seriousness of the various stipulations.

"You must give me any identity documents you have. You will hand me any weapons you have in your possession, including firearms, and also including cameras."

"I'm not carrying a firearm."

"These are standard regulations, Archer. You will hand me any money in your possession above the amount of £5, as well as any valuables. Now, letters. If you wish to send a letter, you will present it to me in an unsealed addressed envelope. All mail will be censored, and you must not mention in any communication that censoring takes place. The same applies to any incoming mail. Telegrams may only be used in an emergency and will be subject to censorship. You will not use the telephone here or in this locality. Is this clear, Archer?"

"Yes, it's clear."

"Good. So, first of all, Archer, welcome to Special Training School 5. I am going to explain to you the nature of the organisation to which you now belong. The principal purpose of SOE is subversion, which, if properly applied, is an extremely potent weapon. We employ subversion in four different ways. The first aim is to damage the enemy's material and their means of communication and production. Modern warfare depends entirely upon material and communication. A strike against their material assets and communication is a strike at the heart of the enemy's war effort.

The second aim is to deprive the enemy of human resources. As casualties mount, manpower becomes a critical factor. We will force the enemy to divert essential forces to provide escort and guard duty. Wherever we inflict damage upon the enemy, they will have to respond with manpower."

She looked up from the manual, ensuring I was paying full attention.

"The third aim is to undermine the enemy's morale. An army with low morale will soon be a defeated army. There are many ways we can affect the enemy's morale. Letters from home which tell of misery, poor food supplies, poor supplies generally. Then there are those who collaborate with the enemy in France. We want them to feel exposed and uncomfortable.

The fourth aim is to raise the morale of those who might help us in the occupied countries. So, how do we achieve these objectives? There are many options available to us; this is subversion, Archer, these are the methods we teach here."

I had no idea how far-reaching SOE was; it sounded like an enormous undertaking. This was not what I expected when I watched the agents training at Middlebourne. It suddenly became perfectly obvious why agents needed to pass as French nationals. Something I would never be able to do. She probably noticed my expression.

"Don't worry, Archer, you will not be expected to do all of these things. In fact, I suspect whatever your role is with Station M, it's likely to be very specific."

That I didn't have a role with Station M had not escaped my attention. The problem was, I had no option but to continue the deception. How would it all end? I had no idea, but I intended to stay the course.

"Are you lot ATS then?" I asked.

"No, all the uniformed women here are FANY."

"Well, yes, I'm sure you are, but does that make you different from ATS?"

"You must have heard of FANY, Archer."

"Well, kind of. Perhaps you would tell me again."

"We are The Princess Royal's Volunteer Corps. Founded in 1907 as the First Aid Nursing Yeomanry, hence FANY. We are not only the longest-standing voluntary all-female unit, but we are also one of the most highly decorated."

"When you say voluntary, are you a part of the British Army?"

"No, we are integrated now, but still keep our independence. We have a presence in many areas. Most of the female military drivers you see will be FANY. They are a part of the ATS, but we wear our own flash on the ATS uniform sleeve. We are attached to the British Red Cross and drive ambulances. FANYs work as radio officers, wireless operators, encryption specialists, radar operators, some work as personal assistants. This is where our close association with SOE was formed. Most of our female SOE agents are FANYs, and we help run these training establishments. As your House Commandant, I will be your conducting officer during your stay here."

"I don't know what to expect; how does this work, how many of us are there?"

"You will be with us for about three or four weeks, for what we call initial training. It gives you training, but it also shows your suitability. Things are not rigid here - the training is very flexible depending on needs. You are part of an intake of ten, two women and eight men. The others are all F Section recruits, so that might be a problem."

"Why should that be a problem, then?"

"Because theory lectures will be given in French."

"Yes, that is a problem."

"We make exceptions all the time, Archer; a way will be found. Some of those who graduate from here will advance on to paramilitary training. The men go to Arisaig in Scotland; and it's being discussed whether women might go there as well. From what I understand, this might apply to you, Archer. From there, if you stay the course, you will go on to parachute training at Ringway in Manchester. Finally, if you succeed in all these things, you will go to yet another stately home in the New Forest, what you might call finishing school."

"Why are all these places in stately homes?"

"Yes, it's a bit of a joke in F Section. Most of our training schools are requisitioned manors and estates. They provide excellent facilities combined with the perfect cover. Some say it's what SOE stands for, "Stately 'Omes of England". You will share a room with the other female recruit. You will not discuss your personal life, and later you will only be known by your code names. This establishes your security routine right from the start."

"What happens if recruits drop out. Not that I will, I can assure you, but what happens to them?"

"It depends; you already come from an SOE section. It's different for others who find themselves in possession of secret information. Some are sent away on "gardening leave" in Scotland."

"Wow, it's all very serious, isn't it?"

"It's a case of life and death, Archer. It doesn't come any more serious, but you already know that. If you have questions your trainers can't help you with, or anything of a personal nature, you come to me. Do you understand?"

"Yes, I understand. I may not speak French, Lieutenant, but in all other respects I'm going to be the best recruit you ever had."

"What makes you so sure of that, Archer?"

"I might not have much going for me, I may not be the sharpest knife in the drawer, but I've learned how to make up for that. I'm determined, I'm more determined than anyone you've ever met."

She made notes in my file, and she smiled while she was doing it. Not sure if she was laughing at me or pleased with the look of me. Either way, her kindness put me at ease. The next thing was the guided tour. There were rooms for different training functions, a Mess Hall, and communal sleeping rooms. Outside, the grounds were extensive, and people were receiving intensive training in small groups. There were some military officers and non-commissioned officers (NCOs) as well as several FANYs overseeing everything that went on.

Last of all, she showed me to my room. It contained four beds, two on either side of the room. Between the beds were large lockers for personal effects. The room was huge, it might have housed another two beds, and I had to share with just one other woman. The Lieutenant left me to unpack my things, and I had my choice of beds.

A short while later, the same FANY officer escorted the other recruit into the room. A timid-looking woman entered. Elegantly dressed in a black dress with a tailored jacket, she didn't look like an English girl. From the one or two words I understood, the two of them spoke French together. When the Lieutenant left her, she turned and spoke to me.

"*Bonjour, je m'appelle Eliane. Êtes-vous nouvelle ici, comme moi*?"

"I don't speak French, I'm sorry."

"*J'ai bien peur que mon anglais ne soit pas très bon.* I'm sorry… English… not good."

"It's better than my French," I joked.

We had been instructed not to discuss our personal life, which I thought was a bit daft when I shared a room with her. Discussing anything at all was a bit of a problem at first. But as it turned out, Eliane and I got on extremely well together. I'm afraid we broke a rule immediately, we inevitably talked a little about our lives. From what I understood, she came from Marseilles where she had been a member of the French Resistance. When the Germans became aware of her, she had to flee the country via one of her own escape routes.

Her timid appearance belied the fact that she was obviously an incredibly brave woman. Upon arrival in Britain, she immediately became a prime candidate for F Section. She might have spent the rest of the war as an exile in Britain, but nothing was going to stop her from going back to France as an SOE agent. Eliane's lack of English proved to be no more a problem than my lack of French. We improvised, I learned French from her, while she learned English from me. In every respect, Eliane was a typical SOE recruit; I was the outsider.

Chapter Seven
Eliane

That evening, in the Mess Hall, Eliane and I sat at a table together. We were obviously not encouraged to sit in large groups; the men sat spread out on small tables just like us. A long table was reserved for the NCOs and FANYs. The food wasn't half bad, it certainly exceeded my expectations. I'm not sure that Eliane agreed, but if she complained, I didn't understand her anyway.

She intrigued me; there is a certain style that French women have, and she had it in spades. Her dress, her hair, her manner, everything about her was French. My first impression of her as a timid little woman could not have been more misguided; scratch beneath the surface and a giant figure emerged. The courage she displayed with the French Resistance placed her among the few. Eliane had learned to be quiet and unassuming but given the smallest encouragement, she became a joy to be with.

I remember wondering if her unassuming manner had been the secret of her success while working with the resistance. That possibility worried me because I was her opposite. I didn't do unassuming; I always took it for granted that I could throw myself at people and they would love me for it. Scratch beneath my surface, and unlike Eliane, all you would find is a tramp from the East End. I really liked her, but she made me feel inadequate.

I sat pondering what life would be like after the code names had been issued. Would I cope being someone else? The prospect of the theory lessons being taught entirely in French really worried me. I spoke to some of the men while we queued for our food, and they were happy enough to answer me in English, so I wasn't entirely isolated. Towards the end of our meal, our House Commandant came over and sat with us.

"How are you two getting on?" she asked.

"We're fine," I said, "at least we can't argue!"

"This must be difficult for you, Archer, the language I mean."

"It is, but I've already started picking up a few words of French."

"There's a good reason for all this, you know. We need recruits to behave as if they are in Occupied France already. It must become second nature to you; one word of English in the wrong place might put you in front of a firing squad."

"When you put it like that, I can understand," I said. "But it's going to be difficult at first."

"We help each other," Eliane said in her faltering English. "Dotty teaches English."

The Lieutenant smiled. "You will be issued codenames tomorrow, so forget Dotty and Eliane. It is so important that you only respond to your code name, especially you, Eliane. You are known in France; answer someone who calls your real name and it might cost you your life."

"I hadn't thought of that," I said.

"Don't worry, Dotty, I suspect you will be fine."

It was a nice thing to say; I wondered if she realised how much those few words boosted my confidence. The Lieutenant didn't act how I expected an officer would. She didn't hide behind her authority; her warm personality reassured us both. Perhaps this was the difference between the FANY and the regular army; I didn't know. Not speaking the same language as my room-mate, and not being encouraged to mix with the rest of the intake provided a strange introduction to STS 5. Our last instruction was to be ready at 06:30 hrs for early morning exercises. They issued us with the kit to wear before effectively sending us to our rooms.

The next morning, Eliane really struggled to get up. Without me there, I suspect she would not have got up at all. The pair of us reported as instructed in our shorts and plimsolls. I stood wide awake and ready to go while she stood staring into the distance with a blank face. An NCO met us who dressed in his shorts and vest, was unmistakably the fitness instructor. Maybe in his late thirties, his arms and legs looked like they had been sculpted out of marble. The rest of the male recruits were similarly kitted out in shorts and vests. They might have been younger, but it was obvious at a glance which one was the instructor.

"I am Sergeant Cummings; you will call me Sergeant." He spoke in a loud, aggressive voice. "My job is first, to assess your fitness, and second, to make you fitter. You two women will be treated exactly the same. I want no excuses, and no complaining from anyone. Is that clear?"

"Yes, Sergeant," came the timid response.

"I need to know if you lot are as pathetic as you look. Fitness and endurance can save your life. It's better to fail here than to fail in the field. This is your first test. If you fail, you will go no further on this course. Is that clear?" The response was even more timid. "Is that clear?" he repeated.

"Yes, Sergeant," came the reply.

We started off with some stretching exercises, and he pushed us all hard. Most of the men smiled at us two women as if we were a curiosity. It didn't bother me; here at least I knew I'd be able to compete with all but the very fittest of them. Eliane appeared to be intimidated by them which only made me more determined that we should both succeed. What followed the stretching exercises, he described as a little stroll around the grounds.

He set off at quite a pace and we all followed. After just ten minutes, the strain began to show among some of them. There was a lot of heavy breathing and red faces. I found it all very reassuring, none of the men were fitter than me. After forty-five minutes, some of them seemed to be in genuine distress, including Eliane. I dropped back and ran next to her. She was struggling and gasping for air. Eventually, her eyes glazed over and she could no longer run in a straight line. One more stumble and she would collapse.

I instinctively put my arm around her waist and stopped her, whereupon she collapsed in my arms. The rest of them ran ahead and probably didn't notice we had stopped. Half supporting and half carrying her, we walked on for several minutes, until I saw the Sergeant running back towards us. He just stood there with his hands on his hips, looking at us. He breathed heavily but remained far from exhausted. I couldn't fathom his expression; it seemed to be somewhere between pity and contempt.

"Right, no point you two continuing, go back and pack your bags."

"*What*! Hang on a moment," I said. "I'm just trying to help her."

"What help have you been, Archer? Had you been in Occupied France, you would have been captured by the Germans. You're a bloody liability."

I argued my case, but to no avail. Eliane and I made our way back to the main building. By the time we finally arrived, she had regained some of her composure, and I told her what the Sergeant had said as best as I could. She understood me well enough and her expression took me completely by surprise. What she lacked in physical fitness, she more than compensated for with sheer defiance.

Her attitude quickly escalated into downright hostility. Our House Commandant met us, and immediately found herself on the receiving end of a torrent of French vitriol. I didn't need to understand exactly what had been said - I got the message. Eliane had no intention of going anywhere! Whatever the Lieutenant said calmed her down a little, and then she turned towards me.

"I'm sorry we're losing you, Archer, but a lot of people drop out at the first hurdle. You're very calm about it, I must say."

"I'm calm about it because I'm not going anywhere either. I told you, I'm the most determined person you will ever meet. You'll have to beat me into submission, tie me up, and drag me out of here, and I'll just come straight back again."

The Lieutenant just stood there, smiling at the pair of us. Just at that moment, the Sergeant appeared running towards us, followed in the distance by six of the men struggling behind him. Two were absent. When the six arrived, they all sank to their knees on the grass, forming a circle. To a man, they were gasping for air. The Sergeant had lost little of his composure and whispered with the Lieutenant before joining us.

"What a sorry bunch of individuals you are," he barked. "I've seen fitter pensioners than you lot. One of you men sustained a minor injury, so I'm giving him the benefit of the doubt. Your other colleague turned out to be a whimpering baby. I never want to see him again. This just leaves you two ladies."

He stood in front of Eliane, trying to intimidate her. "You got as far as I would normally expect a woman to go, and your House Commandant tells me you're made of the right stuff. So, for the moment, I'm going to give you the benefit of the doubt. But you, Archer, you made the wrong decision, you let the team down."

I allowed his attitude to get under my skin. "I would never let the team down," I shouted. "She was close to collapsing, and we're all a part of the same team. I didn't let her down because this isn't Occupied France. Had it been, I might have acted differently. I'll always put loyalty first wherever I can. If you don't value loyalty, Sergeant, then you need to think again."

"Who the hell are you to tell me what to think, Archer. On your feet, let's see what you've really got."

With that, he grabbed me by the arm and started running. We were both already tired, but he set off at a fast pace. I matched his pace stride for stride. After ten minutes, he slowed down to a long-distance pace and kept going. Being a middle-distance runner, I wasn't built for long distance running, and neither was he. We kept going for nearly an hour. We covered the circuit twice, and each time we passed the main building, the team cheered me on. My legs throbbed and my lungs ached, but I would have died on my feet rather than admit defeat.

As we approached the building for the third time, he beckoned me to run alongside him. We looked at each other, and beneath our exhausted and pained expressions, we each revealed the glimmer of a smile. The pace gradually slowed to a walk during the final hundred yards. I momentarily lost concentration for a second and stumbled. He put his arm round my shoulder, and without realising, I put mine around his waist.

"Who do you think would have dropped out first?" he asked, between heavy breaths.

"You would, of course. I don't know how to give up."

"If you had given up, Archer, I would have carried you back, you know that don't you?"

"But then if this was Occupied France, Sergeant, you'd have been captured by the Germans!"

"Fuck the Germans, Archer; this is Surrey."

As far as my breath would allow, I laughed, and he laughed back. We finally sat down on the grass, filling our lungs as if there wasn't sufficient air in Surrey to go around. The Sergeant pretended to be a heartless sod, but I quickly saw through that. He had to build our fitness and character, and he was good at it. I liked him and I think he felt the same about me. It had all been a test, and one that I also passed in the eyes of my fellow recruits. Eliane and I were not about to be thrown off the course. They wanted to see our reaction to a stressful situation. This had been the first of many such tests.

The shower facilities were excellent, and the breakfast which followed turned out to be even better. The morning exercises had taken longer than expected, so breakfast had to be rushed. Nothing was allowed to upset the timetable. When the time came for our first lecture, we left the Mess Hall and headed off together. We were immediately a team; it was no longer the men and us two women. The first priority was the issuing of code names. Eliane became Gabrielle, while they designated me as Angélique. They made it abundantly clear that from then on we must only use those names. We must never use any other.

They had also given thought to my French language problem. The instructor handed me the written transcript of each lecture which had been taken straight out of the SOE manual. This proved incredibly helpful. Not only was I able to understand the lecture, I could hear the French language being spoken while reading the words in English. I had to absorb a huge amount of information, because it provided me with a crash course in French as well as SOE doctrine. The first lesson took up where the House Commandant's introduction left off. First, we concentrated on material damage.

The enemy in occupied countries should be made to feel as uncomfortable as possible. In the first instance, this can be achieved by innumerable minor acts of defiance. This is the fundamental principle of non-cooperation - passive resistance by another name. The second stage is industrial sabotage, where everything possible is done to prevent workers from attending factories. Many of the foreign workers having no allegiance to the Boche, as SOE called them, those workers can be influenced.

The third stage of industrial sabotage can be achieved by workers omitting to carry out essential maintenance. Alternatively, lubricant can be laced with abrasive, thus shortening the life- span of equipment. Lastly, workers can waste time by applying an excess of over-caution and stringent adherence to regulations. Workmanship can be shoddy. We then moved on to the next level of sabotage, which is direct intervention. This involves the destruction of road and rail links.

The ramifications of these actions were then fully explained. All successful sabotage applies a strain to the enemy's resources and manpower.

Faulty workmanship needs to be put right. The replacement of complex and expensive machinery prematurely destroyed by the inclusion of abrasives in the lubricant is enormously costly and disruptive. Attacks on rolling stock, railway lines, and infrastructure place enormous demands upon the enemy's industrial capability. The inevitable consequence is a shortage of material and military equipment.

The final desirable outcome is achieved as a consequence of the enemy's reaction to acts of sabotage. Such attacks invariably result in the enemy increasing its military presence to protect vital infrastructure. Every German soldier on guard duty is a soldier not on the front. Next, the morale of those troops must be undermined. They taught us how to employ psychological methods, by exploiting existing grievances and dissatisfactions. Finally, our instructor explained that all these actions must be coordinated. He explained how minor acts in isolation can be ineffective, but when combined in a comprehensive plan, the effect of minor acts of sabotage can be magnified.

The complexity of detail proved to be enormous. We had to consider the neutral status of some countries and how that might affect an operation. In the occupied countries, working with the population through the existing resistance is always the essential priority. This, we were told, was an extensive subject that would be dealt with in detail at our final finishing school. For now, we had to think in terms of two phases. There was the pre-invasion phase and the invasion phase. I had followed every detail up to that moment, but the instructor's last point lost me. I dared to put my hand up and ask a question.

"What invasion are we talking about here?"

The instructor put his SOE manual down and spoke in English. "Everything SOE does in Europe and elsewhere should support one ultimate objective. That objective is the total eradication of the Third Reich. The only way we can achieve that is by taking the fight directly to the enemy in the occupied countries, and eventually into Germany itself. We have to launch a full-scale invasion of Europe. It will, of necessity, be the largest amphibious invasion in history. The details of such an invasion will remain the most closely guarded secret in this country's military history. The function of SOE is to help facilitate that invasion and contribute towards its success."

It was quite a rousing little speech, and we all responded with a cheer of approval. I realised I hadn't reasoned it through before. I thought agents worked individually to cause disruption and hinder the German war machine. I didn't realise we were to be part of a coordinated invasion of Europe. Quite what my role might be, I hadn't worked out yet. I suspect if I'd seriously thought about it, my confidence would have been dented enormously. Everything we had learned so far required fluent French, and try as I might, that was not going to be me.

In the afternoon, we moved back outside again and quickly found ourselves standing in the firing range. Here we were introduced to weapons and explosives. If I tried to imagine a weapons expert, he wouldn't have looked remotely like the instructor who met us. A grey-haired bespectacled man in his late fifties greeted us with a warm smile and a kind word. His soft voice belied the fact that anything he didn't know about weapons, was not something worth knowing. He introduced us to the MK II Sten Gun.

"Should any of you find yourself in a serious confrontation with the enemy, this is your weapon of choice. This is the MK II Sten Gun. This is a submachine gun, it fires a 9mm cartridge, and in the right hands it can fire 500 rounds a minute. As you can see, it is not a sophisticated weapon; it comes with many advantages as well as some disadvantages. Its light, compact design combined with the folding stock, make it ideal for subversive activities. It is also very cheap to produce, this weapon cost £2 6s, and the rate of production means we can supply resistance movements with large quantities. Within its effective range of 100 yards, this is a lethal weapon."

He paused, holding the Sten Gun aloft for us all to see.

"The advantage of light, compact design combined with ease of production means this weapon is not sophisticated. If it is not properly maintained, or if it is misused, it will jam. Furthermore, it will not jam at a convenient moment; it will jam when the enemy is pointing a gun at you. Should you wish to avoid that situation, you will need to become intimately acquainted with this weapon. The MK II Sten Gun has 62 components; get to know every one of them."

I never forgot those words. Sten Guns did have a knack of jamming, but thanks to my training that never happened to me. The problem lay within the magazine which had to be loaded with two columns of ammunition in a staggered arrangement. The problem occurred where the two columns had to merge into a single column before entering the chamber. Any dirt or grit at this crucial point and it jammed.

The lip of the magazine could be another potential problem. It was manufactured with an eight-degree feed angle; if that lip became deformed in any way due to rough handling or wear and tear, it jammed! The weapon kit they issued with each gun enabled you to keep it in perfect condition, and I did. I remember later in the war some of the French Resistance boys making fun of me because of the attention I lavished upon my Sten Gun. They said I treated it like a baby, and they were right.

Chapter Eight
Guns and Interrogation

Firing the Sten Gun for the first time that day made a big impression on me. I hesitated and flinched; apparently I closed both eyes. It recoiled into my shoulder and the noise and smoke invaded my senses. Our instructor had a very methodical approach to safety, explaining that there were disciplines we forgot at our peril. He assured me that as I became familiar with the weapon, my fear would be replaced with confidence. At first I found it to be a frighteningly powerful weapon, but he was right, I did become confident. That cheap, mass-produced piece of equipment gave me the power of life and death over another person.

None of us had handled the weapon before so it was a novel experience for all. Some embraced their newfound power, while others accepted it with a degree of trepidation. In a way, I'm sorry to admit it, but having such power handed to me seemed to fill a void waiting to be filled. As a child, I hated my father and learned to despise him because I couldn't fight back. I wonder now if those feelings ever left me, because when offered the ultimate power over men, I didn't simply embrace it; I relished it.

In subsequent lectures, we touched again upon the importance of organising local resistance and other organisations. Everything we were being trained to do worked towards the final invasion, which the lecturer referred to as the great day. They taught us how to sabotage the enemy's road, rail, and telecommunications. We touched upon how to demolish bridges and vital infrastructure. The detail would be an essential part of our advanced training. One lecture even covered the eventuality of attacking an enemy HQ, explaining how a small highly trained group would easily overcome a provincial headquarters. Little did I realise then just how important that particular lecture would become.

Back on the firing range, the next weapon we had to become acquainted with was the handgun. SOE would potentially source just about any handgun, with the standard issue at that time being the Colt M1911 automatic. At .45 calibre it fired a large round and weighed two and a half pounds. We had smaller guns like the Colt pocket hammerless that fired a .32 round. It's a strange thing handling a gun for the first time. Like the Sten Gun, holding the power of life and death in your hand is frightening at first. For our instructor it was all very matter of fact, and by teaching me to take them apart and reassemble them, I gradually came to see them as functional pieces of equipment.

The moment he introduced me to the Colt Super .38 Special it immediately became my favourite. It felt right for me and my instructor agreed, saying I should not consider changing. He said I should practise with it until it felt like an extension of my hand. By the end of initial training, I could group an entire magazine into a six-inch target at thirty feet. Nobody else on the course managed to do better than that.

Our lecturer moved on to our individual security. He made the distinction between an Allied Soldier in an occupied country and an SOE agent. The soldier's position is clear, he is protected by convention, and he knows who his friends are. An agent has no friends, does not have the protection of a convention, and is surrounded by the enemy. The agent's life hangs by a thread, that thread is his own wit and guile. Our lecturer achieved his first objective; I looked around at my classmates and we each gave a collective swallow! He continued to list the essential rules designed to keep us alive. Cover, information, alertness, inconspicuousness, discretion, discipline, and finally, planning for emergency.

We covered each rule in great detail, some made up a lecture in their own right. I found some details overwhelming. They told us never to drink real coffee in Occupied France; it suggests a connection to the black market. For women, never wear makeup that is not commonly available in your area. Adopt a local hair style and always wear authentic local clothing. Even your underwear must be locally sourced. Never drink too much, if at all. Avoid routine in your movements. Never voice an opinion in public. Always carry identity documents, and never carry incriminating documents. Avoid any close relationships, especially those of a romantic kind. If anything goes wrong, have detailed plans prepared for alternative action or flight.

Eliane did not excel at any of the combat training exercises. She reluctantly mastered the use of the small Colt .32 but remained resolutely opposed to handling the Sten Gun. I assumed this would all count against her, but I had missed the bigger picture. I excelled at all the physical activities, and combat training, but I gradually came to realise that those qualities faded into insignificance when compared to the abilities Eliane offered SOE.

Her first-hand experience of working with the French Resistance made her the stand-out trainee. The lecturer constantly looked towards Eliane when he wanted to confirm points he needed to convey. It amounted to a wake-up call for me; I realised I would have to re-double my efforts if I wanted to succeed. Especially my French. I accepted I wouldn't become a fluent French speaker, so I reasoned I had to become the best at what I could do.

There was a moment during the third week of training when a light came on for me. I got on well with the Drill Sergeant; he seemed to have taken me under his wing. He pushed me harder than any of the other trainees. I had to compete with the men on an equal footing. He didn't once make any allowance for me, but all the while I realised he did it for my benefit. Our hand-to-hand combat training at Wanborough only covered the basics, but it was during one of these sessions that the Drill Sergeant turned that light on for me.

"You're a very attractive woman, Angélique," he said casually.

"You wouldn't be making a pass at me, would you, Sergeant?"

"No, it's just an observation. You've got especially lovely eyes; do you know that?"

"What *is* this, Sergeant?"

"I want you to do something for me. When you attend the next combat session, put your makeup on, especially your eye makeup."

I looked at him in astonishment. It seemed to be such a strange request in those surroundings, but for some reason I trusted him implicitly. He said nothing more about it, and the following day I did as he requested. We'd reached the stage where we had all acquired a rudimentary skill in the martial arts. All of us attained the same basic level, but most of the men were bigger and heavier than me, and more often than not, I found myself lying flat on my back. The Sergeant put me up against the biggest and most aggressive of all of them. Just as I stepped forward, he had a word in my ear.

"Remember your timing. Get in close and only look him in the eyes when you're ready to make your move. When you do, don't hesitate, not for a second. Tai-Otoshi."

Tai-Otoshi is a judo throw, it means body drop. Like all judo throws, it's all about timing, using your opponent's own body weight and momentum to your own advantage. The man he put me up against had good balance, he'd knocked the wind out of me on several occasions. I still didn't understand what was going on, and so I fully expected to be lying flat on my back within a few seconds. The Sergeant's words had been very precise, and I trusted him, so I did exactly as he told me.

I placed a loose hold on my opponent's jacket lapel and right arm sleeve. He applied a similar hold on me. We pushed back and forth for a moment as I mentally rehearsed my move. I lifted my head and looked him straight in the eye, at the same time I rotated my body and extended my right leg across his while pulling him towards me. I executed the throw as I had practised many times. This time, rather than finding myself being counter-thrown, this big man rolled over my shoulder and hit the deck with a satisfying thump. We shared two reactions, astonishment, and jubilation. His astonishment, and my jubilation.

"What just happened?" I asked, looking towards the Sergeant.

"Timing," he replied. "You have just exploited a fundamental weakness that most men possess. When you looked him in the eye, there was a brief moment when he didn't see you as a threat. He only saw a lovely woman. It only gave you a second, but you used it well. The lesson for you, Marcel, is to never fall for that again. When confronted by a woman, treat her exactly the same as you would a man. Your weakness just cost you your life."

What an awakening that proved to be! I had just overpowered a man much bigger than me. It didn't require great strength; it only required a smile and swift action. The Sergeant smiled at me, and with good reason. There had always been a doubt in the back of my mind; I had to compete with the men in an unequal contest of strength. The realisation that I could compete on my own terms proved to be a revelation. I didn't have Eliane's skills, and never would, but I had something else.

I spent most of my younger life trying to stay out of harm's way, trying to evade my father and keep out of trouble in the East End. I developed the instincts of a prey animal without even realising it. I understood instinctively how to avoid a dangerous situation. When confronted, I learned to misdirect someone with a simple gesture of the hand or even just a movement of the eye. I subconsciously influenced people into thinking one thing while I did another. Having spent my childhood developing those skills, I suddenly realised it was time for the prey to turn predator.

The following day, the lecturer explained what happens if you are interrogated. In Occupied France it usually started innocuously enough. An agent might be questioned by the local police. This would usually be confined to four questions. Who are you? Where do you come from? What papers do you have? What are you doing? If an agent is unable to satisfactorily answer those basic questions, or simply looks suspicious, the German authorities may become involved. At worst, this may be the Gestapo.

Their interrogation methods were described in lurid detail. It would initially include solitary confinement, awful food, sleep deprivation, bright lights, and constant threats. Interrogators would swap between a sympathetic approach and an aggressive one in order to disorientate the victim. Women, especially, are likely to be stripped and humiliated if not sexually assaulted. As a last resort, we would be beaten and physically tortured. It painted a terrifying prospect that had been compounded by all the physiological nuances the instructor detailed.

As an SOE agent in an occupied country, we would automatically be in possession of secret information. Some of that information included agents' names, codes, and networks. They made it abundantly clear that we must never divulge information. There are no circumstances where a single life can be traded for many others, perhaps entire networks. Being told we might suffer severe torture, the lecturer's comments sent a chill down my spine. I noticed we all looked at each other.

The lecturer continued to detail how we should resist interrogation. If we fully understood the physiological techniques being used against us, we would be able to resist them. They taught us techniques to deceive interrogators, and how to avoid various traps. As long as the possibility existed that our story might be believed, then hope remained. If, however, we had been apprehended in the act, then we had no hope. This is why we all carried a suicide pill!

I slept fitfully that night. I confess the lecture frightened me. Then in the early hours of the morning, while fast asleep, a group of men burst into our room shouting. Eliane screamed, and I sat up immediately. They overpowered me and dragged us both out of bed in our nightclothes. I had a hood placed over my head as they marched me away. Coming as it did without warning in the dead of night made it absolutely terrifying.

They forced me down into a wooden chair. My arms were tied to the chair before they removed the hood. I recoiled at the bright light shining directly into my face, unable to see beyond it. A man and a woman shouted at me continually. Both dressed in German uniforms, they immediately struck fear into me. They wanted to know my real name.

It continued for hours. The woman would speak quietly to me, saying how sorry she was that this had to happen. If I just told them my name, it would stop. She would leave me and then the man would shout at the top of his voice. They slapped me several times, it really hurt. I told myself repeatedly that it's just an exercise, none of it is real. The fact is, that's not how it felt; it seemed very real, and it had a real effect on me. Then with no warning, they poured a bucket of ice water over me from behind. The shock completely took my breath away. I only had my nightdress on and it clung to my wet body, I might as well have been naked.

As I grew colder, I began to shake. The trembling became uncontrollable, and they repeatedly slapped me. I desperately wanted it to stop. I kept telling myself this is just an exercise, but in my desperation strange thoughts entered my mind. Is this actually real? It continued on and on for hours. They seemed to recognise when my low point came. I thought I might be about to pass out, so I welcomed the prospect. They poured another bucket of ice water over me. I can't describe the shock and fear, as I struggled to breathe. The woman forced my legs apart and tied my knees to the chair legs. I sat there trembling, completely broken and utterly humiliated.

"This is suddenly going to get a whole lot worse for you," she said. "For the last time, what is your real name?"

They so completely broke me, I absolutely believed her. I became convinced something really horrible would happen to me. My inner belief in it being an elaborate exercise slipped away from me. The woman in front of me looked like a German soldier, in my tormented mind she became a German soldier. I whispered a reply to her.

"Speak up, I can't hear you?" she shouted.

I whispered again. The trembling became so bad, I really had lost my voice. She shouted at me again and lowered her head to hear me speak. The cold had almost paralysed my body, but when her head came close enough, I leant forward and sank my teeth into her ear. She recoiled, almost tearing a chunk of her ear off. Blood splashed everywhere. I summoned up my last ounce of strength to say the only thing I had said right from the beginning.

"I'll die first!"

Everything changed in an instant. The woman left clutching a towel to her ear, another replaced her, dressed in FANY uniform. She untied my ropes and wrapped me in blankets, congratulating me all the while. Another FANY officer came in with a mug of tea and put her arm around me.

"Well done, Dotty. That was really impressive," she said.

"No, you've made a mistake," I replied. "I'm Angélique."

The room emptied and my House Commandant walked in.

"They don't normally take it that far," she said, "you were testing them as much as they were testing you. I nearly stopped it two hours ago. You've got guts, Angélique, you kept your head right to the end. You would be amazed how many recruits get caught out by that last little trick."

The relief that it was finally over overwhelmed me. Tears welled up in my eyes, but I remained determined not to show even a hint of weakness. I drank my tea with great difficulty, struggling to move, the cold permeating every muscle. The Lieutenant showed enormous concern for me; I am convinced she hated what I went through as much as I did.

"Let's get you into a hot bath," she said.

I put one foot in front of the other with great difficulty, but with her help we made it. As she filled the bath, I asked her a few questions.

"How did Gabrielle do?"

"I'm not supposed to say anything but she will tell you, anyway. She didn't crack, she's much tougher than she looks, isn't she? They didn't take her as far as they took you, but she's not as physically strong as you. But for all her experience, she fell for that final deception."

"I'm sorry about that woman's ear, I don't understand what came over me."

"Don't worry about her ear, you displayed absolute defiance. She'll admire you for that."

"What about the men?"

"I can't tell you. What I can tell you is, I'm giving you a commendation."

"Yes, I'm nothing if not pig-headed. Did they really have to take it so far? I've never been so terrified."

"You probably think it's been cruel and unnecessary; but let me tell you, if you are ever unfortunate enough to find yourself in that position, this experience will be invaluable to you."

I simply took her advice at face value, realising they based every aspect of the course upon hard-earned experience. When I did find myself in that dreadful position later in the war, the wisdom of those words came flooding back to me. My training undoubtedly saved me.

We worked relentlessly for ten hours a day. The course proved to be both physically and mentally exhausting. We enjoyed nothing as luxurious as a day off. We next had a detailed explanation of how the Germans administered Occupied France and controlled the population. The whim of local commanders often decided the fate of French individuals and entire villages. They left us in no doubt about the risk faced by those who helped us.

Surveillance techniques taught us how to observe others, how to be aware if we are being observed, and how to avoid it. They detailed the use of various premises as well as all the precautions we should take. Communication is another huge topic, occupying three lectures. Internal coded communication, particularly within a cell, all in great detail. We covered everything from Morse code to carrier pigeons. The radio operator was the vital link within SOE, especially for external communication.

We were all taught the basics, but to be a top-class wireless operator required an enormous amount of practice; it became one of the most dangerous jobs undertaken in Occupied France. Radio signals could be tracked and triangulated. The early sets weighed about 30 lbs, with a 70 ft long cable aerial. The operator had twenty minutes to send the signal and to be long gone from the area, carrying the heavy transmitter. Basic training told us not to carry incriminating evidence about our person. And yet the wireless operator had to carry a heavy suitcase transmitter from one safe house to another. People like me stood on the shoulders of operators like Noor Inayat Khan who received a posthumous George Cross.

Gabrielle, as I became used to calling her, had not been the same since our interrogation. The terror of our mock interrogation had a deep effect on both of us. Our language problem had all but gone; we became very close, and I realised something deeper troubled her. Whenever she forgot herself and laughed about something, another deeper emotion would erase it. One evening in the Mess Hall, she finally broke her silence and spoke about it.

Over time the Germans got ever closer to her and therefore closer to her resistance colleagues. She had no option but to make her escape. The attention which had been directed towards her, then led the Gestapo to her brother Emmanuel. She said nothing else; nothing else needed to be said. Poor Gabrielle, she blamed herself for what happened to her brother. I doubted that anything she did directly led the Gestapo to him. More likely, she had the simple good fortune to escape while he didn't.

Her courage astounded me. She sat through all the lectures about interrogation, and she experienced it first-hand herself. Nobody understood better what her brother's fate would have been. When I asked if she knew for sure that he had died, she gave me a slight nod of the head. A tear rolled down her face. Now I understood her dogged determination to return to France. The hatred she felt for her brother's murderers became palpable. It actually concerned me. Everything we were being taught required self-discipline; a reckless SOE agent is unlikely to survive.

The fourth and final week at STS 5 continued just as intensively. The topics we covered included the selection of drop zones. We had to calculate parachute drops in various wind conditions. We learned how to communicate with pilots and their reception when landing. This tied in with map reading and navigation, and endless hours studying codes and ciphers. Our breadth of knowledge became enormous, and I worried about retaining it all. One of our instructors seemed to understand my apprehension without me mentioning it. He presented us with yet another revelation during our last day of lectures.

"You're nearing the end of your course now, and no doubt you feel it has all been a lot to take in. What you must remember is that this has only been a preliminary course. You will go on from here into various advanced training courses in a variety of disciplines. Some of that will be completely new to you, but mostly it will build upon what you have been taught here. We have given you your basic grounding, now you must build upon that knowledge. The last requirement that all SOE agents must have is the one thing we cannot teach you. It takes great courage to undertake the work you are being trained for; but never doubt yourselves, your presence here shows that you already possess that courage. Take the knowledge we have given you and serve your country with distinction. Good luck and Godspeed to you all."

Our group met his words with total silence. We enjoyed no end-of-term celebration, just the cold reality of what lay ahead of us. The time rapidly approached for us to go our separate ways, the problem being that I didn't know which direction that might be. I needn't have worried, our House Commandant called me into her office.

"Sit down, Angélique. Where do you want to go from here?"

"I don't know, you tell me."

"You have surprised many people on this course. Sergeant Cummings has nothing but praise for you. The question is what Station M wants you to do. I can't advise you because I've not even heard of it."

I suddenly realised I was still bluffing with the same hand of two cards. In fact, I had forgotten the General's name I used before, so that left me with only one card.

"My French has come on in leaps and bounds, but we all know I wouldn't pass for a French national. Perhaps it's just as well Station M requires those other skills I've acquired."

"Sergeant Cummings has put forward an unusual recommendation. Some of the men here are going on to Arisaig in Scotland to develop paramilitary and hand-to-hand combat skills. Women do not currently undertake that course, but it's under discussion. Your Drill Sergeant has recommended that you should take part in a trial to see if a woman can stay the course at Arisaig. What do you think?"

"I'll do it!"

"I thought you would, so did he, that's why I've already prepared your paperwork."

"That's great. If I can stay the course, will I be the first of many women?"

"Yes you would, so it's quite a responsibility."

"I *can't* fail, then."

"When I first interviewed you, Angélique, you told me you were the most determined person I would ever meet. Do you know what? You are! I don't doubt that you will succeed."

"Well, thank you. And thank you for being there for me, I appreciate it."

"It's been a pleasure; I wish you all the luck in the world."

I left her office feeling quite buoyed up. If she had confidence in me, then so should I. We all understood that Wanborough simply provided a step on the ladder, but it proved to be more than that. We built up a camaraderie that would be hard to leave behind. Gabrielle and I had become extremely close, I wanted to believe our friendship would outlast the war. For all that they told us not to socialise with the men, we did! We were all there on equal terms; by the end of the course, none of us had anything to prove. Inevitably, one man seemed to pay me extra attention, and I confess I always had a smile for him. I only knew him as Gaston.

Despite what anyone said we had no intention of letting our last evening together just slip away. You wouldn't call it a party, but that evening in the Mess Hall we let protocol drop, just a little. We pulled some tables and chairs together, and we had what one "wag" called the last supper. They were a good bunch of lads and three of them went with me to Arisaig, including Gaston. They came from a wide range of backgrounds, not all what you would expect.

One of them had been a bank manager; Gaston had been a factory production manager. They all had one thing in common, they'd spent time in France before the war, the odd one out being an Army intelligence officer. He insisted his job amounted to a glorified clerk, but I didn't believe him. They were about to ask me about my background when an officer came over and gave us all a bollocking for discussing our private lives. That evening remains a lovely memory of my time at Wanborough, especially my time with Gabrielle. We all hugged each other. Saying goodbye had a considerable poignancy during the war, especially for people like us.

Chapter Nine
Arisaig

They organised everything for us the following morning; we had transport to take each of us to our various destinations. We had rail passes, maps, and timetables, as well as a small amount of money if we needed it. Cars waited outside to transport us. Our collective journeys nearly all started at Guildford Station, and so having said our goodbyes at Wanborough, we found ourselves saying them all over again at the station. Finally, we would each go our separate ways. Several of the group headed south for Beaulieu in Hampshire, including Gabrielle. Others went on to various specialist training centres. My group needed to go to London Euston, en route to Arisaig.

My last and final goodbye had to be with Gabrielle. She finally called me Dotty again, and I called her Eliane. We pledged to keep in touch and reunite after the war. One last hug and she kissed me, apparently that's what French women do. It became a tearful farewell. After the war, I tried desperately to get back in touch with her. Lily contacted Vera Atkins for me. Vera ran F Section alongside Colonel Buckmaster. After the war, Vera Atkins took it upon herself to find out what happened to each and every one of the female agents she sent to France.

It broke my heart to be told Gabrielle had been parachuted into Occupied France directly into the unfolding disaster of the "Prosper" network. Gabrielle was far from alone; the German exposure of almost the entire network proved to be a devastating blow for the SOE. It has always been assumed that an informer had been responsible. After the war, in 1948 during his trial, the chief suspect Henri Dericourt was acquitted due to insufficient evidence. Vera Atkins established that Gabrielle died in Dachau concentration camp during 1944, much the same fate as Noor Inayat Khan. My memory of Eliane never fades, but it's always the same memory. She is waving goodbye with a smile, and a tear is running down her face. She smiles with all the innocence of a person who has hope in their future. I know what that future was, and still I see that smile.

We arrived at Euston just in time to catch the overnight sleeper to Glasgow. There we had to change for a train to Arisaig. I had not been in uniform outside of a military establishment before. The public, as we now referred to them, were very courteous towards us. That also applied to the attendant who kindly found me a sleeping compartment. The food on the train can only be described as grim, but my three companions compensated for that. We had already been through a lot together; a steadily growing bond developed between us.

Marcel, the military intelligence officer, said he had become tired of paperwork. While Gaston left an important job as a production manager in an armaments factory. Pierre worked in a bank before working as an analyst at Bletchley Park. He was the clever one among us. They had one important thing in common; they all spoke French. Marcel had a French mother who married an Englishman. Although Marcel never lived in France, his parents brought him up to be bi-lingual. The other two had both spent some time living in France.

Our strict instructions not to socialise at Wanborough did not, as far as we were concerned, extend to the four of us on that train. That evening in the dining carriage became the first occasion when we became really close to each other. As part of a very secret organisation, we already knew far more than the public would ever be told. That made us different to all the other passengers; we formed an exclusive club of four, inextricably bound.

"I'm Dotty, can we just be ourselves for this evening?"

"Bloody good idea, Dotty, I'm Joe," said Gaston.

We understood the imperative that we adopted our French code names as our own. But we were also real people who shared a common bond. Pierre became Donald, and Marcel was Harry. Suddenly we became even closer. When I turned in for the night, I found it comforting. I didn't stand alone in that venture; we supported each other. I slept like a log. Far from keeping me awake, the motion and clatter of the train seemed to rock me to sleep. The attendant knocked on my compartment door at six o'clock in the morning; we were stationary in Glasgow station. The next person to knock was Joe.

"Come on, Dot, get your arse in gear, they want us off the train."

"I'm coming, I'm coming, wait for me, Joe."

"No, we thought we'd leave you to travel back to London," came the reply.

Joe came from London, but not from the East End, so I said he didn't qualify as a proper Londoner. I noticed him looking at me at Wanborough, perhaps it's because I looked at him. I'm 5ft 10in so I'm kind of attracted to tall men. Joe stood shorter than me with a great mop of curly brown hair. I don't think his mouth even had a down-turned position; he just always smiled. He had thick eyebrows and eyelashes that I would have killed for, and yet on his smiling face it suited him.

We obviously liked each other, but I remained determined that nothing like that would happen - you know, stuff like that. I quickly put on a bit of lipstick and eye makeup; I was with three handsome fellas after all. I rushed out to find Joe waiting for me on the other side of the door.

"I thought you lot had left me behind."

"As if! Come on, Dot, the boys are waiting."

In the early hours of the morning, the station was relatively quiet. We walked along the platform as a group with me in the middle, the hope being that we would find a place for breakfast. A cheerful porter gave us the nod about a "greasy spoon" just around the corner. It only took us five minutes, with two hours before our next train departed. It's funny how you remember little things from all those years ago. I remember that cooked breakfast as if I'm sitting there now. In a time of rationing, it was a treat to have any bacon, let alone a plateful. Had it been the dead of night, I reckon the locals would have seen us glowing when we left there.

The train to Arisaig passed through some breath-taking Scottish countryside. All the while, the boys poked fun at me; they said I behaved like an over-excited kid at Christmas, looking out of the window. The fact is, I hadn't seen Scotland before; I didn't know it would be so wild and mountainous. Arisaig station served the village of Arisaig and if you blinked you'd miss it. A more remote station I couldn't imagine. I felt terribly important when we stepped outside the station. We were met by a military vehicle, a Humber staff car.

Don sat in the front, and three of us squeezed into the back. I sat half on their laps with their arms around me, they thought this was a wonderful idea. What the driver must have thought of us, I can't imagine. We swayed back and forth into each other's arms as the car bumped in and out of the ruts. I think the driver's expression indicated disapproval.

We drove along a narrow single track road seemingly coming from nowhere and going nowhere. On either side of us, forest trees reached for the sky, but the sky in the distance became occupied by mountains. The fun stopped abruptly as we approached what I thought at first glance to be a castle. We arrived at STS 21, Arisaig House. None of us had seen anything like it. Perched not far from the edge of the sea, slap in the middle of nowhere, the word remote doesn't do it justice.

Coming from Wanborough, we were accustomed to enormous country houses being used as SOE establishments, but by any measure Arisaig is impressive. Built as a Victorian hunting lodge, all I can say is that the Victorians knew how to live! Initially, as we entered via the drive, it looked a little like a collection of buildings, seemingly random rooflines and dormer windows. Only later did we realise that the full majesty of the building faced the glorious vista in the other direction.

Arisaig functioned very much as a military establishment. During the summer of 1942, I became the first and only female trainee at Arisaig; in fact there was only one other woman, the station nurse. It would be nearly a year later before female agents routinely went to Scotland. That placed me in an uncomfortable position. None of the instructors had dealt with a woman before, so I entered an exclusively male world. And not just any man's world; here only the fittest and strongest were trained to be the SOE's elite agents. They also trained to be ruthless killers.

We were not billeted in the house itself. The entire area had been requisitioned, including various estate cottages. They made no allowance for me, I had to share with the boys in a cottage with two bedrooms. It would have been awkward if not frightening with strangers, but we were mates, so I had no fears in that regard.

At least they gave me one of the bedrooms; Don and Harry top and tailed in the other bedroom. Joe lost the toss and had to sleep in what passed as the living room. I hadn't lived with a man before, let alone three of them. Talk about a rude awakening to the habits of the opposite sex. I didn't realise men changed their sweaty underwear so infrequently and wore their "almond rocks" until they walked away by themselves!

We reported to the house for meals, as well as showers. I basically only slept in what I called the "fume cupboard". That first evening, we met the others of the intake in the Mess Hall. It surprised me to see only two of them, our band of four became six. They introduced themselves.

"Hello, I'm James Hollingworth," the blonde haired one said.

"And I'm Robert Bartlett, everyone calls me Rob," the tall one said.

The blonde one looked very smart in every respect, terribly nicely spoken and polite. The tall one turned out to be a Londoner with a very infectious smile. He looked at me with a real glint in his eye. We introduced ourselves to them and exchanged the usual pleasantries. The one with the glint in his eye stood looking at me. Finally he spoke.

"I probably shouldn't mention this, but you're… um… not what I expected."

"Did you expect someone shorter?" I replied.

"Well, no, I can't quite put my finger on it, someone different."

"Different how, what did you have in mind?"

"I'm not sure, maybe someone a good deal less attractive."

That was my introduction to Rob, he flirted with me from the first second we met. I had no doubt he behaved in exactly the same way with every woman he met. When you're dressed in a FANY uniform and not feeling remotely attractive, a bit of flirting goes a long way. I had to smile at him. I probably shouldn't have, but then again, I'm glad I did. We all got on well together right from the start. James had the look of an ex-army officer. He swept his blonde hair back from his face and looked at me with piercing blue eyes. If ever a man had been designed to sweep a lady off her feet, it had to be James.

Robert is the kind of bloke who can't disappear in a crowd. Despite being kind of ordinary looking, he stood 6ft 1in tall. He had light brown wavy hair and hazel eyes with those little crows-feet in the corners where he continually smiled. He remained ordinary looking until he looked at you and spoke. I reckoned Rob could charm the birds out of the trees. Joe had that same personality, but whereas he maintained a polite reserve, Rob had "more front than Selfridges"! I poked a bit of fun at him.

"So tell me then, Rob, what did you do for a living before you joined this outfit? Don't tell me, with your charm, I bet you worked as a door-to-door salesman. What did you sell, insurance or brushes?"

"You're close - soap."

"Really?"

"Best job I've ever had," he replied, looking really upset. "White King granulated laundry soap. You know the one, longer lasting suds. It may not be much but you shouldn't take the piss; I'm proud of my job."

"Oh, no. I'm sorry, I didn't mean being a salesman is demeaning or anything. Oh dear, that sounds awful, I mean what I said sounds awful. I'm sure it's a wonderful job."

"No, actually it's a rotten job, but it's my old mum, you see, she can't get about much now. And since Dad's been gone, well, I had to work seven days a week, I didn't earn much selling soap."

"Oh, Rob! Me and my big mouth, I'm really sorry…What are you two laughing at?"

With that, the pair of them collapsed in laughter, and the penny finally dropped. Then the rest of the boys burst into laughter, leaving me holding the wooden spoon. I soon saw the funny side of it and pretended to give him a good slap but he grabbed my hand. I had known Rob for five minutes, and we stood close to each other with him holding my hand and the pair of us laughing like drains. It turned out he was actually a builder and lived in France for a while. He said he did it for a laugh, so I reckon a woman had to be involved. Then he had a spell in the Marines before SOE found out he could speak French.

"I didn't realise women did this course, Dotty," said James.

"They don't, I'm the first, probably the first of many."

"Well, you must be here by right, so well done."

They accepted me without question, so at least I cleared the first hurdle. I have to admit being the first female recruit was daunting. My team were all lovely, but I realised I would have to work harder than any of them. The atmosphere in the Mess Hall that evening felt very relaxed. Another group of men sat together and seemed to be having as much fun as us lot. The NCOs accepted our high spirits without complaint. Everything about Arisaig seemed less formal than Wanborough. We had a pleasant introduction to STS 21. They told us to report for breakfast at 06:00 hrs the following morning and to be dressed in full military uniform.

Our alarm clocks rang soon after 05:00 hrs and I found Joe knocking on my door offering me a cup of tea. I knew Joe's game; any excuse to enter a girl's bedroom. However, at 05:00 hrs a cup of tea in bed is irresistible. We liked each other, Joe and I, and in other circumstances I think I might have been tempted to more than just the tea. But in the circumstances, I ushered him out of the door and quickly made ready.

As we walked together towards the house, the surrounding views took my breath away. The smell of pinewood hung in the clean damp air as low clouds pressed fingers through the branches. Above us, an enormous bird soared high in the sky with no effort from its wings. Its plaintive call didn't seem to belong to such a big bird. It was less a squawk and more a squeak, but somehow it filled the air. I had never experienced such sights and sounds before. My senses filled to overflowing, as if I had been deaf and blind before that moment.

Those same sights and sounds became my companion for the day, but a new sense was about to invade my body. We reported in full kit as instructed and met our new Drill Sergeant. He made it immediately clear that everything we learned at preliminary training amounted to the first rung of the Arisaig ladder. He told us this would be where our basic skills would find their practical application. He issued our additional kit for the day, the principal item being a Bergen backpack. It looked heavy, and it proved to be even heavier when I picked it up. It contained everything we might need to survive; we must never be parted from it.

"This is only your basic kit," the sergeant said. "When I'm satisfied you are sufficiently competent, you will also carry weapons and ammunition."

He explicitly ignored me, or rather he paid me no special attention. I thought being the first woman at Arisaig, I would be on the receiving end of all kinds of comments. In fact, they had immediately instigated the policy that women would not be treated differently in any way. That policy remained unchanged for the duration of the war. I struggled to put the Bergen on my back, but I was not alone. We set off on what proved to be the most gruelling day of my life. It started as a hike in the surrounding forest. When we reached open grassland, it became a run, and slowed back to a walk again in the next forest. Some of the hills became mountains and every stride up the gradient sent a searing pain down my thighs.

Had I been dressed in shorts and running shoes, and had the course been flat firm ground, I don't doubt that I would have been fine. However, the course was anything but flat. We crossed streams and bogs, often knee-deep in mud or water. The weight of the Bergen seemed to push me into the ground, and my wet boots were made of lead. As I staggered over one of the streams, I slipped over and became soaked from the waist down. Two of the boys rushed to my assistance only to be shouted at by the Sergeant. It took my last ounce of strength to struggle back onto my feet.

There came a point when, for the first time in my life, I realised I might have to give in. I would never voluntarily give in, but my legs buckled beneath me. Just at that moment, the sergeant shouted to stop. I heard the most wonderful words I ever remember hearing, "rest" and "food." Rob, undoubtedly the strongest of the men, immediately helped me off with the Bergen. We all slumped into a heap, legs throbbing, lungs bursting. Not one of us remained standing; I didn't appear conspicuous in any way. The Sergeant walked around assessing his trainees. He had a brief conversation with each of us, I suspect he wanted to be sure we were still conscious.

"You did well, Archer. How are your legs?"

"I had very attractive legs, sergeant, I left them back there somewhere."

"They served you well, Archer, you'd better go back for them."

We both laughed. But really my legs had become no laughing matter. The blisters on my feet hurt and the dull ache in my thighs submitted only to the cramp in my calf muscles. We ate army rations survival food, and we drank water from a stream. None of that mattered, all that really mattered was sitting down. Forty-five minutes later we had to resume.

He told us to stretch our muscles, heave on our packs and get going again. My heart sank to depths I didn't even know existed. I remember three low points during the afternoon, starting, finishing, and everything in between. Perhaps the very worst part was starting again. The cramp and the blisters filled my head to the exclusion of all else until even that became replaced with a kind of delirium. I got to the point where I almost felt nothing.

Somehow I stayed the course, we all did. The Sergeant's job at Arisaig had not been to sort the wheat from the chaff, we were all supposed to be wheat. His job was to build us up, to get the best out of us. When we staggered to a halt at the end of the day, we found him full of praise. Apparently we had done well. Too weary to stand in the shower, I sat beneath it. My legs looked white and wrinkled having been wrapped in my wet trousers. I sat there looking at my blisters until my whole body matched my legs. Joe collected our flock together, and I found them waiting for me.

"You didn't have to wait for me," I said.

Their reply came in the form of a weary smile. We didn't even have the strength for our usual banter. Despite that, they looked out for me. I didn't want to be treated differently to anyone else, but the boys would have none of it. They had my back, every one of them. When I thanked them, it came from the heart. We had a quiet evening in the Mess Hall; even Rob lacked the energy to flirt with me. The walk back to the fume cupboard became the last leg of a marathon. We struggled through the cottage door and went directly to our beds, hardly a word passing between us.

Chapter Ten
No Holds Barred

The following day, we were introduced to a diminutive Japanese gentleman wearing voluminous black trousers that looked like a dress and a heavy white open jacket, very similar to a judo gi. I realised the clothes formed some kind of traditional martial arts dress, and I assumed this would be judo that we had been introduced to at Wanborough. He asked for a volunteer to step forward and attempt to strike him. Before anyone did, he pointed towards the tallest of us. Rob stood nearly a foot taller than our diminutive instructor. The mismatch seemed almost absurd; Rob could probably pick him up with one hand.

He stepped forward as instructed and attempted to grab the little man. What followed had to be seen to be believed. It almost appeared to be an illusion. Rob found himself flying through the air, destined for a collision with the ground. One by one, he did this to each of us. I stepped forward, and he gave me a short stick to use as a knife. Having seen the likely outcome, I tried my utmost to stab him. In judo, we maintain our hold during a throw - not so this little gentleman.

Like Rob, I found myself flying through the air quite independently of him. All the while, I remained unaware of any particular force being applied to me. This was our introduction to Mr Tanaka and Aikido. Right from the beginning, we had to understand the importance of our state of mind before even beginning to coordinate mind and body. I confess I loved it and maintained an interest long after the war.

It wasn't all physical training. We had lectures which went back over some of the ground we covered at Wanborough but were more intensive. We dealt with everything from concealing our identity, to fieldcraft and navigation. It also seemed to be very important that we became familiar with the enemy's uniforms and structure of command. We would also familiarise ourselves with German weapons during our weapons training. There would be some form of physical training nearly every day, some equally as gruelling as our initiation day. Every one of us sat during lectures with our bodies aching.

The next major revelation arrived in the form of Eric Sykes and "Buster" Fairbairn! These two unlikely looking gentlemen had both worked for the Shanghai police where William Fairbairn gained the nickname "Shanghai Buster Fairbairn". At the outbreak of war, they both presented themselves at the War Office offering their help training the British armed forces. Having described their particular talents, I can just imagine what went through the mind of the senior officer interviewing them. Two middle-aged bespectacled men of unconventional background, self-confessed experts in some very underhand and dubious practices. The man from the Ministry told them the British Army did not descend to such ungentlemanly conduct, and they should clear off! Well, they might have been unfit for the Army but they were exactly what the SOE wanted.

Buster especially looked like a formidable character. Short of stature but long in the arms, he made a good impression of a monkey. His neck appeared to be as thick as my waist and he had shoulders like Rob but minus the height. He had thick black curly hair, and a broken nose. To complete this image, you can add a scar that ran from his ear down to his mouth. We all agreed, we would hate to meet the person who gave him that scar!

Eric Sykes was far less physical than Buster, with his hair parted in the middle, wearing small round glasses. You would not have guessed that he had an encyclopaedic knowledge of firearms. Between these two gentlemen, they understood everything there is to know about self-defence, small arms, and how to kill people. Everything we learned about pistol shooting at Wanborough, they told us to forget! We didn't learn how to withdraw our pistol and calmly hold it with both hands while taking aim at a nice convenient target thirty feet away. Instead, we learned how to quick draw our pistol and shoot from the hip. Apparently Eric held the title "the fastest draw in the East". He could draw his pistol from a shoulder holster, cock it, and fire it accurately on target in one third of a second.

The reason for all this is that if you are confronting the enemy at a distance, you would not use your pistol. You would use your Sten Gun within its hundred-yard range. The pistol is primarily for close range self-defence rather than offence. If we needed our pistol in those circumstances, we would likely need it quickly. When we practised these scenarios, it all fell into place. By the end of training, I managed to draw my weapon and fire at close range within a second. That meant that even if I'd been confronted by someone with a drawn weapon, I still had an excellent chance of firing first.

When Buster said he would teach us to fight no holds barred, he really wasn't kidding. An expert at the martial arts and every other art of self-defence and silent killing, he mixed the martial arts with his own unique blend of fighting. Those who mastered his techniques might almost think they had become invincible. His approach was absolutely clinical. He viewed the human body as a collection of bones, muscles, nerves, veins, and arteries. While he didn't necessarily use the correct terms, he understood the human body in every detail. He could pinpoint every vulnerable area.

We learned how to defend ourselves against any kind of threat. In all instances, we were dealing with the enemy, and no quarter should ever be given. If we could successfully defend ourselves against a knife or a fist, then we should immediately follow that up with a blow or manoeuvre to incapacitate or kill our attacker. Buster taught us how to kill people with our bare hands. We learned how to kill silently and in ways that left no trace, such as stopping a man's heart with nothing more than a hand pressed in the right place. I knew how to break a man's neck or strangle him without leaving as much as a mark. With a knife, I could sever an artery to kill the victim in seconds.

I confess I revelled in this aspect of our training because counterintuitively I competed on level terms with the men. Of course, brute strength can be a great asset, but technique and timing are more important. Mr Tanaka taught us that the greater the level of attainment in Aikido, the more the application of strength is a handicap. Brute strength stands as an obstacle between the coordination of body and mind. Our greatest attainment comes from the mind. In Aikido, we call it the "unbendable arm". I really took that on board. Mr Tanaka told me I was his most promising student because of the way I applied my mind.

Buster was a man of very few words. His work became his life; he seemed to have little room for anything else. When he took me aside one day and started asking me some personal questions, it really surprised me.

"You're a natural, Archer. Why is that?"

"What do you mean?"

"I've taught enough people, including women, to know what the most difficult thing is to teach. It's that thing that you have."

"I'm not following, Buster."

"You're either being dumb or modest, Archer. Which is it?"

"I realise I'm not the sharpest knife in the drawer, but I'm not exactly modest, am I?"

"Well you're not dumb either are you! When you confront someone in training, you've got more tricks to misdirect them than even I know. You're also not a bad-looking woman, Archer; you use that as well, don't you?"

"That's a trick the Drill Sergeant taught me at Wanborough. Use my eyes to the best effect."

"It works. Do you honestly not realise those other things you do? I've watched you closely. You intuitively draw your opponent's attention away from your next move. It's an old magician's trick. A movement of the eyes, or a sleight of hand. When we trained in the use of everyday objects as weapons, I matched you up against Hollingworth. You glanced at that bottle for a split second and moved your body just slightly towards it. You had no intention of trying to grasp it, did you? Hollingworth shifted his weight to the right foot, and in that instant you had him."

"I don't think about it, it's just what I've always done."

"That's why I say you're a natural. Don't overthink it, Archer; just keep practising what you're doing. You're a very rare commodity, perhaps we should call you the 'lipstick assassin'."

That unfortunate name stuck, but he certainly made me think. When you come from a background like mine, achievement is not a word I would have been associated with. I could run all right, but that didn't empower me. At Arisaig, I really achieved something, I had a sense of self-worth, albeit as a lipstick assassin. I didn't always manage to compete with the men in the Arisaig environment, because they became wise to my feminine charms. Outside of Arisaig, it would be a different story.

Physical training remained the hardest, they spared me nothing. I regularly struggled home last on most of the cross-country exercises. Nevertheless, I proved I could carry the same weight and stay the course. The problem was living with the injuries and the blisters. We had a resident doctor and nurse who probably tended me more than anyone else. When the MO told the Drill Sergeant I should miss an exercise, I went anyway, turning out equipped with bandages and painkillers. The boys had to help me the last mile home. That's the first and last time I gave in to anything.

The SOE recruited experts to teach us things that you might describe as specialist knowledge. For instance, we had a convicted forger teaching us the finer arts of forgery. We had a burglar-cum-safecracker, and a locksmith who taught us the most amazing things. I had the distinct feeling these people were unable to leave even if they wanted to. The local poacher was exactly that. He taught us how to catch or steal anything that moves or flies. Anything that would sustain our lives in open country.

Not everything happened at Arisaig. The whole of northwest Scotland had been requisitioned for the purpose. Other smaller specialist training schools were spread over the area. We spent time at another hunting lodge in Mora, called Garramore House. At STS 25a, we had an architect, and an engineer, as well as Army experts. We learned about explosives, fuses, and detonators. Every kind of explosive and fuse imaginable became familiar to us. Much more than that, they taught us exactly how to use them. Demolition of railway lines, bridges, and buildings were the primary focus of our attention. In all cases, it is never just the size of the explosion that determines the outcome. We needed to fully understand how things had been constructed before we could deconstruct them.

We visited various railways and buildings where we had to assess the problem and explain where and how we would place our charges. They conducted exercises at night when we went out in pairs to place dummy charges on real railway lines and bridges. We did the same in factories in Glasgow, where we had to creep in and out without being detected by night watchmen and workers. In addition to all the dummy runs, we also made a lot of enormous bangs.

We had a brief stay at STS 23b. Swordland Lodge lies on the shore of

Loch Morar, with a base at Tarbert Bay. Here the Navy crew taught us essentially how to get ashore in a small dinghy launched from a ship or submarine. With hindsight, we should have spent more time at Swordland; we barely scratched the surface. The accepted doctrine at SOE had been that agents would be parachuted into occupied countries, and so they placed less emphasis on amphibious landings. This proved to be a mistake for Norwegian operations, and also a mistake for our operations from Station M. Rob and I nearly drowned getting ashore in Normandy. More extensive training would have prevented that.

Final weapons training happened back at Arisaig where we became familiar with just about every weapon available to the British military as well as to their German counterparts. We completed the course with extensive exercises where they dropped us off in remote areas, fully kitted with weapons. We had to make our own way to various objectives under the cover of darkness. Only then did I fully appreciate what all that physical training had been for. We struggled miles over mountainous terrain in driving rain in the dead of night. When we reached our objective, we mounted an assault with live ammunition. On another exercise, we might place charges and blow an old bothy sky high. The last exercise proved to be the longest and hardest.

They sent us out in pairs halfway across Scotland with the ultimate aim that we should all rendezvous together at the same time to mount a joint assault. Towards the end, my heavy load nearly crippled me. If there had been an option to give in, I might even have thought about it, but if we stopped, exposed and alone on a desolate mountainside, I would have died. The triumph of completing the last exercise cannot be adequately expressed. Somewhere between relief, and unrestrained elation would sum it up. The following morning, we said very little, but the expressions on our faces said it all.

Come the end of our long stay at Arisaig, the team once again had to be broken up. The powers that be made decisions about us with no consultation; they just informed us. Rob and James stayed at Arisaig for advanced paramilitary training. Don had to go to another secret establishment, something to do with codes and ciphers. I found it to be one of the cruelties of war; they threw us together in circumstances which united us in ways that simply didn't exist in peacetime. As friends and comrades, we shared a reliance on each other that seemed unbreakable. But when our orders came, something did break.

The last supper remained cheerful and upbeat, but it hung over us like a descending cloud. Our conversation always came back to reuniting after the war. We didn't admit it, but we all accepted the probability that a reunion was unlikely. I dreaded the end of the evening; saying goodbye would be awkward. The boys would have put a brave face on and said things like 'good luck, old boy'. But as the odd one out, the team centred around me. They might be tough boys between themselves, but not with me. James put his arms around me and kissed my cheek. He didn't let go for ages. When he finally spoke, the emotion in his voice rang in my ears.

Rob just stood there waiting his turn with a sense of anticipation on his face. When James finally put me down, I looked at Rob wondering what to do and say. Standing in front of the others tempered any thoughts I might have had. I didn't want to embarrass him or myself. I should have known Rob would share none of those concerns. He scooped me up in his powerful arms and kissed me on the lips like I didn't recall having been kissed before. A kiss can tell you a lot about a person. His lips explored mine in search of a response. Looking at his reaction, I think he found one. Despite standing in front of the others, I became lost in the moment. It would be fair to say he took my breath away.

"Wow, where did that come from Robert Bartlett?"

"When this is over, Dotty, I'll find you; wherever you are, I will find you."

"I won't be hard to find, Rob. I'll be the one with the red nails and lipstick looking out for you."

I don't understand why I said that; it amounted to a commitment, and I never made commitments. The words hung in the air in big bold letters. Rob looked at me, we each explored the other's thoughts during an unspoken conversation. It might have been just as well that Donald didn't hear our conversation, he didn't realise what he interrupted. He gave me yet another hug - another sad farewell.

Chapter Eleven
Ringway And Beaulieu

From Arisaig, the three of us moved south again, this time to STS 51 Ringway, next to Manchester airport. Here we would undertake parachute training, the only discipline that absolutely terrified me. The prospect of jumping out of an aeroplane positively filled me with dread. Joe pretended otherwise but felt nearly as terrified as me. Harry surprised us, seeming very unconcerned. They billeted us together in a house close to Ringway. Actually, it proved to be a lot better than the fume cupboard at Arisaig. Our stay at STS 51 would be relatively brief; ours wasn't the full training course. We were not intended to be paratroopers, we only had to land safely in Occupied France.

During training, they mixed theory and practical, with all the emphasis on the practical. We started kitted out with the parachutists' smocks and foam helmets. There seemed to be a rush to get us in action on the jump tower. The sooner we managed to overcome our fears, the sooner training could begin in earnest. They called the first exercise "swing landing". It still required you to launch yourself from a platform. With everyone else looking on, I didn't have the option of backing out; I had to do it. It's not natural to step off from a high place, your brain sensibly tells you not to do it. I wanted to follow my own advice, but I jumped.

With hindsight, swing landing is like riding a bicycle, but that didn't apply the first time. My heart jammed itself in my throat, and my stomach almost joined it. For the second part of that training, we had to get out of the harness, rather important in some circumstances. The next level increased the fear factor. We practised dropping through what they called the “Joe hole”. On some British planes, you dropped through a hole in the aircraft’s belly.

When I asked why “Joe hole”, they told me it was slang for an outside toilet. That seemed to sum up my fate very well. Beneath the hole, a huge fan simulated the sudden rush of air as we left the aeroplane. At only three feet wide, the danger of injuring yourself on the way down should not be underestimated. Some people ignored the warnings, and if you struck your face, you would be in for a very nasty injury. They even had a term for it. They called it, “ringing the bell”.

With all of those fears in my mind, it took a lot of willpower to take that irrevocable step. Harry jumped first without incident. “Piece of cake,” he shouted. I looked down at the Joe hole, hoping I wouldn’t end up in the shit. Remembering all the training, I took the plunge.

“Come on, Joe, what’s wrong with you? It’s a piece of cake,” I shouted.

It’s amazing how your bravado increases after the event. When we became reasonably confident with the basics, the next and obvious level loomed large. I assumed it would be an aeroplane, but it wasn’t. The first proper parachute drop is from a balloon. A standard barrage balloon they called “Bessie” hovered, tethered to a truck. Beneath it, a large wicker basket swung back and forth. The three of us climbed aboard with an instructor. I found myself shaking. We were about to float up into the heavens standing in a glorified shopping basket. Everything about it seemed unnatural. My knuckles turned white clinging to the sides. As the winch played out the cable, we floated ever higher into the heavens. I hardly dared to look down. I realised it needed to be high enough for the parachute to deploy, but I just kept thinking: this is high enough.

The instructor told me to go first; apparently if a “mere” woman managed to do it, the men would be obliged to follow. He opened the Joe hole, and I sat with my feet dangling through it. Beneath me, the landscape looked like a patchwork quilt. It looked like the place where I should be, and where I belonged, not dangling in a shopping basket. I was absolutely terrified, scared witless, and petrified all at the same time. When the order came, I held my breath and did as the training had taught me. I dropped through the hole. Those first few seconds before the parachute deployed are the longest few seconds of my life.

When it opened, the sudden jolt sent my stomach back to where it had come from. It took several more seconds before I collected myself, the violent swinging back and forth ceased and I looked up at the most reassuring sight in the world. The moment I realised I would be all right, the training kicked back in. I rehearsed my landing procedure as the ground loomed larger, racing towards me. When the moment arrived, it did so with a bang. To my immense relief, I managed a perfect landing. I wanted to raise my arms in the air and jump up and down for joy, but I resisted. I released the chute and gathered it together. An instructor had followed me down and stood waiting for me.

"Well done, Archer, perfect landing, you should be pleased."

"Pleased, I'm over the bloody moon."

I watched Joe and Harry follow me down. Harry landed perfectly; Joe made a mess of it. He mistimed his landing and ended up being dragged across the ground like a rag doll. Once we saw he would be okay, we might just have taken the piss a little! They winched Bessie back down, and we did it again. This time I still felt terrified but a little less so. After those balloon drops, the first drop from an aeroplane didn't seem so bad.

For the last of the drops, we trained in total darkness. We only did that when we had a little moonlight. The darkness added another whole level of danger. Come the end of training, I couldn't say I ever enjoyed it, but it no longer filled me with dread. It came as a surprise on our last day when they presented us with our wings. I sewed the badge onto my lapel with more pride than you can possibly imagine.

From Ringway we continued south to STS 31, Beaulieu in Hampshire. Beaulieu acted as the SOE finishing school. By the end of the war, over 3000 people had been trained there. The boys and I were quickly split up, entering a new regime of strict code names and no socialising. They billeted me in a small house on the estate with another woman. Our training by that time had become so advanced, we were not about to break the rules. I knew nothing about her, and she knew nothing about me. I only learned much later that Lise was the code name given to Odette Sansom. If either of us had been captured, we could reveal nothing about the other. A strange situation, but we accepted it.

They divided Beaulieu into separate sections, each teaching specialist skills. In all respects we entered a finishing school. Here they taught us the finer arts of an agent's work. What they called "tricks of the trade" and field craft, leadership skills and numerous gadgets. Some of those gadgets were everyday items designed to conceal maps or a means of secret communication. Others concealed ingenious devices for killing people like the shoelace which contained a blade.

Having lost the boys I felt in need of a friend, and Lise became that person. We formed a close friendship, as close as strangers can. Even without knowing her background, I recognised the enormous confidence that she carried with a calm dignity. Like Eliane she made a huge impression on me. After the war, she became the other person I wanted to trace through Vera Atkins. When her story became known it did not entirely surprise me.

The only revelation I didn't anticipate is that she didn't come from the WAAF as I assumed. Odette had been a housewife living in Somerset. She responded to a general request for photographs of France that she had taken while on holiday there. As fate would have it, she sent them to the War Office and not to the Admiralty. They interviewed her, and that interview was later followed up by another; SOE had spotted her. She bravely accepted the offer to join SOE despite knowing little about it. That happened in 1942, when I met her at Beaulieu.

Later that same year, she dropped into France and acted as a courier for the "Spindle" network. Her exploits have since become legendary but her ultimate fate was to be captured by the Germans and horribly tortured. Along the way, she had fallen in love with the head of the Spindle network, Captain Peter Churchill. Despite horrendous treatment by the Gestapo, Odette stuck to her fabricated story that she and Peter Churchill were married, and that he was the nephew of the Prime Minister. None of it was true, but she used it as a bargaining chip, she never once let go. Sent to Ravensbrook concentration camp, the Germans condemned her to death twice. Her treatment in Ravensbrook was unspeakable, but somehow her unbreakable courage saved her. Against overwhelming odds, Odette survived the war.

Odette became the first female SOE agent to be awarded the George Cross. The citation ends with the words: "*During the period of over two years in which she was in enemy hands, she displayed courage, endurance and self-sacrifice of the highest possible order.*" For her work with the resistance, the French awarded her the Legion d'honneur. After the war in 1947, she married Peter Churchill. And in 1950 she became immortalised in the film that bore her name. Odette is but one of the many women who served with the SOE. We all served our country one way or another, but only the few were recognised.

A different person ended her training at Beaulieu. That person had become fitter and stronger and possessed skills I'd never dreamed of. It gave me new confidence, in all respects except one. My French had improved enormously, but I could never be embedded in French society. Nearly everyone including Joe and Harry went to F Section as a formality. When they summoned me to the office, I feared my gamble had finally caught up with me. The officer in charge summoned me in and left me standing. He sat looking at my file without a word. Finally, he lifted his glasses off and raised his head.

"Well done, Angélique, you have received a commendation at each stage of your training. You should be immensely proud."

"Thank you, sir."

"It appears those commendations have not gone unnoticed. There is a most unusual request from an anonymous section of SOE. The authority for this request comes from General Gubbins. Are you acquainted with Major McBride?"

"No, I'm afraid not."

"Well, you are instructed to report to him."

"Where do I have to go?"

"You will report tomorrow to this address."

He produced a small envelope and removed a card without looking at it, and while doing so he lit his lighter and set fire to it! I only just had time to read it before it became reduced to ash. The second I saw it my heart jumped. I could hardly believe my eyes. It said Middlebourne Manor, Middlebourne, Kent. I tried to prevent the smile that appeared on my face, but to no avail.

"You appear to be very pleased with this posting, Angélique."

"I am, sir, I intend to make you proud."

Chapter Twelve
Hello You Lucky Boys

I didn't return to Middlebourne until the spring of 1943. The first person I went to see was Gran. The welcome I received brought tears to my eyes. A welcome home might be a simple thing, but I had never experienced it before. Gran wanted to know everything and of course I could tell her nothing. What an absurd situation, but none of it seemed to matter; we were back together. I asked her about Lily and Fiona; Gran said they were working long hours at the manor; beyond that they didn't tell her anything. I understood - I understood everything now. Sat in Gran's kitchen with her tea and cake, everything I had been through seemed to come into perspective. I apologised that our reunion had to be so brief.

I needed that moment in the real world, but I also had to report to Major McBride. My other life existed somewhere quite different; when I entered the manor, I would step back into it. Before my training I had never heard of SOE and understood nothing about the activities at the manor, nor Lily's part in it. As I walked along the drive towards the sentry, I now had a pretty good idea. My face lit up on seeing it was my old mate, Corporal Harris.

"As I live and breathe, is that you, Dotty?"

"None other, Brian, it's been a long time."

"Far too long. What's all this, soldier Dotty?"

"That's me, I'm one of you lot now."

I always got on really well with Brian; we were mates, although I suspect he would have liked it to be a bit more. For just a moment we almost hugged each other, but of course we didn't. He drew back and noticed my wings.

"What's this badge then, Dotty; that's not what I think it is, is it?"

"It bloody well is, but don't ask me, Brian."

"Crikey! Perhaps if I'm lucky, you might float down from heaven and into my arms."

"I'll tell you what, you stand there with your arms out and wait and see."

"I'd wait forever," he replied with his usual irrepressible smile.

"You might have to," I said as I carried on towards the manor.

I hadn't been told where to report but I had a pretty good idea. All those months ago, from Reg's top field, I noticed one hut which was obviously the centre of things because I regularly saw Lily there. I headed straight towards it. Nobody noticed me coming, I opened the door and marched straight in.

"Hello, you lucky boys, my name's Dotty."

"*Dotty*, what the hell are you doing here?" exclaimed a very surprised Lily.

"I've come to see you, Lily; give me a hug."

The boys instantly stopped what they were doing. They pushed their papers, maps, and files to one side. Each one sat there with his mouth open, gazing at what had just burst in through the door. I confess I intended to make an impression. You didn't see many women in uniform wearing red lips, nails, and lots of eye makeup. Lily threw her arms around me and for the moment we were just elated to be together again.

"Introduce me to these lovely men, Lily."

"You're not supposed to be here, Dotty! You must leave immediately!" she said, almost in a panic.

"I thought this was Station M, where I'm supposed to be! So I came to look for you."

"Do you mean you've been stationed here, *with us*?"

"You can't believe your good luck, can you? I told you I'd be good at this; they reckon I'm the best. You ask your Major McBride; he wanted me and nobody else."

"I understood Mac had been concerned that he had no female agents, but it just hadn't occurred to me for a moment it would be you."

Another smart looking woman came into the hut, astonished to see me there.

"This is Maggie," Lily said. "Maggie's our photo reconnaissance analyst."

"Which one of these lovely men do you have your eye on, Maggie?" I asked.

I was only joking but Maggie replied, "That one," pointing towards one of them.

"Fair enough, he's yours!"

Lily introduced me to the boys. She called them her boffins, and I instantly saw the relationship between them. The one Maggie pointed towards was Patrick, a most delightful Irishman with a wicked sense of humour. He didn't look like a boffin to me; he had a day's stubble on his chin and wore an old woollen waistcoat with more holes in it than a tea strainer. One word and I could tell he had a spark about him. Corky shook my hand and said more with his smiling eyes than he said in words. He looked like a rugged adventurer to me, one of those quiet types who can also be a real livewire. I liked him immediately.

Woody stood out from the others with his smart jacket and bow tie. Older than the rest, he was the epitome of a proper English gentleman. He kissed my hand graciously and treated me like royalty. Woody made me feel privileged to meet him. Rolo was quite another matter with his frizzy hair and thick glasses. None of the others looked how I thought a boffin should look, but Rolo certainly did. I can usually pull a man's strings, but not Rolo. He acknowledged me from across the room.

I immediately recognised the atmosphere in the hut. Nothing brought people together more than the war. People united with a common purpose always form a special bond. I wanted to be a part of that. Lily suggested we go over to her office to see Fi and I instantly agreed.

"Bye-bye, boys, you'll miss me, but I promise I'll be back."

They all seemed to agree with that sentiment, I really enjoyed the warm welcome they gave me. Lily and I talked non-stop all the way to the manor, each full of questions. I wanted to understand about the boffins, sensing something special about the atmosphere in Hut 3. There seemed to be no chain of command, but they all looked up to Lily.

"What am I joining here, Lily, what's going on? You seem to be in charge but nobody has any rank."

"That's right, we're all civilians. Our only military are the guard and Major McBride. Edward has been very clever; the manor hasn't been requisitioned. As a senior member of the SIS, the Prime Minister asked him to set up a top-secret intelligence unit away from SIS. Edward volunteered the use of Middlebourne Manor as an unofficial section of SOE. We don't exist, Dotty!"

"What's so secret that no one must know?"

"The invasion of Europe!"

"Bloody hell. This is what I've been trained for. What's your part in it?"

"We have one specific task. We are to advise the Prime Minister which beaches will be the most suitable for the invasion of Europe. Our job is to analyse every inch of the European coastline. We have to study the geology and topography of both the coast and inland. The tides and prevailing weather all have to be considered. Then we need to be aware of every permanent defence, every gun emplacement, infrastructure, communications, bridge crossings, and German troop movements."

"And you can do all that with just those boys in the hut?"

"Edward can call upon the intelligence of MI6 as well as all the aerial reconnaissance that is undertaken from Medmenham. But don't let our size fool you. We have a lot of resources and we have our own reconnaissance pilot who works with Maggie. As we narrow down the search, the amount of suitable coastline is reducing all the time."

"And are you in charge of all this?"

"Good Lord, no! Edward is in charge; he created all this. I'm his assistant, and Fi is my assistant. Edward says my job is to be the glue that holds us all together."

"I've seen you, Lily, you're more than that."

"Well, I'm called the Chief of Staff. I do what I can, we all do."

"What makes the boffins so special?"

"Between them they cover every expertise we need. Corky is a geologist. Woody came from Oxford university, he's a history professor and military expert. Rolo is a mathematician and cipher expert. He can speak seven languages. Patrick is an all-round academic, and cartographer; he draws all the information together. What isn't obvious is that they all came to us from Bletchley Park, they're some of the cleverest people in Britain. Maggie was the top photo reconnaissance analyst at RAF Medmenham."

"You speak so warmly about them, Lily, you all seem really close."

"I can't be like them, but they accept me completely. I love them like family."

"I can see that."

Lily wanted to hear everything about me, but she had no idea how much I had to tell. As we approached the manor, we noticed the guard changing. Corporal Harris walked back in the process of taking over door duty.

"Dotty, what have you been up to now?" he said.

"Thanks to you, Brian, I'm an indispensable part of this outfit now!"

"Blimey! Is this true, Mrs Heywood?"

"I'm afraid so, Corporal, it's all your fault," Lily replied.

"Yes, it's your fault, Brian," I said, "but don't worry, I haven't forgotten I owe you one."

He smiled approvingly as we walked inside. Lily then had to explain to William the doorman, and then to Albert the young footman, that I would likely be a regular visitor. Lily then put her head around the office door.

"Guess who's here, Fi?"

With that, I made my grand entrance. "Ta-dah! It's me! Hello, Fi."

"*Dotty*, what the hell are you doing here?" she exclaimed.

She got up from her chair and rushed towards me with her arms open. We three had so much to talk about, and so little time available. It had been months; we had a wonderful reunion.

"Look at this office!" I said. "Wow, you two must be so important, you're really posh now, Fi!"

We talked and talked. I thought I had an idea what they did at Middlebourne, but I didn't know the half of it. I told them about my training, how SOE agents were trained primarily to help facilitate the invasion, and that my lecturer said the invasion would be the most closely guarded secret in British military history. Everything made sense now, this explained the total secrecy surrounding Station M. The pieces of the jigsaw puzzle now fitted together perfectly. I had been trained to help ensure the success of the invasion, and here I was, at the very heart of it. Lily reminded me I should report to Major McBride, or Mac as they called him.

"I'd better go, I don't want to get into trouble again, not on my first day. What about the pub tonight?"

"Perfect," said Fiona, "I'm meeting Johnny there tonight. What about you, Lily?"

Just at that moment the telephone rang. Lily answered it and immediately her expression changed. We both overheard her.

"Do you have any details; did he bail out?"

That was all Lily said, but Fiona realised instantly what that meant. Johnny had been flying over Normandy, it meant only one thing. The fear in Fi's eyes sent a chill down my spine. I instinctively put my arm around her. I knew Johnny was a fighter pilot but hadn't realised he was Station M's reconnaissance pilot.

"He's most likely bailed out okay, Fi. I'm sure he'll be all right," Lily said, slightly unconvincingly.

Fiona screamed, her pain filled the room, no amount of comfort helped her. Hearing her scream, His Lordship rushed into the office.

"What's happened?" he asked.

"It's Johnny. He's been shot down, that's all we know," Lily replied.

The way Lily reacted to that crisis reminded me of Rudyard Kipling's poem that had been required reading on my training course. "*If you can keep your head when all about are losing theirs.*" I understood then why she held the position she did. I had been trained not to panic, to think rationally, to make a decision under stress and act upon it. Lily had no such training, she just did it instinctively. I witnessed her bring Station M together as an effective force with the sole aim of finding Johnny. Every connection they knew became involved; every ounce of their expertise became channelled towards this one objective.

That proved to be the start of an extremely long day, and certainly not the day I had expected. The crushing burden of Fi's anguish weighed heavily upon everyone. The possibility that the worst might yet be confirmed became a prospect so terrible I dared not think it. I comforted Fi, but there is no comfort for a person whose loved one is in peril. His Lordship and Fiona seemed to be much closer than I expected. He held her in his arms in the kindest possible way. One by one, just about everyone came into the office and offered what hope and reassurance they could. Mr Jennings and several of the staff did the same.

All the while, Lily ran back and forth between us and Hut 3. When she wasn't there, she was in the communications hut. What I witnessed that day reaffirmed my belief in the human spirit. They were not just work colleagues; I saw the unbreakable bond which existed between them all. Fiona's pain had become everyone's pain. When the long-awaited phone call finally came, all of our fears coalesced together. Lily answered with her usual controlled and authoritative voice. Almost immediately her command of the situation melted away, and tears welled up in her eyes. All she managed to say was, "He's safe."

Fi completely lost it, she jumped up shouting, "He's alive." She kissed and hugged everyone in the room, including His Lordship. Just as Fi's pain had been shared among us, so was her joy. I had never witnessed anything like it. Even the household staff became involved. Mr Jennings brought us all champagne; and I met everyone I hadn't met before, all in one go. Major McBride introduced himself as Mac, everything was so informal. I stood in the middle of an outpouring of emotion, the likes of which I hadn't seen before.

"This is quite an introduction to Station M," Mac said.

"You can say that again. You've created something special here."

"Yes, I'm proud to be a part of this. We are a very small autonomous section of SOE, what you see is all there is. I guess that brings us close together."

"Why me, Major? Why did you select me? Is it because I'm close with Lily and Fi?"

"I didn't know about your connection, I can assure you. We need a female agent, and when they allowed me to look at your file, who else was I going to choose?"

"You mean I'm still the only woman who's been to Arisaig?"

"Yes, and no. You received four commendations, one from each training centre. I would have chosen anyone with your record."

"You realise I'm not a fluent French speaker?"

"Yes, but that's not what we do here,"

"Are you going to tell me then?"

"When we finally narrow down the invasion beaches, do you realise how many people will know the location of the invasion?"

"A handful."

"You're right, a tiny handful. Our field agents will be the only agents in SOE who will know where the invasion will be. Even we won't be told when it will be, not until the very last moment. None of this information can be shared with the normal networks, and neither can we risk our agents being captured. All of our operations will be seaborne, quick in-and-out surveillance missions."

"I've been trained for a lot more than just surveillance."

"That's the first phase. When the day comes, we need agents who can inflict maximum damage on the enemy, and in exactly the right places. SOE will operate all over France, they will be coordinated at the last minute. F Section will arm and coordinate FR, they'll disrupt and sabotage the German war effort all over Europe. We will act as the spearhead of that operation on the day of the invasion itself because we'll be the only group who knows in advance where the invasion will take place. That gives us the unique opportunity within SOE to plan ahead. It's quite possible that we will be called upon to provide direct intervention behind the lines to support the invasion. That's why I need you."

"You two are deep in conversation," Lily said.

"Yes, Mac is just filling me in."

"Good. Right now Johnny's our first priority. Bring him home, Mac; send Dotty."

Chapter Thirteen
Bring Him Home

My training just slipped into place. It was 20:00 hrs, but I immediately asked Mac if we could leave the party atmosphere, I needed to be fully briefed. I had so much to catch up on. Mac had been with the SAS before an injury removed him from active service. Nobody could be more effective as Head of Operations. We left immediately, hurrying directly towards Hut 3. Woody joined us, Maggie quickly followed. I studied the maps and Maggie's reconnaissance photographs. Rolo joined us and pinpointed where the FR message about Johnny had come from.

Everyone understood their job; whatever information I needed became immediately available. Maggie selected a small sandy cove on the Normandy coast for my landing site. Rolo seemed to know everyone in Occupied France in possession of a wireless set. He knew every cell, everyone to trust, and more importantly, who not to. He would establish a contact for me, together with contact codes. My job would simply be to go in and retrieve Johnny. The outline of a plan had been formulated within the hour.

I might have been ready to go the next morning, that's how quickly things were organised. Unfortunately, the weather turned against us, and we lost three days. Those days were not wasted. Mac didn't want the Germans to suspect the resistance had assisted us, or that local people had hidden our pilot. If we were discovered at all, it must appear like a straightforward British rescue with no local involvement. The penalty for harbouring a British pilot would be dreadful. Appearing as one of the locals in those circumstances might be counterproductive, so I would be armed. Mac issued me with a Sten Gun, and a Colt .45.

"This looks like a nice Sten Gun, Mac, it's unused, isn't it. Can you make sure no one else uses this? I'd like it to be mine alone. Is it possible to have it modified? I would like a front pistol grip added. I can use this .45 but can you get me a 38 Special for another time?"

Just as important as my weapons were my clothes. I wouldn't pass for a French national carrying a gun, but neither should I stand out in a British uniform. Not wearing a uniform with the conventions it bestowed upon the wearer was the price an agent paid. Mac showed me a choice of authentic French clothing. I didn't ask how, or from where. I selected what fitted me. There would be no radio, no way to be traced.

I would be ferried across the Channel in a fishing boat, courtesy of the Navy. Having retrieved Johnny, I would then rendezvous back with the same little boat at the same time the next night. Failing that, the following night. What could go wrong? I was impressed with the efficiency of Station M. Training taught us that the planning of an operation is always the key to success. Being a part of a great team was the best asset you can have. Three days later, I called in to the office.

"I'm going down to Portsmouth now. I'll get your boy back for you, Fi, don't you worry. Can you imagine the look on his face when he sees me!"

We all laughed. It was true, I'd be the last person on earth Johnny would expect.

"Is this really you, Dotty, where has the old Dotty gone?" Fiona asked.

"Yes, I know, I'm no longer dotty by nature. I realised something on the training course. I've never been good at anything before, so I had nothing to take myself seriously for. The thing is: when you're good at something, it gives you confidence, doesn't it? I've not had that before, not really. So whenever you send me over there, whatever it is, you can rest assured I'll get the job done."

"Please don't get complacent, Dotty," Lily said, "we need you to always come back to us."

"I've learned that one; complacency is the word Mac hates most of all. Seriously, that will never happen."

Mac arranged my transport down to Portsmouth, an army car waited for me outside the manor. My final checklist was done, and Mac declared me good to go. Without hesitation from either of us, I boarded the vehicle and the FANY driver immediately set off. I recognised the flash on her ATS uniform. She must also have realised my role, being dressed in French clothing.

The two of us chatted away like old friends, but she never once asked about my operation. We stopped at the barrier to Portsmouth Naval Base, and when my papers were approved, she delivered me to a small nondescript building on the quayside. "Goodbye, good luck," she said. A sailor met me, and after he checked my identity we entered the building, where two more sailors greeted me in a very matter-of-fact way.

"Haven't seen you before, luv, this your first time?"

"Yes, fresh out of training."

"You don't get seasick, do you?"

"I don't know. I hope not."

They were obviously a team selected to deal with SOE. Mac briefed me on what to expect but they were more prepared than I imagined. They went through everything I needed to know. Emergency procedures, and what to do in every eventuality. Their primary concern was German E boats. These fast attack craft would represent a real problem if we were discovered. Our small French fishing boat offered us one principal means of defence - camouflage. Even if spotted, we would not appear suspicious. If we raised suspicion, our last resort was to attack the E boat. I didn't like the sound of that.

We boarded the fishing boat at last light and I set off accompanied by two of the sailors. The half-moon gave us a tiny amount of vision in between the broken clouds. One sailor said I must have good luck; the conditions were perfect for a Channel crossing. They were very professional; I felt completely safe with them. The crossing had been timed to perfection; we reached the rendezvous point at 02:00 hrs. For our code signal, we used the letter D in Morse code. One long and two short flashes of a small torch. The torch had a hood around it, the beam would hardly be visible, other than to someone in direct line of sight. The signal came back immediately, everything worked like clockwork.

They took me as close inshore as possible before sitting me in a small rubber boat. I paddled ashore exactly as I had done in training. I quickly jumped out, and they roped the dingy back. When I made contact ashore, I flashed the code for the letter R. One short, one long, and one short flash. I heard the engine start and the fishing boat quietly disappeared into the night. My reception party was with another woman. She didn't appear to be more than eighteen years old. I asked her immediately where our pilot was, but her instructions were to take me to a farmhouse, nothing else.

We walked over fields that she obviously knew well, keeping close to hedgerows. Neither of us spoke. The velvet silence made the call of a male Tawny Owl seem incredibly loud. Moments later, a distant female responded. My training taught me to listen for nocturnal birds like the owls. They would react to sounds long before I would hear them. The reassuring call told me all was well. I kept a mental picture of the map in my mind. We travelled southeast from the cove, so we must be heading towards a small village called Le Bouffay.

Sure enough, I just made out the shapes of some farm buildings, assisted by a dim chink of light visible along the lower edge of the blackout at one window. The young woman pointed to a barn, the outline of which I just recognised in the dark. "There is a door at the end," she said, "go inside." I looked back from the building and she had gone, vanished into thin air. A field edge directed me almost to the door. I slipped inside expecting to find someone there.

Standing inside a coal-black strange building is not for the fainthearted, especially when there is the sound of breathing. I spoke quietly, and when no reply came, I had no option but to use my torch. The barn contained what I might have expected, farm equipment, drums of oil, an ancient tractor, and a horse! I lowered my Sten Gun; the horse would live to pull a plough another day. It must have been asleep, my torch didn't as much startle it as quietly disturb it. My sigh of relief seemed to reassure it.

A convenient bale of hay provided a comfortable seat away from the doors. Waiting is another discipline you have to learn. Sitting in the dark gives your mind a chance to play tricks on you. There are ghosts and ghoulies around every corner, not to mention the Gestapo. Rather than submit to those thoughts, I rehearsed every eventuality methodically in my mind. Just as dawn broke, I heard someone approaching. The door opened, and the silhouette of a man stood against the dawn sky. I pointed my Sten Gun at the centre of his body. He said the code name Rolo had given me - Anna. "*Oui*," I replied.

The man opened the door wide and for the first time my surroundings came into view, including my contact. A man of my age walked towards me. He stopped abruptly when he saw my gun pointing at him.

"*Tout va bien, je suis ami. Nom de code, Anna,*" he said nervously.

I lowered my gun and smiled at the man; he responded with obvious relief. Despite my French being limited, it proved to be perfectly adequate, and my first question was: did he have our pilot? He didn't, but he knew who did. Excellent news indeed. The details were sketchy, but this is how things worked, no one person needed to know any more than necessary. The person I needed to talk to wasn't that far away in Cussy. I asked how I would get there.

Being in a sparsely populated rural area, I didn't consider the risk to be high, but he offered to guide me across the fields rather than go by road. We set off immediately. I concealed my weapons and suggested we hold hands. The walk proved to be almost entirely uneventful, except for one moment. An open-top German transport lorry carrying a small contingent of troops appeared on the road next to the field we were crossing. They were about seventy-five yards away and not even likely to notice us, but just in case I said to my new friend, "Kiss me."

He obliged rather enthusiastically. It might have been fortunate, because one of the German soldiers did notice us. They waved and jeered as the lorry carried on its way. Two lovers alone in a field, what could be more innocent. We continued using the same pretence as we walked into Cussy. He sat me down at a table outside a pavement cafe, while he disappeared inside. Another man came and spoke to me. Once satisfied with my identity, he took me inside and down into a cellar. Hidden behind boxes and wine bottles, I found Johnny looking very sorry for himself.

"*Dotty,* I can't believe it! What on earth are you doing here?"

"I'm your guardian angel, Johnny. You may consider yourself rescued!"

"Good God! How, what's happening?"

"I've been sent over to get you home. You're in big trouble, I can tell you. You've lost an aeroplane, and even worse, you stood up Fi the other evening."

He laughed; I suspect he hadn't done that for a while. Our host kindly agreed to us both staying there until the evening, which was no small thing. Collaborators and informers were potentially everywhere; these people were taking a tremendous risk on our behalf. Johnny and I made ourselves comfortable for the rest of the day; it gave us time to answer each other's questions. Johnny had been caught by a Messerschmitt 109. He simply didn't see it until too late. The German pilot followed him down and watched him bail out into the sea, just off the shore. Johnny had the good sense to lie motionless face down in the water as the 109 sped over him. It's possible the pilot might have reported Johnny as a 'kill', in which case they may not be searching for him. I praised his quick thinking.

Needless to say, my appearance took a bit of explaining; Fiona hadn't explained the reason for my recent absence. He wasn't in the best of spirits, some of his ribs were bruised or broken, and he had a badly sprained ankle. The fact he had come within inches of death had shaken him up badly. I assured him nothing like that would happen with me in charge. As the light faded, we prepared to depart.

I thanked those brave people for their help, especially the man who took the decision to hide us. I kissed him, it might have been a scant reward, but it was all I had. Another man gave us a ride in the back of a horse-drawn cart part of the way towards our destination. I supported most of Johnny's weight, but the final few miles on foot must have been agony for him. Despite everything, Johnny didn't complain once. I thought back to all those hours spent in training struggling with a heavy backpack; it really had been for a good reason.

We sat breathless in the dunes waiting for a signal to appear in the blackness. The night turned chilly, and a mist rolled in off the sea. It appeared first as a grey blanket draped over the black expanse of the English Channel. As it rolled towards the shore, it appeared to reach out with ghostly fingers until we became consumed by it, our visibility reduced to a uniform grey in all directions. Time appeared to slow down for us, I worried my sailors wouldn't find us.

I needn't have worried; they were nothing if not punctual - at precisely 02:00 hrs the coded signal flashed in the darkness. I flashed my return code and breathed a small sigh of relief. Fifteen minutes later, the sailor reached the beach in the dinghy. My first mission had gone like clockwork. The next day, we arrived at Middlebourne in the back of an army lorry. Lily obviously saw us arrive because she came rushing out to greet us.

"Don't you ever do that again, Johnny Albright!" she said, as she hugged and kissed him. "Are you okay?"

"Sprained ankle, and a couple of bruised ribs, but apart from that only damaged pride," he said with a grimace on his face.

"Come on, Dotty, let's get him to the office. There's someone over there who might just want to see him."

We helped him towards the office with his arms over our shoulders. Obviously in more discomfort from his injuries than he wanted to let on, only the prospect of seeing Fiona kept him going. Both the guard on duty and Albert the footman offered to help, but I dismissed their good intentions out of hand. Eventually we arrived at the office, where we stood outside the door.

"Can you take your weight if you lean against the door surround?" Lily asked Johnny.

"I expect so, why?"

"Because this is as far as Dotty and I go. This is a moment for you and Fi."

I opened the door, and we left them alone. As we turned our backs, we heard Fiona's cry of "*Johnny!*" I looked at Lily and we both smiled as we headed off to Hut 4 where I would be debriefed.

"I've never seen two people so in love, have you, Dotty?"

"No, I haven't, it's kind of wonderful, isn't it?"

"It is. I'm envious, I'd like some of what Fi's got."

"Wouldn't we all, Lily! Maybe one day."

"Did you find him okay?"

"Eventually. FR only communicate when they have to. My contact knew someone, who knew someone else, who knew where he was."

"Promise me, Dotty. When you go back, please take no more risk than you have to. I've overcome a lot in this war. I just can't face the prospect of losing you as well."

"Don't worry, Lily. I've found the first proper home I've ever had here in Middlebourne. I'll drag myself back here by my fingertips if I have to."

Chapter Fourteen
I'm Rob Bartlett

I followed events in the early war years like everyone, but only listened to the wireless occasionally or read the odd newspaper. As soon as I joined Station M, the progress of the war became my daily diet; and I arrived just when events were turning in our favour. The invasion of Sicily on 10th July 1943 proved to be a significant turning point. It paved the way for the invasion of the Italian mainland which would begin on 3rd September 1943. These events were important because all these strategic advances brought the main invasion of Europe ever closer.

Winston Churchill met with President Roosevelt at a secret meeting in Quebec, code-named "Quadrant", where a provisional date for the invasion was decided - May 1944. That was when "Operation Overlord" finally became a reality. This is what everyone had been working towards, what Station M had been created for. I didn't think the team could be any more focused, but when they gave D-Day a provisional date, everything changed.

Reality is an unyielding master. Our reality was that the sands of the Normandy beaches had become the sands of time. The hour glass had been turned over, time was running out, the tension sky rocketed. The responsibility for our part of the planning became overwhelming. I saw it in Lily's face every day. Their collective sense of responsibility became a crushing burden.

Our surveillance operations in Normandy were relatively straightforward at that time. We could have used the local resistance movement to reconnoitre our targets of interest but it was deemed far too risky. The location of the targets all indicated Normandy, between Cherbourg and Caen. The nature of the targets all indicated an advancing invasion force. The D-Day secret would be compromised. We had no other option, we must carry out the critical surveillance, but Mac was resolute that we should take no unnecessary risks. It remained imperative that a Station M agent must not fall into the hands of the Germans. Even if we said nothing, our very presence in that sensitive area was informative in itself. For that reason, we operated under strict instructions - do not get taken alive!

The resistance would remain unaware of our presence in all but an emergency. With no radio, we each memorised a name or point of contact where we might be able to contact the resistance but it never proved necessary. Our training fully equipped us to remain invisible. As well as reconnaissance to assist the advancing Allies, we needed up to the minute intelligence in order to disrupt and hinder the enemy. Key targets were identified for destruction, both before, during and immediately after D-Day. Road and rail networks, as well as telecommunications and power supplies.

It might be a single target or several in the same area. We went in, under the cover of darkness, using a different landing site every time. If the target could be reached on foot, we did so under the cover of darkness and returned in the same way. For more distant objectives, we went equipped with a bicycle. As D-Day pressures mounted, the number of targets of interest grew, but I only experienced two close calls.

The fast coastal patrol boats were our most significant risk. You heard an E-Boat long before you could see them, but usually they remained just that, a sound in the distance. Our fishing boat was complete with nets and tackle. We looked exactly how we should look, a small French fishing boat. The seamen had learnt a smattering of French, perhaps enough to get by when speaking to a non-French speaking German. On one occasion we did hear the sound of an E-Boat in the distance, but this time one headed directly towards us!

"What do we do?" I asked, trying to sound relaxed about it.

"Keep out of sight in the cabin," came the reply. "Have grenades ready and your Sten Gun prepared to fire."

"Oh, shit! Have you experienced this before?" I asked the sailor.

"Once or twice, it's all a part of the game," came the reply.

My sailors were consummate professionals, they remained resolutely calm. Our instructions were to never allow a German inspection of the boat. We were to bluff our way through regardless of what happened. That is until an attempt might be made to board. In the dead of night with a patrol boat steering directly towards us, all of our precautions suddenly felt inadequate. My sailors carried a box of fish onboard during every crossing. They were in varying states of decay and stunk to high heaven. They immediately removed the lid. This is all we had, perfect camouflage.

The E-Boat pulled alongside us. I placed my finger in the ring of the Mills grenade. These boats were 114 ft long and carried a crew of twenty-five men. I was very conscious that the E-Boat vastly outgunned us. We never actually discussed it but we all realised our orders to attack them as the last resort had nothing to do with us overpowering them. It had everything to do with us not being taken alive.

The sea had been relatively rough that night, the wind whistled through the tackle. The Germans maintained a reasonable distance as they trained two powerful spotlights on us. We were lit up like Gran's dining table on Christmas Day. They shouted across to us and one of the sailors shouted back. The two languages struggled against the sound of the wind and the waves breaking against the side of the E-Boat. Their powerful engine provided a convenient drone. The sailors feigned frustration at being stopped for no reason, waving their arms in apparent disbelief. The Germans shouted even more but we genuinely did not understand them. My sailors' preparedness never ceased to amaze me. They didn't only carry rotting fish! They also had some really nice bottles of French wine.

The sailor with the best French shouted across words to the effect that the captain should be satisfied with a good bottle of wine and leave hard-working fishermen alone to get on with their fishing. A Scotsman, his name was Archie. Believe it or not he made a convincing Frenchman. He carried out his part as if his life depended upon it. The Germans shouted back a comment and he answered, "Chateau Lynch Bages" hoping it was the correct answer. As we rose up and down in the swell I would catch momentary glimpses of the E-Boat. It appeared enormous compared to our little boat. I held my breath and gripped the grenade even harder.

After some discussion the Germans threw a rope over. Archie secured the bottle and dropped it over the side. Once on board, the captain of the E-boat came forward to inspect his trophy. We held our breath. The next thing we knew the engine roared back into life and they pulled away from us shouting something about stinking French fishermen! I slumped back down in the corner of the little cabin, slowly removing my finger from the grenade pin. My life didn't exactly flash before my eyes but there was a moment there when I thought I had reached the end of the road. My sailors obviously felt the same. We looked at each other, breathing a collective sigh of relief.

"You were brilliant, Archie, you saved our bacon."

"Och aye, it's all part of the service. Just think yourself lucky you don't have to do our laundry."

We laughed as only people relieved of such fear can laugh. The three of us stood with our arms around each other's shoulders enjoying every second of the new life we had been given. The rest of that operation became entirely mundane in comparison.

We had four operational field agents at that time. They told me about the disaster of operation "Skua" when they lost three agents. Their fishing boat was also intercepted by an E Boat. All three agents were killed in what they assumed must have been a firefight. It was in all respects a terrible setback. Lily felt personally responsible, it affected her very badly. When Mac arrived he only replaced two of them; they were recruits intended for F Section, so the four of us were under increasing pressure.

Come the autumn of 1943, military planners confirmed our landing beaches between Cherbourg and Caen. Originally three, they expanded the number to five, and now we had our five code names - Utah, Omaha, Gold, Juno, and Sword. We continued reconnaissance, because we needed to know every grain of sand and blade of grass on those beaches and beyond. Above all, we needed to pinpoint any changes the Germans made to their coastal defences.

As soon as the beaches were confirmed we had to be sure the advance from the beachheads would not encounter any unknown obstacles. Aerial photography will show where advancing troops and heavy vehicles might advance over open ground unhindered. What it doesn't tell us is the state of the ground, is it soft or firm, are there any hidden dangers. It was during one of these reconnaissance operations that I had another close shave.

We were not given any strategic details; the military planners used our intelligence as they saw fit. Just occasionally a specific request might come down from the top which quite obviously would have originated from the military strategists. One such request was to reconnoitre the bridges over the Caen canal and Orne river. It didn't take a brilliant strategist to realise these bridges were vital for the British advance from Sword beach.

Mac gave me the bridges. A significant part of my training was about identifying structural weakness in buildings and bridges. The architect and engineer at Arisaig taught us well. My training taught me to use my knowledge to destroy bridges; now I needed to confirm the bridges would not fall down. It would be a planning disaster if a bridge collapsed under the weight of an advancing Allied tank column.

My sailors put me ashore quite close to Sword Beach. It was one of those operations that went very smoothly. Conditions for the crossing were ideal. I had some moonlight to guide me, and during my cycle ride to the bridges I didn't encounter a single problem. The two bridges are quite close together. The Benouville Bridge over the canal was of particular concern. It opened to allow boat traffic, like a drawbridge. I concealed my bicycle and studied the structure at first light with my binoculars. We didn't make written notes in case we were intercepted, so I developed a mental technique of drawing the structure in my mind, as if drawing on paper.

The same applied to photographs. I could not risk being captured and offering the Germans such vital information. I moved around freely in the half light of dawn and studied the bridges from different vantage points. My only companions were the birds providing me with a dawn chorus. As the sun rose higher, the song birds grew quieter to be replaced by the arguing waterfowl. Gradually local people appeared as I withdrew into a concealed position. I remember thinking how well the operation had gone. From my position I could observe the Benouville Bridge in complete safety. Plenty of time to commit it to memory before I cycled back to the rendezvous point that night.

The Germans certainly had a presence there. I saw plenty of vehicles, and more troubling, I spotted a foot patrol. Two soldiers walked the far bank. They were not a problem, but their Alsatian dog was! Straining at its lead, alarm bells rang in my head. When they crossed the bridge to my side those alarm bells became deafening. Dogs are one of those "what if" unknown quantities that we did not want to encounter. They walked in my direction and I knew the dog would smell me. I had options - you always have options. I carried my .38 and a knife, if I chose to kill them it would be easy, given the element of surprise. The location was quiet, I might get away with it, but they would be missed and subsequently found. The time to run had passed, so I decided to bluff.

I concealed my gun, knife, binoculars, and torch in the undergrowth and crawled away from them. Away from the undergrowth I found an area of short grass and laid down, hands behind my head, as if asleep. With only seconds to spare the dog found me, dragging its handler behind him. I pretended to wake up terrified of the dog, shouting for them to control him. My clothing was authentic and my papers were good, I bluffed with a good hand of cards. Neither of the soldiers raised their weapons, they didn't see me as a threat, rather as a curiosity.

What was I doing there? Where did I come from? They demanded to see my papers. I worked in the town hall, just on the other side of the river. This was my afternoon off, I liked to watch the boats, I must have fallen asleep. It sounded credible to me! The wretched dog didn't stop barking which made conversation conveniently difficult. For some reason they were suspicious. One of them studied my papers intently, while the other one demanded to search me. His hands were all over me, for a brief moment I considered another option but that didn't appeal to me. Pretending outrage, I pushed him away. In my best French I suggested his commanding officer would hear about his conduct. That didn't seem to bother them, but it troubled me. He pursued me again and I fended him off trying to appear as helpless as possible.

All the while I made sure I remained in a position to kill them both. I could incapacitate the soldier threatening me in a way that his colleague would probably not notice. It would look as if I had slightly hurt him but nothing more. That would give me more than enough time to approach the other one. If I allowed myself to be forced down onto the grass I would lose that advantage. I pretended to become hysterical, shouting as loud as I could. My benefactor turned out to be an old lady walking not far away. She heard the commotion and walked towards us. Bless her, she was outraged. That kind of conduct was all too common among the German occupiers. Faced with two irate women, the soldiers finally thought better of it. He gave me a parting slap for my trouble which I accepted as a small price to pay.

The lovely old lady suggested I should go with her until we were sure they had gone away. We walked in one direction while the Germans walked in the other. She realised I was not French almost immediately, she even asked if I was English! What could I say, I put my finger to my lips and whispered yes. I hesitated - had I jumped from the fat to the fire? "Come with me," she said. We walked to her house on the outskirts of Caen where she gave me a cup of their awful chicory coffee. The old girl reminded me of Gran, she had that same knowing look. She said I should stay there until dark, but after that I should go. Such an invitation I was not about to refuse. That bridge became quite famous after the war, they even renamed it Pegasus Bridge.

Come nightfall, I thanked her profusely and melted into the cover of darkness. First I retrieved my weapons, and then my bicycle. After a day like that I expected trouble at every turn but Lady Luck must have taken pity on me. I needed to avoid one German patrol, but apart from that I arrived at the beach unscathed. My reliable sailors flashed the signal and I flashed back. It was Archie who offered me his hand from the dinghy.

"Any problems?" he asked.

"No, a walk in the park!"

We had far-reaching capabilities, but all the while secrecy limited what we were allowed to share. As the only section that knew where D-Day would take place, it made centralised planning difficult. F Section (France) was the largest SOE Section by far, but crucially the networks relied upon the French Resistance. There was always the risk that captured resistance fighters might talk. This, combined with the fear of infiltrators, meant that F Section had to plan its D-Day tactics without knowing precisely where or when that might be.

Military planners dealt with all aspects of strategy; only they saw the bigger picture. SOE were not there to add to our military might - what we provided would be more like a surgical incision. We alone in SOE were the only people on the ground who knew where the Germans would have to respond following D-Day. That gave us a unique advantage. We now devoted considerable time exploring various scenarios that would follow the invasion. What would the German response be, and critically, where would it come from, and how might we disrupt it? There was only so much that we were capable of doing with our limited resources, so decisions had to be made. Mac wanted more agents, while Lily and His Lordship needed to coordinate more with F Section.

They formulated a plan. We would designate an area around the landing sites as our most secret and critical. Then, going further out within areas of ever-increasing radius, we gradually reduced that critical designation. We had to ensure that RAF or SOE operations did not inadvertently draw disproportionate attention to the Normandy beaches. Finally, there were time-critical operations that had to be actioned just moments before, or else during the landings.

Mac had difficulty putting his full trust in the French Resistance. The problem, as he explained, was the fragmented nature of the resistance in a country where loyalties were divided. We decided that our own agents would carry out operations in the critical zone. Although French involvement would be essential, they would not be told about the invasion details until it was almost in motion. We needed to orchestrate our clandestine operations with F Section; that meant closer ties with Colonel Buckmaster and Vera Atkins. We would now put our full weight behind the invasion effort.

The last weeks of 1943 ticked by, and each tick added new urgency. Surveillance shifted towards infrastructure targets. Targets we would sabotage. The landing beaches covered a vast area; if we were going to be an effective force during the hours leading up to D-Day we needed more agents. Mac told me he had it all in hand, I had nothing to do with it. The first I heard was when Mac told us as a group that he had selected another five agents to join us. Four men all highly qualified and a woman wireless operator.

The four of us greeted the news enthusiastically, especially regarding the wireless operator. My other fellow agents were good lads, and we got on really well, but Mac had selected them more for surveillance and intelligence gathering. Their peacetime careers indicated their skills. Neil had been a primary school teacher in France. He was a warm, empathetic man, the ideal agent to assimilate into any French community. Bertrand, we called him Bertie, spoke several European languages, he came from academia. Nigel had been a bus driver. His motivation to join SOE resulted from his French wife being killed during the Blitz.

They had all been through various parts of the system, and they were all extremely brave and capable agents within their limitations. Mac made it clear he wanted agents capable of taking the fight to the enemy, should it prove necessary. Neil, Nigel, and Bertie were not trained to be commandos; I could outrun and out-shoot any of them. Mac understood this when he made his selection.

The new agents arrived one at a time. When the second one arrived, I had the shock of my life. A tall man with fair hair, broad shoulders, and an outrageous smile stepped out of the back of a lorry. I couldn't believe my eyes, it was Rob! I realised I had a candle burning for Rob, but I didn't appreciate how bright it still burned between us. As he stepped out of the vehicle, I have to confess my heart skipped several beats. I followed him into Hut 4 without him seeing me. The first he knew about me was when he turned around. He got the shock of his life! You should have seen the expression on his face. He pretended we were strangers.

"Hello," he said, "I'm Rob Bartlett."

"Yes, I'm sure you are. I'm Dotty."

"Yes, I'm sure you are. I met someone like you once."

"Did you? Perhaps we should get to know each other better then."

"Maybe you're right. No rush though, we've got the rest of our lives to do that."

He stopped me dead in my tracks, what did he just say? We both had so many questions, like what the hell are you doing here, but neither of us said anything. He leant forward, broadcasting clearly that he intended to kiss me. Then thinking it might be the wrong thing to do, he backed off.

"I thought our training taught us to make a decision and act upon it," I said.

"You're right, it did," he said, and he kissed me.

It wasn't your average kiss; it didn't come with a time limit. Neither of us noticed Mac come into the hut.

"Oh, I'm sorry about that, Mac; Rob and I trained together."

"Yes, I can see that. Is this going to be a problem?"

Rob was hugely embarrassed. "I apologise, Major, that won't happen again."

Mac disliked relationships between agents; he said it affected judgement. He had a point, but I disagreed. I made a decision and acted upon it.

"Don't worry about Rob and me, Mac, it will never be a problem, I promise you. You can trust me on this, just like you can trust Rob."

Mac had a lot of respect for me, he frequently made that clear, but he remained conflicted over this issue. He thought before answering.

"Welcome to Station M, Rob. You can drop the Major, and may I say you look ridiculous with lipstick on your face."

"Thank you, Mac," Rob replied. "Dotty's right, this won't be an issue."

When Rob and I were at Arisaig, we didn't exactly have a relationship. We might have thought about it, but we didn't. Now, suddenly, we were making allowances for the relationship we obviously shared but neither of us realised we had! I didn't understand any of it, but I accepted it without question. After Mac left us, I turned to Rob.

"What just happened, Rob?"

"I don't know, but something did. There hasn't been a day when I haven't thought about you; and now this, I'm posted here."

"You thought about me, *every* day?"

"I did! Tell me you didn't think about me the same?"

"I did, every day, but I don't do relationships, Rob, not serious relationships."

"Yes you do, you're doing it now, you just don't realise it."

"I am, aren't I. If you let me down Rob Bartlett, if you break my heart, I'll kill you."

"I decided at Arisaig, Dotty, I'm never going to let you down, I daren't."

It all happened so ridiculously quickly, but I doubt it could have happened any other way. If he had given me time to think about it, I would have run a mile. I'm not sure if Rob ever really understood what a giant step it was for me. I had lots of casual relationships with men but I always kept them at arm's length. The prospect of a proper relationship terrified me. Perhaps he realised what a fruitcake I was and decided to sweep me off my feet anyway. As we walked towards the accommodation block together, I realised I had made a life-changing decision.

ooOoo

Christmas of 1943 proved to be a quiet affair. Lily felt obliged to spend Christmas Day at the manor, and her parents Pam and Jack had to go to Jack's sister. Fiona had been terrified at the prospect of spending Christmas Day with Johnny's parents, albeit the right thing to do. This left me and Rob at Gran's, to share Christmas with Jim, Aunty Mavis, and Aunty

Mildred. It might have been quiet, but I wanted to be with them. Gran had not met Rob before and sat smiling at me throughout our Christmas lunch. When we were alone, she made it clear that she approved of Rob.

"I like your young man, Dotty."

"He's lovely, isn't he?"

"He better not break your heart, luv, he'll have me to contend with if he does."

"I'll tell him, Gran."

"I'll tell him myself; I'm not having one of my girls upset."

And so she did. Poor Rob didn't know what to say in front of everyone. Gran's stamp of approval meant a lot to me. We returned to Gran's on Boxing Day so Lily and Fi both met Rob properly for the first time. For reasons I didn't understand, I felt a bit silly when they were so happy for me; I didn't want to make a fuss about it. Lily wasn't at her best, I noticed something was wrong. When I had the opportunity to talk to her alone, I asked what troubled her.

"No, I'm fine," she said.

"Lily, this is me, look, it's Dotty. Tell me what's wrong."

"It's silly, you'll tell me I'm being daft."

"If it's what I think it is, then yes you are daft. I've never seen anyone so crazy in love as you are with Edward, and you know it can't work. You've got Greg; why do you torture yourself like this?"

"I can't help it, honestly I can't. You wouldn't guess who I had to meet yesterday. Lady Beatrice! She's the one who Edward is supposed to marry. You should see her, Dot, she's young, she's really beautiful, and she's a Lady. I couldn't wait for it to end, it was horrible."

"So she's the reason you're upset. You know this is daft, don't you? Why can't you be happy with Greg, he's adorable; what more can you possibly want?"

"I want to be happy with Greg, I'm trying to put Edward out of my mind. I am trying Dotty, but it's so hard… I love him."

"I know you do. I wish I could help you."

"You do, you're always there for me."

This is how 1943 ended. For the first time in my life, I was the happy one and my dearest friend was the one with tears in her eyes.

Chapter Fifteen
Build-Up To D-Day

When I replaced the calendar on the wall of Hut 4, every one of us realised that 1944 would be the most significant year of our lives. The decision had been taken; Utah, Omaha, Gold, Juno, and Sword were now a reality. I could not imagine the responsibility Lily and the boys carried. They now had to maintain constant surveillance to ensure nothing material changed. Our side of Station M had a completely different role. Winston Churchill told SOE to "set Europe ablaze". Our role was to disrupt the German response to D-Day in any way possible. We were the clandestine invasion force. My part in D-Day was only just beginning.

The months of reconnaissance and collaboration with the French Resistance gave us our list of targets. Telecommunications remained high on the list; they would be destroyed all over France. Power lines, transformers and distribution hubs would all be targeted. The railways were a key means of transport for German troops, munitions, and equipment. The entire network would be disrupted. Industrial sabotage would be stepped up. Many German vehicles would prove unreliable. Industrial production of essential hardware became a constant and ongoing target.

The huge contribution made by SOE required exact coordination. We were to strike the match that would set Europe ablaze in the moments leading up to D-Day. Not a moment sooner, and not a second later. This became Station M's unique contribution, because only we knew where the invasion would take place, and we would be among the first to be told when. With the location of the invasion remaining a secret, the job of coordinating the rest of SOE with the French Resistance became a considerable challenge.

To answer that challenge, an elite team of specially trained commandos would parachute into Occupied France. Provided with our country's most carefully guarded secret, they would arm and coordinate the French Resistance who were not already working with SOE. The call went out for troops who could speak European languages, especially French. Volunteers endured extensive and vigorous training, many of them at Arisaig. The majority didn't make it. The best of the best came together to form what became known as the "Jedburghs". American, French, and British commandos combined into groups of three. They numbered 83 American, 90 British, and 103 French.

In order to maintain absolute secrecy, the Jedburgh teams would not be sent in until the last possible moment. That moment would prove to be June 5th. All over the occupied countries, just 276 commandos would supply additional weapons and explosives to the resistance. They would set Europe ablaze moments before and during the invasion. Station M's field agents working with the French would light the brightest blaze of all behind the beachhead.

Time-sensitive targets within the critical zone became our specific responsibility. Targets further away from the beaches were designated to F Section working with the resistance. Some heavily defended targets, such as gun emplacements, were to be dealt with by Bomber Command, or by Marines who would be parachuted behind enemy lines.

Our reconnaissance remained up to date - it had to be. Johnny Albright flew over Normandy three or four times a week, sometimes more. At the beginning of May, he struck lucky when he spotted a high-ranking German officer in an open vehicle. Mac asked our agents on the ground to enquire about this officer, because Woody thought the appearance of such a high-ranking officer in a remote French village might be significant. Our agent quickly reported that the resistance recognised this man. He was Otto Schneider, *SS-Gruppenführer und Generalleutnant der Waffen-SS.* He commandeered a remote Chateau near Brutelles for his headquarters, and this Chateau placed him just two miles from the landing beaches.

This appeared to be extremely significant. Why did such a high-ranking

SS officer set up his headquarters in this area? We thought this only meant one thing; he must be the senior commanding officer in charge of local coastal defence. The Germans expected the invasion, they just didn't know where or when.

Within the week, we obtained reports of a general clampdown on the local resistance movement. Six people had been rounded up. They were interrogated and eventually shot for being suspected members of the resistance. Communications with our two agents immediately became extremely limited. This confirmed Woody's suspicions. Hut 3 went into an immediate huddle; they all sat around a table together to discuss the matter, and Lily included me.

"Do you think we're compromised, Edward?" Fiona asked.

"I don't think so. They assume we are coming but they still don't know where or when; otherwise, we would see reinforcements."

"What about the poor bastards the SS have tortured?" Patrick said. "We have no idea what they might have told them."

"No one in the resistance has been told where or when the invasion will occur," His Lordship said. "So those poor devils couldn't have told them anything. The danger would be if they had been aware of our agents, but we must assume they have said nothing, because the SS would have picked up our people by now."

"That's true, old boy," said Woody, "but I'm still concerned about this SS officer. His rank bothers me; I think they must have some suspicions to send an officer of that rank to an otherwise unimportant area, especially Schneider."

"Plus the clampdown on the resistance," said Rolo, "I think that confirms Woody's concern."

"We must reduce our activity in the area," Mac said, looking worried.

"Can we afford to do that, Mac," I replied, "when we're only weeks away?"

"We have no option but to keep our heads down. Our agents mustn't be compromised."

"Even if we're not compromised," Lily said, "we still don't want an SS General right on top of one of the invasion beaches organising counter measures!"

"You're right," replied Rolo, "especially a nasty bastard like Schneider; we need to kill him." He said it with a completely expressionless face.

"A job for the paratroopers?" suggested Corky.

"No," replied His Lordship, "paratroopers are too obvious; it would give them vital minutes of warning. No, this is a job for you, Mac. It needs to be done quietly, just moments before the invasion begins. His telecommunications can be cut, but his headquarters will have radio. We must destroy that before they can raise the alert."

"Why not just bomb the Chateau instead?" Fiona asked.

"We could," replied Woody, "but it's only a small target in the dark. The RAF might easily miss it."

"Can you do it, Mac?" Lily asked.

"I don't know, we need intel. Give me a detailed drawing of the building, and the whereabouts of all the personnel, and yes, maybe my agents can do it. This is what we train for, but without that kind of intel, I can't guarantee anything."

"Then we must get what you need, and fast. Who do we have there now, Mac?" Lily asked.

"I've got two agents only a few miles away. I must risk sending them a message."

During the build-up to D-Day, Mac steadily increased our number of field agents. We now comprised ten operational agents, and our people only rarely crossed the Channel on "day trips". Our missions grew longer as we formed sustainable links with the resistance. Two of our agents posed as man and wife, living as a part of the French community. These were the agents Mac referred to, and the sudden change of circumstances placed them in additional danger.

"If this operation is possible, Mac, will those agents carry it out?" Lily asked.

"Not by themselves, no, I'll need the help of the resistance and at least two other agents. We'll need the best we have. Only a few are trained to this level."

"You mean me and Rob, don't you?" I asked.

"It has to be, Dotty; no one can bluff their way past a German guard like you can, you know that, and you and Rob are specifically trained for an operation like this."

"I agree, I've practised this exact scenario. This is why you chose me in the first place, isn't it, Mac?"

"You're right, it is. This isn't all about clandestine operations assimilating with the French. Sometimes you need someone who can go in and get a specific job done. I wanted that capability, and now we need to use it."

I always wondered why Mac wanted me when I wasn't a fluent French speaker. Now I knew! Lily and Fi hated the prospect, but that's what we trained for; I wanted to do it. In the following weeks, we gathered all the intel we could. Agent Starling risked several communications with us. Between each transmission, she would have to move her location. Each message risked her life. Best of all, she somehow organised a microdot film to be sent to us. How she got the film in the first place we didn't know. But we knew how she got it to us. It flew across the Channel attached to a carrier pigeon! It arrived with us just like a telegram via special messenger. Maggie processed it and ran to Hut 4 with it.

"Mac, look at this. You won't believe it."

None of us could believe it. Starling obtained photographs of the architectural drawings of the Chateau the Germans were using as their headquarters. It gave us everything we needed. I looked at Rob, and we both looked at Mac. It was on! In the following weeks, we went over every probable scenario. Occasionally, our intel might change, but essentially we had a plan in place. Patrick made a scale model of the Chateau, the detail following the drawings precisely. A beautiful symmetric building it had four floors, including the attic and basement rooms. The classic design featured the usual steep pitch roof with eight little dormer windows on the front elevation. There were numerous chimneys, always symmetrically placed.

The front of the Chateau had six tall windows on each floor, Three on either side of a full height central portico. Entrance steps swept up from either side leading to a raised front entrance. An ornate balustrade followed the curve of the steps. At the level of the second floor, a frieze and label moulding ran around the entire building. Above the entrance on the second floor, there was a tall glazed double door. Designed in keeping with the windows, it opened out onto a tiny balcony and balustrade. This important feature would be my way in.

The smooth-faced stone quoins built into each corner of the building provided a prominent architectural feature. They were recessed between each quoin, allowing a toe and finger hold. Somehow, the boys managed to find a grand house in Tunbridge Wells that had a very similar feature. I practised climbing there and found it to be both dangerous and difficult. The importance of this stage of the operation escaped none of us, so we spared no effort to get it right. They found an experienced rock climber to help me with technique, and a local builder erected a scaffold on either side of the corner with a pulley wheel placed at the top. The owners of the building must have been completely bewildered.

I climbed the corner stones attached to a safety rope. This built my confidence enormously. I fell off several times, and they gently lowered me to the ground on each occasion. When I watched the assurance with which the rock climber scaled the wall, I realised I should be able to do it. The main thing with rock climbing is finger strength. Following that exercise, I practised everyday pulling myself up by my fingers. There were no doubts in my mind, the operation had every chance of success.

Mac's problem became reorganising agents and FR to work around those of us now involved in what became known as "Operation Top Hat". Over twenty operations were planned behind the beachhead. Every operation was designed to impede the German response and facilitate the Allied advance. Each carried its own risk, depending upon the importance of the target. Mac designated Top Hat as our number one priority.

The importance of the operation could not be underestimated. The fact that the Germans set up a provincial headquarters with such a senior officer meant only one thing. As the Allied ships appeared on the horizon, the local German chain of command would have this man at the top. The response to the invasion would not come from Hitler or any of his cronies; it would come from local commanders. And it would be unlikely that any were of higher rank than our *SS-Gruppenführer und Generalleutnant der Waffen-SS.* If we got him, the local German response to the invasion became a bicycle with a wheel missing. Countless Allied lives would be saved.

Given the element of total surprise, the Chateau would not be a problem. What worried us was the troop contingent less than 500 yards away. The Germans commandeered an agricultural building and farmhouse in the grounds of the Chateau to use as makeshift barracks. Our intelligence told us they numbered about twenty-five. Besides those, they had a personal staff in the Chateau and wireless operators. We thought a total of seven.

That the barracks had been hastily commandeered showed a sense of urgency, and there was only one urgency in German minds at that time. Our two agents on the ground were brilliant. They coordinated with the local resistance, trying to form an effective fighting force to tackle the barracks. Mac wanted a full-on assault to quickly eliminate the threat. He wanted overwhelming firepower. FR, however, were not trained or equipped to carry out such an assault. We discussed the possibility of a small contingent of paratroopers being brought in to deal with it. In the hours before the invasion, that proved to be a bird that would not fly.

Mac then requested an air drop of heavy weapons, machine guns and bazookas. That bird flew but didn't lay a golden egg. It became a disaster! With time of the essence, the RAF flew in less than favourable conditions. The pilot swore he saw the signal light through the broken cloud. It probably came from a farmhouse. They dropped the canisters in the wrong place. The resulting panic went right to the top. What message did we send to the Germans? Not knowing whether the canisters fell into their hands, that possibility remained. Another drop became out of the question. We next discussed who would carry out the assault on the Chateau with me.

"Me and Rob," I said immediately.

"No, Dotty, not Rob."

"Yes, Mac. I'm going with Rob. He's by far and away the best, you know he is. We work together as a team without thinking. We trust each other."

Mac was starting to see Rob and me as a couple and he didn't like it. He thought it might be a distraction but I had no doubts whatsoever; Rob and I made a formidable team. More to the point, Mac knew that as well and I left him no option. The bigger problem remained creating a large enough force to tackle the barracks. We couldn't afford to take any more resistance fighters away from the sabotage operations already planned for so long. The maximum force our agents might realistically muster amounted to five, plus one of them. They could be armed with submachine guns, but without the heavy weapons Mac intended, the odds did not favour them.

At that point, we knew where, but we still didn't know when. We decided that Rob and I must only go over at the last moment. The German security clampdown made our assimilation into the local community far too risky. The fact we would take as much armament as we could carry confirmed that decision. We rehearsed the plan a hundred times; the armaments were ready; we were ready. With nothing more to do, we had to wait. All of our agents, not already embedded with the French, were in the same position. The same applied to the Jedburgh teams.

The waiting became awful. I had sympathy for the 156,000 troops who would be in the first wave, plus all the airmen and sailors waiting to cross the Channel. In total, one and a half million people were counting the days. The Prime Minister himself advised His Lordship that the invasion would take place on June the 5th.

Chapter Sixteen
Getting Ashore

He gave us two days' notice, which became three when the invasion had to be postponed. Portsmouth became one of the busiest places in Britain, so they moved our little fishing boat to Chichester, courtesy of the Navy. When the word finally came, Rob and I wasted no time departing. Everything had been ready for weeks.

In the rush to go, I missed saying goodbye to Lily and Fiona. Not seeing them that last time really troubled me. Sitting in the back of a lorry is very uncomfortable, but this is the transport that arrived. Rob sat on one side and I sat on the other. Our kit covered the floor between us. Neither of us wanted to show fear to the other. We laughed and joked, pretending we were involved in just another routine operation. In truth, the tension became unbearable. My stomach knotted, and my heart seemed to be fighting its way out of my chest.

It was so much more than just fear. The enormity of the events about to unfold overwhelmed everyone involved. Lily and Fi were the same, I saw it in their faces. I doubt there was a person at Station M whose hands were not trembling. Everyone realised we were on the verge of one of the most momentous days in world history. The weight of responsibility pressed down on every fibre of our bodies.

Rob dealt with it better than most, but the stress imprinted itself upon his face. If you allow fear to dominate your thoughts, it rapidly becomes self-doubt. Our plan for Operation Top Hat had been mentally rehearsed so many times it felt more like the memory of a past event. This is how we conquered our fear. I didn't once have a moment of self-doubt.

When we arrived at Chichester, it wasn't a moment too soon. My body ached where I tried to brace myself against the movement of the lorry. The moment we jumped down from the tailgate, the tension eased. The pair of us stood there stretching and rubbing our backsides. Waiting is always harder than doing. We carried as much kit as we could manage; those days in training carrying the heavy Bergen now proved its worth once again. It wasn't far to walk, but we both breathed a sigh of relief to get there. Our designated sailors met us with a cheery smile. They too welcomed the start of the operation; waiting did nobody any good.

Having arrived at dusk, our timing was perfect. When I passed my backpack to the sailor, he momentarily buckled under the weight. He looked at me with some astonishment. I presented them with our destination coordinates, and they consulted their map. Any crossing of the Channel at night carried a certain amount of risk. My sailors, as I called them, did it repeatedly. Statistically, they reduced their chances of coming home safely with every crossing. I thanked them on each occasion when I crossed over with them, but I now wish I had said more. That proved to be the last occasion I would see that crew. They were extremely brave men, and like so many people during the war, completely unrecognised.

They warned us it would be a very rough crossing. The weather had turned unseasonal. Rob and I both thought the same thing. Rough seas might delay the invasion. On the morning of D-Day, our crossing point would become the busiest shipping lane in the world. Not all of it would be seaworthy vessels, like our fishing boat. Landing craft especially were not designed to plough through the waves. This made the weather a critical factor. When the sailors said it would be a rough crossing, I don't think Rob or I really understood quite what "rough sea" implied.

The little fishing boat chugged out of Chichester harbour, as stately as a galleon. As soon as the harbour became the Solent, our stately galleon lost much of its composure. Our sailors suggested Rob and I remain in the little cabin, a suggestion we gladly accepted. Our route took us along the Solent, and while the sea provided a few entertaining moments, it wasn't desperately bad. Not desperately bad until we rounded The Needles on the western tip of the Isle of Wight. Suddenly, the full force of the weather hit us.

I had experienced nothing like it before. Rob and I braced ourselves in the small cabin, and I honestly thought every minute would be our last. The little boat climbed a sheer wall of water one moment, only to fall almost vertically down the other side. Then, when I thought the worst moment had passed, it did it again, and then again. When people ask me what the worst part of the operation was, I tell them the crossing.

Our luck held out. My wonderful sailors got us to the other side. It might have been routine for them, but that is not how I would describe it. Our last problem would be getting ashore. The moment we stepped outside the little cabin, the problem hit us in the face. The waves threw us around the boat and horizontal rain and spray lashed into our faces.

Although we were close to the beach, I had no idea where to shine my torch signal. I couldn't see anything. One of the sailors guided me with a compass, and I sent the signal. A coded signal came back from our contact ashore. They were there waiting for us.

The navigational skills of our sailors had performed yet another miracle. Having got us there, somehow, we needed to get ashore. Our plan called for the contact to remain concealed. We alone would be exposed on the beach. Unbeknown to us, the French boys ashore changed the plan. The howling wind combined with the pounding rain to virtually exclude conversation as the sailors shouted at us, inches from our ears. They advised us to remove our backpacks. The rough sea would be too dangerous for us to be strapped to a heavy weight. Rob shouted back pointing out how dangerous it would be to complete our mission without the guns and munitions in those Bergens. We made what proved to be a disastrous decision; we said we would risk it.

The sailors' words echoed louder in my ears with every passing second. Our little fishing boat tossed like a cork in the wind. We struggled to stand, let alone move. The rubber dinghy rose and fell with every wave; one moment it crashed into the side of the boat, the next moment it fell out of sight. The sailors held Rob as he struggled over the gunnel. As the dinghy rose up towards him, they pushed him off. He fell on his side and grabbed a hold of the rope. Safely aboard, he braced himself for my undignified entrance. My sailors launched me overboard shouting the words, *good luck.*

Rob and I struggled wearing our packs. With our centre of gravity dictated by the heavy loads, we had no control over our balance in the tossing dinghy. We had to sit flat on the bed of the dinghy with our packs pushed against the sides. The noise of the wind and rain now combined with the surf to make it impossible to hear each other speak. The driving rain seemed to hit us full in the face, regardless of trying to turn away from it. I held Rob by one of his straps and he held mine as the dinghy repeatedly crashed into the side of the boat. The sailors pushed us off into the night.

Only then did the full reality of our situation impose itself upon me. I realised we were in serious danger! The heavy cloud cover and rain prevented even the slightest night vision. The wind roared in our ears. We had no sense of where we were or which direction we needed to go. I began to think our sailors would have to rope us back to the boat when I saw a light. Our shore contact broke all protocol by continually flashing their torch. We could only paddle with one hand each, as we clung to the dinghy with the other. As we reached the surf, it propelled us towards the beach, but the waves became steeper. The waves tossed us about and the dinghy spun around. I lost all sense of direction. It all happened so quickly. One moment we were clinging to the dinghy, the next moment we were both thrown in the sea.

Of all the things to happen, our moment of crisis had been the one thing we didn't account for. My heavy backpack immediately dragged me straight under the waves. I did the one thing I shouldn't have done. I panicked. The sudden shock of being underwater in complete blackness causes an involuntary reaction to gasp. I breathed in water. My life didn't flash before my eyes. There was no last moment of tranquillity. I just remember the blind terror as I panicked uncontrollably, trying to separate myself from my backpack.

I don't even remember the hand that saved me. My next conscious moment became filled with coughing and gasping for air. Only then, lying on the beach, did I realise I was still alive. I immediately looked for Rob. When I didn't see him in the dark, terror visited itself upon me again. If you think terror is self-limiting, you would be wrong. I tried to scream his name, but I just coughed. Seeing my alarm, one of the French boys said, "He's okay."

The local resistance who worked with our agents all had experience of the sea. They understood how difficult our landing would be. They used the cover of the foul weather, but nevertheless, they risked all for us. A team of them stood waiting in the surf with rope and floats. They swam out and grabbed both of us, and quite obviously, they saved our lives with seconds to spare. Pinned under the water, we were lucky to be found, let alone saved. I later fought with some of those same boys. They were heroes to a man.

They got us both into the nearest safe houses in the small village of Le Vieux Bourg. Still badly shaken up, I shivered with the cold. The wife of the house ushered the boys away and immediately stripped my clothes off me. She wrapped me in a blanket and sat me by an open fire. What felt like just a moment ago, I lay beneath the waves in absolute blackness. Now I sat in front of a fire, warm and safe. My change of fortune was so extreme, so overwhelming, I just lost control and burst into tears. I couldn't understand my reaction. Lily's the one who cries all the time, she's very emotional, not me. I tried to control it but just couldn't. Renée assured me I was in shock, that it would pass. She proved to be right, but not before I made a spectacle of myself. A large glass of cognac seemed to help no end. We had so much to do; we needed every second to organise. Instead, I got into a comfortable bed, and with the help of the cognac, slept until the morning.

The weather remained quite stormy into the next morning. I woke to the sound of the windows rattling, making me react with alarm. An entire night had been lost, with every minute vital. My wonderful host, Renée, told me to calm down, I needed time to recover. Even as the wife of a resistance fighter, she knew nothing about Top Hat, but her advice was well-founded. She prepared breakfast and gave me back my dried clothes.

Renée could not have been more charming. About thirty-five years old, she looked like a fashionable Parisian, rather than a housewife in a remote country village. She appeared slightly incongruous, dressed in her expensive-looking dress drawn in at the waist with a narrow belt. Even her makeup proclaimed a sophistication which belonged in a chic Parisian nightclub. In Occupied France at that time of heightened tension, and with a platoon of German troops barracked not three miles away, helping me required yet another act of heroism. The regular patrols represented an ever-present danger.

Her husband, Henri, saved me at the beach. Now he came into the room and assured me Rob was safe in a house in the village. We both needed to leave as soon as possible. They organised a meeting outside the village in a farm building. He assured me our backpacks had been opened and their contents cleaned and dried. Everything would be taken to the farm building. We should meet up, organise our plans and disperse as quickly as possible. He would guide me. His calm, sharp mind reassured me. Looking at that lovely man, I realised what attracted a beautiful Parisian lady to that provincial part of France.

I thanked Renée profusely, and we left without further delay. He avoided the roads; we walked between and behind houses. When we had no option but to walk in the open, we did so as casually as possible. Two German soldiers appeared out of nowhere. Dressed in authentic French clothing, I didn't look suspicious so, provided I didn't have to get involved in a long conversation, there should be no problem. One of them spoke to us in German. Henri calmly answered in German while I felt for my handgun. It wasn't there! They spoke for only a minute. I nodded as if I understood. Both the German soldiers possessed nice boyish looking faces, only their uniforms made them the enemy. When they moved on, I breathed a sigh and asked Henri what they talked about. "The foul weather," he replied.

They chose the farm building well. With a long open access track we would have plenty of warning if anyone approached. Everyone was there, including Starling, our radio operator, and Kingfisher. We only used our code names for wireless broadcasts to Station M. In France, their operational names were Nicole and André. We hugged each other warmly. I stood in Rob's arms until it became embarrassing. Reunion over, it quickly came down to business. Nicole received a specially coded message that night. It mentioned my code name, Sparrow, in normal code. Nicole responded with a single code word of acknowledgment that confirmed my safe arrival. A single word is too short to trace. The return message from Station M came back as gobbledygook.

I guessed its meaning. SOE used various communication systems, such as the Playfair Cipher and the Double Transcription Cipher. We even had the Innocent Letter code, and code 53. Nothing could be described as being infallibly safe. Before we left, Rolo told me we should have a secret code, just in case he had to send anything too sensitive to send by normal code. He meant anything to do with D-Day. We needed a perfectly safe, unbreakable code. Rolo handed me a tiny pocket book of poetry. He took the precaution of covering it in a waterproof wrapping.

Little did he know how important that turned out to be! Thank God it was still in my pocket.

The message comprised a series of numbers. A number for the page, the line, and the word. A simple system, a one-off cipher that only related to that one little obscure book. As I transcribed the words a message appeared. *Your mother regrets she will be late arriving. Expect her the following morning.* It didn't surprise any of us. D-Day had been postponed for a day. The weather was still terrible. Although the wind had slightly moderated, we greeted the decision to go ahead with some surprise, but an additional day provided us with valuable time; we needed it. If Rolo used the book, I needed to destroy it. This is how closely we guarded the most important secret of the war.

The munitions we brought with us were distributed among the boys. There were six of them in total, André, Henri, and four other French Resistance fighters. The packs nearly cost us our lives, but now it felt worth the risk. Rob handed them two additional Sten Guns and bundles of ammunition magazines. We also carried some handguns, with as much ammunition as possible. Besides that, we carried more than a dozen hand grenades. The standard No. 5 Mk.1 Mills grenades. Best of all, Rob carried a Bren Gun broken down in his pack. It came with as many magazines as he could carry. The gun alone weighed 25 lbs.

The Bren gun and grenades increased our chances enormously. We considered every detail of the plan again. Provided we achieved complete surprise at the barracks, we should overwhelm them quickly. As for Rob and me, we rehearsed it a hundred times. Armed with the element of surprise, we remained confident we would achieve our principal objective. All that remained was for us to see the Chateau first-hand in daylight. The meeting broke up, and we all dispersed. We would meet again on D-Day.

Henri arranged a guided tour around the Chateau. Our position in the horse-drawn cart was not without its problems, and we needed to keep our distance. From a less than ideal concealed position, we both studied the magnificent building with the aid of binoculars. It looked exactly like the scale model we worked with. My view of the front of the building through the binoculars confirmed the value of the training. It looked just as we assumed it did. I felt I knew the building as if I had been there before.

Rob studied his point of entry through a ground-floor window directly into the communications room. I would require absolute stealth right up to when I confronted the target; Rob would only require stealth to get into his initial position. When he heard my shot, his first action would be a Mills grenade through the window. That explosion would be the signal for the assault upon the barracks.

The layout and room plan remained clear in our minds. I saw it in my sleep. Our access route through the grounds would take us through a copse of trees before a quick dash across open ground to the perimeter of the ornamental garden. We would then climb over a low stone balustrade wall and follow that to the building. Rob and I worked through every scenario, every eventuality. If everything went according to plan, I would eliminate the target. From that moment, all hell would break loose. Rob's job was first and foremost to eliminate the wireless operators and destroy the equipment. He then needed to seek out the remaining soldiers on his level before they were able to regroup. I would search my floor, followed by the attic rooms.

A nearly full moon would rise an hour and a half before sunset on June 5th. It would be at its highest point at 01:19 hrs on June 6th. The first Allied gliders and paratroopers would hit the ground at 00:05 hrs. We timed our assault to be moments ahead of them. Cloud permitting, the moonlight would give us more than enough night vision. With everything in place, we could not have been more prepared.

Chapter Seventeen
Operation Top Hat

We were each spread out around the village to reduce the risk of detection. I stayed again with Henri and Renée. I felt so sorry for Renée; she knew full well her husband would soon take part in a dangerous operation, but she could not be told any details. Fear of the unknown can be worse than fear of the known. They struck me as being the perfect couple. A beautiful and sophisticated woman, Renée obviously adored Henri. He didn't share her Parisian sophistication but his presence went far beyond any rustic appeal. Henri was a man as big in stature as he was in heart. They loved each other with a passion they could not disguise. Photographs of their two little girls adorned the mantelpiece and bookshelf. When it came time to leave, I saw the pain of separation between them. Renée kissed me goodbye and I could taste the fear on her cheek. I left them alone to share a final tear-filled au revoir.

We assembled in that same farmhouse. As the hour approached, we all sat quietly in the dark, each secluded in our own contemplation. Our eyes gradually attuned to the soft glow of moonlight streaming in through the small window. Shadows reached out across Rob's face, and I couldn't tell the shadow from his face camouflage. With the endless discussion over, the only questions remaining were those we asked of ourselves. What if I hesitate? What if I let everyone down? Will my fear overwhelm me? Am I going to die? Those thoughts, and many more, inhabited the dark recesses of everyone's mind.

My heart seemed to be beating in my throat, but I amazed myself with my relative calmness. Rob removed a small box from his backpack and opened it. He gave a suicide pill contained in a matchbox to every person. I put mine in my pocket with little thought. Rob's expression changed as he picked his own up; his hand visibly shook.

At that moment, I looked at a true reflection of myself. Before I joined SOE, I didn't amount to much of anything. In my mind, I had become an SOE agent and nothing else. What did I have to lose? When the time came to go, I eagerly welcomed it. Waiting is the worst part. We had no doubts about André, Henri, and the other French boys; we shared one important understanding. They relied upon us as implicitly as we relied upon them. They would not let us down.

The cloud cover continued thin and broken. The breeze ensured that a break in the cloud would always be only a moment away. We wished each other good luck before Rob and I stepped out into the cool night air, our eyes fully adjusted to the darkness. A passing cloud unveiled the full moon like a fortune teller lifting a silk cloth from her glass globe. The cold reflected light bathed the landscape in stark shades of light and dark. It provided both our vision and concealment in equal measure.

Quickly away from the farm building, we hastened into the adjacent field. Concealed against the coal black shadow of the hedgerow, our progress continued predictably safe and rapid. The wooded area next to the Chateau provided even more reliable concealment. Sharply defined ghostly fingers of shadow extended from the base of each tree, while above them their leafy canopies sparkled as a profusion of moonbeams found passage through them.

When the outline of the building came into view, we stopped behind cover and just observed. Through our binoculars, we saw exactly what we expected to see. In daylight, the architecture of the Chateau provided a wonderful balance of symmetry and elegance, its roofline and chimneys restful on the eye. Now it sat bathed in moonlight which offered neither warmth nor flattery. The cold, austere light cast long straight-edged shadows violating its perfect lines. The once elegant building now presented an altogether unfamiliar face, it neither welcomed nor invited us. We circled around, ensuring no surprises lay in wait for us.

The Germans were extraordinarily lax in their security. A sentry stood front and back, as we expected, but neither of them was alert. The sentry at the back was sitting on a low wall and lit up a cigarette. The one at the front sat on a wrought-iron bench in the garden. He leaned back, arms folded, his straight legs crossed. We could hardly believe how extraordinarily lax they were. A gap in their blackout allowed light to pour through one of the basement windows. We saw at least three soldiers inside the room. Two sat at the radio transmitter. A shaft of light came from the adjacent room. From what we could see they were laughing, completely relaxed. Their only effort towards security appeared to be staying awake.

The weather contributed towards the Germans' complacency. They assumed an invasion was out of the question. With the high winds and rough seas only just abating, the German logic was not entirely misplaced. That proved to be a very serious mistake reflected across the whole of German High Command. We expected to see only the radio room occupied, so immediately a change of plan became necessary. This eventuality like so many others had been considered. Rob understood what he needed to do. His task had always been more onerous than mine. In no more than a minute, he had to eliminate any armed resistance on the ground floor. At least five soldiers had to be accounted for, it might easily be more.

On my floor, we only knew of one, possibly two, officers. A single inconsequential flaw remained in our plan. We didn't know for certain which bedroom suite the target occupied. Sometimes a light had been seen in both bedroom suites. A central hallway ran the length of the second floor, with a principal bedroom suite at each end. I guessed the target occupied the bedroom offering the best view across the Normandy countryside. It didn't greatly concern me. I needed to eliminate whoever occupied the second floor, regardless of rank. Carefully watching the time, we took up position next to the stone balustrade. From there, we would each go our own separate way across the open ground. I was about to climb over the low wall when Rob placed his hand on my arm, preventing me.

"I need to tell you something, Dotty."

"What is it?"

"I love you! Whatever happens, I will always be there for you."

"You love me?"

"I do. I need you, okay? So no more of this talk about nothing to lose."

I climbed over the wall and looked back at him. "What a time to tell me that," I said, walking away.

What a strange but wonderful moment. I crossed the grounds towards the sentry, with Rob's words ringing in my ears. I had no room for fear. We trained to silently kill guards and sentries so extensively, I'd developed the confidence of someone who had done it a dozen times. The silent killing techniques we learned at Arisaig were frighteningly efficient. While we should never allow ourselves to be complacent, the training equipped us for exactly this moment. That my man chose to sit down meant he had no chance at all.

The approach is the dangerous part. If an SOE agent can reach the sentry without being detected, the man is dead. Obviously, I approached him from behind. I had practised a range of techniques, all of them silent. This sentry had his back against the wrought iron seat. That decided my plan of attack. The first and absolute requirement is silence. I carried a Sten Gun with several magazines. My Colt .38 sat in its holster ready for an instant draw, with three Mills grenades attached to clips. Each item had been thoroughly secured, nothing can be allowed to clunk or rattle. Even minor items in my pockets are packed with cloth handkerchiefs to prevent movement. My shoes, being specially selected to enable the wall climb, also ensured silence.

I just followed the training, watching every step to ensure I didn't stand on a twig or anything which might make the slightest noise. Not even the resident tawny owls were aware of my presence; they confidently called out into the velvet silence. My heightened senses were acutely aware of everything around me. Approaching from down-wind, even the damp night air felt viscous against my face. It carried with it a heavy scent of lavender from the garden borders. One silent step followed another until only two steps separated us. A final breath before even my breathing became silent.

I slipped my fighting knife from my left hand into the right. Two more steps and I instantly grabbed him by the chin and yanked his head back forcibly. At the same time, I thrust the long stiletto blade of the knife into the side of his neck with the blade edges parallel to the ground. Even if I missed the carotid artery first time, a thrust backwards and forwards would sever it. The tip of the blade protruded slightly from the other side of his neck. With the blade through his throat, and my hand over his mouth, he didn't make the slightest murmur. The instant shock renders the victim virtually immobile. There is only token resistance. It takes five seconds for a man to become unconscious when the carotid artery is severed. When his five seconds expired, he crumpled into his final resting place. Another seven seconds, and he became the first German soldier to die on D-Day. Only then did I withdraw the knife.

I had no time to consider the consequences of my action. The sentry only amounted to a minor part of the operation, a means to an end. I needed to move on immediately, but first I remembered to wipe the blood from the blade; a necessary requirement before returning it to its scabbard. I stroked it across the shoulder of the dead soldier's uniform. From the sentry to the foot of the entrance steps, took only five seconds. Here, I paused for another second. All remained quiet. Six quick steps and I stood at the corner of the entrance portico. Nothing would give me away now. Nothing unless I fell off!

I reached up and placed my first finger hold, just as I practised. My kit added many extra pounds, but that's how I practised. One finger hold followed a toehold, and then another. Gripping either side of the corner, I prevented myself from falling backwards. A hand at a time, a foot at a time, I made progress. With the second floor tantalisingly close, a sharp pain shot down the middle finger of my left hand just as I negotiated the frieze and label moulding marking the second floor. I grimaced but couldn't let go. I paused for a moment until the pain in my toes and ankles became an even greater problem.

During practice, aching muscles were an ever-present discomfort to be overcome. The label moulding projected about six inches. It made my last couple of steps difficult. But once above it, I managed to stand on it and momentarily rest. It might have been a precarious position, but just thirty seconds eased the muscles in my feet. The next manoeuvre would be the most dangerous.

I needed to let go with my left hand and take a step along the label moulding. Away from the corner I had to grip the face of the ashlar stones. The technique involved jamming your fingers in the recess. It gave me a modicum of balance as I let go of the corner. My next step was always going to be the critical one. I let go with my right hand and stepped three feet along the six-inch wide label moulding with only two fingers jammed into a slight recess to prevent me falling backwards.

The balcony appeared so close but so far away. In practice, I fell from that position about a third of the time. I had two options. Maintain balance and reach for the balcony. Or push off from the label moulding and grab the balcony on my way down. It wasn't as difficult as it sounds, but it came with the extra likelihood of noise. If I lost balance, I remained confident about still grabbing hold of the balcony. I took that last step with my face and body pressed against the wall. Reaching as far as possible, my fingers touched the metal balustrade. It felt like I had taken hold of Rob's hand; I immediately felt safe.

One more long stride and I stood on the balcony; I made it! Rob would have dealt with his sentry and returned to watch me gain entry. This is when he would manoeuvre himself into position next to the radio room window. I didn't see him, but I knew where he would be. The double door presented the next challenge. Our training taught us how to pick locks. That should have been my first option, because it's quiet. Unfortunately, the key remained in the lock on the other side, which made it slightly more difficult. I decided to jemmy the door open, hopefully with the minimum of noise. The door had not been designed for security; it offered little resistance.

The wooden door frame gave way with an audible crack as the lock broke free. It wasn't a loud noise but in the velvet silence of the night it was the only sound. I hesitated for thirty seconds. Our reconnaissance reported seeing no dogs, but I listened for a movement, just in case. Everything remained reassuringly silent. The moonlight shone brightly onto the balcony but the moment I stepped through the drapes nearly all the light was gone. Inside I find a round pedestal table directly in front of me. A vase of flowers sat in the middle. I could so easily have walked into it, instead I committed it to memory in case I needed a hasty retreat. A clock ticked rhythmically somewhere in the hall. Guided by the sound I found a long case clock and memorised its position.

A moment to take stock of the situation, and all remained quiet, no one heard me. My watch said 00:12 hrs; I knew the first paratroopers were landing at precisely that same moment. D-Day had begun! One of the most momentous days in world history was unfolding, and we were a part of it. Only the thinnest shafts of moonlight entered the hallway around the drapes. I needed my torch but muffled the light with my hand. With the torch in one hand and my .38 in the other I continued along the hall towards the southwest-facing bedroom suite. Treading carefully, always landing on the ball of each foot, never the heel, I hoped to remain totally silent. A floorboard creaked; I grimaced in response. Everything remained quiet, still no one heard me.

When the moment came, it arrived without fanfare. I stood outside the door knowing that like a line of dominos I was about to instigate a chain reaction. Once that first domino fell, nothing would stop the others following. The man I hoped to find on the other side of that door was the enemy, nothing more nor less than that. So without a moment's hesitation I reached for the door handle. Some door handles can make a noise, but this one didn't. The door hinges made a slight squeak. Opening the door just enough, I stepped inside.

The curtains had deliberately been left open to invite the early morning sun. The tall south facing window allowed the glow of the full moon to bathe the room in colourless light. The target, or at least a target, lay fast asleep in his enormous bed. An army uniform had been carefully placed on a hanger in the room. A pair of high boots sat beneath it. One glance at it with my torch and I knew I had him. I had no further need for the torch, so I placed it quietly back in my pocket. Five silent strides across the room left me standing next to the bed.

The elimination of the man lying in front of me would accomplish the prime objective of Operation Top Hat. My training taught me never to hesitate, always seize your advantage. I didn't hesitate, not for a second. I raised my .38 from about three feet away and fired a single shot. Blood ejected from the other side of his head splattering the pillows and bed linen. It created a strange surreal scene that I had not expected. The blood glistened black as tar in the moonlight. His body barely moved. I might just as easily have killed him silently, but the sound of the shot toppled the first domino. The retort rang in my ears and the acrid sulphurous smell of black powder filled my nostrils. D-Day really had begun.

I left the room instantly and took up a position in the hall. Two almost simultaneous explosions came from the floor below, followed by rapid fire from Rob's Sten Gun. Had there been an occupant in the other bedroom suite, then he would likely rush out of his bedroom door in response to the noise. I knelt in position in the hallway with my Sten Gun aimed at the other bedroom suite. The occupant abruptly flung open the door. I resisted firing until he rushed out carrying a handgun. One quick burst of my Sten Gun and he instantly fell to the ground. He looked like a ridiculous figure, dressed in night attire with his jackboots on.

The gunfire below me continued, and it wasn't all from a Sten Gun. The noise echoed and reverberated around the building. Rob had met opposition. Every instinct told me to rush down and help him, but the plan called for me to clear the second floor and then the attic rooms. I did it instinctively. I ran between rooms, following every lesson my training taught me. With no one else on my floor, only the attic remained. The stairs to the attic rooms were narrow, a dangerous place to be caught out. I fired a long burst of fire as I ran up the stairs. At the top landing, the lights had been turned on. A terrified elderly man in nightclothes confronted me.

During training, I mistakenly shot several friendly targets; I tended to be over-eager. The man standing in front of me presented one obvious difference, he wasn't cardboard. I hesitated for a fraction of a second. He raised his hands, saying, "We are French." He sounded like a Frenchman telling me the truth. Three more people appeared all in their nightclothes, two women and another man. They assured me there were no Germans on that floor. They were the domestic staff. When they realised what had happened, they erupted in celebration. One of them shouted "*Vive la France*." I shouted the same back as I raced back down the stairs, "*Vive la France*."

The gunfire stopped abruptly. Apart from the celebrations on the top floor, the Chateau fell silent. I approached the ground floor cautiously. The body of a soldier lay at the foot of the stairs. Smoke rose out of the radio room. Two bodies slumped over the equipment, their uniforms peppered with ragged holes. The door to the adjacent room lay splintered on the floor. Inside, another German soldier lay back in a chair. A thin waft of smoke rose from his uniform. Sensing movement behind me, I spun around to see Rob walking towards me.

"Have you got them all?" I asked.

"Yes, three more than we thought. Did you get him?"

"Yes, I got them both."

"Right, let's get out of here fast."

As we left the Chateau, we immediately became aware of continuous gunfire in the distance, obviously the assault on the barracks. The noise sounded close; it sounded like a pitch battle.

"This should be over by now," said Rob.

"I know, they must need help."

We followed our instinct and ran to help our comrades, realising something must have gone wrong. The noise and flashes of machine gun fire filled the air. From our position, it became clear that our people had been forced to move back and take up a defensive position. Something had indeed gone horribly wrong. We circled round behind the conflict and were forced to crawl towards them keeping as low as possible. The air above us was filled with gunfire. The solid resistance offered by the small copse of trees seemed to amplify the sound of the striking bullets. A continuous drumming echoed through the trees, splinters of bark and wood sprayed everywhere. I recognised the sound from training; it came from an MG-42 machine gun. Our Sten Guns were no match.

We only made faltering progress against the almost continuous hail of bullets. Rob shouted to them as we crawled closer between the trees. We were relieved when they finally heard us. Their covering fire allowed us to crawl a little faster. Bullets ricocheted off the trees hitting the ground around us. When we joined them, we realised they were sheltering behind a low stone wall.

We entered a scene of utter confusion. No one wanted to put their head up to take stock of the situation; we didn't dare put our heads above the cover of the stone wall. The situation appeared hopeless. The German forces were in control, not us. There were only four of them, Henri and three other French boys. When Rob asked where the others were, the expression we received in return told us everything. Rob and I looked at each other, our comrade Nigel (André) had been killed along with one of the French boys. We were in the middle of an unfolding disaster.

All the while, the terrifying roar of the MG-42 filled the air. The unmistakable sound could not be confused with any other machine gun during the war. The rate of fire was so fast at over 1,500 rounds per minute, the sound of each individual round merged into a continuous roar. This led to its terrifying nickname - Hitler's buzzsaw. We became familiar with it during training. The rate of fire created two problems. The barrel would overheat rapidly and its consumption of 7.92mm ammunition was prodigious. To overcome those inherent problems, the Germans fielded each gun with a crew of ten soldiers. The gun crew would ensure an almost continuous rate of fire with only one exception. The barrel would overheat to the point of failure, but the design allowed for it to be replaced quickly and easily in the field. A good gun crew could replace a hot barrel in 20 seconds, and each machine gun came with a stock of replacements to allow time for them to cool down.

"Where's our Bren Gun?" I shouted.

"We've lost it," came the reply.

"It's hopeless, Dotty!" Rob said. "It's only a matter of time before they advance across the open ground towards us. We have to retreat back into these trees."

The French boys didn't know about the need to replace the barrel. They say knowledge is power. Well, our knowledge didn't so much empower us, but it offered a glimmer of hope. If we waited for a particularly long burst of fire, we might reasonably guess that it would be followed by a change of barrel. We'd still be subject to submachine gun fire, but even a 20 second respite from the buzzsaw increased our chances.

The trees offered some cover, but they didn't extend very far. Someone needed to stay behind and keep the Germans at bay long enough for the rest to get some distance between us. Rob immediately said he would do it. I argued with him, but we could hardly hear ourselves think, let alone talk. He wouldn't change his mind even though I pleaded with him. Henri pulled me by the arm. A long burst of fire strafed its way along the wall. Shards of limestone flew into the air.

When the buzzsaw abruptly stopped, I shouted for us to go but Rob filled my mind. As we crawled away, I kept shouting 'Rob, Rob' but I doubt he heard me. He risked all by firing continuously over the stone wall. Rob just kept firing. Each time his magazine ran out, my heart stopped, only to start again when he quickly replaced it. In that adrenalin-filled moment of maximum danger, my body propelled me away from Rob, but a part of me stayed behind. It's the bravest thing I have ever seen. He offered his life for ours without so much as a second thought.

Having crawled perhaps forty yards from the wall, we stood up on our feet crouching low and attempted to run. The terrifying roar of the MG-42 resumed and Henri immediately staggered and fell. I stopped and looked back. Rob still fired continuously. In a matter of seconds, another of the French boys fell, followed by another. One of them was almost cut in half by the MG-42 and Henri lay on the ground injured but alive. In the confusion, the only remaining Frenchman didn't notice me go back.

Drill Sergeant Cummings at Wanborough proved to be right all along. I *am* a liability! Henri saved my life on the beach. Just as I couldn't leave Eliane in training, neither could I leave Henri and Rob. I dragged Henri behind a tree and started firing over Rob's head. I wanted him to crawl towards me under the cover of my fire.

Rob saw what I wanted him to do, but he had other ideas. He threw his last grenade towards the German position and disappeared along the length of the wall. I knew what he was doing. He wanted to draw the Germans away from me. Rob maintained bursts of fire as he progressively moved away from us along the wall, intentionally making his position known. I pulled Henri up from the ground, intending to get him out of there. A hail of bullets from the buzzsaw passed inches above my head. Bark and wood splinters erupted from the trees. So many bullets hit Henri that his body was yanked from my hands and his head seemed to explode directly in front of me. Something hit me full in the face, the impact knocking me to the ground.

In that instant, I assumed I had been shot and I would soon be dead. I lay on the ground in confusion thinking it would soon be over. I had lost Rob; I wanted it to happen. Lying there confused and disorientated, I wanted death to make it all go away. It didn't! The next thing I knew, German soldiers were lifting me up and dragging me away. The realisation that death denied my request left me feeling strangely terrified. I still assumed I had been shot in the head, unable to see, blinded at the very least. Worst of all, my fate now rested in German hands.

Chapter Eighteen
The Darkest Hour

They bundled me into some kind of vehicle and drove me away. I felt them searching me. They removed my weapons and my suicide pill. When I struggled, they hit me. When I kicked one of them, they really laid into me. I must have lost consciousness because I have no memory of the rest of the journey. I remember being forced out of the vehicle, and two of them dragged me a considerable distance into a building. Unable to see, the sound of panic all around me spoke volumes. I could hear vehicles moved in all directions. A German officer shouted orders that no one seemed to respond to. Eventually inside a building, forcing me to sit, they tied my hands to the arms of a chair.

After what seemed like an age, someone came into the room. I heard the footsteps. A woman spoke in a French voice. She bathed my eyes and face. "This will hurt," she said, pulling splinters of wood out of my face. I was afraid I had lost my vision and so, even in that dire situation, I felt a moment of joy as my vision returned. I realised grit and congealed blood, Henri's blood, had stuck my eyelids together. The young woman looked extremely nervous.

"Where am I?"

"You're in Caen," she replied. "You're in the municipal building."

"Are the Gestapo here?"

"No, not yet. They are all panicking. Is this the invasion?"

"No, not yet."

I worried she may not be what she appeared to be. When German uniforms strutted into the room, the woman appeared to melt in fear.

I suspect she had not been working against me. The uniforms were followed by a man in plain clothes. He did everything to intimidate me. I found out much later that he might have been Harold Heyns, the head of Caen Gestapo. He appeared to be what is left of a person when all humanity has been removed. His eyes were sunken and dead. They sat beneath a wide expanse of forehead which accentuated his soulless eyes. A weak jaw and thin lips painted a picture of a little man emboldened only by his position of power.

Dressed in plain clothes he would go unnoticed in the street, but in his own environment he commanded power and dominance. His cold eyes didn't see me as a frightened human being; he just saw me as a source of information. If I disclosed that information, I would become as disposable as a scrap of paper. He intended to frighten the shit out of me, and he succeeded. We trained for this eventuality, but no amount of realistic training can remove that fear.

The two uniformed SS people acted subserviently while Heyns remained in attendance. The instant he left, however, their moment of power and dominance had arrived. They both removed their jackets, effectively preparing for work. When they turned to face me, they were both smiling. The expression on their faces portrayed a sense of eager anticipation. These two men took pleasure in their work; I was about to become the source of that pleasure. They were either sadistic bastards or clever interrogators. Both eventualities terrified me.

All the while, I concentrated on my training and the techniques they taught me. I expected they wanted information about the invasion. At that early stage in all the confusion, they would know very little. In the event of capture, Mac told us to resist as long as possible. When we were unable to take any more, we were to confess that the Normandy invasion had only been a diversion for the actual invasion to take place in Calais.

It started with ritualised humiliation. They ripped my blouse open and enjoyed playing with me. Then they progressed to shouting and slapping. When that didn't work, they progressed to the next level. They beat me with a heavy electrical cable. They concentrated on the arms and legs. The last thing they want is to knock you unconscious. I said nothing. They placed a hood over my head, so when they hit me, I didn't see it coming. The element of shock made it much worse. This continued for a couple of hours. All the while, German soldiers ran in and out of the building. With the invasion in full progress, my interrogators left me at regular intervals. Each time they returned, they appeared more desperate.

I remembered at 00:30 hrs the RAF intended to bomb Caen. I assumed that happened. We were told to suspend SOE operations in Caen just prior to D-Day. They only gave us the details we needed to have. I knew the advance from Sword beach depended upon the Caen Canal and Orne River bridges being taken intact. I reconnoitred those strategic bridges. Looking at the areas they told us to avoid on D-Day, it seemed obvious that they intended to liberate Caen on the first day. It didn't take a strategic genius to assume that those bridges would be taken by paratroopers or troops in gliders. Knowing the area, I realised the fighting would be close to the city itself. No wonder the Germans were in a state of panic.

My interrogators seemed unable to concentrate on their task. I feared they would be overtaken by events and simply shoot me where I sat. Normally an SOE agent in the Gestapo's hands would be assured a short and brutal life. I clung to the fact that my circumstances were different. With D-Day going on around me, anything might happen, and I had Rob. If anyone would be able to get away from the Germans after Operation Top Hat, then it would be Rob. If he got away, I knew for certain he would come for me. In that case, heaven help the people interrogating me.

Our training taught us to overcome the pain by employing clever mental techniques. Always remain positive, keep looking for an opportunity. If I got my arms untied, they would be easy to overpower. We had to expect an opportunity to present itself at any moment. I convinced myself that Rob would come for me. The aim is to keep a sense of hope and optimism. Your interrogators want you to lose all hope. People break when they find themselves staring into the abyss. I attempted to turn that around. I kept telling myself, I wouldn't like to be in your shoes when my Rob arrives.

I heard all sorts of things going on outside the building; my interrogators came back into the room looking even more grim-faced. The clock on the wall said 13:30 hrs. Just as they started to lay into me again, planes flew overhead and bombs started falling. One or two must have fallen quite close because the building rocked. I managed a smile; unlike them,

I had nothing to lose. The bombing seemed to change everything; they became increasingly more concerned. Another two soldiers rushed into the room and untied me from the chair, immediately retying my wrists. They forced me out of the building and dragged me a short distance along the road. For the first time, I saw the bomb damage and general panic among the Germans.

The latest air raid only increased the damage caused by the night-time bombing. A veil of smoke hung over much of the city. The smell of death and destruction entered your body with every breath. Many buildings lay in ruins. Debris blocked the roads and pavements. The injured struggled, some scarcely more able than the dead. Some of the dead wore German uniforms but so many were French, innocent men, women, and children. Lives were shattered simply because they were in the wrong place at the wrong time. I had seen this all before, during the Blitz. Whoever the innocents are, it's the same vision of hell that visits itself upon them.

They dragged me a short distance to the City Jail. Somehow, I didn't think they intended to imprison me. They stood me in a small courtyard within the prison. Immediately, the reason for me being there became apparent. Blood and bullet holes splattered the wall opposite me. On the ground, blood trails showed where numerous bodies had been dragged away. Even when I realised my fate, I still clung to the hope of Rob coming for me. I remember thinking, 'you better come soon, Rob'. Either in fear or exhaustion, my legs gave way beneath me. Two of them held me upright, one on either side.

Prison guards dragged six bewildered prisoners into the courtyard with their hands tied behind their backs. They brutally lined them up against the wall. Those poor bewildered people suddenly realised their fate. Three soldiers with sub-machine guns stood in front of them. The look of terror in the eyes of those poor people sent a chill right through me. The soldiers holding me seemed completely indifferent, as did the execution squad. A quick burst of fire and all six fell back against the wall like so many rag dolls before crumpling to the ground in a lifeless heap. Yet more blood flowed. I wanted to scream and turn away, but I did neither.

They dragged the bodies away, adding to the trail of blood. I assumed my turn had come. Minutes later, another six people were dragged out and placed against the wall. A different Gestapo officer strutted towards me. Dressed in the black leather greatcoat so beloved by the Gestapo, he looked at me with all the cold anticipation of a psychopath. With a hand painfully gripping my swollen face, he spoke in quite good English.

"You can end all this. These people will be spared if you tell us what we want to know."

I didn't have the slightest difficulty appearing to be broken. "All right, I'll tell you everything, but let these people go."

They marched me back to where I came from and slammed me back into the same chair. The same Gestapo monster then proceeded to slap me about, apparently for the sheer fun of it. He assured me I'd made the right decision; all those people would be spared if I cooperated. A part of me wanted that to be true, but I realised the fate of those people had nothing to do with me. The truth is far worse. Faced with the prospect of being overrun by the Allies, the head of Caen Gestapo, Harold Heyns, decided to execute all the French inmates of Caen prison. Mostly suspected of being French Resistance, they killed 87 people in the prison that day. Even if I had known that it wouldn't have made any difference to my circumstances.

I gave them little pieces of information. I hinted about minor operations like mine being only a token gesture. If I made a full confession, my usefulness would have been lost, and I would have taken my place against the wall. I saw how good they were at that. I tried to keep enough information to make the day last. You must never ever lose hope, so I clung to my belief that Rob would save me. As the day progressed, they became more and more desperate. They rapidly lost patience with me; I realised the beatings might only be the first stage. The Gestapo had an unenviable reputation for their hideously inventive torture techniques. Despite knowing that, I refused to dwell on it.

The misinformation programme that the cloak-and-dagger people put in place during the build-up to D-Day had been so successful the Germans became convinced the invasion would be directed towards Calais. "Operation Fortitude" is undoubtedly the most successful misinformation campaign of all time. If Hitler believed it, my interrogators had to believe it. This gave me a slight edge. They wanted to be told the major invasion would be at Calais. I didn't need to convince them. I gave them hints and clues, playing for time. They became ever more eager to get it over with. We reached a point in the early evening when my delay tactic expired.

The Gestapo officer, who seemed to delight so much in slapping me about, rushed into the room. Events were overwhelming them and their time was running out. That meant my time had run out. Two of them held my hand while he pushed something up under my fingernail. The pain seared right up my arm and seemed to explode in my head. They didn't ask me anything, they just did it again with another finger.

This continued until a wooden cocktail stick protruded from each finger on my left hand. He then delighted in pushing them harder. When they started on my other hand, something inside me broke. Unable to take any more, I confessed everything. The landings in Normandy were not the actual invasion. They had been right all along. A large force was intended to draw the Germans away from Calais, with the actual invasion waiting to land in the Pas-de-Calais. I knew that I signed my own death warrant the moment I told them.

I learned something that terrible day, something that, thank God, few people need to know. There comes a point during torture when your humanity has been stripped away. There is nothing left, nothing more to lose. The life you once had is so unbearable, you willingly let it go. That's the moment when you welcome death; that's when you break.

They threw water at me because I must have passed out. As I came around, I heard a loud explosion. It rocked the building. I assumed it must be another air raid. My interrogators appeared terrified. Seconds later, another smaller explosion sounded much nearer. Within seconds I heard gunfire. I recognised the sound; it came from a Sten Gun. The gunfire rapidly came ever closer. *Hell had come to Caen*! The door burst open and shots rang out. My interrogators were dead before they hit the floor. Rob rushed in and when he saw the state of me, his expression frightened even me. He had no time to ask me anything.

He pulled the cocktail sticks out of my fingers and cut my ropes, saying, "Come on, you can't just sit there."

Rob had a team of French boys with him; I recognised some of them. One of them gave me a Sten Gun while another strapped a belt of ammunition magazines on me. Where I found my reserve of strength, I do not know. It proved to be another lesson. However broken you are, the human spirit has an incredible capacity to cling to life. You just need a reason to hope. One moment I sat semiconscious waiting for death. The next moment, with hope restored, they escorted me out of the ruins of the municipality building.

I realised all these men had risked their lives for one reason. They risked everything for me. I felt a tremendous responsibility. I had to find a reserve of energy for them, anything less added to their danger. As we climbed over the rubble of the municipality building, we came across the psychopathic Gestapo officer who delighted in my torture. His good fortune was to be lying dead on the ground. Had Rob found him alive, he would have ripped his heart out.

In times of immense danger, most people behave irrationally. They might take the fight to the enemy, but they do so without thinking clearly. Rob never did that. When he saw what they did to me, I have never seen such anger in anyone as I saw in Rob that day. But only he could channel that anger to such an effect. He led us out of there like a one-man army. The explosions drew the attention of every German soldier in the area. Within two minutes of leaving the building, we became engaged in a full-on battle in the street.

Perhaps as many as twenty-five German troops advanced down the road towards us. Rob signalled to his five Frenchmen, and although vastly outnumbered, we charged toward them. The German troops didn't appear to be hardened veterans, some appeared to be no more than Hitler Youth. Faced with a hail of bullets running towards them, the soldiers turned tail, but to no avail. Rob pursued them and gunned them down. We intended to move north, towards the English and Canadian forces, who we knew would be advancing from the beachhead. Little short of a Panzer division would stop Rob, but that's exactly what we confronted.

The Germans realised if the invasion landed anywhere in Normandy, then Caen would be strategically placed to block the advance. Troops and armour had been concentrated there. We faced opposition at every turn. Our only option would be to head south instead. The bombing caused considerable damage. Amid the chaos, both French and Germans wandered the streets in shock and bewilderment. As the day turned into evening, we hoped it might be possible for us to disappear among the crowd of displaced people. We stayed out of trouble for a while, but eventually we ran headlong into German troops who were looking for us.

An intense battle ensued. We stayed together as a fighting unit, moving from one building to another. One group would advance under the cover of fire. The other group would then provide covering fire, and so together we advanced from street to street, and building to building. These were tactics we learned at Arisaig. Despite vastly superior numbers, the German troops had not been trained in this kind of urban warfare. As their casualties mounted, ending our "insurgence" became an ever-increasing priority. More and more troops were brought in. A contingent of twenty or more forced us to shelter inside a building.

Our position inside that bombed building appeared relatively secure for the moment, but we were pinned down. I fired my Sten Gun until it became too hot to handle, and my ammunition ran low. Then I realised how clever the designers of the Sten Gun had been. It fires the same 9mm ammunition as the enemy. They lay all around us; we just had to collect their ammunition and load it into our magazines. More and more German troops appeared at the front of the building. Albert, one of the French boys, said what should have been obvious.

"They think we are part of the invasion force."

"They're right," said Rob, "we *are* a part of the invasion. But we need to get out of this building before they bring up artillery."

"We've done well to get this far," said Émile. "You and Angélique make a break for it; we can try to disappear among the people."

"I'm not leaving anyone behind," I replied. "We all get out, or we all die here."

"It looks like the whole German army out there," said Michêl.

When the Gestapo murdered those French prisoners, they made a serious mistake. It wasn't only Rob fuelled by rage. The resistance boys possessed a steely courage born of their hatred for the enemy. If the truth be told, none of us thought we would get out of there. When courageous people are placed in that position, the term reckless no longer applies. You take chances because it's all you have left. With German troops massing in front of us, we decided to make a run for it out of the back of the building. If we left immediately, we would face fewer troops because they were only just taking up positions. We would punch through those troops and then go our separate ways. We remained positive, we could do this.

Of course, we couldn't do it, and everyone quietly realised that. Maybe with luck, one or two of us might make it, but not all of us, perhaps not any of us! When confronted with men who are prepared to die for each other and for me, it's a humbling experience like no other. I kissed and hugged each one of the French boys. They were only there because of me. I would have stepped into the line of fire to save any one of them.

Rob gave the order. We rushed at them, guns blazing. We caught them completely by surprise. They were still taking up positions, some of them in the building opposite. From the German perspective, Rob must have been a terrifying spectacle. He seemed to be invincible; he ran towards them at speed still firing with accuracy. Faced with that coming towards them, they flinched. It might have only been for a second, but that was all Rob needed. One of their own grenades went into the building, followed by another. We didn't stop to mop up, we just ran towards the next road intersection.

A hail of bullets followed us. Albert became the first of us to be hit. He staggered and finally fell. I stopped and as I looked back, they hit him again. Another few yards and Michêl in front of me was hit in the head. It happened as if in slow motion. I still can't erase that terrible image. He obviously died instantly. Terrified local people ran away or cowered behind windows. Rob reacted as he always did. He waved us on and then stopped to return fire. Émile joined him. The two of them lay behind some rubble, firing continuously. I ran on with the two other French boys. We then took up positions in doorways, providing covering fire for Rob and Émile to run after us.

An elderly French woman found herself between us and the advancing Germans. I don't know if I shot her or if it was one of the German troops. I tried desperately to avoid her, but she slumped to her knees in front of me. Her expression said only one thing. Why? The last shot was not mine. The woman fell forward, she would never have her question answered. Only Rob sprang to his feet, Émile didn't move. The sound of bullets ricocheting off the road and buildings filled the air. It sounded like a swarm of bees all around us.

Rob made it. His Sten Gun became so hot it jammed. He was firing a German MP 38. We reached the road junction and turned away from the gunfire. The two remaining French boys ran one way, and we went the other. We had no time for any recognition, much less a word of goodbye. Then I realised three of us had fallen. Even at a time like that, when the body is fuelled with adrenalin, a terrible sorrow overwhelmed me. It seemed to remove my last remaining resolve.

Rob saw that whatever kept me going this far had now gone. He put his arm around me and virtually carried me down the road until we disappeared down the side of some houses. I wanted to rest. In fact, I wanted to just fall down. Rob would have none of it. As we approached the next road junction, a personnel carrier with two occupants confronted us.

The Germans called it an *Adler Panzerspahwagen*. It looked more like a bathtub on wheels. My first thought was to avoid them, but Rob had other ideas. For whatever reason, they sat there alone. Then I understood Rob's idea, we could use the vehicle. With German troops still looking for us, we didn't want to draw attention to ourselves with gunfire. We needed to deal with them silently.

"Are you capable of taking one of them?" Rob asked.

"I'll have to be. I look like a bomb victim, anyway. Give me your knife, I'll approach them asking for help."

"Draw them both away from the vehicle so I can approach from behind. Don't worry, I'll shoot them if you end up in trouble."

Rob is as close to being invincible as a human being can be. I approached those two Germans with no fear whatsoever. I staggered towards them with half of my body exposed. "Can you help me?" I asked in French. I guessed they would do one of three things. They would ignore me, shoot me, or take pity on me. A part of me thought I was still attractive and I would only have to reel them in. The reality couldn't have been more different; I was a terrible mess.

One of them wanted to ignore me, but the other one approached me. I fell into his arms begging for help. That effectively disarmed him because he was no longer able to fire his MP 38. I waited until the other one approached. As he moved around the *Panzerspahwagen*, Rob moved in silently from the other side of the vehicle.

I kept my left arm around the German but I swung my body away from him. "Look at me," I said, looking down at my exposed body. I tracked his eyes while I reached for the knife behind me. As he looked up again, the knife entered his heart. At the same time, Rob grabbed the other soldier. He fell dead to the ground with a broken neck. Fearful that we would be seen, we acted quickly. Rob took the jacket off one soldier and put it on, together with his helmet. I did the same with the other one. We dragged the bodies into a building and climbed into the vehicle. It took a moment to work out how the thing worked. It helped that we had seen plans for most German vehicles during training. Suddenly, it seemed possible that we might actually get away with it.

We were both disorientated in the dark. In truth, we didn't know our arse from our elbow. Rob just drove, trying to stay in the same general direction. As we left the city behind and entered the surrounding countryside, we tried to follow Rob's compass and head north towards the advancing Allies. German activity became concentrated towards the north and west of the city. Our encounters with small columns of troops advancing in the opposite direction pushed us southwest. We kept out of their way, but they effectively dictated where we could go. On one occasion, with nowhere else to go, we just drove towards them. They obligingly moved off the narrow road for us, and we drove on. Everything continued well until the unmistakable sound of advancing tanks filled the air.

It took a moment in the dark to be sure they were German and not Allied tanks. Three of them advanced towards us. These were not just any old Panzers, these were the Germans' very latest Tiger II tanks, all 70 tons of them. With three of those advancing towards you at nearly twenty miles per hour, you get out of the way rapidly. Rob pulled over off the road, and we bumped to a halt on some rough ground. The noise of the Panzers became quite terrifying. With massively powerful engines, the air seemed to vibrate to the sound; the rhythmic clunk, clunk, clunk, of the sole plates, and the screeching of metal on metal as the sprockets engaged the tracks. They passed us by with only inches to spare. Our vehicle shook like a leaf at the mercy of the wind.

My hand momentarily reached down for the MP 38 until I realised the utter futility of such a gesture. The tanks were travelling at pretty well their top road speed; we had a good idea why. Behind them came dozens of armoured vehicles. One or two drivers gestured towards us; we waved back. Fully ten minutes elapsed before the slower members of the column passed us. I think I must have held my breath for all of those ten minutes, because when the last of them passed us by, all of Normandy must have heard my sigh of relief. They left behind a silence that overwhelmed our senses.

"I can't believe we got away with that," I said.

"Nor can I. We've enjoyed some good fortune tonight."

"Not all of us, Rob."

"I know. Don't think about that now. We've been handed the advantage. We must use it."

"I can't go on much more, Rob, if I don't lie down soon, I'll fall down."

"After everything you've been through, don't make me laugh, Dot. You're not about to give in now, or ever."

He was right, but I don't know how I did it. We managed to get the bathtub out of the rough ground and drove on into the dawn. Rays of sunlight gradually brought colour back to the landscape. The events of the last twenty-four hours seemed to belong to an underworld where only one colour existed. In my mind I could only see red armbands, and red blood. That was the real world, not this place with its warm sunshine and bright colours. It seemed impossible that these two worlds existed at the same time.

The sun rose behind us, which meant we had been heading west. Each time we tried to head northwards, the movement of German troops prevented us. When our fuel finally ran out, the bathtub coughed to a halt in the middle of nowhere. A road sign showed we were only six kilometres from Colleville-sur-Mer. We ended up not far from Omaha Beach!

The distant sound of battle hung in the air. We couldn't determine where it came from. It seemed to be everywhere. Our priority was to get into a French town or village, perhaps there we might disappear. Everywhere we drove appeared to be involved in the battle, the scale of events bewildering us. German forces regrouped everywhere. Our German uniforms served us extremely well, but perhaps they had now outlived their usefulness. As we discussed that issue, we heard a vehicle approaching. In that location, it might have been either side. Imagine our indecision as we stood there in German uniforms. It appeared to be a lone vehicle travelling quite fast. Rob made the decision before we could identify them.

"Take it off quick. If they are German, open fire as soon as they're in range."

We both threw the jackets and helmets behind us. Using the bathtub as cover, we stood ready to open fire. The vehicle turned out to be an

American Jeep. The second they saw the German personnel-carrier, they swerved off the road. Rob and I ran out from behind the bathtub with our hands held high in the air. It was an extremely tense moment. The two young Americans were minded to shoot us, but seeing us in plain clothes, they advanced cautiously with guns aimed at us. They shouted for us to put our weapons down, which we did. Only then did they approach us.

"Thank Christ for the Yanks," I said. "Are we pleased to see you guys!"

"Are you both Brits?" one of them asked.

"You bet your bloody life we are," Rob said.

What we didn't realise was that the Germans placed a lot of English speaking fifth columnists in the area. They caused havoc with road signs and sabotage. The Americans were on the lookout for them. We fitted that criterion perfectly. I showed them my cable bruises and fingers, but they had their orders. They were just a couple of scouts; they didn't know what to do with us. In the end, they tied Rob's wrists, and for some reason didn't tie mine. They bundled us into the back of the Jeep and headed back towards the American lines.

Chapter Nineteen
Back to Blighty

We soon realised the bathtub had conveniently run out of fuel within a few miles of the advancing American forces. Despite being alert to the possibility, the danger of driving our German personnel carrier into Allied lines had always been a significant risk. No doubt it would not have been well received. Within no time at all, we seemed to be in the thick of it. The sound of battle filled the air both near and far. It appeared that by good fortune we had ventured into the only sector not contested by the Germans. The two American soldiers took us to their temporary Field Headquarters. It didn't amount to much, just a couple of farm buildings overlooking Omaha beach.

Rob and I stepped out of the Jeep with guns pointed at us. It wasn't staring down the barrel of an American gun that made our jaws drop. The vista spreading out before us took our breath away. Omaha beach itself is a vast expanse of flat sand, and nearly every inch was covered with soldiers and equipment. Ships of every shape and size dotted the sea in front of us; they disappeared far into the distance as far as the eye could see. Huge numbers of enormous landing ships lined the water's edge, each one with its cavernous bow doors open.

Vehicles of all descriptions spewed out of them in a never-ending stream. Armoured vehicles, supplies, and tanks. Among them, truckloads of troops. Columns of vehicles formed grand processions along the beach. Armoured vehicles in one column, tanks in another. A third column comprised troop carriers, each laden with over twenty soldiers.

Floating above it all, barrage balloons drifted high in the sky tethered to the beach and to ships.

We had to remind ourselves that this same scene was being repeated along all five landing beaches. The scale of the D-Day operation had to be seen to be believed. I found it impossible not to be moved by the scene before us; it was an achievement without parallel. I thought of the planners, and the logistics people. All the unseen people like those at Station M who contributed so much to its success. I thought of everything SOE had done and continued to do. Rob and I were a small part of that achievement; our contribution had been but one of many, but together SOE had been a vital element of the invasion. One of our captors walked away, endeavouring to find out what to do with us, while the other watched over the pair of us as we stood in awe. He remained unsure about us but didn't appear to consider us as a threat.

"It's quite a sight, isn't it?" he said.

"All the years of planning have paid off," Rob replied.

"How many casualties were there here at Omaha?" I asked.

"Not sure I can tell you that," the soldier replied.

"You can tell us, soldier, we've contributed more to this invasion than you might imagine."

"Well, I'm not sure, but there is talk of 2,000. I've never seen such carnage."

"Oh my God!"

I was unable to say anything else. Upon reflection I now realise the events during those three days had taken their toll on me. My physical injuries were one thing, but the mental trauma had been even more damaging. The lovely Henri flashed into my mind, and I thought of his poor wife Renée and their children. Her life would never be the same again. Michêl, Émile, and Albert died for the liberation they would never see. They also died for me, Rob risked his life for me, and there I stood, alive!

They call it survivor's guilt today, and it hit me like a 70-ton tank. After all we had been through, the scene before me represented so much more. I just fell to pieces. Rob became alarmed at my reaction and shouted for a medic. The Americans really didn't know what to make of us. Above all, they didn't have time for my problems.

Another soldier returned with a low-ranking officer, and they discussed what to do with us. The enormous number of German soldiers who had surrendered were an inconvenience to say the very least. The Allies had no time to house and guard prisoners, and the same applied to us. The German prisoner problem was overcome by loading them into landing ships and shipping them to England. They discussed that possibility for us, but if we were German saboteurs, we would not fall within that convention. They might also want to interrogate us. We were low priority, nothing more than a nuisance as far as they were concerned. They decided to lock us up somewhere and hopefully forget about us.

The farm buildings being used as temporary Field Headquarters had an unused storeroom with a secure door. They untied Rob and locked us both in it. An hour or two later, a medic attended us. A man in his late thirties came in wearing a blood-stained apron. His expression told of hours spent tending the wounded, and inevitably the dying. The poor man looked like a casualty himself, his eyes were bloodshot and sunken, and his stubble had traces of blood in it. Sheer exhaustion and mental trauma had reduced him to a barely functioning automaton. He didn't want to be wasting time with German saboteurs. Rob shrugged off his many minor injuries, and the doctor agreed with only a cursory inspection. When he came to look at me his attitude changed. He looked at the bruises on my arms and legs, and my fingers. That I had been tortured shook him out of his malaise.

"Did you do this?" he asked the soldier guarding us.

"No sir, she came in like this."

"Who did this to you?" he asked me.

"The Gestapo in Caen," I replied.

"Who are you?"

"We are both British SOE agents; we prepared the way for you guys."

"Why are you being treated as prisoners?"

The guard stepped forward. "They were found hiding German uniforms, sir. We have picked up several German infiltrators. They all look and sound very convincing."

"Look at this woman, Corporal; does she look like a German agent to you?"

"Well no, sir, but it's not up to me."

"For God's sake man, we're not the Gestapo. Get these people beds to lie on and blankets. Make sure they are properly fed and taken care of. Do you understand?"

"Yes, sir. Sorry, sir. I'll attend to it right away."

Needless to say on day two of the invasion, our doctor had more patients than he had energy to cope with. He gave me all the attention he could and I have never forgotten his kindness. We hoped perhaps a word in the right place might have shortened our incarceration, but we became lost in the fog of war. The German attempt to infiltrate the Allies with English-speaking saboteurs continued with some success. No one understood better than us the workings of a good saboteur; we understood the reason for their doubts.

Our salvation finally arrived when an American officer came to interrogate us. The Major gave little away, but we quickly realised he must be OSS. I knew they worked closely with SOE. Most, if not all our D-Day operations behind the beachhead would be concluded, so I saw no harm in giving him one or two details. Operation Top Hat would be straightforward to confirm; Rob and I gave him specific details that only SOE would know. He listened intently. Our conversation started based upon his assumption that we were a part of the German operation but he quickly changed his opinion.

"We owe you guys a huge vote of thanks, and what do we do - we lock you up!"

"Yes, it's ironic, isn't it," I said.

"Does SOE know about you? Are there any arrangements to extract you?"

"No. We're not with F Section. It's likely our section thinks we're dead. If they realised we were alive…" I had to stop for a moment. "If they knew, there's nothing that wouldn't be done to get us out."

"You seem pretty sure about that. Which section are you with?"

"I can't tell you, you wouldn't have heard of it, anyway. But if you can get an open message out, they'll hear it, and things will happen."

"If I had authority to release you, I would, but it's not up to me. I'll do what I can, and I'll make sure your section hears an open message, whoever they are."

"Thank you, Major," said Rob. "They will confirm our code names. Sparrow and Goldfinch."

"It's been a real honour to meet you," he said. "Good luck to you both."

We knew the second he left us that our ordeal would soon be over. Rob sat smiling at me.

"This is all about you and Lily, isn't it?"

"I suppose it is. It's like I didn't doubt you would come for me. When Lily finds out we're alive, she will move heaven and earth for us. That's what she does."

"How did you two get to be so close?"

"You know Lily, she's amazing. We both come from the East End. I'm just a typical East End girl, I came from nowhere, and I'm going nowhere. But look at Lily, she's shown everyone just what a girl from Stepney can do, she's my hero. She makes me feel proud to come from East Ham."

"Who is this woman you talk about? The one who is going nowhere and regards Lily as a hero. This isn't the woman I've just fought my way across France with. This isn't the woman who came back for me and nearly died in the process."

"No, I suppose it's not."

"Why do you not see in yourself what everyone else can see, Dot?"

"I don't know, what do they see?"

"You're incredible! You've got the heart of a lion and the soul of an angel. You don't need a hero to look up to, you stand taller than anyone I've ever known."

"Don't be daft, I was the one who needed saving, remember. You were the one who saved me."

"Yes, and I would do it again tomorrow, and so would Michêl, Émile, and Albert. You have that effect on people."

"I knew you would come, Rob. Knowing you'd come kept me going. It's the others, they died trying to save me. I'll never be able to live with that."

"Is this what has been troubling you so much?"

"It's all of it, Rob, but especially them. I'm not worth the lives of those men. And I think I shot that old woman. I can't live with that guilt."

"Everyone who has been killed in this war has died for someone back home. You're not alone."

We discussed the matter, and Rob tried to reassure me but my guilt became overwhelming. At least our conditions improved immediately after meeting the OSS Major. We were victims of circumstance, as much as anything else. Our location became demoted from field command centre, to supply coordination depot. Things moved on around us, and we were largely forgotten. It wasn't so bad; they fed us army rations and treated us well. We were also in the right place for soap and bars of chocolate. Our captivity only amounted to five days, but I found it a difficult time. I tried to fathom what troubled me, but it's impossible to see your toes when your head is enveloped in a black cloud.

The great news didn't come from OSS, or even a senior officer. It came from their supply depot. A captain from logistics simply informed us he had orders to put us on a returning supply ship. We'd be in Southampton before the end of the day! We ended our stay in the same way we started it, in a Jeep. The Captain drove us down onto the beach where we joined the never-ending movement of traffic. Everywhere buzzed with activity. Huge landing ships still unloaded onto the beach, but now a Mulberry harbour had been built at Colleville-sur-Mer. Known as Mulberry A, it had been towed over the Channel and put together on Omaha Beach. Another called Mulberry B provided a harbour facility at Arromanches, Gold Beach.

Between the two harbours, 22,000 tons of supplies and equipment were being unloaded every day. The only load going the other way was the wounded, and us. It appeared to be such a permanent structure. I can hardly imagine the ferocity of the storm that swept up the Channel on the 19th of June, when both Mulberries sustained dreadful damage. Engineers managed to repair Arromanches, but Omaha had to be abandoned.

Rob and I can fairly say we are among the few who started their journey from the Colleville-sur-Mer Mulberry harbour. The Captain dropped us off with instructions to board the waiting ship. He promptly departed, leaving us both standing there looking at each other. Our departure from Omaha could not have been more anticlimactic, we were not even a foot-note in history. The battle for Normandy had moved inland. We were just another piece of flotsam left stranded by the receding tide.

Our return to Blighty was in complete contrast to our outgoing journey. The English Channel remained calm for the crossing. Ships of every description stretched as far as the eye could see. The true scale of the invasion and the battle for Normandy was laid out before us. As our merchant ship steamed away, intense activity continued to take place on the other landing beaches. I realised more than ever that industrial might is the ultimate winner of wars. Men die, but industry supplies the means. The two SOE agents who set sail on June 4th did not return. We came back as entirely different people.

Southampton appeared to be in total confusion, but I suspect it operated as one more cog in a giant wheel. We had no money, no passes, no orders, nothing. It took a while, but we got ourselves onto a train, and then changed onto another, before finally arriving at Tunbridge Wells West. Rob talked his way into a bread van, and that's how we arrived at Middlebourne. Tired and exhausted, we walked towards Hut 4, but the boys in Hut 3 noticed us first. They were all there, including Mac.

The welcome they gave us knocked me sideways. Maggie burst into tears and Patrick wasn't far behind her. He put his arms around me and wouldn't let go. Rolo kissed me! I'm not sure if he has ever kissed even his mother! They were all so pleased to see us back. Mac stood with his arms around Rob. I hardly knew how to respond, nothing like that had ever happened to me before. The next thing they insisted, we should all go to the manor. I expected to see Lily, Fiona, and His Lordship.

What we found instead was the Great Hall covered in bunting with a banner draped across from one side to the other. It said, "Welcome home Dotty and Rob." Rob struggled to keep it together, I didn't even try. None of them had the faintest idea what we had been through. Mrs Morgan hugged me, and then Mr Jennings shook our hands. The two maids, Mary and Florence fussed around us. I coped with it all until Fiona appeared.

"Oh, Dotty, we thought we had lost you both," she said, never letting go of me.

"I'm sorry, Fi."

"You look terrible, has it been awful?" I only managed to nod my head but my face must have said it all. "You know what Lily would do at a time like this?"

I knew exactly what she meant. It was as if I needed permission, and Fiona provided it. I wanted to cry, but I couldn't. They were all so kind and understanding but I felt really embarrassed; I just didn't show vulnerability, not like that. Lily wasn't there, and so Fiona did what she always does when she's allowed to shine.

"I think that's enough, everyone. These two need to step out of the limelight. Mr Jennings, would you be so kind as to bring a bottle of champagne to the office? And Florence, ask cook to make some sandwiches, and can you also bring us tea and cake. Come along, you two."

"I'm sorry, everyone; Fiona's right, I'm not coping very well, am I?"

Fiona whisked us away. I couldn't thank her enough; she understood me so well. When they worked together Fiona and Lily made such a formidable team, but on those occasions when Lily wasn't there, Fiona always seemed to rise in stature. Her wavy blonde hair and impeccable dress sense combined with her posh voice to make her a natural authority figure. In Lily's absence, nobody ever questioned Fiona. She understood my distress that day and knew exactly what to do. I used to poke fun at her because she went to finishing school, but I really admired her. She walked with perfect poise and grace as we followed her to the office. Just her presence made me feel safe. Rob hadn't seen the office before and sat with wide eyes looking at the splendour of the room. I just sat staring into oblivion.

"Where's Lily and His Lordship?" I asked.

"That's a long story," Fi said. "Have you encountered one of the V1 flying bombs yet?"

"What's that?" asked Rob.

"That's what we said, only a week ago. It's a new weapon the Germans have developed. It looks like a small pilotless aeroplane, but it's powered by a thing called a pulse jet. They are flying over us all the time now, you'll hear one soon enough, they make a horrible sound. Edward attended a meeting in London last week to discuss what to do about them. And well, one of them fell very close to him."

"Oh, no! He's not dead, is he?" I asked.

"No, but he has been badly injured. He needed an operation to relieve the pressure on his brain; Lily is with him."

"This is terrible, how is Lily? She must be beside herself!"

"You know how she feels about Edward. I can only imagine how she reacted. They took him originally to St Thomas', and apparently a doctor there told her Edward's chances were not very good. Can you imagine someone telling Lily that!"

"I wouldn't like to have been in his shoes."

"No, exactly. She must have been absolutely distraught, but the moment she was told that, nothing was going to stop her. Lily found the name of an expert brain surgeon, and I found where he works. She told me to do everything to ensure that Edward received immediate attention. I had to use all our contacts, and to stop at nothing. So I did exactly that, I telephoned the Prime Minister's office, and Elizabeth, his private secretary, assured me it would be taken care of. Lily couldn't believe the reception Edward received when they arrived. The Prime Minister himself spoke to the hospital Principal."

"You can do that? You got Winston Churchill to telephone the hospital!"

"I did. I was so proud. But it's really because of Edward, they are family friends of the Churchill's. But it's also Lily, she's had lunch with him, he calls her Lily."

"I realised His Lordship had high-level connections," Rob said, "but you're telling us Lily knows the Prime Minister."

"She does. I met him and shook his hand."

"So what happened to His Lordship, is he going to be all right?" Rob asked.

"They performed the operation immediately, and it went really well. He came out of a coma the day after the operation; it sounds like he should make a full recovery."

"Oh, thank God," I said. "So where are they?"

"They are in St Hugh's Hospital in Oxford. Lily has taken the place over. She sings to the patients."

"She what?"

"Don't ask me, but by all accounts they think she's a star."

"That sounds like our Lily."

Mr Jennings appeared with a bottle of champagne and glasses. Then Florence arrived with tea, cakes, and sandwiches. Fiona knew better than we did just what we needed. We drank a little of the tea, but we drank all the champagne. It didn't remove the black cloud I stood in but did lift it a little from my shoulders. Eventually Fiona asked the inevitable question.

"Can you tell me what happened over there?"

I didn't say a word. Rob told her about Operation Top Hat, and how it had gone wrong. He skipped the details. Fiona is no fool, she realised he was being 'economical with the truth'.

"You're not telling me, Rob; has it been terrible?"

Fi kept looking at my fingers and arms but waited for Rob to explain more, rather than ask. It was only then that I realised how badly my capture had affected Rob. He struggled to talk about it, his eyes welled up.

"They tortured her."

Fi jumped up and put her arms around us both. We didn't mention that again. We didn't talk about any of it. Mac would demand a complete debrief, I couldn't face doing it all again, so we said no more about it.

Chapter Twenty
The George Cross

The debrief with Mac seemed to take forever. We both just wanted it over; every second we had to relive was another second we would sooner forget. Each revelation came with yet another vivid memory. Mac could hardly believe our story, looking at us in astonishment. He had received various reports about the "uprising" in Caen; the realisation that we were the uprising left him momentarily speechless! Mac wanted to record every single detail, making copious notes. As painful as it was, we understood why. Every SOE operation provided valuable information for the future. Operation Top Hat comprised two halves. Our half of the operation went perfectly. Mac did not mince his words.

"Top Hat will go straight into the SOE manual. What you two achieved has saved the lives of countless troops. All the research and training paid off; I can't think of a more flawless operation. Congratulations, I could not be more proud. *But*, what the hell went wrong at the barracks?"

"We still don't know, Mac," Rob replied. "By the time we got there, the situation had already become hopeless."

"Had they achieved complete surprise as we intended, none of it would have happened," I said. "Either they were detected or someone informed the Germans."

"I agree," replied Mac, "this is something we need to know."

"We may never know," Rob said, "a battle is being fought over the entire area now. The local people are probably dispersed."

"That's true, but I'll do my best to find out. Now, I realise it's painful, Dotty, but I need to know about your interrogation."

I was able to talk to Mac; he was one of the very few, other than Rob, in whom I could confide. He might be as tough as nails but his narrow eyes and tight lips spoke of a man with enormous empathy and understanding. We spoke as comrades-in-arms; he shared my anguish and fears. Above all, he wanted to understand how I resisted my interrogators for so long; why I never gave up hope.

"I just knew Rob would come for me. I clung to that belief."

"No, there's something else, Dotty; you couldn't be certain Rob would come."

"Maybe you're right. Perhaps it's something I've carried with me from childhood. The one thing my parents inadvertently instilled in me is defiance. I left home at fifteen years old with only one intention in life - no one would ever mistreat me or abuse me again. When the Gestapo crossed the line, they roused that childhood defiance, it brought it all back. It's just who I am, Mac, I'll never bow down to anyone again."

Mac listened intently, his emotions torn between the tough professional soldier and the caring man I knew him to be. He wanted to understand me as a person but he needed to record the account of an SOE agent. The more we talked, the more I looked into a mirror of my own reflection. No one else can ever understand what we went through in Caen, Mac being the only exception. There were details I told Mac that I hadn't even told Rob before. The debrief is a necessary process, we all understood that. But more importantly, on that occasion it provided me with absolution. Mac's genuine empathy encouraged the light to return to those very dark corners of my mind.

My account of the Caen prison massacre filled Mac with horror which gradually gave way to anger. "The day will come", he said, "when people like Harold Heyns will face justice." I hoped he was right. What I witnessed that day still haunts me. It's of little consolation to those poor souls, but they will live on in my mind until I get to meet them again. Heyns was sentenced to death in absentia by a British military court in 1948. The French sentenced him to death in absentia in 1952. Sadly he escaped justice, he's still alive. (Heyns enjoyed a long life. He died in Berlin, 2004)

Rob came back from the ordeal of debriefing a different person, we both did. When people talk of men being tough, they mean different things. Some are physically strong and can endure all kinds of hardship. Others are mentally strong in the face of adversity. There are even a few who combine all those qualities with selfless courage. Rob is that person, and yet even he struggled in the aftermath of Caen. We both suffered recurring memories, flashbacks of horrors that we couldn't erase.

Worst of all is the guilt. Scores of people died in Caen because of our actions. The German soldiers can be dehumanised and labelled as "the enemy", but the innocent bystander always remains innocent. Even more insidious is the guilt of the survivor. Might we have done more to prevent the deaths of our comrades? Did we make the right decisions? In some respects, the debrief reopened the wound, but in other ways it started the healing process. Mac didn't dress in priestly vestments but his confessional provided a degree of absolution.

Mac's advice was to get back to normal routine as soon as possible. There was no such thing as counselling in those days. We should resume training and exercise and enjoy a few pints in The Forge. I didn't disagree with his advice about resuming normal routine, but I had difficulty remembering what normal looked like.

The next person I wanted to see had to be Gran. She marked the boundary between my world and that place people regarded as normal. I realised it would be difficult when I was unable to tell her anything about what had happened to me, but I desperately needed to inhabit her world. I walked home to the cottage that evening not knowing what to say. Middlebourne village with its pretty cottages, its climbing roses, hollyhocks, and lupins, seemed to exist in a different time. As I neared Gran's, a powerful scent of lavender filled the air. In an instant, I stood again in the grounds of the Chateau, the smell of lavender filling my lungs as the young man in front of me breathed his last breath.

Village people waved as they leaned on fences chatting to neighbours. There were no bodies lying on the ground. The air was full of birdsong, not gun fire. I hesitated at the door, almost afraid to step through that portal into Gran's world but desperate to get away from my own. Spencer Tracy greeted me with such affection, I really think the silly dog missed me. I entered cautiously, almost afraid to greet her. When I confronted Gran in the kitchen, her face lit up. As always, she understood more than I gave her credit for. She hugged me for an age, seemingly unable to speak.

"Thank God you're home safe, Dotty; I've been worried sick about you."

"I told you I'd come back in one piece."

"But you're not in one piece, are you?"

She took one look at me and immediately wanted to know where I had been and what happened to me. I tried to be evasive but keeping things from Gran was like trying to push water uphill. She always used to say, the longer you live, the more you see, and the more you see, the more you know. Well, she had seen it all, and she saw through me like a pane of glass. She put two and two together and combined it with what Lily and Fiona had told her.

"I understand why you can't tell me, luv, but it's not a coincidence, is it, you being away during the invasion. You've played an important part in D-Day, haven't you? It's written all over your face. You've had to do things you would sooner forget, and you have seen things you can't forget."

"How can you understand so much, Gran?"

"I've seen it all before, after the last war. Men who came home but left a part of themselves in those fields of Flanders. It's not your fault, Dotty, that you came home and people you knew will always remain there. You will all be reunited in the end, but until then you have a life to live. Do you imagine for one moment that those people you left behind would wish to deny you that?"

"I suppose not."

"It's because life is so precious that we can't bear to see people lose it. But that's also why you have to live your life. Anything less is a betrayal to those who didn't return."

She put her arms around me and said nothing else. She didn't need to. I just sat there with her, wondering how I had lived nearly twenty-seven years without her. Gran was my adopted family, the keeper of all wisdom, and my lifelong inspiration. Nothing else was said about it but I continued to marvel how Gran's silence spoke as loudly as her words. Things reverted to normal when Fiona arrived home and she came with wonderful news. Lily and His Lordship would be home in two days' time.

The evening became just like any other evening, except for me it wasn't ordinary. Gran complained about the rationing and Fi told us again how wonderful her evening with Johnny had been. I listened and raised the corner of my mouth in an attempt to smile. In Gran's mind, there was no connection between rationing and Reg's black-market sausages; I envied her for that ability. I listened to their conversation but I only heard the sound of machine gun fire. They looked down at the golden-brown sausages knowing they would taste as good as they looked; I saw the last second of life in Henri's eyes. Fiona shook the bottle of tomato ketchup before allowing a large viscous blob to slowly creep its way around the sausage; I only saw blood.

I hoped that like a sacred building my demons would not enter Gran's cottage. Demons do not respect boundaries; they live within you; they inhabit your past and wait for you in the future. The next couple of days were difficult for Rob and for me. We didn't discuss it, but it lived behind every look and deed. At least my reunion with Lily would raise a smile on my face. With the three of us together again, I would have to smile. They knew me as that brash, insatiable woman I always pretend to be. I wanted to be that woman again, even if it wasn't real.

They would have so much to do when they first arrived, I decided I should wait an hour but no longer. When the moment came, I rushed over to the manor like a kid entering a toy shop. A quick laugh with Corporal Harris and a brief chat with William at the door and I was on my way towards Lily's office. Wanting to surprise her, I just put my head around the door.

"I told you I'd drag myself back by my fingernails, didn't I!"

"Dotty!"

Lily jumped up and almost threw herself at me. We stood hugging each other. I didn't stop to question why we were both so emotional, but in our own way, we had both returned from a horrible place. Lily had tears rolling down her face. Tears are normal for Lily, but this was much more.

"So, what's all the fuss for then, Lily? I hoped you'd be pleased to see me."

"Pleased! I've never been happier to see someone return from the dead in my entire life. We thought we'd lost you. Fi and I have been to hell and back in a handcart. We must never lose each other again; we must make a pact, the three of us, we can't go through that again."

"Well, it's kind of nice to be back, I must say."

"I guess all of us have been to hell and back," Fiona said.

"I've heard all about Edward from Fi," I said. "It sounds like a close one. Imagine that, one of those V1 things hitting His Lordship."

"It was a close call, Dot. I nearly lost him."

"Well, that wouldn't do, would it? Fi tells me you dumped Greg."

"Oh, don't put it like that, Dotty. I had to; we just couldn't go on as we were."

"So it's finally official then, you are gooey eyed over Edward?"

"God, I've missed you, Dotty! Yes, it's official, I am gooey eyed over Edward. Now, enough about me, what did they do to you?"

"They messed up my nail polish! Can you imagine, of all people, they had to mess up *my* nail polish."

"Seriously, Dotty, what did they do to you?"

"Oh, it's nothing that won't grow back. They stick things down your fingernails, that's all."

"That's horrible, are you sure you will be all right?"

"Of course. I tell you what though, they made a terrible mistake, they left my trigger finger alone, that cost them dearly!"

"How did you get away?"

"It's all in the debrief report. Rob saved me, I knew he would. I just sat there waiting for him to come for me."

"How did you know he would come?"

"What did you do, Lily, when you were told about Edward? Nothing was going to stop you going to him, was it? Well, it's the same for me and Rob."

"We didn't realise you and Rob were that serious!"

"Don't sound so amazed, I'm a bit of a catch. You can't blame Rob for being gooey eyed about me!"

"You're the same, aren't you?"

"Well yes, he's not so bad, is he?"

"Not so bad! He's lovely, why didn't you tell us?"

His Lordship came into the office, obviously late starting his day.

"Dorothy!" he said in surprise. "How lovely to see you back with us."

"It's lovely to be back, My Lord, and may I say how good it is to find you in one piece."

He then completely surprised me with a hug. I mean he really hugged me. I stood in his arms for an age. He then looked at me, and I suppose I looked a sorry sight with my bruises and bandaged fingers. Mind you, he didn't look so hot with his head bandaged. I asked about his head, and he asked about my fingers. Then, of course, he asked about Operation Top Hat. Not content with that, he then asked Fiona to hand him the debrief report. He sat reading it, occasionally looking up at me. Finally he placed the report on Lily's desk, and what he said stripped me of my brash Dotty facade. He removed every pretence I ever had.

"Bravery above and beyond the call of duty only applies to His Majesty's Armed Forces. The valour that you and Rob displayed goes way beyond any call of duty. I intend to use this report as the basis for a recommendation to the Prime Minister. It will be my honour to advise him. I think you should both be awarded the highest civilian award there is, the George Cross. The recipients of this award wouldn't fill a tea shop, and the female recipients would fit into a telephone box. You should both rightly take your place in that exalted company, and it will be a privilege for me to put your names forward."

Completely flabbergasted, I floundered for words. I felt utterly exposed.

"Are you serious? You'd recommend me for such an honour?"

"Without hesitation. Do you not realise, Dorothy? You and Rob stand amongst the bravest of the brave, it would be the nation's way of paying homage to you."

I completely and utterly fell to pieces. Unable to understand my reaction, I just looked at him, and when he smiled so warmly, I really made a fool of myself, a tear rolled down my face. The poor man didn't understand, and who would blame him.

"Did I say something wrong?" he asked.

Lily assured him he had done nothing of the kind; it was a matter for her and Fiona. It would be best if he left us alone. As he left, I became determined not to let him leave without a word.

"What you said, Edward, it was wonderful. Thank you."

He closed the door behind him, and I turned to face the girls.

"I don't understand what came over me. I've never heard such nonsense, recommending me for a medal. I'm not worthy of a gong, or anything else; I just did my job."

"Edward made you realise something about yourself, didn't he, Dotty?" Fiona said.

"Well, I mean, treating me like some kind of hero. That's Rob; it's not me, is it?"

"That *is* you," Lily said. "You just caught sight of the person we know and love. You should become acquainted with each other, Dot. That woman is the bravest person I've ever known."

That just started me off again. I felt more vulnerable in Lily's office than I did in the hands of the Gestapo. Was I really the person they said I was? I reached for my other brash, impetuous self, but that persona never fitted quite the same again. They took me over to the Canteen and asked Brenda to produce a round of her finest bacon sandwiches. Brenda's smile was always irresistible, but never more so than that morning. She was a large woman with a permanently happy disposition, the canteen would not have been the same without her. Her notorious smile had a way of convincing you that her bacon sandwich was utterly irresistible.

We sat the three of us with mugs of tea and tomato ketchup on our faces. Was this the "normal" Mac told me about? Lily's ordeal ended the moment they left St Hugh's Hospital. With Edward by her side, the future was larger than the past. I only ever lived in the past; the future always seemed to belong to other people. We laughed and joked but all the while my present remained in the past.

I had never seen Lily look more radiant. She always turned heads with her great shock of auburn hair, but now her smile filled the Canteen. Lily's sharp mind reflects in her eyes, they broadcast clearly that she misses nothing and sees everything. That day I saw something else, her lovely eyes sparkled. Edward had returned from the dead, and I suppose in my small way the same might be said for me.

I thought her relationship with Greg Norton had the look of permanence about it. The revelation that she had ended it came as a big surprise to me. Greg is every woman's ideal man, so to cast him aside for a dream that didn't appear to have a future seemed like a terrible decision to me.

"Are you sure you're doing the right thing, Lily, I mean about Greg?"

"Yes, I had to; it couldn't go on."

"You know what I'm going to say about Edward, don't you?"

"I know, Fi tells me all the time. The truth is, I simply can't help myself."

"You really are crazy about him, aren't you?"

"It's true, I've finally admitted it to myself. He's my world; it's as if I didn't exist before I met him."

"So what happens when he marries some titled Lady, because even if he feels the same way, that's what he has to do. The Ninth Earl simply can't marry a woman from the East End - can he?"

"Do you know what, Dotty," Fiona said. "I nag Lily constantly about this because, like you, I don't want her to get hurt. But I work with them both every day, and I see how Edward looks at Lily. The poor man is as tormented as she is."

"If anyone can change the system, it's you, Lily. I hope it works out for you."

"It has to work out, Dot! I've laid all my cards on the table, I'm nothing without him."

Lily's sparkling hazel eyes dimmed at the prospect, and she drew her lips together. Fiona tactfully changed the subject.

"How serious is it between you and Rob?"

"Rob wants it to be serious, it's just me."

"What do you mean?"

"He's the first man I haven't run away from, so I suppose that's a start."

"You need to stop running, Dotty. It's time you moved on."

"That's easy to say, Fi, but it's hard to do."

I suspect that conversation had much further to run, but we were stopped in our tracks by the strangest of sounds. Brenda left us immediately and rushed into the kitchen. Two of the guards sitting on a nearby table put their cups down abruptly. Lily and Fi looked at each other.

"What's going on?" I asked.

"That's the sound of a V1," Lily replied, "if the noise stops, dive under the table."

We sat silently as the rasping sound grew louder. It obviously flew directly over our heads. The second it had passed over, Lily rushed me to the window. That was my first sighting of a V1. The menacing looking thing flew on short stubby wings, and behind it a streak of flame lit up the sky.

"What does that thing carry as a warhead?" I asked them.

"I don't know," replied Lily, "but it's an extremely large bomb. The boys will learn all there is to know about it soon enough. Edward is very concerned; I expect there will be a meeting about it tomorrow, why don't you sit in, Dotty?"

"Would I be allowed to?"

"Don't be ridiculous."

"Okay, I will. By the way, I asked Mac what will happen to Station M now that D-Day has been successful, and he's in the dark, like us. So what's going to happen Lily?"

"Edward has told us to continue reconnaissance because we need to learn all the lessons from D-Day, but beyond that we don't know either. Edward fears we might be decommissioned; he thinks our agents will be moved over to F Section."

"So what will happen to you and Fi?"

"As I said, I've played all my cards, I really have no idea."

"I can't imagine all this not being here."

"I'm trying not to think about it," Fi said. "I know it's selfish with all the sacrifices everyone is making, but the truth is I've never been happier than I am here with you two, and with Johnny."

"What, even though we're a couple of Cockney girls!"

"I have to close my ears sometimes, but yes, even though."

We ended our afternoon together in complete agreement.

Chapter Twenty-One
The V1 Threat

Rob and I took Mac's advice, we walked over to the pub that night, just the two of us. We both needed cheering up; we weren't in the best of spirits. An ever-increasing number of V1's constantly flew over our heads, which only added to our tension. Both of us were in a dark place, but it was mostly me. I inadvertently brought things to a head by telling Rob I wanted to spend some nights at Gran's and not in the accommodation block with him. I didn't mean every night, but as always with these things, assumptions were made and feelings were hurt.

Rob is a man who never shows weakness. I saw his hands shake as we prepared for Operation Top Hat. He's human like all of us, but when the chips are down, his ability to overcome fear is the true mark of courage. I doubt Rob had ever felt weak in his life, but he did that night. I should have realised he loved me and he wanted us to be together. My rejection left him feeling abandoned. If only I had the sense to realise! For Rob, feeling rejected amounted to weakness, he didn't know how to cope with it.

There were few people in The Forge that night, the only ones I recognised were Florence and Albert, the young footman. I sat at one of the rickety round tables while Rob went to the bar. He looked decidedly crestfallen. Roger stood behind the counter polishing glasses as he always did. The brasses on the pump handles glistened and the array of copper and pewter beer mugs hanging from the beam above the bar played with the light. A second beam supports a collection of china mugs, while another is adorned with decorated chamber pots. Everywhere the British way of life covers the walls. Hunting horns, horse brasses, and reminders of the pub's previous history as a working forge.

Seeing Rob standing there at the bar should have been so ordinary, so quintessentially English. But for me the ordinary had become the extraordinary. My flashbacks were all in Normandy. The Forge Pub seemed like another parallel world, like Gran's. I still expected German uniforms to march in at any moment. When Rob returned with our beer, we raised our glasses without a word.

"This is a strange time, isn't it?" I commented.

"It is. I'm like a fish out of water."

"I know. They created Station M with only one objective. What do we do now that D-Day has been a success?"

"Mac reckons we'll be seconded to F Section," Rob said, looking even more dispirited.

"It's all such an anti-climax. I feel so sorry for Lily, it's been her life these past years. If she has to leave Edward, I really fear for her."

"What do you mean?"

"She loves him, but it goes way beyond that. Lily says she has no life without him."

"I didn't realise that. I've noticed them together. What does His Lordship say about it?"

"Nothing! He says nothing. What can he say? They're socially poles apart!"

"A bit like us then; we say nothing."

"It's my fault, Rob, I'm sorry."

"I really believed we had something together. I made a commitment to you; I've never done that before."

"You know how I feel about Gran, I just need to spend some evenings with her."

"No, it's more than that, you need time away from me."

"It's not what you think, Rob. None of it's your fault. I've never made a commitment in my life. I don't know how to trust anyone. Give me time."

"You trusted me in Normandy to come and save you."

"I did, but that's different. We both trust each other with our lives. You're asking me to take an even bigger step."

"What can be greater than your life?"

"There are things in my past that frighten me more than the Gestapo. I can't expect you to understand because I don't understand myself."

"What are we to do then?"

"Can we just wait and see? I don't know my own mind at the moment. I can't leave Normandy behind."

"We can agree on that. I can't sleep, I keep having vivid dreams."

"So it's not only me. I can't get the image of Henri out of my mind. Such a beautiful man, I hoped I would get him out of there. One moment he looked me in the eye as I pulled him up. The next moment, he was blown to pieces right in front of me. It was his blood and goodness knows what else that covered my face."

We both learned a lesson that night, we were not yet ready to talk about Normandy. For someone who didn't cry, I certainly made up for lost time. Florence made it even more embarrassing by coming over to see if she could comfort me. Florence is such a sweet young girl - I invited her to sit with us.

"What's wrong, Dotty? I've never seen you so upset."

"I'm afraid it's not a problem we can talk about, Florence."

"Problems only exist for one purpose. They exist so that we can overcome them. Mrs Heywood told me that."

"Well, if Lily said it, then I'm sure it's true."

"This isn't like you, Dotty, to be so upset. When we thought we'd lost you, Mrs Heywood said you were the bravest and most special person she had ever known. So I think you'll be all right."

"You're supposed to be cheering me up! You're very close to Lily, aren't you?"

"I like to think I am, especially now that I'm her lady's maid."

"How can you be her lady's maid, when Lily isn't a lady?"

"Oh believe me, Mrs Heywood is every bit a lady."

"This doesn't sound like her at all. She wouldn't ask for a maid."

"She didn't. Between you and me, I sneaked up on her. No one has ever been as kind to me as Mrs Heywood, so I made it my task to do everything I could for her."

"Well, I think she's very lucky to have you," Rob said.

"And I think it's the other way around, so we're both happy."

Florence's revelations changed the atmosphere completely. I wondered about her relationship with Lily and now I knew. Several weeks later, I found out she was pregnant. And furthermore, her boyfriend Harry and his family had deserted her just days before that evening. She had all the problems in the world, but still took it upon herself to comfort me. I will never forget that.

Rob and I resolved nothing that evening, but we understood each other a little better. The cross he had to bear was that he interpreted the pain he felt as weakness. The cross I had to bear was that I allowed my past to be my weakness. We were both flawed people, scarred by terrible memories. Our circumstances would not be easily resolved, but we were both determined to see it through together.

The next day as I walked towards Hut 4, I noticed Lily and Edward going into Hut 3. I guessed they were going to the meeting she told me about. Hut 3 was supposed to be out of bounds for agents but having been given a special dispensation, I walked in and joined them. I found them all taking the V1 threat seriously, and I soon realised why. They had all the facts before them.

On June 15th, when Edward's car had been hit, 244 V1s were launched. In just three days, another 500 were launched, and on the 18th of June, they hit the Guards Chapel at the Wellington Barracks. It killed 121 people with another 68 wounded. Those figures sent a deathly chill down my spine. A new deadly weapon now rained down on the southeast of England, on a daily basis.

The dreadful carnage at the Guards Chapel left everyone in little doubt that we should prepare for the worst. The news activated them in the most extraordinary way. I watched them at work as they bounced ideas off one another, and how they brought all the information together. For the first time, I saw how Lily motivated them. The boffins talked among themselves, and they often discussed technical issues Lily couldn't possibly understand, but all the while they spoke as if directing their conversation towards her. She just had that power, it flowed through her commanding presence. She didn't demand it, far from it; she didn't even realise she had that effect on people.

She had always been in awe of the boffins, never understanding why her intellectual superiors accepted her so wholeheartedly. Lily often spoke about their special bond. When she said she loved them like family, I understood why. During the build-up to D-Day, they came together to form a well-oiled machine. That machine sat ready to spring back into action. The atmosphere crackled in the room.

"Right," said Patrick, "let's get some background; when did we first find out about these things?"

"I think it will amaze you when I say we had an idea about them in early 1942," Edward replied.

He then continued to describe the work of the Polish Home Army Intelligence Unit, Armia Krajowa which we knew as AK. The Poles had a unique relationship with the British secret intelligence services throughout the war. Perhaps best known for supplying us with our first German Enigma machine, they were also our first source of intelligence about the development of both the V1 and the V2. The Polish reports were both many and authoritative.

"It's all here," said Rolo. "These are AK reports going back to 1942, and several reports about launch ramps, from a French field agent, Michêl Hollard. And there is aerial reconnaissance."

"Let me see," said Maggie.

"It says a WAAF Flight-Officer called Constance Babington-Smith was the first to spot the ramps pointing out to sea," said Rolo.

"I heard about that at Medmenham," replied Maggie.

"What did we do about it?" Lily asked.

"Eventually we sent 600 bombers to Peenemünde and bombed the hell out of it," replied Woody.

"Well, it obviously didn't work, did it, Woody?"

"No, they moved all their research and production under the Harz Mountains, totally impregnable. And when launch ramps started appearing in northern France at the Pas-de-Calais, we bombed those as well, but they just rebuilt them."

"So what do we know about the actual V1 itself?" asked Maggie.

"We know quite a lot already, we've defused one," replied Rolo. "I've got a detailed report from Bletchley."

He handed the documents around. While they were concentrating on the documents, we all suddenly stopped and instinctively looked at each other. The now familiar sound of an approaching V1 filled our ears. We were directly under the flight path between the launch sites and London. They were now flying over us regularly, but the sound of the pulse jet engine never failed to fill you with fear. You quickly learned to listen for the change of sound as it receded away from you.

Rolo explained it all to me. It's called the Doppler effect, the difference in frequency between a sound approaching, and a sound receding. I didn't understand a word of it, but the moment that sound changed, you knew it was not about to kill you. That it would go on and kill some other poor sod offered a guilty comfort of sorts.

They discussed one technical issue after another. This thing had a warhead full of 1800 lbs of Amatol, but it was quite another thing to deliver it onto a target. So the guidance system became the critical thing for them to understand. We already understood quite a bit about that, courtesy of AK. It amounted to an arbitrary weapon, a completely blind assassin. The orientation of its launch ramp determined direction; it required nothing more complicated than that.

"There must be more to it than that?" Lily said.

Rolo looked up from his paperwork. "It's a simple autopilot with yaw and pitch controlled by a pair of gyroscopes. It has a magnetic compass to control azimuth, and a barometric device to control altitude."

That all went above my head but I understood the range mechanism. It had a simple counter, driven by a vane anemometer mounted on the nose of the missile. Every thirty rotations of the propeller produced one click of the counter. When the counter reached its pre-set number, a series of automatic sequences came into effect to reset the elevator and rudder, putting the missile into a dive. A random number decided the fate of thousands of innocent individuals. In effect, it amounted to a lottery. For those in the wrong place at the wrong time, their number was up.

The buzzing sound of the pulse jet engine gave rise to the names "buzz bomb," and "doodlebug." When that terrifying noise stopped, every Londoner cowered in fear, knowing only too well it meant the flying bomb would fall close by. Ironically, the additional level of terror which the sudden silence imposed upon its victims, had been unintentional. The engine wasn't designed to stop; the German engineers created a design error which caused the fuel to cut off when the missile went into a dive. They later changed it.

"Right, it's an effective, arbitrary killer; so how do we stop it?" asked Patrick.

"We need its accurate speed and altitude," Woody replied.

"Initial estimates tell us it cruises at about 340 mph at 2000 to 3000 feet," Edward said. "Anti-aircraft batteries along the Downs have not been effective."

"Not surprising, that's just above the effective range of our light guns," commented Woody.

"We can improve that," said Corky.

"There's a lot of development going on with gun-laying radar, and proximity fuses," said Rolo. "Bell Labs are developing a new fire control system."

"We can do the calculations; it should be possible to shoot these things down," Corky said.

"What about aircraft?" asked Edward. "340 mph, we can do that."

"Yes," replied Woody, "a Mosquito has already shot one down. We need additional speed to catch up with one, but if we can, they're vulnerable."

"Right, let's get to work on the numbers," Edward said. "We can work out an optimal strategy for the fighters, and we need all the technical details about the gun-laying radar."

"That's right," said Corky, "we must find out where they launch them from. Once we know that, combined with altitude and speed, we can plot the most likely interception points. Correctly placed anti-aircraft guns with radar guidance should prove very effective."

"We need reconnaissance," Edward said. "Rolo, give Maggie all the recon we have and let's get Johnny over there again as soon as possible. We need up-to-the-minute location of launch sites, as well as their research, development, and manufacturing sites."

"There's another consideration," Rolo said. "The arbitrary nature of the targeting means they're still trying to perfect it. So they need to plot precisely where they are falling."

"Excellent, Rolo," said Edward enthusiastically. "They need spies on the ground reporting back to Germany."

"Of course, well done, Rolo!" said Corky. "Misinformation, we can feed them misinformation!"

"MI5 has an operation called Double Cross," Edward said. "It has been incredibly successful at rounding up German spies. I'll put this to them immediately."

I thought it best as a lowly field agent not to contribute, but I must say they hugely impressed me. I wanted to be a part of it, a part of the process. Walking back to Hut 4, my head was spinning with facts and figures. Gyroscopes, timers, barometric devices, and above all, 1800 lbs of Amatol. I had seen what one pound of Amatol could do, the prospect of 1800 lbs of it dropping out of the sky didn't bear thinking about. Seeing them at work, it seemed improbable that Station M might be decommissioned; their work was far too important.

The V1 had the potential to change the war, but surely we could do something about that. If we managed to destroy a German regional headquarters, then we could sure as hell destroy one of those V1's. When I told Rob and Mac about it, we were of one mind. Later that afternoon during a break in training, Rob and I sat for a while and discussed it further.

"Would you go back over there?" he asked.

"I'd go tomorrow. A part of me hasn't left, I need to go back."

"I'm the same. What's wrong with us, Dotty, why do we need it?"

"I can't settle, I'm on edge all the time. This isn't real here; the war is over the Channel."

"It's all the uncertainty about Station M. If we're to go over to F Section, I would just like to get on with it."

"They'd split us up, Rob."

"Perhaps that would be for the best. If you and I can't sort ourselves out, perhaps SOE can."

"I don't want us to split up. Not after all we've been through."

I'm not sure where that conversation was headed, but we didn't get the opportunity to finish it. Mac came over and sat with us. He always wore plain army fatigues on duty. Although he held the rank of Major in the SAS, he rarely used it at Station M. I suspect few people saw past the battle-scarred face he presented to the world. A veteran of many daredevil raids in North Africa, he commanded absolute respect among the agents. After Top Hat, I suddenly found myself even closer to him. Rob felt it too; whatever we shared in common, it brought us together.

"I'm concerned about you two."

"Why's that, Mac?" asked Rob.

"We're all in the same boat not knowing what the hell is happening, but it's more than that, isn't it?"

"There's nothing wrong with us, Mac."

"That's bollocks, Dotty, and you know it. I've been where you are.

All the while I lay in hospital with my leg shot up, I remained desperate to get back to it. When they told me my combat days were finished, it nearly killed me. My last operation, we went against a heavily fortified airfield in North Africa. There were six of us in three Ford GPW Jeeps armed with mounted Browning machine guns, and everything we could carry. We achieved complete surprise and armed to the teeth we went in there, guns blazing. The plan sounds daring, but it was sound. We acted as if we were bloody invincible.

Within two minutes, we destroyed or damaged every plane on that airstrip. Their fuel tanks blew up in giant balls of flame, we lit up the whole place like daylight. With our job finished, we just had to get out of there. The Germans were slow to respond because we'd surprised them but when they did, we came under heavy fire. My Jeep almost reached the safety of darkness but we received a hit that stopped the engine. I waved the others to go on and we returned fire. We had no time to say anything, but we each knew it looked like the end of the road. I got hit four times, but I kept firing. My driver, Dave, got it straight through the head.

It was against my orders, but the rest of my men came back for us. Teddy passed me and drove straight at them. I don't know if they thought they might get away with it or not, but they didn't. My guess is that when all was lost, they pulled grenades because their Jeep blew up right next to one of the German armoured vehicles. Digger got me into the remaining Jeep before he bought it. Somehow two of us got away. I live with the sacrifice those men made every day. I see them every time I close my eyes. So don't tell me you're all right, Dotty. I know you're not."

Mac had never spoken about that raid to anyone before. We each sat immersed in a deafening silence. I finally recognised the bond that only people like us can understand. For that moment, Mac ceased to be my Commanding Officer, he became my comrade-in-arms. I stood up and put my arms tightly around him. Tough guys like Rob and Mac are afraid to show emotion. That didn't apply to me, I had to do it.

Chapter Twenty-Two
In Limbo

The well-oiled machine that Edward and Lily created now brought its full intellectual might to bear upon the V1 threat. Johnny flew reconnaissance flights over France and Maggie analysed the photographs. They were looking for the launch ramps. It became a constant game of cat and mouse. Combined with all the reconnaissance from the RAF at Medmenham, and the intelligence work of MI6, the launch ramps were easily spotted. Once found, they were a target for the RAF, but as quickly as we destroyed them, they sprang up like weeds elsewhere. They plotted and charted every detail, but all the while Edward had no authorisation from above. Station M's future hung in the balance despite the work they were doing.

Without authorisation to send our agents into Occupied France we had no option but to continue training in a virtual state of limbo. Mac expected to receive orders any day, we just waited to be seconded into F Section. The uncertainty played on everyone's mind; it became something else that widened the gap between Rob and me. In Normandy the Allied advance had stalled. Caen had become the gateway to the rest of Occupied France, and the Germans were intent on keeping that gate closed.

Operation Epsom, planned for June 19th, was intended to break through the German front, skirting the city of Caen to the west and taking the bridges over the river Odon. The operation had to be postponed because of the storm which also destroyed two of the Mulberry harbours so vital for Allied resupplies. The British and Canadians finally launched Operation Epsom on June 26th. When the operation failed in its objective, it felt like a personal loss.

The success of D-Day had been an unprecedented achievement, not least for SOE. The Americans had taken Cherbourg but the price they paid was almost too terrible to contemplate. When Operation Epsom failed, it rapidly became clear that Normandy had now become a killing field. We had eight highly trained SOE agents. Each and every one of us could inflict damage upon the German war machine. We had unfinished business, but for Rob and me it felt like so much more. If we failed to capitalise upon what we had achieved, then what was it all for?

"We can't go on like this, Mac. You've got to get me into F Section, I have to go back."

"It's not up to me, Dotty, but I've spoken to Edward about it."

"What did he say?"

"He feels Station M should be held together for as long as possible. He has a point. Look what we achieved on D-Day. This is a unique section of SOE, there is no other section like it."

"But what good is that when all we do is train and sit in the sun?"

"We were set up for one very specific purpose and we have more than proved our worth. Edward has a hunch that the Prime Minister and General Gubbins are keeping us intact as some kind of special reserve."

"Reserved for what, I don't need a bloody suntan."

"That's the whole point of a reserve. When a special situation arises, that's not the time to build a specialist team. Besides, they're doing some brilliant work over there against the V1."

"Yes, I'm sure they are, while I just sit here."

Mac obviously took my complaining to heart because two days later he called Rob and me into his office. We called it his office, but it amounted to nothing more than a sectioned off corner of Hut 4. He had no wife or family, so his private little domain contained none of the usual personal reminders. In so many ways I felt a great empathy with Mac, and it all reflected in his office. The small room contained no hint of his private life. There were no knick-knacks or ornaments of any kind. A bare light bulb hung from the ceiling. What little filled the room was all Station M related, maps, reports, and reconnaissance photographs. A telephone sat on his desk, and a filing cabinet overflowed in the corner.

Tellingly, his only personal collection hung on one wall. It comprised several photographs of his SAS unit based in North Africa. Images of his men, none of them in uniform. Everyone looked as if they had been roughly hewn from granite. A line of the heavily weaponised Jeeps they used in the desert, and a photograph of a column of them raising a dust cloud. They say you can't get blood from a stone, but it seemed obvious to me that his men of granite were the exception. If I had an office, it would have looked like Mac's.

"I'm going to be straight with you two," he said. "You're not yourselves, either of you, and I'm concerned. I know you've been to hell and back and I know what you're going through, but you're not dealing with it, are you?"

"What do you mean - nobody trains harder than us!"

"Yes, but why do you train harder than everyone else?"

"It's what we do, we like to stay on top."

"Bollocks, Dotty! You two are the best we have, you know that; you don't have to prove it. You train hard rather than face your troubles. And this relationship between you, it's a problem, isn't it?"

"That's our business, Mac."

"It's your business, Rob, until it affects this unit, and that's what's happening."

Rob and I looked at each other like two school children brought up before the headmaster. Through his rank and war experience, Mac wielded great authority. He seldom used it - he didn't need to; he commanded enormous respect without it. The dressing-down Mac gave us cut through me like a knife. He was right, I just needed to admit it. In Normandy we shared a bond so powerful, not even the might of the German Army could break us apart. We needed to admit that we were no longer those two people.

"I'm sorry, Mac. I know you're right, but this is so hard to deal with. All this waiting about, it's just making it all worse."

"I know, Dot, I've watched you. The new Commanding Officer at STS 21 is someone I served with for a while, he's a good man. We have spoken on the telephone and I've arranged for you two to go back to Arisaig. They're still training and you can be really useful mentoring the new recruits."

"What!"

"You heard me. I'm sick of you two complaining, so you can clear off to Scotland. Seriously, instead of sitting around waiting, you might as well use your time constructively."

"What have we got to offer them?"

"You don't get it, do you? They're still training people to set Europe ablaze. Just occasionally people like you two come along. You didn't just start a blaze; you created an inferno. Do you seriously think they couldn't benefit from your experience?"

"Bloody hell, what do you think, Rob?"

"I say go for it. As Mac says, we have done it all before."

"You mean we're to train people? We're not qualified to do that."

"That's where you're wrong, Dot! Sure some of their experts have more detailed knowledge than you, but there is no one at Arisaig with more overall active experience in the field as an SOE agent than you two. The course is now open to women. That decision has a lot to do with you. You both know how vital your training has been, that's the experience they want to tap into. It's one thing telling people what to do, it's another when someone like you explains why."

There were few if any people more highly trained than Rob, he even finished advanced paramilitary training. Combine that with our experience and Mac had a point. When he said he had spoken to the Commanding Officer at Arisaig, I knew there was more to this. I trusted Mac with my life; I knew his priority was our welfare. If he wanted us to go to Arisaig, then it would not result from a whim. I left Rob to go home to Gran's in a thoughtful mood.

Lily stepped out of the Grand Entrance that evening just as I passed by, the look on her face told its own story.

"Evening, Lily, you look glum, what's the matter?"

"Oh, it's Edward's sister, Elizabeth, she's arrived from America."

"You look like you need cheering up. I've got a bit of news, why don't we go for a drink?"

Corporal Harris overheard us. "Can I come?" he asked.

"Do you know what the penalty is for desertion, Corporal Harris?"

"A night out with the two most desirable women in Middlebourne, it would be worth the penalty, Mrs Heywood."

"Dream on, Brian," I said. "I don't know why the Chief of Staff puts up with you."

"It's my natural charm and good looks isn't it, Mrs Heywood?"

"Well, there must be a reason. You stay alert now, and don't desert your post." We left him with smiles on our faces; he did it again.

"I can never get used to this, Lily. Just a few miles across the Channel all hell's breaking loose and we're going for a drink."

"I know. Patrick calls it the Devil's coin. The slaughter of the innocent on one side, and the laughter of children on the other."

"We really need a drink," I said.

A V1 could fall anywhere, other than The Forge pub. It seemed obvious to everyone that such an oasis of calm would always remain that way. We sat inside, steeped in the contentment of our invulnerability. Roger pulled us a couple of pints and we deluded ourselves that all was right with the world.

"So, what's the problem with Edward's sister?"

"Wait until you see her, Dotty. She's what you could only describe as glamorous. She's got short dark hair just like yours, big eyes, big mouth, big teeth, big tits, and she hates me!"

"Why does she hate you?"

"She told me straight. She said I've weaselled my way into Edward's family. Then asked why she had to dine with a member of staff!"

"Crickey, you have got off on the wrong foot."

"Oh, it gets worse. The ghastly woman insisted I call her *Lady* Elizabeth. I said she only had a courtesy title, and courtesy had to be earned."

"Sounds like you've put your foot in it right up to your knee."

"I did. I basically told her what I thought of her in front of Edward and Lady Caroline. It was unforgivable."

"What did Edward say?"

"He said he told me so. He said I didn't need any help to deal with her. But then Lady Caroline tore a strip off both of us. That was the worst thing of all. I didn't mind causing Elizabeth offence, but Lady Caroline, that's a different thing altogether. I felt awful."

"Don't get all teary about it, Lily. The woman doesn't know you. She's obviously jumped to conclusions; give her time. Let's be fair, she comes home from America and finds someone from the East End of London acting as Chief of Staff in a top-secret SOE establishment in what used to be her home. Then she finds you dining with the family and making eyes at her brother."

"I didn't make it obvious."

"You can't do otherwise. You might as well walk around carrying a banner saying, I'm crazy in love with your brother."

"Is it really that obvious?"

"I'm afraid it is, Lily, you wear your heart on your sleeve."

"Oh, Dotty, you know me so well. You're right, I'm such an idiot. I'll have to try harder with her. Wait until you meet her, you'll see what I mean. She's shaped like an hourglass, and the dress she wore must have cost a fortune. Everything about her says she's a titled lady, I can't compete with her."

"I think you're wrong about that. You do have a title, you're the Chief of Staff, and that's a title you've earned. She might be terribly posh and talks down to you, but that's her mistake. I bet Elizabeth has done nothing with her life; look at what you've done with yours. People like that have difficulty accepting successful people like you, so they resort to putting you down. You're a leader, Lily, she's a follower. Elizabeth will not be used to that, but with you she has no option. If you did but know it, Lily, you probably tower over her; I bet that's a difficult situation for her."

She sat in silence looking at me with eyes like saucers. Everything she is, she has achieved herself. It's true that her Uncle George paid for her private education but only because he saw her potential. Some people say she's gifted, perhaps that's true as far as her singing is concerned, but I know she worked incredibly hard for what she has become. Lily never ceases to amaze me - I so admire her; by any measure she is an extraordinary woman. Everybody knew and understood that; everyone except for Lily. Why she felt inferior to Lady Elizabeth, I couldn't understand.

"Coming from someone like you, Dotty, that's quite a compliment."

"Even someone like me can see your situation for what it is."

"I didn't mean it like that. Edward has put you forward for the George Cross, Dotty. When I said someone like you, that's what I meant."

"I can't believe he's done that. Anyway, it doesn't change my opinion."

"No, but it's why I value your opinion so much. If you tell me I need to change my approach to Elizabeth, I believe you - I will. So, what's this news of yours?"

"Rob and I are going back to Arisaig, we have to mentor the new recruits. It's Mac's idea."

"After what you and Rob did in Caen, I think that's a great idea."

"Well, I'm not sure about it. I suppose I am the first woman to do it, that's something isn't it?"

"We haven't done badly for a couple of Cockney girls, have we, Dot?"

"I suppose not. Who would've thought this awful war had anything good to offer anyone. It's brought you, me, and Fi together. And it's brought Edward, Johnny, and Rob into our lives."

"You're so right, Dotty. We really are the lucky ones."

Chapter Twenty-Three
Return To Arisaig

Rob and I boarded the train bound for Arisaig, not really knowing why the hell we were going there. Our doubts revolved around what the benefit might be. We both wanted to be in France, not training. Neither of us realised at that stage that we had anything else to offer. Without an operation to use our skills - what was the point of it all?

When we arrived, we found ourselves among another group of six, but that was where the similarity ended. We were given something of a red-carpet treatment. The Commanding Officer, Lt Col Greyson greeted us. Operation Top Hat remained top secret but nevertheless it seems that our exploits in Normandy had somehow gone before us. They introduced us as SOE agents with operational experience. The new recruits greeted us warmly without question. There was a woman doing the course. When they said I'd been the first woman to complete the course, she looked at me in awe. I felt sure our reputation had grown larger than the reality.

The routine at Arisaig had not changed. Mr Tanaka was still there. He presented himself with a deep bow. Buster Fairbairn had gone by then but his replacement Sergeant Beddington was equally expert in his own right. The other routine that hadn't changed was the first-day route march which was effectively an initiation ceremony. We were met by the Drill Sergeant who looked at us as his latest victims. I remembered my own first day so well. How I finished the course that day I do not know. When the woman asked me if it would be difficult, I smiled sweetly.

"Trust me, you have no idea how difficult! Don't make the mistake of trying to keep up with the men. It's fine to come in last. The cardinal sin is not coming in at all. You will have to dig really deep. Don't let the pain dominate your mind, just remain determined not to give in."

"Did you finish the course?"

"I did, I surprised myself and so will you."

Isabel was a fit-looking woman, she wouldn't have been there otherwise, but I knew the ordeal that lay ahead of her. Rob and I were probably at the peak of our strength and fitness; I welcomed the challenge as a kind of personal test. The moment she lifted the heavy Bergen, the realisation of what lay ahead showed on her face. I stayed with Isabel and led by example. We set off at a slow pace that I didn't vary. She started off feeling frustrated watching the men disappear in front of us. As the morning progressed, she increasingly struggled to keep up. I saw the pain written across her face.

She gasped for air through gritted teeth while shaking her head, trying to shed the sweat which ran into her eyes. I remembered that stage of the march when the pain in your feet and legs seemed to rise up and join with the pain descending from your shoulder straps. Every so often, Isabel looked up to see me apparently striding away in front of her. I felt the pain as much as she did but just didn't show it, trying to provide an extra element of motivation; if I could do it, then so could she. We made it to the rest site.

Rob stood there looking as if he had just been for a stroll. Only then did I realise we were standing talking together. All around us the trainees lay on the ground gasping. When I did the course for the first time, I was flat out on the ground just like Isabel. I felt her pain with every step she took during that afternoon, but to her credit she did not give in. The boys cheered us in on the last leg where we all collapsed into a circle around the Drill Sergeant.

"Why do we do this, Archer?" he asked.

"Because you're a sadistic bastard, Sergeant."

"Apart from that, Archer."

"We do it because when you're in an enemy occupied country, the situation can arise where you might need to carry a heavy load some considerable distance. Weapons or explosives, for example. You might need to support an injured comrade. Whatever it is, your life can depend upon your physical fitness. You probably saved my life, Sergeant."

I think the Sergeant appreciated me saying that. I received a slap on the back and the words "well done." In Drill Sergeant language that means, "thank you, Archer, I really appreciate that." The men looked up to Rob who could have run the course a second time. They placed him on a pedestal but rather than being discouraged, they wanted to join him there. It hadn't occurred to me that we might have a positive contribution to make. We ended the first day enjoying the unfamiliar feeling that we had inspired and motivated people.

Of all the disciplines, we were probably most accomplished with the martial arts. Rob and I practised almost every day; we both enjoyed it. When it came time for Mr Tanaka, I felt much more confident. He used me immediately as a demonstration; he put me up against one of the biggest of them. His instructions were for him to attack me with a knife and spare me no quarter. They were well trained in the basic use of the fighting knife at Wanborough, and he confronted me correctly. I knew he would hold back if only for a second because he looked at me as a woman. None of them would make that mistake a second time, so I knew I should exploit it to the full. We danced around each other with him changing the knife between his hands.

I stared only at his feet and hands. He would move in close and not seeing an opportunity he would take a half step back and change his knife hand to confuse me. A natural right-hander, I waited for him to take his half step back and pass the knife into his left hand. As he attempted to change hands, I misdirected him with a false body movement. My misdirection shifted his body weight towards his right leg which was the opposite of what he intended. That placed him off balance. That was my opportunity, I looked him straight in the eye for the first time while his hands were close together. I grasped both wrists and executed a manoeuvre called *Ushiro Tekubi-Tori Ikkyo*. In a flash I had disarmed him, much to Mr Tanaka's delight.

When Mr Tanaka asked me to explain exactly how I achieved the manoeuvre, it became something of a revelatory moment for me. What I took for granted, those subtleties of mind and movement, made the difference between life and death. The more I explained, the more I learned about myself. The instructors used us to demonstrate many things, and each time they asked us to explain why it was important. We told them and they listened intently. I realised that even I had something to contribute. We couldn't discuss anything to do with Operation Top Hat, we always used general terms, but they knew we spoke from recent experience. Things came to a head when we discussed the tactics for open conflict.

"The hardest battle you fight is in your own head," I said. "If you lose control, if you panic, you're finished. Always think back to your training, and never forget the basics. Check your weapons and ammunition, be constantly aware of your surroundings. Keep a mental image of local buildings and inhabitants. When the time comes to confront the enemy, remember they will not be as well trained and motivated as you are. Always believe you are better than them, always.

When the enemy has you outnumbered, and under fire, they feel they are in control. That will be their greatest weapon - confidence. Never allow that to happen! Your superior training and skills will always give you the advantage. Show maximum aggression, counterattack against them. A retreating soldier fills the enemy with confidence, an advancing soldier fills them with fear. It's all about fear; theirs, not yours."

"Were you not afraid?" someone asked.

"When you live in a world surrounded by death you see things differently," replied Rob. "We were not about to let each other down; we did what we did for each other. Your body's pumped full of adrenalin, your heart is racing, so yes, you're frightened, but you overcome that for your comrades."

"This is where your training steps in," I said. "You can't show fear, and there's a fine line between not showing it and not feeling it. Whatever the situation, you have to dominate it. The enemy has to regard you as invincible, so give them reason to think that."

For the first time since Caen, we both analysed our thoughts. Before that moment I dared not look back but confiding in the others forced me to confide in myself. What I saw was someone who followed the training. Someone who took the fight to the enemy because it was the best tactic. Someone who didn't get it wrong!

The quick-draw pistol techniques developed by Sykes and Fairbairn were a revelation to them just as they had been to us. Equipped with blank ammunition, Sergeant Beddington demonstrated how to draw the pistol and fire so quickly that even when confronted with someone holding a weapon, he could still fire first. Rob proved to be even faster than Beddington as one by one the trainees went toe to toe with him. The dirty-tricks people took the quick-draw to a different level with the rotating holster. Beddington demonstrated to an unsuspecting trainee how the holster placed on the outside of the hip could be rotated into a forward firing position by the operation of a cable hidden down his sleeve. Another operation of the cable fired the pistol at the totally unsuspecting victim.

The silent killing techniques were another very important part of training. Beddington was extremely good, having completely mastered all of Buster Fairbairn's techniques and more besides. Even Rob had met his match. Isobel had a sharp intake of breath when she realised everything Beddington taught the group also applied to her. He used me to show some of the methods. I think it surprised more than just Isabel to realise that a woman could kill someone, just the same as the men. More to the point, using to my advantage the fact that I was a woman gave me a distinct edge in some circumstances.

Even though women were now regularly going to Arisaig, Beddington failed to exploit the more lethal aspects of feminine charm. I showed them some methods I had worked out for myself. My first demonstration was against Beddington himself. The ground rules were simple. He would not protect himself until I clearly represented a threat. We all realised the element of surprise was the key factor which a demonstration clearly lacked, so I had to improvise. Having prepared in advance, I put on some makeup, especially eye makeup. I wore a jacket over a blouse that had several buttons undone. I gave the gathered trainees a running commentary in order to distract Beddington and restore a small degree of surprise. Approaching him without eye contact, I turned my head towards the group as I described my approach. When I came into striking range, I opened my jacket to reveal my open blouse.

I turned again to the group and started a sentence, words to the effect that Beddington's eyes would be drawn to my cleavage. Beddington had been caught doing exactly what I told them he would. That momentarily put him off guard. Mid-sentence and with my head still turned towards the group, I opened my jacket further as if showing them how to reveal more of yourself. In fact, I reached inside for my knife. Continuing the conversation with the group, I looked up for the first time into Beddington's eyes. His split second of hesitation allowed me to press my knife between his fourth and fifth ribs.

Though I say so myself, it was a master class! We all agreed, if Beddington fell for it, even though he expected it, imagine what would happen to a totally unsuspecting German soldier. To my surprise, he was delighted and asked me what other little tricks I had up my sleeve. So I showed them another one. I said a German soldier on guard duty would typically carry a rifle. Beddington stood before me holding a standard issue Lee Enfield 303. I pointed out that it was a relatively heavy two-handed weapon.

I said I would be dressed as a French woman and would act as if I had drunk just a little too much wine. My appearance would be as provocative as possible in order to distract him. Above all, I must look like a vulnerable, defenceless woman. The reason I would approach an armed guard is that I am slightly drunk and the cigarette dangling from my mouth is unlit. I ask the soldier if he has a light, so naturally I approach closer so that he can light my cigarette. Men keep their lighter or matches in their trouser pocket. So the guard, who does not see me as a threat, reaches into his pocket. Beddington played along with me.

"Right, did you see what the Sergeant just did? In order to hold his rifle with one hand, he moved his right hand towards the point of balance to make it easier to hold. His finger is nowhere near the trigger. He has one hand in his pocket and the other holding a weapon he can't use. I can now easily kill him with my knife or my bare hands if I need to."

It was a revelation for Beddington but one that he took on board with relish. Female trainees from that day forward were taught to use every asset they had. It seemed a strange irony to me that the cloak-and-dagger boys of the Secret Services had long since used attractive women to lure men into compromising positions, the so-called honey pot trap. And yet they failed to exploit that asset in the lethal environment. I had a hand in changing that.

The hardest part came when we attended the lessons about interrogation. Even without giving them the details, it quickly became obvious to everyone that I had suffered torture. My fingernails were not fully grown back, it didn't take long for them to put two and two together. What followed were a lot of awkward questions that they didn't want to ask and I didn't want to answer.

"No, I wasn't raped if that's what you're thinking. That's on their list but in my case they were short of time. That's all about control and humiliation. They went some way down that road but you must close your mind to the prospect."

"How do you close your mind to something like that?" asked Isobel.

"You always know something far worse than humiliation and degradation is coming, so just think about that. Fill your mind with what they teach you here. Look for ways to escape, look for ways to break free and attack your torturers. It doesn't matter how unlikely that is, cling to the possibility. As an SOE agent in enemy hands, you're probably dead anyway, so all that matters is how you go."

"What does it matter? You might die a hero but you still die alone and no one will know."

"It mattered to me and it will matter to you. I didn't want to die a hero, but I would have died defiant; I would have died on *my* terms."

"You talk as if you expected to be killed. I couldn't be that brave," said Isobel.

"You can be driven to the point where death becomes a better place. That's what gives you the power to be defiant."

"Did you crack, did you tell them what they wanted to know?"

"No, and that's a valuable lesson. The time comes when most people simply can't take any more. But remember two things about that moment. As an agent, if you tell them what they want to know you lose your usefulness and they will kill you. So hang on as long as you possibly can. If you can take no more, then tell them what they want to know. But, and it's a big but! What they want to know is often what they have been told to expect. You can exploit that, tell them what they think they want to know, not what they don't know.

If you can maintain a credible story, saying that you're innocent, don't ever deviate from it. If you have anything to gamble with, any plausible story, stick with it. Never believe what they tell you. Whatever inducement you are offered, it will be a lie. Even then, when you know they will kill you, remain hopeful. They will most likely take you somewhere to be shot. However weak you may be, remember they might untie you before moving you. Seize that moment! Attack your torturers, grab a weapon if you can. Fight for your life and believe you can succeed."

They looked at me in some amazement. Being taught by instructors is one thing. Being told first-hand is quite another. You don't join SOE thinking you might end at the hands of torturers. You also don't consider the possibility that you might be cornered like a rat, fighting for your life. What I said made an enormous impact upon those trainees. Heaven forbid they should find themselves in that position. But if they did, they would remember me, and I would be there supporting them. In return, they invited me to face my darkest demon. I doubt any of them realised who benefited most.

One trainee came from an unlikely academic background. He had a degree in psychology from Cambridge University and inevitably asked most of the probing questions. During our last night together, he made something of a speech on behalf of everyone. A speech I found deeply moving.

"On behalf of all of us, I would like to thank you both for what you have contributed to this course. We've learned more here than I would have thought possible. The expertise available to us has been quite remarkable, but you have taught us something over and above basic training. You have given us a human insight into that place where other humans would fear treading. We know all SOE operations remain top secret, so it's not what we have been told, it's what we haven't been told about you. I speak for all of us when I say you are both a true inspiration; it has been a privilege. Thank you."

Rob thanked them for their kind words while I fought back a tear. I had never considered myself capable of teaching anyone anything. I was a tramp from East Ham who started out in life looking up at everyone. Now suddenly, people were looking up at me! If I'd been capable of speaking, I would have thanked them for changing my life. I thought about it all during our long train journey home. For the first time since returning from Normandy we had both spoken about our innermost feelings, we saw our actions within the context of our training. It was the first step on the long road towards recovery, and I knew exactly who to thank for it. I owed Mac a lot.

Chapter Twenty-Four
Home Again

It's a long journey from Arisaig. We were tired and exhausted before we set off; we were even more exhausted when after three changes of train we finally arrived at Tunbridge Wells West. I can't tell you how delighted I was to find that Mac had sent someone to pick us up from the station. After the stark landscape of Highland Scotland, the picturesque, sleepy village of Middlebourne looked and felt like heaven to me. Rob didn't have that same connection, he lived in Hut 5, the accommodation block. I see it all now, but I didn't see it then. I came home to Lily and Fiona, and Gran. Rob came home to Mac! It was hardly the same.

We slowly ground to a halt outside the manor. Private Thompson on duty at the entrance stepped forward and opened my door. He wasn't supposed to do that, but he made me smile. Every part of my body ached, especially my legs. Both dressed in filthy old army fatigues, we probably looked like something the cat dragged in. I looked at Rob and we both managed a grin. I don't suppose I stood outside of the car for more than thirty seconds before Lily and Fi came running down the steps. They greeted us as if we had won the war! I must have smelt like a dustbin but they hugged me anyway and Rob the same.

"Come into the office and tell us all about it," Lily said.

"We will, but I need a bath first, I feel foul."

"Are you going back to Gran's or Hut 5?"

"Oh no, we'll clean up here, give us an hour."

The accommodation block only had one bath. There were showers but Rob being a gentleman insisted I take the bath. The facilities were spartan but functional. It comprised a deep enamelled bath, washbasin, and a lavatory in an otherwise bare room. The walls were painted white, but the paint flaked and bubbled with what looked like patches of cotton wool, the only concession to luxury being a hook on the door for your clothes, and a mirror. But best of all, hot water came out of a tap and you didn't need to empty the bath with a bucket, you pulled the plug out.

During the winter, the cold would condense the steam from the bathwater turning it into droplets which ran down the walls. Water collected at the bottom and soaked into the concrete floor. It gradually crept towards the bath like so many fingers reaching towards you. That day at the end of July, the weather turned gloriously hot, and I sat in that bath until my skin wrinkled. I doubt anyone has ever enjoyed a bath more than I did that day.

We were technically still on duty; I probably should have dressed in my FANY uniform or clean fatigues. Instead, I dressed in a nice skirt and jumper. I only had four good fingernails, but I made a point of painting those. The others were growing back, so I gave them a bit of encouragement as well. When I looked at my face in the mirror I hardly recognised myself. I'm not sure if the wind or the sun had provided the tan. I put on my usual red lipstick and spent a few extra minutes on my eyes. They are my best feature, so why not make the most of it. I couldn't remember the last time I had gone to so much trouble with my makeup. In fact, I couldn't remember when I last used makeup at all. For some strange reason, I needed to look like a woman again.

Rob insisted we should report to Mac. I agreed, but first I also needed to see my friends. He smiled and said he would cover for me; he always did that. Be it trivial, or life and death, Rob always had my back. I wish I had loved him more for that. Walking away from Hut 5 in a pair of low heels I felt strangely wonderful. I tried to remember when I last wore a skirt, and I couldn't. The demons that haunted me with flashbacks and dreams were still there, and so was a frightened little voice from a previous life. But then another voice whispered in my ear. Look what I've achieved, look at this woman I've become. I may not be much, but I'm Dorothy Archer, and I'm someone. I strolled into Lily's office as if I owned the place.

"Dotty!" Fiona cried out.

"Wow, is this really you, Dot?" Lily asked.

"This is me cleaned up, not bad eh?"

"I can't believe my eyes," said Fi, "you come back from learning how to kill people and you look like this."

"Perhaps that's why I need to dress like this. If I have to be the lipstick assassin, I might as well look the part."

"We've missed you, Dot, it's not the same when you're away," said Lily.

"Well, I'm back and what an experience it's been."

"How did this differ from your basic SOE training course?"

"Let's just say it was different. We did all the things we did before, but we were helping the others. It's been an amazing experience. I've learned a lot."

I talked probably more than I should have done; it took some time for me to realise that Lily looked especially sad, almost tearful.

"You wouldn't have heard any of our news, Dotty, but a lot has happened here. Gran has had a really bad turn, its apoplexy."

"Oh no, she's not…you know?"

"No, not at all. She's recovering well, but I'm afraid she's not the same."

"You're not just saying that; she is recovering?"

"Oh yes, she's doing well. Her speech is starting to come back but she has lost the use of her left arm. Florence is living there and taking care of her."

"How did you manage that?"

"It's a long story," replied Fiona. "The silly girl's pregnant."

"Oh, for goodness' sake, she's only seventeen. Don't tell me, it's that young soldier she's been going out with, and he's done a runner."

"Absolutely right. I had to do something for her," Lily said, "so this works out well for everyone."

"Where is she sleeping, have we lost our room, Fi?"

"Well, the thing is, I won't be needing my room soon."

Fiona held out her hand and my eyes fixated on the ring.

"Well, about bloody time!"

How Fiona contained herself up to that point I do not know. Once she started telling me the story of how Johnny proposed there was no stopping her. I have to say, as far as romantic proposals go, Johnny's tops them all. Fi couldn't hide her joy as I listened to every detail. I had no intention of telling them about me and Rob, but they seemed to guess.

"You're going to tell us something, aren't you?" Lily said.

It was something that Rob said at Arisaig. I always wanted to avoid talking about our relationship, but he insisted. He didn't propose, not in as many words. He said we had a future together if I wanted it. I did what I always did, I neither committed nor declined. I avoided the question; how stupid was that? Then I compounded my stupidity by pretending otherwise to Fi and Lily.

"I am, you're not the only one with a proposal, Fi!"

The moment I said it I realised I had made a mistake. They asked many questions, and I had to evade every one. I welcomed a change in the conversation, not realising what it was. Lily told me that a V1 had struck the village not a stone's throw from the manor. I knew the row of cottages she referred to. It was difficult to believe a V1 was capable of destroying the entire row of houses. She described how most of Station M had run to help search for survivors. When Lily told me only one survived and eight people had died, it filled me with rage.

"What are you doing about it?"

"We're making a lot of progress with countermeasures. The boys think we are gradually reducing the numbers that get through."

"It's not enough, Lily. It could have been Fi, or you and Gran. Hitler has gone too far this time; this has become personal."

Edward came into the office soberly, carrying some papers. As our eyes met his face lit up. He did no more than put his arms around me! He always wore a perfectly tailored three-piece suit. Combine that with his impeccable manners and the aristocratic way he speaks - and well, frankly, he frightened the life out of me!

I likened him to a mediaeval knight in shining armour. I finally came to realise it was my own reflection I had been looking at. He didn't hide behind the armour. I chose to see what I wanted to see. Beyond being the Ninth Earl, he's just Edward, and is exactly what Lily says he is. Best of all, despite our disastrous first meeting I realised he liked me, and I certainly liked him.

"It's lovely to have you back, Dorothy, you must tell me about Arisaig."

"It's nice to be back, Edward."

"Have you brought us news, Edward?" Lily asked.

"Yes, it's not awfully encouraging, I'm afraid. Operation Goodwood has ground to a halt."

"Everyone at Arisaig has been following progress in Normandy," I said. "They get a report every morning. We all followed the progress of Operation Goodwood."

"How bad is it?" asked Fiona.

"It's difficult to say. The Germans fell back from Cagny, regrouping around Guillerville and Émieville."

"Did we reach any of our objectives?" Lily asked.

"Yes, we reached Bourguebus. The Canadians are mopping up German infantry south of Saint-Martin-de-Fontenay."

"What about the 21st Panzer division?" I asked. "The last I heard they were counter-attacking."

"That's right, we have pushed them back," replied Edward.

"So is it over, Edward?" Fiona asked.

"Not so much over, as ground to a halt. The weather is appalling, it hasn't stopped raining."

"That sounds like a disaster to me," I said.

"I spoke briefly to the PM this morning," Edward replied. "The debate has already begun. It has, however, prevented a massive counterattack against the Americans when Operation Cobra is launched, so perhaps we can say it's a strategic success."

"It's been over six weeks, and we're still confined to Normandy," I said.

"Yes, it's not what we expected," replied Edward. "Let's hope Operation Cobra can capitalise upon the situation."

"When does that begin, Edward?" I asked.

"The weather has delayed it - I expect tomorrow or the day after."

Lily's telephone rang, it was Mac asking for me. Lily attempted to cover for me, saying I had already left. They laughed as I hurried towards the door. I had a parting word.

"What about a drink in the pub tonight after I visit Gran?"

"Great idea," Lily replied. "You ask Maggie and I'll suggest it to Elizabeth. Are you taking Rob?"

"I doubt he'll want to come if it's a crowd of women. I take it you're on speaking terms with Lady Elizabeth," I joked.

Lily looked at Edward and they both smiled. I assumed that indicated bridges were being built.

Chapter Twenty-Five
Drinks In The Manor

The summer of 1944 proved to be a frustrating time for the Operations Section of Station M. We were set up at the behest of the Prime Minister for the sole purpose of providing intelligence and support for the D-Day landings. The build-up towards the invasion and the events that followed in its wake were so monumental in scale, it was always going to be difficult to accept that our role was over. The anti-climax and lack of purpose gnawed at us like a festering wound.

We lived on a lean diet of rumour and disappointment. Rumour had it we might not be disbanded; that we were still there only added fuel to the rumour. The tantalising suggestion was that we were being kept in reserve for a special assignment. But what special assignment, Edward didn't know, and so the Operations Section certainly didn't. In the absence of a new directive, Hut 3 was unofficially giving full attention to the V1 threat. Their contribution was considerable, and no doubt delayed any thoughts of our being subsumed into F Section. The war raged on in Normandy and the Operations Section of Station M trained! That's all we did, we trained relentlessly, day after day.

The secret world of intelligence is always based upon the need-to-know principle. Until the need became apparent, the operations section didn't need to know. This is how Station M should have operated, and mostly it did, but not always. Whenever I breezed into Hut 3, the boys would always chat about what they were working on. I noticed the atmosphere changing as 1944 progressed, and I understood why. However great the V1 threat, we now had an even greater threat. The Germans were developing a new vengeance weapon - the V2.

I really wanted to understand more about it, so when Lily asked me if I would like to join her and Edward for a drink before dinner at the manor I eagerly agreed. Lily often invited me and Fi, it was very kind, but I seldom accepted. The invitation even included dinner on a couple of occasions, but I always felt uncomfortable and declined. Everything about Middlebourne Manor is so grand, I would be out of place. You had to dress for dinner and pre-dinner drinks. The days of black tie and evening dress had been suspended, but it still required me to posh up in a dress. I hardly ever wore a dress; they made me self-conscious. That evening I made the effort. Because people were unused to seeing me in a dress, I always attracted comments that only made me more self-conscious. It just had to be Brian Harris on duty at the entrance!

"Dotty! Wow, look at you," he said. "This can only mean one thing. You're going to ask me out."

"You wish; I'm having a drink inside."

"How the privileged live, eh."

"Between you and me, I'd sooner be down the pub."

"Sounds like we've got a date then."

"Not tonight, Brian. Now clear off, I'm coming through." He stepped aside with his infectious grin while looking me up and down. "Don't say it," I said, as I brushed past him.

William saw me from across the hall and approached looking very grand in his livery. "His Lordship is expecting you, Miss Archer."

"Since when do you call me Miss Archer, William?"

"You're an invited guest, Dotty. This is how these things are done."

"I see. Will you announce me properly?"

"Yes, of course."

"I was joking."

I thought he was having fun at my expense, but he did announce me. "Miss Archer, my Lord."

As I entered the Drawing Room Edward leapt to his feet to greet me. "I'm so pleased you can join us, Dorothy."

He put his arms around me as if I hadn't seen him for a week. Edward is the real deal, an aristocrat from tip to toe, but I knew him well by then. Wonderfully dressed in a navy-blue blazer and light tan cavalry twills, he sported a matching navy-blue bow tie. Even his white shirt exuded an obvious elegance with its lustrous Egyptian cotton. I easily understood why I initially found him a daunting prospect, but how wrong I had been. Edward and I came to share something that I regarded as special. What it was I could never explain, but it was something we both enjoyed.

"One of these days, Edward, you're going to call me Dotty, like everyone else."

"But I'm not everyone else, Dorothy."

"Couldn't you make an exception?"

"Well, I suppose if you insisted, I might let protocol slip."

"Let it slip, Edward."

"Lily tells me there isn't a man alive who you couldn't charm, I suspect she's right, Dotty."

"Well, it worked on you, didn't it?" I laughed.

"It certainly did, although we did get off on the wrong foot."

"You promised you wouldn't mention that again."

"I hold it in reserve to counter all those audacious comments of yours."

"Audacious, me? That's a big word, you must be mistaken."

"Not at all, you're all those big words, Dotty, and more besides. Would you promise me one thing?"

"What's that?"

"Promise you will never change."

"I promise."

Lily sat smiling at the pair of us. She wanted nothing more than for me to approve of the man she loved. Well, I did; I wholeheartedly approved. That I thought she was heading towards the greatest heartache of her life was not something we talked about any more. I understood the evening ritual they shared each day. The tension and responsibility they both shouldered during the build-up towards D-Day must have been all-consuming. After an endless day, they each changed for dinner and sat together in the opulence of the Drawing Room. It was their way of stepping as far away from the war as possible.

I saw it that evening, they drew strength from each other, but even more they seemed to be invigorated by everything surrounding them. For Edward, that was five hundred years of family history. It overwhelmed me, but not Lily. Either through Edward or by her own connection, she embraced Middlebourne Manor. Dressed in her lovely black cocktail dress with the sheer lace top, Lily took nothing from the opulent surroundings, she enhanced it. The building intimidated me, as did Mr Jennings who entered the room.

"What would you like to drink, Miss Archer?"

"Have you got a beer, Mr Jennings?"

"I'm sure I can find one, but may I suggest the rather excellent single malt whisky His Lordship and Mrs Heywood are drinking?"

"What do you think, Lily, will I like it?"

"I don't see how you couldn't, you must try it. It's a twenty-five-year-old Bowmore."

Mr Jennings pootled off, and I marvelled at this world that Lily embraced so perfectly. She arrived there in 1941 as an East End girl from Stepney. Admittedly, her background had been nothing like mine - she managed her uncle's shipping agency for nearly ten years; but nevertheless, Lily would have been a piece of a jigsaw puzzle searching for her place in a picture she had never seen before. I so admired her. When Mr Jennings returned, he came with a silver tray adorned with a glass of whisky and a tiny water jug. I immediately showed my ignorance.

"What's the little water jug for, Mr Jennings?"

"You may prefer to add a little to your whisky, Madam. It's just personal preference."

I smiled as if I understood. I was as out-of-place sitting in the Drawing Room of Middlebourne Manor as a pork pie at a bar mitzvah. But the wonderful thing was that it didn't matter. My closest friend and the man she loved made me so welcome, I felt as if I belonged there. I didn't hesitate to ask them about what amounted to top secret intelligence.

"What can you tell me about this new V2 threat the boys were discussing?"

Edward immediately took me into his confidence. The first thing he told me was that we had intelligence about the development of the V2 a couple of years ago. Nearly all of our intelligence came from the AK. None of these things had been launched yet, but MI6 now considered the threat so great that every effort was being made to find out about them. MI6's communications with AK were well established, and Edward's connection with MI6 ensured he also had access to that intelligence.

AK informed us about the development of this new rocket as early as 1942, but sadly the intelligence was not considered worthy of further investigation. AK described the test rockets as being forty feet long and taking off vertically. Someone decided a rocket that size would be too heavy to take off because it was not possible to burn fuel that quickly. That mistake cost us valuable time. As Edward pointed out, if Station M had seen that information they would have come to a different conclusion. MI6 is an intelligence organisation; they can call upon experts to advise them, but we had that expertise under one roof - the roof of Hut 3! Station M was uniquely placed to investigate the V2. The Prime Minister understood that, which is why he asked Edward to put the full weight of Station M against it.

I never ceased to wonder at the contact Edward and Lily had with the Prime Minister. For average people like me, Winston Churchill was our national hero, second only to God himself. I couldn't even imagine speaking to him, but Lily did; he called her by her first name. It all went back to Edward's family; the Churchill's were long-standing family friends. As Edward described his conversation with him, it was like I might describe a conversation with Rob.

"Winston studied the reports I handed him," Edward said. "He looked up over his glasses and pursed his lips together. Winston always reacts with indignation, and usually anger, whenever his beloved country is threatened. I had seen that look in his eyes before, he thumped his fist down onto his desk and said: 'I don't care how you do it, Edward, you can have every resource at my disposal, just stop the bloody things'."

This was all great news for Edward and Lily, removing all the uncertainty surrounding the future of Station M. The intelligence section finally had a clear mandate, but that didn't necessarily apply to the operations section. We were like a kite with no string, never knowing from one day to another where the wind might blow us. At least now I knew everything, and it looked very much as if we were working towards some form of sabotage. I had more questions but Lady Elizabeth joined us and I thought better of it. She didn't disguise her surprise at finding me there. We'd met before when Lily organised a girl's night out at the pub. That didn't go as well as it might.

"Oh hello, Dotty, I didn't expect to see you here."

"Just having a drink with Edward and Lily."

"Discussing all your daring deeds, are you?"

"No, not at all, we don't do that."

She was dressed in the most fabulous dress I had ever seen. A red creation she called her crossover wiggle dress. The similarity between us stopped abruptly below the neck, but with her distinctive short black hair and red lipstick it was almost like looking at myself. I found it really disconcerting, like looking at a fantasy image of myself. Lily obviously felt obliged to make a special effort as well. Feeling something of a drab wallflower, I started looking at my watch. The moment Edward's mother, Lady Caroline, entered the room, I became a wilting wallflower.

I had met her once but not in those circumstances. Lily told me she always dressed for dinner, regardless. And wow, did she dress for dinner! Her evening gown would have been breath-taking on a manikin but seeing her float effortlessly into the Drawing Room was a sight to behold. The Dowager Countess of Middlebourne looked every inch a Countess. Lily adored her, and I understood why. She terrified me the first time we met, but I quickly came to agree with Lily.

Why they treated me so kindly I couldn't imagine. Lily went on about the social divide between her and Edward, but compared with me, the divide that concerned her was little more than a crack. I was like a swan crossing a fast-flowing river. I did my best to appear composed but below the waterline I paddled like crazy. I had already told them I had arrangements made for dinner, so when Mr Jennings called them through to the Dining Room, it was my time to go. I remember thinking as I left, 'I wonder what my mum would say if she saw me here'. Not that she ever gave a shit.

The summer days drifted by in lockstep with the white fluffy clouds. Station M's attention now became directed solely towards the V2. If everything went according to plan it might result in a sabotage operation deep inside Germany. If it didn't, the operations section would be reduced to casual onlookers, watching the progress of the war from a safe distance.

In Normandy, the deadlock centred around Caen still continued despite Operation Goodwood. Although its objectives were not realised, Goodwood paved the way for the American Operation Cobra on the 25th of July. The success of Cobra, as elsewhere in Normandy, came at a terribly high price. In London and the southeast, the death toll inflicted by the V1 increased by the day; and all the while we continued training in the relative safety of the green fields of Kent. We were eight highly trained SOE agents wthout a purpose. Rob felt the same as I did, there seemed no end to our exasperation.

"Do you think there will ever be an operation, Rob?"
"I'm beginning to wonder. Why don't we go and see Mac again?"
"Good idea; I can't bear this waiting any longer."

Chapter Twenty-Six
My Funny Turn

I'll never know if it was the divine hand of providence or the roulette Wheel of Fate, but our conversation was abruptly interrupted. Mac shouted across the field towards us.

"Everyone in Hut 4, now!"

His voice carried a sense of urgency, we all dropped what we were doing and took to our heels. An RAF Battle of Britain fighter squadron would not have scrambled quicker. Mac stood with his hands on his hips wearing his beige beret and fatigues. Beneath the beret, he wore a very obvious smile.

"What's the panic, Mac?" I asked, wondering at his expression.

"There's news. Sit down everyone. Do you remember the rumour that we're being held in reserve just in case a special operation came along? It's not just a rumour! It looks like we have that operation."

I suppose in some respects we were like turkeys cheering for Christmas, but that's exactly what we did. A spontaneous cheer erupted in Hut 4.

"Must be something pretty important," said Rob.

"It is," replied Mac. "The countermeasures against the V1 are gaining ground every day. There are people on the ground from F Section and MI6 finding the launch ramps, and there's RAF reconnaissance as well as our own. The new threat is the V2 rocket, and it's now apparent that we have no countermeasures."

"When you say no countermeasures Mac. Do you mean we're powerless to stop them?" asked Phillip.

"Yes, that's precisely what I mean. Once they start launching these things, there's bugger-all we can do about it."

"Are we sure these things are going to be launched; it's not happened yet?" asked Lofty.

"Hut 3 are quite certain," I said. "Don't doubt it, they're coming."

"So we attack the launch sites?" suggested James.

"It's not like the V1. This thing has a much longer range so they'll launch them from well within Germany."

"Can the RAF bomb the launch sites?" asked Ray.

"This is another problem. They drive these things around on the back of a special lorry and can launch them anywhere."

"You make this sound impossible, Mac," I said, "but there has to be a way we can sabotage them."

"The boys next door are still working on this problem but they've put forward a suggestion and it sounds plausible. Lord Middlebourne put the idea before the Prime Minister personally, and he agreed. The threat is so serious he has ordered that Station M is to direct all its efforts towards the V2, and now that includes us. This is the special operation we're waiting for, so you're right, Dotty, we are going to attempt to sabotage the production of the V2."

"Patrick told me they're being manufactured in an underground site at Mittelwerk right next to the Dora concentration camp. He said it's impregnable."

"It is! If the boys next door are correct in their assumptions, their idea is nothing less than genius."

"So how do we do it?" asked Lofty.

"Do I look like a genius? It's all top secret at the moment, we only know what they decide to tell us. There are no details but I can tell you, if it comes off, we'll demolish a few German factories. So we prepare on the assumption that it will go ahead. I want explosives practice every day. I've asked Lily and Fiona to find us a list of bomb-damaged factory buildings in and around London that are due to be demolished. We can work with local police to cordon off these places and we can go in at night to practise demolishing them."

An hour ago our morale was scraping the floor, now there were six smiling faces. Of the eight of us, only Rob and I didn't smile. We had experience of directly confronting the enemy in Occupied France. This operation presented the possibility of confronting the enemy on his own soil deep inside Germany. Rob and I exchanged the same expression, and it wasn't a smile. We would do it, we wanted to do it, but our days of cheerfully rushing into the Christmas turkey queue were over.

"All of our training, Mac, has been directed at operating in Occupied France. This is very high risk and we don't have a fluent German speaker between us."

The atmosphere in the room changed immediately. Rob nodded in agreement. The cold light of reality illuminated the room in stark shades of black and white.

"None of that has escaped me, Dotty. You know me and how I operate. I've told Edward I will consider it and nothing more. I will never put my people in harm's way unless we each know and accept the risk. The odds of success must be in our favour or we don't go. We can move the odds in our favour by being as prepared as we can. You're right about the language. I'll arrange language tuition here, starting as soon as possible. Not a question of fluency, but you may need the basics in an emergency. If this comes off, we'd work with the Polish Resistance, so that's another language."

"How important will an operation like this be when you factor in the Allied advance?" asked Phillip.

"I asked the boys next door that same question. The consensus is that the Mittelwerk site might be overrun early next year."

"So why not leave it to the troops on the ground?"

"They've calculated the death toll the V2 might inflict at its predicted launch rate. They estimate at least 4000 people might be killed and thousands injured. We can't stop production, but if we can reduce their numbers for just a few months, they calculate we could save at least 1000 lives, perhaps many more. More importantly, there are still many things we don't understand about it. They might produce more than we estimate. And the big worry is how accurately they can make the guidance system. Imagine if they can hit specific targets!"

"If that happens, and we can't stop it, that doesn't bear thinking about." said Rob.

"That's precisely why the Prime Minister has given us this personal directive. This is the special operation we are being kept in reserve for."

"I know the boys are working on the rocket engine design; they want to understand exactly how it works," I said. "But if it's made underground, how do we get to it?"

"They don't think all the parts are manufactured at Mittelwerk. They're reasonably sure some components are manufactured elsewhere."

"How on earth can they find where they are made?" asked Rob.

"I don't know but I trust Edward's judgement; he says they have nearly solved the problem. He has called a meeting tomorrow morning in Hut 3, everyone attends."

Rob and I left that meeting with mixed emotions. My thoughts supported the old adage that you should be careful what you wish for. We wanted an end to the waiting, and we wanted to be engaged in the war. With both ambitions about to be achieved, the stark reality of an operation deep into Germany focused our minds. Neither of us said very much as we walked towards Hut 5 but our silence spoke volumes. I intended to go to Gran's that evening, and although Rob had long since stopped openly brooding over the matter, I realised I had created a rift between us.

Like it or not, Mac's news raised our stress levels, and when that happens everything else that troubles you seems to take greater prominence. For us, everything else that troubled us was ourselves, our relationship. It simmered just below the surface like an unopened letter. When Rob suggested we go to the pub together, I anticipated he wanted more than just a pint. I would rather face an armed German soldier than try to explain myself to Rob, but I realised I had to. I often went to the pub dressed in my FANY uniform; I suppose I probably adopted it as my less feminine option. I consciously wore it that evening. Rob dressed in a jacket and open-neck shirt, looking very smart. When he saw me emerge in my uniform, I sensed he was disappointed.

I needed to call at Gran's on the way to the pub, to tell Florence that I would have a bite to eat in The Forge and not to prepare any dinner for me. One thing led to another, and we ended up sitting at the kitchen table with Gran. Her ability to hold a conversation had improved enormously. Although not back to normal, she obviously enjoyed her regained ability. All the while we chatted, I noticed her looking at us both with all the inscrutable wisdom that only a ninety-two-year-old can possess. She liked Rob; she told me so. Gran called him "dear", which meant she liked him a lot.

"What's troubling you two this evening?" she asked.

"You don't miss much do you, Gran; it's to do with the war, nothing we can talk about."

"Nothing you can't talk about, or nothing you don't want to talk about."

"You understand, Gran, I know you do. It's all secret stuff about the war."

"I don't mean that, I mean you two."

"What do you mean?"

"I know you, luv, like I know my own daughter and granddaughter, and I'm getting to know this lovely young man of yours. Do you remember that first day, Dotty, when you knocked at my door. We sat here in my kitchen just like we are now. I saw it then, and I see it now; do you remember, I said 'you're safe now'."

I have never forgotten those words. There I was, a complete stranger, and Gran understood those were the words I really needed to hear. I don't know how she knew, but she did, and she knew it that day as well. Rob didn't realise what was going on, but he saw my discomfort as he glanced between us.

"Are you going to let me in on this conversation, Margaret?" he asked.

"I think you should ask Dotty."

The wisdom of her years sat opposite us like a colossus. In one short sentence, her words opened me up like a surgeon's scalpel. She placed the question on Rob's lips and the answer in my throat. Rob looked at me, expecting an answer without needing to understand the question. Gran sat back wearing a satisfied smile. Had anyone else done that to me, I would be annoyed, but I had only love for her.

"What Gran is saying is that when I first arrived here, she saw right through me. I arrived as bold as brass and twice as confident, except I wasn't. You saw that didn't you, Gran? I was running away, and when you run away, it means there's something in your life you have to get away from. I hate my parents, Rob! That's a terrible thing to say, but I do. They made my life hell, and the way I survived was by pretending I didn't care. All I had was the person I pretended to be. That's the woman who arrived at Gran's door, but Gran saw the frightened little girl who'd never left London before. Gran said the only words I ever wanted to hear, 'you're safe now'."

"Why do you hate your parents, what did they do to you?"

"There was something badly wrong with them, Rob. They should never have had a child. I've not spoken about it to anyone, I can't. Maybe one day, Rob, when I'm ready."

They both looked at me with sad eyes. The world I had created for myself was collapsing in on me. There were no tears, no genuine emotion at all, that part of me was dead. It took a moment for the enormity of my situation to sink in, but when it did, Rob's eyes changed. Almost from the first day we met, Rob took it upon himself to guard my back. There I was, exposed and vulnerable, and Rob's instinct was to protect me. The problem was that the demon taunting me remained beyond his reach.

Gran sat looking at us with a satisfied smile. We never discussed that subject again, but she knew my past had come between Rob and me. She understood as I did, if we were to save our relationship I had to share my past with Rob. Florence came down from her bedroom at a timely moment. One hand clasped the bannister rail while the other supported her ever-increasing belly. Her face wore a healthy glow, no doubt the result of the extra weight she carried. It was no longer the timid housemaid who hugged and kissed us; it was this new confident expectant mother. We chatted briefly, but it proved to be an opportune time for us to continue towards the pub.

As we left, I whispered into Gran's ear, "Thank you."

"Be sure not to lose him, he's a good man."

"He is, isn't he?"

We said little as we walked away. Spencer Tracy followed us, looking as if he understood every word of our kitchen conversation. He eventually returned to Florence's call, leaving Rob and me alone with our thoughts. Middlebourne village is rarely more inviting than on a late summer evening. The soft breeze settled into stillness and the scent from the fragrant garden flowers filled the air. One or two people waved to us, but mostly we walked to the sound of honey bees and birdsong. It was easy to believe all was right with the world.

Roger greeted us at the pub with a broad smile and a cheery welcome. He started pulling the first pint before we reached the bar. Reg walked over, he gave me a hug and shook Rob's hand. I recognised several people there and felt very much at home. Rob and I immediately spoke in hushed voices about the proposed German operation.

"Are you happy to go back?" he asked.

"I'm not happy, no, but I'll go."

"You're still traumatised; are you confident you'll be alright?"

"There's a part of me that needs it, Rob. It's what I do best."

"I know what you mean, I'm the same."

Without knowing what the operation might entail, we talked around in circles and drank more beer. All the while, an elephant sat at the table with us but we both pretended it wasn't there. Eventually as the beer got the better of our inhibitions, Rob asked the inevitable.

"What you said about your upbringing, I'm sorry. It's a heavy burden, isn't it?"

"It is, but it's who I am, Rob; I can't change it."

"We all did what we had to do in Caen, you fought like ten men, you showed no fear, never a second's hesitation. You were full of anger. Does all that anger have anything to do with your parents?"

"I suppose it does. I've spent my entire life angry. I was angry at them, angry at everyone else for not helping me, and angry at myself for putting up with it."

"Why are you angry with me? I would never hurt you. I'm always there for you."

"I know you are, Rob. It's not you, it's everyone. I learned how to depend on myself by needing no one else."

"Are you saying you will never need me?"

I sat in silence for a moment. "I want to need you, I want to commit to you, but you can never understand what that means for me."

"We haven't shared a bed together for ten days; is this how it is now?"

"You're counting the days?"

"I am, because every day pulls us further apart."

"I'm sorry, we'll be together tonight."

"How can you when it's not really what you want? I don't want that."

I started shaking. I noticed my fingers trembling and my heart racing. My head spun, and I felt sick. For a while I pretended I was fine, but all the while I struggled to maintain control. Suddenly it became too much to ignore, I felt as if I was going to pass out. Trying to stand up to go to the ladies, I lost my balance and fell onto the table knocking both of our glasses onto the floor. I lay on the table soaked in beer with sweat forming on my forehead. For a moment, I had no idea where I was.

It caused quite a stir in the pub. People must have thought I was as drunk as a lord, but I wasn't. Roger behind the bar realised something was wrong and quickly telephoned the local doctor. Rob realised I wasn't drunk; he looked petrified. Conscious of making an even bigger fool of myself, I tried to regain control, but I couldn't. The room spun around me and the only thing I remember was my racing heart. Roger and Rob carried me into Roger's living room and sat me down. When Dr Harrington arrived, I assumed he would dismiss me as a drunken fool but he didn't. He diagnosed a case of acute anxiety.

Rob didn't understand, but the Doc assured us both that what I was experiencing had a psychological origin, not a physiological one. Today, of course, I realise it was a panic attack, but that term didn't exist in 1944. He asked lots of questions, had I experienced recent stress or trauma; did I have any history of psychological issues. When I answered yes to all those questions, he peered over his gold rimmed reading glasses and gave me a reassuring smile.

"These symptoms can feel life-threatening but I promise you, my dear, it will pass. Have you experienced this before?"

"No."

"Well, I hope this will prove to be a one-off, but don't be alarmed if you experience it again. The fear of this happening again can become an additional stress. I'll give you some pills which will help you in the short term, but you need to address whatever troubles you."

He reassured me, but the symptoms persisted. When Rob asked if I wanted to go to Gran's or with him, I answered with him. I remember walking some of the way, and then Rob carrying me. The guard at the barrier assumed I was drunk and told me I would be better the next morning. Fortunately, I avoided seeing anyone else as Rob carried me into Hut 5. At six foot one and broad shouldered, Rob didn't appear capable of gentle kindness, but his appearance was deceptive.

He undressed me and washed the beer off with a warm flannel. I raised my arms as he slid my nightdress over my head. When my face reappeared, he kissed me and my arms fell naturally around his neck. I had never been closer to him than I was at that moment.

"Do you want me to stay with you, or do you want to sleep it off by yourself?"

"Stay with me."

He came back later wearing pyjamas; I didn't even realise he had any.

We lay there saying nothing, just the reassuring warmth of his body next to mine. Whatever Dr Harrington had given me certainly put me to sleep. I remember nothing else until Rob woke me the next morning. The entire episode felt like a strange dream but we both had things to learn from it. When the Doc asked if I had mental issues I answered 'yes' without thinking. Perhaps I always knew, or perhaps he prompted me to admit it. Either way, I realised my past was like a cancer eating away at me from the inside. If I accepted that, admitted it to myself, then maybe I could fight it, because that was the one thing I was good at.

"You say you haven't experienced anything like that before," Rob asked.

"I think I might have done, once. It was Christmas of 1942 at Gran's. It wasn't like last night but I had a funny turn. Lily and Fi took care of me, and I told them some things."

"About your childhood?"

"Yes, I couldn't stop crying."

"Does anyone else know about this?"

"No, I've told you more about me than anyone. So what are you going to do now that you realise I've got problems?"

"I'll tell you what I'm going to do. I'm not giving up on you, Dorothy Archer. We'll fight this together, and we will beat it. And when we do, you're going to tell me how much you love me."

"I want that more than anything, Rob."

"Good. You realise you'll not be going on the German operation, don't you?"

"Why not?"

"Mac will never allow it."

"Mac won't know. I need this; Rob, please say nothing."

"We'll have to see; you can't put other people's lives at risk."

"You're right, but I might not do it again; give me a chance."

Chapter Twenty-Seven
The V2

As we walked together towards Hut 3, it felt like a brand new day. For the first time in my life, I shared my burden with someone else. It might only be a small part of it, but it felt a lot lighter. My heart rate had returned to normal and my hands were steady. I dreaded it happening again but didn't dwell on it. Rob had my back as always and now that was an even greater comfort. We were the last to arrive at Hut 3, a fact that Patrick quickly jumped upon.

"Ah, the two lovebirds have finally torn themselves away from the nest. Me Mammy doesn't approve of these shenanigans, you know."

"If you don't tell her, I won't."

"He's just trying to divert his Mammy's attention away from himself," said Maggie.

"Is it working?" asked Lily.

"Sadly not, Mammy says I'm beyond redemption."

Edward had the last word on that subject. "Sounds like your Mammy is a lady of sound judgement."

Here we were, about to discuss a deadly threat and we were all in fits of laughter. This was how Hut 3 worked. Edward called us to order and the other side of Hut 3 fell seamlessly into place. Obviously used to speaking in the House of Lords, Edward had a wonderful command of the English language. When he spoke, everyone listened.

"As you all know, the Germans are developing a new and highly sophisticated weapon. The V2 rocket represents a threat to this nation like no other we have faced. The V1 can in some ways be likened to a pilotless aeroplane, a flying bomb. And like an aeroplane we can defend against it; we are achieving ever greater success shooting them down. The V2, when it becomes operational, will be a totally different proposition. We shall have no countermeasures."

Edward gestured towards Woody, who stood up to speak. "This weapon is a rocket-propelled missile. We believe it can achieve speeds over 3000 mph. At such a speed it will reach the edge of space and fly in a ballistic trajectory. In other words, it flies undetected and will drop out of the sky at supersonic speed with no warning."

In 1944, such a weapon was the product of science fiction. The Operations Section sat with their mouths open, including me and Rob.

"Are we sure about this?" asked Mac. "A weapon that can fly into space; it hardly sounds credible!"

"That is precisely what British intelligence thought when AK presented us with their evidence in 1942," Edward replied. "They made that mistake because they didn't understand how such a large rocket would develop sufficient thrust. We haven't made that mistake because we understand how the Germans achieved it. Will you explain, Rolo?"

One by one, they each added to our understanding of the V2. The technical challenges the Germans had to overcome sounded almost impossible. At the heart of the rocket lay its engine which, on an elementary level, they had long understood. Burn sufficient fuel in a combustion chamber and the outgoing gases provide thrust. The problem increases with the size of the rocket. The heavier the payload, the more fuel is required, and more fuel means even more weight. It had long been thought there had to be a natural limit to a rocket's performance, a point where the weight of fuel becomes impossible to counter by the thrust it generates.

The boys explained it all in elementary terms, as if the solution had been obvious all along. The correlation between the weight of fuel and the energy required to lift and accelerate the rocket remained constant. The German breakthrough came when they realised the answer was to burn the fuel faster, much faster. Rollo explained that part with great relish.

"So, to improve the efficiency of a rocket engine you need to burn the fuel quicker. In order to do that you must increase the rate of fuel delivery into the combustion chamber. And this, my friends, is the crux of the problem."

Edward continued. "There is more intelligence from AK than we ever dared to hope for. They are in possession of engine parts; they have scientists studying the parts which they manage to collect from the test site. With everything they tell us about the size and weight of the rocket, we calculate the engine must generate about 56,000 lbs of thrust. In order to achieve that, using an alcohol fuel and liquid oxygen as oxidizer, it's straightforward to calculate how much fuel it would need to combust every second in order to maintain that degree of thrust."

"So why did MI6 disregard the intelligence?" I asked. "What aspect of it did they not believe?"

"Good question, Dotty," replied Rolo. "In order to achieve a combustion capable of producing that amount of thrust you would need to burn the fuel at the rate of 33 gallons per second! And all of it is forced at extremely high pressure through some kind of fuel injection system. In other words, 33 gallons per second being forced through a series of nozzles. The next complicating factor is that the fuel must be delivered at that rate with an oxidizer, in this case liquid oxygen, at minus 297 degrees Fahrenheit. This is what we didn't understand - fuel delivery."

"There's another factor," said Patrick. "Burning fuel at that rate generates an enormous amount of heat. Would you believe it's between 4000 and 5000 degrees Fahrenheit?"

"Hot enough to melt steel," added Corky.

"Right - I get the picture," said Lily. "Incredibly difficult technical challenges, so I'm thinking from the look on your faces you've narrowed down some essential components."

"Come on now, Lily," replied Patrick, "you're not keeping up, even me Mammy can work this one out."

"I'm guessing the critical factor is how to deliver such vast quantities of fuel, and oxidizer. They must have developed an amazing high-volume pump."

"That took you just long enough, Lily," said a mischievous Patrick. "Any sooner and you might sound like a smart ass."

"Oh, bugger off, Patrick, what chance have I got of sounding smart amongst you lot?"

I loved to listen to the banter between Lily and the boys. A room full of some of the sharpest minds in Britain, and a woman from Stepney. A more unlikely coupling I couldn't imagine. Somehow by sheer force of character, Lily stood shoulder to shoulder with them. Edward was the lead soloist in that orchestra, but Lily was the conductor. Now I was a part of it as well.

Lily had been correct in her assumption; the rocket engine had many components, but the essential breakthrough was understanding the fuel pump. Corky described it as a fuel pump with a V2 rocket engine attached to it. This was no ordinary pump; it amounted to a twin-turbo pump with its own power supply, capable of delivering fuel at a hitherto unbelievable rate. Even I realised the turbo-pump was the most complicated and advanced component of the rocket. When Edward explained the relevance of our newfound knowledge, everything became clear.

"The turbo-pump is revolutionary; by definition most of its components will be completely innovative. Specialist components require specialist manufacturers; we do not believe those capabilities can be contained within the underground works at Mittelwerk. With the help of AK we have compiled a list of essential components. The next stage of our effort is being directed towards finding the German manufacturers of those parts. I would emphasise two words, essential and specialist. If we can locate these suppliers and knock them out, those parts will be very difficult to replace. I hope this explains why you are practising your explosives and demolition skills."

It might have been a case of the triumph of hope over expectation, but we left there in high spirits. Everything Edward said made perfect sense. Until we understood what, and where, we were unable to plan anything; but finally we would go back to training with a purpose. As we walked away, Rob put his arm around me. Lily and Edward walked with us but there was no contact between them. I found it so sad to watch. Our circumstances couldn't have been more different. I felt totally unable to commit to Rob, while he pursued me at every turn. For Lily and Edward their roles were reversed, but worse still, neither of them would admit to it.

As we walked together I saw her look at Rob's arm around me, and I saw what others might not notice. In that moment, Lily's eyes dimmed with an all-consuming sadness. There is something exquisitely sad about the agony of unrequited love. It tore Lily apart, and I hated to see it.

She remained far too strong to ever admit it, but I knew. Edward shared that same expression. For him it was not so much an unrequited love, it had become an unattainable love. I wanted to hug the pair of them and tell them how much they loved each other, but of course, Edward being Edward, I never once felt able to.

oo0oo

During the following weeks the research in Hut 3 continued apace, as did the plans for Fiona's wedding. I approached the wedding with just a tinge of trepidation. The entire business of dressing up in a posh frock and putting myself on parade did not appeal to me one bit. For Fiona, Lily, and Elizabeth, dressing up in their finery was something to be celebrated. They seemed to be consumed by the entire process. I tried to avoid it, but to no avail. Lady Caroline's dressmakers had been commissioned to make Fiona's wedding dress out of the finest parachute silk. I blame Lily entirely; she forced me to have a gown made for the occasion at the same time.

I had to be measured, prodded, and poked, much to everyone's amusement. Fiona thought it was wonderful, I thought it an awful waste of time. When the time came for us to go to the seamstress for the fitting, they were like children at Christmas time. We had to make an afternoon of it, the four of us. The two seamstresses were young girls not more than twenty years old, but they had much older heads on their shoulders. They had recently rented a small shop in Tunbridge Wells; it was rumoured Lady Caroline was their benefactor. Even I could see they were wonderfully capable and talented young women. It came as no surprise when after the war they developed their haute couture business into a household name. They whisked Fiona away while we stood in expectation. When she reappeared, I had to admit, it was a sight to behold. It seemed incomprehensible that the wonderful shimmering silk came from a parachute; she looked amazing.

She didn't want to break with tradition, so it had the usual long sleeves, and full circle skirt which fell from the waist to the floor. It had a fitted ruched bodice, a sweetheart neckline trimmed with lace and the long sleeves were gathered at the shoulder. Most of the decoration went into the veil and headpiece. Fiona's joy seemed to fill the room; we were each lifted by it. The girls fussed around her, a pin here, a tuck there, but in reality their creation was perfect, as reflected in Fiona's smile. When we all agreed it was perfect, they looked at me in unison.

"What?"

"It's your turn, Dotty," said Lily. "Get those horrible fatigues off."

The next thing I knew the girls were undressing me in front of everyone. I stood there in my bare feet, bra, and pants, as they produced their creation. I stepped into it; they pulled it up, fastened numerous buttons, and stood back to admire their work. That was when I noticed the others; they stood open-mouthed in silence. When I looked in the mirror, my own jaw dropped.

"You look absolutely beautiful, Dotty!" Lily said. "How does it feel?"

"It feels strange! This doesn't look like me, does it?"

"You're right, Dot, it doesn't look like you," Fiona said, "but you still look wonderful."

"Do you think so? Would I need to wear pearls or something with it?"

"Yes, of course you should," Elizabeth said. "I've got lots you can choose from and borrow if you want."

I had never seen myself in a dress anything like it. All the bridesmaids were wearing a shade of green, and the girls delighted in the fact that green suited my hair perfectly. The dress was made in dark green velour and designed specifically for me; the girls said it would suit my height and 'embrace me in a chic understated elegance'. Well, I don't know about that, but I didn't recognise the person I saw in the mirror at all.

It was gathered tightly at the waist, transforming into soft pleats that fell away over my hips before smoothly descending to just above my ankles. The sleeves were full length and close-fitting. Above the elbow, they transformed into soft pleats mirroring the waist. The shoulders were unlike the usual fashion; they finished neatly with no pronouncement. Above the waist, the material had a backing that ensured it remained smoothly fitting over the contours of my body. Far too smoothly over my contours if you ask me. Just three flat pleats ran up the middle from the waist to meet the low-cut square neckline which had been trimmed in lace. There were parts of me on display that wouldn't normally see the light of day. I couldn't tell if everyone approved or not; they were silent.

"Is this really me? Are you sure about this?"

"This is so you, Dotty," said Elizabeth.

"I'm lost for words, Dot," said Lily, "you really look beautiful."

"Trust me, Dotty, no woman can look as wonderful as you do and not feel good about herself," said Fiona.

I hoped she was right, but I was more comfortable when I put my fatigues back on. It was a strange experience for me. My life as an agent was not compatible with dressing up in haute couture, and the constant presence of the war made fun-days seem strangely decadent. The others loved it, and even I had to admit Fiona looked spectacular. I left carrying a box under my arm. We walked together down the road, three elegant, fashionable women, and me.

Chapter Twenty-Eight
Fiona's Wedding

Saturday 12th of August 1944 was the big day. Fiona and Johnny were married in St Michael's, the village church. They intended it to be a low-key celebration, as they all were during the war, but it turned out to be the opposite. Fiona and I stayed in our bedroom with Florence doing our hair and fussing around us. We heard the commotion downstairs as everyone started to gather at Gran's. Lily told me about Florence's talent with hair and makeup but I hadn't seen it for myself. That all changed as I watched in awe while Fiona became transformed.

Fi is a really attractive woman who bears more than a passing resemblance to Ingrid Bergman. Florence styled her hair to match the star, and the effect was quite stunning. By the time Florence had finished her makeup, Fiona could only be described as breath-taking. There's something about a bridal gown that just makes you want to get married. When Fi asked me how I thought she looked, I struggled to answer her.

"I know it's what people say, Fi, but honestly I think it's true for you. I can't imagine a bride looking more beautiful."

"You're not just saying that?"

"No, I mean it, Fi, you look amazing."

"Well, it's your turn now, see what you can do, Florence."

I submitted to that ritual humiliation because it seemed to be the right thing to do. Florence had become so large by that time she had difficulty standing close to us, but none of that deterred her. She insisted my hair was too short to do much with, but she would cut it some more to make it a bit more stylish. I sat in fear trying to reassure myself she was very capable. She removed very little but the result immediately amazed me. Then she moved on to my makeup.

"I've always wanted to make up your eyes, Dotty."

"Why, what's special about my eyes?"

"You know you've got lovely eyes, they're your best feature."

"You mean my only good feature."

"No, of course not, just let me work on you. I make my own mascara and eyeliner. I don't think you'll recognise yourself."

She was right there! The person who looked back at me from the mirror bore no resemblance to me whatsoever! I looked like something out of a fashion magazine! In keeping with tradition, the bride stayed hidden from view until she would be driven to the church, so I had to make my entrance alone to the gathering crowd downstairs. I struggled to walk in the high heels Elizabeth loaned me. My elegant entrance comprised a stumble on the first step followed by a slightly faster descent down the stairs than I intended. Having only just remained upright, I stood at the bottom of the stairs and looked at them all. They all just stood looking at me.

"What? Haven't you lot seen a dress before?"

"Not like that, not on you, Dotty," Jim replied.

"Don't make me feel self-conscious."

"Dorothy Archer, is that you?" A voice called from the back of the room.

"Oh, for goodness' sake, stop staring at me, Rob! Come and smudge my lipstick."

Rob didn't need telling twice, and they all gave a quick cheer.

"You lot are rotten to me! I'm no more dressed up than Lily is."

"Yes, but we've seen Lily dressed up before," said Jim.

"Come on, Dotty," said Rob, "let me see you do a twirl."

"You'd better behave, Rob Bartlett."

"Give us a twirl, come on," he said, picking me up in his arms.

Lily's mum and dad smiled at the pair of us. They hadn't met Rob before so I introduced them. I treated Pam and Jack as my family.

I planted a kiss on Jack's cheek. "Dotty, you look lovely," he said.

"Well, you don't have to sound so surprised, Jack, you're as bad as this lot. They're all ganging up on me 'cos I've got a posh frock on."

"So where did you two meet, then?" Jack asked Rob.

"We met at work, didn't we, Dot?" Rob replied.

"Do you work on the farm as well, Rob?" asked Pam.

"Is that where we met, Dotty?" Rob asked.

"Yes, that's right, at Reg's."

Every time that kind of thing happened, it troubled me. We obviously didn't tell anyone how we met, much less what we did. I had the same encounter with Fiona's Mum Judith. She was in such a flap that I didn't need to try too hard. Lily took her upstairs to see Fiona, and I wish I had been there to see their faces. Gran complained all the while because Lily organised a wheelchair for her, insisting she wouldn't cope without it. We all told her she was being silly but not until Lily told her she had to use it, did Gran reluctantly accept it.

When the time came, we all made our way down the road towards Saint Matthew's, we could see the spire from Gran's house. William waited outside, sitting at the wheel of the Rolls Royce ready to drive Fiona the one hundred yards down the road. For all that Fi's mum was close to panic, everything went as smooth as a nut. I waited in the church with the other two bridesmaids, Lily and Fi's sister Karen. Fi entered the church on her father's arm and left on Johnny's arm, as Mrs Albright.

Wartime weddings had to be modest affairs, even simple things like flowers were normally scarce. This didn't apply to Middlebourne! I suspected the flower gardens in the village must have looked rather bare, because they were all in the church. Not only did the villagers donate the flowers, but most of them also stood outside the church. I found it very moving; in that time of austerity the village came together in an act of defiance. They would cheer the bride, no matter what. Fiona was well known in the village, but they regarded us all as something of a mystery. Obviously our connection to Lord Middlebourne intrigued everyone. As a result, they treated Fiona like Royalty. For her part, Fi certainly looked like Royalty; when she waved to the crowd they cheered. I doubt the King and Queen would have received a more enthusiastic reception.

The wedding had already been the most memorable day, but what happened next outside the church locked that memory into everyone's mind forever. I noticed the boys in blue, of whom there were many, forming a guard of honour in front of Johnny and Fi, and I realised that something was going on. As they each stood in salute I heard the unmistakable sound of an approaching Spitfire. You have to remember that the Battle of Britain largely played out in the skies above Kent. The sight and sound of that aircraft had become a symbol of British defiance during the war, as were the gladiators who flew them.

To a person, everyone looked up to see the Spitfire approaching at low level. I quickly spotted another behind it, and then another. Five of them in straight formation came directly towards us at high speed. Everyone stood mesmerised, eyes fixated upon the lead Spitfire as it sped towards us. Then at the last moment as it approached, the pilot dipped the Spitfire's wings, first one side and then the other. Only when he was directly above us did he bank away to the left, soaring up into the sky. Our hearts soared into the clouds alongside him. The second Spitfire rapidly approached us and dipped its wings before banking off to the right. There was a third, and then a fourth, and finally the fifth Spitfire approached. This pilot performed a barrel-roll directly above us before joining his comrades high in the sky.

The thunderous roar of the Merlin engines made our lungs shake. You had to be there to experience the effect of the sight and sound of those aeroplanes. Everyone had the same reaction. For a moment we stood in silence, as if mesmerised. Then a spontaneous cheer filled the air, the sound of which would have eclipsed the roar of Merlin engines. I didn't see patriotic fervour like it again until VE-Day. People stood with tears in their eyes, including me. Johnny put his face in his hands, and Fiona comforted him.

His reaction became crystal clear to me when they explained the significance of the five Spitfires. Johnny is a Battle of Britain fighter ace. That meant he had shot down more than five enemy aircraft. The flyers came from his Battle of Britain squadron based at RAF Hendon. The significance of the five Spitfires was their special tribute to him. I doubt there was a person there that day who did not repeat Winston Churchill's famous words that he delivered in the House of Commons in August 1940.

*"*Never in the field of human conflict was so much owed by so many to so few."*

The wedding congregation were the "many" and Johnny Albright was one of the "few"! There are scant memories of the war years which stir the heart in a good way. The reaction of the crowd, the look on Johnny's face, my own tears; this is my abiding memory. It set the scene for the rest of the afternoon, as it became a wedding like no other. We later gathered in the village hall where Mrs Morgan and the Middlebourne Manor staff provided the buffet lunch. Where in that time of rationing, Mrs Morgan found it all remained a mystery. We had the usual speeches, Johnny's best man was hilarious, and Fi's father, Dennis, said some heartfelt words. Johnny then told everyone how they met at The Forge pub. He described Lily and me being there with all the other airmen, how noisy we were with everyone talking and laughing together.

"Suddenly," he said, "I could see and hear nothing else; it was only Fiona sitting in front of me. I knew in that instant she'd stolen my heart. If I was to have any hope of being a whole person again, I knew I had to spend the rest of my life with her."

Needless to say that went down well, we all clapped and cheered. All the while, Fiona sat there looking serenely beautiful. Even as the afternoon turned into evening and the merriment attained new heights, Fiona rose above the crowd; she was a triumph. I rather thought Lady Elizabeth might steal the show, looking as she did in her red wiggle dress. But not a bit of it, Fi's position as queen of the ball remained unassailable.

Elizabeth's moment in the spotlight came when the village band struck up. Rob and I were quite good dancers, not ballroom, but swing. We were so fit, that kind of energetic dance really suited us; we thought we would set the place on fire. Talk about a rude awakening! Elizabeth bided her time, watching for which of the many flyers had the best moves. She then asked him to dance. 'Wow' was all I could say. Elizabeth didn't just set the place on fire; she ripped the floor up and blew the roof off.

Obviously her time in American cabaret had not been wasted. The sight of her, dressed in the wiggle dress, mesmerised us all. I hadn't noticed, but she had the seamstresses alter her dress. They introduced a buttoned seam down the side, which Elizabeth had undone almost right up to the top of the thigh. In 1944 this was about as outrageous as fashion could be. Being the Lady Elizabeth only added to the spectacle. She danced in a way none of us had ever seen before. One by one the dancers stepped aside to watch her, and that included Rob and me. When the music stopped, everyone cheered and shouted for more. Elizabeth obliged.

"You seem lost for words, Edward. Did you realise your sister could dance like this?"

"I am lost for words, Dotty. I can't be sure if this spectacle is a joyous thing to behold or a disgrace upon the family."

"Trust me, Edward, it's a joy. Why don't you give it a try, with me?"

"Don't be absurd, Dotty. I have no more idea about this dance form than I do about Morris dancing."

"I can just see you dressed up as a Morris Dancer!"

"Precisely."

For all that Edward insisted he couldn't dance, when he took to the floor with Fiona during a waltz he might have passed for Fred Astaire. I noticed when he danced with Lily how they had the attention of the entire hall. Lily isn't the greatest dancer, but that didn't matter; the chemistry between them was obvious. This became Edward's opportunity to hold Lily tightly without, as he would see it, public scandal. They enveloped each other with obvious passion. Lily's eyes didn't leave his, and his smile did more than just welcome her gaze. Elizabeth came over to talk to me.

"You will have to teach me the way you dance swing, Elizabeth."

"That would really be fun, I should love to."

"I'll take you up on that. You were amazing."

"I think I shocked my brother, and my mother. They don't really know me, do they?"

"He was shocked, I can tell you. I can also tell you, when he got over the shock, he quietly admired you."

"Really, you're not just saying that?"

"No, it's true."

"Look at them now, the two of them. He's almost making love to Lily."

"I bet Lily wishes he was."

"Dotty, really!

"Well, look at them; can you doubt that Lily's feelings are genuine, and Edward's, for that matter."

"I have never seen my brother like that before; it's completely out of character."

"A bit like you dancing with that dress on!"

"Oh, well yes, I suppose so. He is enjoying himself, isn't he?"

"They're in love, Elizabeth, can't you see that? They might not admit it, they may never be able to admit it, but it's real isn't it? You'd make Lily's life a lot easier if you accepted that."

"You're Lily's loyal champion, aren't you, Dotty? Well, between you and me I have changed my view about Lily. And you're right about them; my brother is broadcasting it to the entire village."

"Will you tell Lily that?"

"I suspect you will break my arms if I don't."

"No, it will be worse than that."

She laughed a really genuine laugh. For whatever reason, Elizabeth and I became quite close after that evening. The only thing we had in common was Lily, but I liked her, and to my surprise she liked me. And she taught me some of those dance moves. Edward even danced with Mrs Morgan which caused Mr Jennings to frown. They had both returned to the village hall out of uniform. Mr Jennings, not being on duty and dressed in an ordinary suit, didn't seem quite so daunting. I thought I would embarrass him by asking him for a dance.

"Take me for a spin, Mr Jennings."

"I beg your pardon, Miss Archer."

"Oh, come on, Charlie, it's Dotty."

"Charles, if you please, Dotty."

"Very well, Charles, take me for a spin around the floor."

"Well, it's been a little while, but I think I can still manage it."

Manage it! He was another Fred Astaire. When I quizzed him about it, he admitted he had been a junior dance champion. It goes to show, you really can't tell a book by its cover. When we stepped off the floor, Lily took over and Mr Jennings surprised everyone again. All the household staff were there in the evening, most of them enthralled by Mr Jennings. I noticed Mary talking to one of the airmen. Lily had taken Mary, the housemaid, and turned her into Greg Norton's assistant in the Estate Office. The transformation was eye-catching. She wore a dress suit just like Lily usually wears. She pulled her hair back from her face and tied it up in a bun. In every respect, she looked and acted like a young professional woman. Where she discarded the housemaid I had no idea, but her new incarnation suited her admirably.

Greg stood by himself looking preoccupied. I felt so sorry for him. Lily had broken his heart, that much was obvious. I didn't blame Lily for it, in the circumstances she had no option; but now his life had been turned upside down again by the arrival of his previous affair. She came complete with the shock of his life cradled in her arms. No wonder he looked preoccupied! It was easy to think everyone's worry centred upon the outcome of the war. For most people at Station M that would have been true, but Greg became my reminder that life goes on with all its trials and tribulations, not to mention heartache.

Gran sat in her wheelchair looking decidedly happy. Lady Caroline spent a lot of time with her; I suspect some of their conversation involved a certain son and granddaughter. When I chatted with Gran, she wasted no time asking me about Lily and Edward.

"They're dancing so close together, does she think we wouldn't notice?"

"She can't help herself, Gran."

"I didn't realise. I hope His Lordship is not taking advantage of Lily."

"It's nothing like that, believe me. I can't see a future in it for either of them but they're very fond of each other."

"That's not being fond, Dotty, that's being in love."

"Well, it's not for me to say, Gran, you'll have to discuss it with Lily."

"I will, I don't want any of my girls hurt, and that includes you, Dotty."

"I'm okay, Gran, no need to worry about me."

"Oh, but I do."

I loved having someone who worried about me. We shared a hug, and I left her wondering about Lily.

Come the end of the evening, Johnny and Fi finally left in Johnny's car. We covered the car with ribbons and a long trail of tin cans attached to the rear bumper. They left with a mighty cheer ringing in their ears, only to drive a few hundred yards down the road to their new cottage. What a day it had been. As we left, inevitably our thoughts turned towards marriage. Rob and I walked together through the village towards the manor, and despite all the preoccupations of the day, I knew intuitively what Rob was about to say.

"Will that be us one day, Dotty?"

"This is probably not the best time to discuss that, is it?"

"Will there ever be a better time?"

"That's something we can agree on, Rob; there will be a better time. And before you ask when, I don't know."

It seemed like a strange time for us to start a row, but then again perhaps it wasn't. We both looked at Fiona and Johnny with envy. If you excluded the war, they had what most people might wish for. Blissfully in love and embarking upon a new life together; they had everything they'd ever dreamed of. Rob shared that vision of the future, and why shouldn't he? I wanted more than anything to share that vision, but try as I may, the future frightened me more than the present.

"You don't know when! That means it may be never. I'm trying not to give up on you, Dot, but I'm beginning to think I should."

"Everyone I've ever known has given up on me, one way or another. Why should you be any different?"

"I could give you a list of reasons why I'm different, but you don't want to know. It's time I accepted that. Perhaps we need to move on."

"You mean move on without me?"

"Yes. If we don't have a future together, what's the point of me waiting for you?"

I said a few more things completely out of turn. Poor Rob, he poured salt onto an open wound without even knowing it. The more he did it, the more I recoiled away. In effect, I flatly rejected him. After the event, I couldn't believe I'd done it. In my own way, and as far as I was able, I loved him. I knew it wasn't enough, but I had nothing else to offer, not then. When Rob said I would be better to go home to Gran's, I stupidly agreed.

"I'll see you tomorrow then. Goodnight, Rob."

How can it be that pride or misguided emotion can make you do and say the most ridiculous things? As I walked away, I knew it was madness. Every step compounded the absurdity of my actions, and yet inexplicably I continued to walk away. The gap between us grew with each stride and my reaction became ever more intense. I recognised the symptoms from last time. My head spun, I felt cold and sweaty, my body trembled. Crouching slightly with my hands resting on my knees, I drew long slow breaths. Panic overwhelmed me; I had just lost Rob. I straightened up, spun around, and shouted, "Rob, don't leave me." But Rob had gone.

Chapter Twenty-Nine
V2 Components

When I arrived at the cottage I found Gran already tucked up in bed and Florence ready to do the same. It gave me the opportunity to quietly disappear. It might have been more sensible not to have taken one of Doctor Harrington's pills. He said not to mix them with alcohol, but I would have required a clear head to recall his words. Once again, a crushing sense of panic overwhelmed me until a drug-induced sleep offered me sanctuary.

Thank heavens the following day was a Sunday. I didn't wake until eleven o'clock. Struggling to fully wake up, I made my way downstairs, blaming everything on an excess of beer. Both Gran and Florence expressed concern; apparently I looked awful. Assuming I suffered from a monumental hangover, they laced their comments with little sympathy. All I could think about was Rob and how stupid I had been. If I ran to him and apologised, he would ask the same question, and I would be left wrestling with the same answer. Gran would no doubt have had sound advice for me, but I couldn't face it. Instead, I spent the day working in the garden trying not to face up to my problems.

The following couple of days were difficult for us both. We couldn't avoid each other even if we wanted to. It almost felt as if we were back to normal, but of course what had been said could not be undone. The prospect of losing Rob became too terrible to contemplate, so I didn't contemplate it; I pretended it hadn't happened. I guess Rob felt much the same because we behaved like a pair of ice skaters dancing around each other, pretending to be unaware of the very thin ice beneath our feet. As was so often the case during the war, events would suddenly put everything else into perspective. On August 15th, the Allies launched "Operation Dragoon".

This was another massive operation. Three divisions of American troops landed on the beaches of the French Riviera between Toulon and Cannes, and 5000 British and American paratroopers landed to the rear of the German defences to support them.

The Germans had concentrated their forces in the north of France; the south was not so heavily defended. The French Resistance working with SOE F Section harassed the Germans all over the south of France. Communications, road, and rail transport were all disrupted. Against weaker forces, the invasion is quickly successful. Within four weeks, most of southern France was in Allied hands. The southern ports became vital for the Allied war effort; millions of tons of equipment, and over 900,000 troops would be landed over the coming months.

Operation Dragoon proved to be an enormous success. We assumed at some point the Germans would launch a last-ditch counterattack, but for the time being at least the war progressed in our favour. The same might be said about our intelligence work with the V2. Each time I called into Hut 3 the boys seemed to be getting ever closer to the information they needed to enable an operation against the V2 manufacturing sites. The ultimate intelligence coup would, of course, have been to get our hands on a V2 rocket. They manufactured these things deep inside Germany under the strictest possible security. Add to that the fact that the rocket was forty feet long, then the prospect of us spiriting one away from under the Germans' noses seemed to be out of the question. Or was it?

It has to be said that as clever as the boys in Hut 3 were, the key intelligence concerning the V2 came from AK. The original German test site at Peenemunde had been badly damaged during the prolonged British bombing campaign called Operation Crossbow in 1943. As a result, manufacturing moved to Mittelwerk, and they carried out testing at Blizna in south-east Poland. Crucially this was beyond the range of British bombers. The magnificent Polish Resistance reasoned that while the test site might be impregnable, this only applied to the launch. The words of Longfellow might have inspired their reasoning:

"I shot my arrow into the air, it fell to earth, I know not where." (Henry Wadsworth Longfellow)

The brave and resourceful Poles understood their homeland more intimately than the German occupiers. While the Germans searched for their fallen arrows, AK frequently beat them to it. The spoils of their resourcefulness became the subject of one of the most audacious undercover operations of the war called Operation Wildhorn. On the 15th of April 1944, a Dakota FD 919 from 267 Squadron took off from Brindisi and landed in a beetroot field near Matczyn near Lubin in Poland.

Right under the noses of the Germans, the chances of success must have appeared slim for such an outrageously impetuous operation. The Dakota, not unsurprisingly, became stuck in the beetroot field. One can only imagine those valiant resistance fighters trying to free the aeroplane and load the crashed rocket on board. Somehow, and against all odds, the remains of the V2 were successfully loaded into the aircraft, and once freed from the mud, it managed to take off. I doubt British Intelligence believed their eyes when they were presented with the crashed remains of a V2 rocket.

It provided us with invaluable information. We then compared our theorising with the actual parts, albeit badly damaged. The boys worked out that the fuel and oxidizer pumps were in fact a twin-turbo pump, independently driven by a steam generator. AK confirmed the power source for the generator to be hydrogen peroxide using sodium permanganate as a catalyst. The turbo pump itself became the key to the whole thing, and the more the boys understood it, the more the various essential specialist components became obvious. The breakthrough came when they realised there was only one specialist designer of turbo pumps in Germany, designing and manufacturing high volume water pumps for the fire service. They were *Klein Schanzlin Becker,* known as *KSB.*

The boys needed to work out what the vital unique components were that made up the turbo pump. Then they needed a list of the specialist manufactures - their names and addresses would be helpful - so we could go over to Germany and blow the factories to kingdom-come. Needless to say, nothing is as easy as that; the Germans didn't publicise their top-secret endeavours. In some respects it sounded like the boys were looking for a needle in a haystack. When they called us over to Hut 3 for a meeting, I had the distinct feeling they had found that needle. The atmosphere in the Hut was palpable, the boffins couldn't contain their smiling faces.

"We've been able to trace some key components directly back to specialist manufacturers," said a jubilant Woody.

"Are you certain?" asked Lily.

"Unequivocally, we finally have absolute certainty." He produced a sheet of paper. "This is our list of targets."

"How have you arrived at this?" Lily asked in astonishment.

"Mathematical and analytical genius," replied Rolo.

"Well, tell me how you did it."

"Rolo is quite right, Lily, it was an act of pure genius," replied Edward. "We gave the Poles a list of likely components to look for amongst their collection of crashed parts, while we looked at the components MI6 recovered during Operation Wildhorn. Between us, we quickly formed a list of manufacturers."

"You make it sound easy," I said. "How did you find out who manufactured them?"

"Easy, we just made a note of the manufacturers' marks on the components!"

"Are you telling me the manufacturers put their names on the parts? Is it as simple as that?"

"There's a certain Irish logic to it," Patrick said. "We searched for the difficult answers and forgot to ask the simple questions."

"This is especially true of metal castings," said Edward. "Foundries always have a maker's initial inside the casting."

"Even better is the fact that the turbo-pump comprises very specialist machined castings," said Corky.

"It's not just the body of the turbo-pump," said a jubilant Rolo. "There are several brass castings, like the oxygen nebulisers."

"And AK knows where these manufacturers are?" Lily asked.

"Casting iron, aluminium, and brass is very specialist. There are only a few foundries capable of doing this kind of work, and we have the list."

This was Hut 3 at its best. Lily regarded them as "her boys", and the look on her face portrayed an enormous sense of pride in their achievement. They all sat there with beaming faces. I'm not sure if they had pride in what they had achieved, or pride that they had pleased Lily. I shared their enthusiasm, but as always it came tempered with the realisation that the Operations Section would have to put it into action.

"Do we have enough to mount an operation?" Mac asked.

"I think we need to go ahead," replied Edward.

"I agree," said Patrick, "but is it possible to assess the risk against the reward, Mac?"

"This isn't like a mission in France," Mac replied. "Our agents can't rely on local support. This is much more dangerous."

"What about AK?" asked Rolo.

"Yes, we'll be working with them, but we don't have such established networks," Mac replied. "There's also an unknown element to this mission. Even if your assumption about these vital components is correct, we cannot know what the German stock level of that component is."

"You're right, Mac," said Edward. "We are dealing with the unknown, but AK has expanded the list of suppliers to four. That increases the odds that one of those supply chains is vital for them."

"Where are these places?" I asked.

"One of them is in the big industrial centre of Dusseldorf. There's one near Hamburg, in Pinneberg. Another is down in the south, a place called Furth. The last and possibly the most important one is at Frankenthal, near Mannheim. So we have one in the Ruhr valley, one in the north, and one in the south, and the most important target near Mannheim."

"So the targets are spread out," said Woody. "How many planes, Mac?"

"I think we need two. We can drop near Dusseldorf and go on to Frankenthal. A second plane would drop near Pinneberg, and go on to Furth, which is down near Munich. This does unfortunately give the second plane a long flight over Germany."

"Can we get aerial reconnaissance?" asked Maggie.

"It would be a big ask for Johnny," replied Corky. "These are industrial areas, plenty of flak, and right at the range limit. Besides, the targets are probably not obvious from the air."

"What about drop zones?" Rob asked.

"Should be okay," replied Corky, "but only if we can get an exact fix from AK. They would rely on torch signals at night for the final approach."

"It all comes back to agents on the ground," said Mac. "Nothing gives you intel better than eyes on the ground."

"I agree," replied Edward, "but how risky do you rate this for our people, Mac?"

"We only have two German speakers, and they're not fluent, so we would depend heavily on Polish Resistance. But make no mistake, AK is very well organised and extremely capable."

"Are you saying the risk is acceptable?"

"We would be putting the lives of our agents in AK's hands, but I think that's a justifiable risk."

"Right, we go ahead," Edward said. "How will you plan it, Mac?"

"We coordinate with AK, and with the RAF, and we get our people safely on the ground over there. I'll designate one team to each of the sites. Phase Two will be for our agents to assess the situation on the ground, and report back. Then we decide the next course of action. We can supply and coordinate whatever additional explosives or equipment they need. Phase Three will be implementation, followed by phase Four, extraction of our people."

"You make it sound easy, Mac," Lily said.

"It is easy for me sitting here, but any mission this deep into Germany is going to be dangerous."

"That's settled, then," Edward said. "Rolo, you coordinate with AK, and Mac, you set it up. I shall inform General Gubbins and the PM."

So that was it, the decision had been taken to put all eight of our agents into harm's way. None of us had much say in the matter, but that's the nature of war. It had been decided; Christmas had come early, and the turkeys needed to prepare themselves. Rob seemed almost enthusiastic, as did some of the others. A part of me shared their enthusiasm, but I seemed to be the only one who kept a healthy scepticism. We had trained precisely for an operation like this. In terms of explosives and the demolition of buildings, we were probably among the most highly trained in SOE. Nobody would be more capable of such a mission than us, I just didn't see the necessity to be happy about it. We all left together heading over to Hut 4. Rob didn't seem to want to walk with me, so I walked alongside Mac.

"This is quite different to France, isn't it, Mac?"

"It is. We have no established connections, and we will have to rely on AK."

"An operation into the heart of Germany, on this scale; has this been done before?"

"No, everything about this will be a first. We'll have to get four teams into four separate locations. It will be important to coordinate all four attacks; we can't give the Germans an opportunity to realise what's going on."

"You mentioned Phase Four being extraction of agents; did you mean that, Mac? It's normal to leave F Section agents to get themselves home."

"Lily spoke to Edward as we left. She wouldn't agree to anything less. We're not like the rest of SOE, Dotty; we've always got our people home."

"I'm pleased to hear that."

I trusted Mac implicitly. He would only send us if he assessed the risk to be acceptable. I also had confidence that his planning would be meticulous. There had always been an air of confidence about Station M. We never regarded ourselves as anything other than just another SOE section, but in reality, and I can say this now with hindsight, we were a pretty special bunch. We had Mac, a masterful tactician. Edward and the boys of Hut 3 were among the sharpest brains in Britain. All eight of our field agents were highly trained individuals. Mac had chosen each one of us for our special talents. We even had Johnny, our reconnaissance pilot, a highly decorated Wing Commander and Battle of Britain fighter ace. If we had a secret weapon, then it was Lily and Fiona. If anyone could pull off an operation deep into Germany, *we* could!

Rob didn't avoid me, no more than I avoided him. With so much else to talk about, we didn't really have time to think about each other. Only when we left for the evening did I realise I had to decide: Hut 5 or Gran's? By the time I realised, we were already on our way and Rob called out, "Good night." I turned and waved, as if to a casual friend. It felt like I had entered a strange topsy-turvy world where nothing made sense. Was I the Queen of Hearts, or the Mad Hatter? I needed to find my way back into the real world, but like Alice, I had lost my way.

I found out the next morning that poor Lily had received a telegram just after the meeting in Hut 3. That telegram contained the worst kind of devastating news. Lily's Uncle George and his wife Marcia had both been killed in Croydon by a V1. The moment I saw Lily's face, I realised she had received terrible news. I didn't know Lily's Uncle George, but I understood how important he was to her. He gave Lily her big opportunity in life. It was his shipping agency she managed for ten years. They were so close, Lily worshipped him.

"I'm so sorry, Lily. I wish I had known; I should have been there for you."

"I wish you had been, Dot, I needed you."

With that she broke down in tears. I held her tightly and tried to console her but the void in her heart could not be filled. We all have a cross to bear in life, Lily's is her close encounter with death. In 1941 a bomb fell directly into Lily's house in Stepney. Thank God, she had been next door at the time with her neighbour. Both houses were razed to the ground, and Lily's best friend together with her twin boys were killed. Miraculously, rescuers pulled her alive from the rubble. Lily insists she had not been intended to walk away, convinced a part of her remains there. She says the hand of death didn't spare her; rather, she evaded it.

That belief then became compounded each time death visited itself upon someone she loved. Death first turned its attention towards her brother, Ian. Then the hand of death pointed towards her friend next door. Recently it came for her husband, Gerry. Now it had been the turn of George and Marcia to suffer the wrath of death's vengeance. I must have told her a dozen times that death is the ultimate fate of us all, and it comes without judgement or the slightest regard for those it leaves behind. But Lily had become obsessed with the notion that death stalked her like a debt collector, prepared to take its payment in any way it could.

I had never seen her so distraught. I would have confronted her tormentor myself had it been in my power, but nothing I did would have relieved her anguish. No one could replace her loved ones; I might only offer her comfort. With Fiona away enjoying her honeymoon and so much happening at Station M, it became a desperate time for Lily. I did everything possible, but with the intensified training programme, I had little time. Mrs Morgan and Mr Jennings were wonderful; all the household staff rallied around her, as did Elizabeth. Above all, Edward stepped up magnificently. He wanted everyone to believe it amounted to nothing more than gentlemanly compassion, but I knew otherwise. It was a pure expression of love, albeit one that must not mention its name.

The time between a death and the funeral is a kind of hinterland for the bereaved. A time when the dearly departed have started their journey but those they leave behind refuse to let them complete it. The last days of August heralded gradually shorter daylight hours and misty mornings. Everything outside of Lily's world continued apace. The Allies liberated Paris on the 25th of the month, and the V2 operation became a reality when Mac gave it an operational name. From that day on we counted down the days to "Operation Cormorant."

Chapter Thirty
The Briefing

On the morning of the 8th of September, we were summoned to Hut 3 for a combined briefing. As we walked over there, Fiona joined us, fresh from her honeymoon. Even a stranger passing Fi in the street would have noticed how happy she looked. It seemed to radiate all around her; it made you want to stand close and bask in the sun. We hugged each other and only had time to exchange a few words, but as we entered the hut, I felt sure some of her glow rubbed off on me. Mac wasted no more time and walked towards a large map of Germany pinned to the wall. Lily appeared late and made her apologies. Mac appeared restless, waiting for her to sit down.

"This morning, the first V2 rocket has fallen on London. It has caused widespread destruction in Chiswick. I don't believe we have the casualty figures yet."

"When did this come to us, Edward?" Lily asked.

"We heard around half an hour ago."

So, it began. The reign of terror the V1 had visited upon us now acquired an even more deadly companion. The era of the ballistic missile began, and we had no defence. Mac obviously planned the meeting before the news of the V2's arrival, so his timing felt uncannily prescient. It certainly concentrated minds. He went through the plan meticulously. They would fly us eight field agents into Germany on board two Halifax four-engine bombers, departing simultaneously from RAF Tempsford in Bedfordshire. Tempsford was a part of the RAF Special Duty Service, the most secret airfield in Britain. It was the starting point for nearly all SOE operations involving parachute drops into Europe.

Mac decided upon the night of September 14th. He confessed that the date was far from ideal. Unfortunately, there would only be a crescent moon, giving the pilots and agents precious little night vision. The next full moon would not rise until the end of the month, and then there was another complication that we had only just been told about. The Allies planned a major offensive to be launched on the 17th, which would involve 40,000 airborne troops. "Operation Market Garden" might have implications for our operations, especially in and around Dusseldorf. He chose the 14th as the first practical opportunity for us. It needed to be before the 17th. Mac confessed he didn't like the sudden haste, but he'd only just been made aware of the pending Operation Market Garden.

"The two Halifax's are to be designated Alpha One, and Alpha Two," he said. "Alpha One will navigate directly to a drop zone west of Dusseldorf. Agents Dipper and Wren will rendezvous at the drop zone with AK. Alpha One will then continue to a drop zone east of Frankenthal, where agents Woodlark and Swallow will rendezvous with AK. Alpha Two will navigate to a drop zone north of Pinneberg, where agents Jay and Swift will rendezvous with AK. Alpha Two will continue to a drop zone southwest of Furth, where agents Goshawk and Osprey will rendezvous with AK."

Lily whispered in my ear, "Which one are you?"

"I'm Goshawk."

We all understood flying over Germany was extremely dangerous but parachuting out of the night sky into exactly the right place, guided by only a couple of torches, was also fraught with danger. The risks to be taken by the Polish Resistance were equally immense. Getting our agents safely on the ground, and into the hands of AK, was one of the most dangerous aspects of the mission. The RAF would navigate the least hazardous route to avoid heavy concentrations of ack-ack, but this remained a very risky part of the mission. Mac went through it all, chapter-and-verse. As always, he had been meticulous. I noticed immediately that Rob and I were on different teams. I raised my hand, but he saw me coming.

"Before you ask, Dotty, I've put you and Rob in different teams. You know my view about couples working together. It's potentially a conflict of interest. Apart from that, I need to spread your experience."

Any pretence we might have about not advertising our relationship had just been blown out of the window. Edward knew me well enough by then to have some fun at my expense.

"You and Rob weren't keeping your relationship a secret, were you, Dotty?"

"No, of course not, Edward; not like you and Lily."

It was a rare day indeed when anyone got the upper hand over Edward, but on that occasion he walked right into it. Lily looked a little embarrassed, but it didn't compare to Edward's discomfort. I realised I'd done it again; me and my big mouth. Whatever I said next would only make matters worse, so I said nothing. Mac saved me from myself by continuing with his briefing. He explained how he considered all other options. Bombing had been ruled out because such relatively small targets deep into Germany would likely not succeed.

He discarded the possibility of sabotaging the components in transit. He decided that the weeks of intelligence required would add too much risk. The aim of the operation was to destroy the factories, and each factory would represent a unique challenge. Our initial task was to reconnoitre the sites, assess the challenge and come up with a plan to put them out of action. There was an excellent precedent for such an audacious operation.

In 1942, the Pessac electrical transformer station near Bordeaux provided an essential power supply for the Germans' Bordeaux submarine base. RAF precision bombing had often proved itself to be more lethal for the flight crews than for the chosen targets. General Gubbins saw the opportunity to show the capabilities of SOE sabotage to his sceptical detractors. Four agents cut through the wire perimeter fence in the dead of night and planted magnetic limpet mines against the eight enormous oil-filled transformers, destroying six out of the eight. The Germans assumed it must have been an air raid, and all four SOE agents returned safely to England. Known as Operation Josephine B, it set an example for future SOE operations, with an outcome that we wanted to emulate.

Mac detailed the many sabotage options available to us, and the equipment we would be provided with. Canisters would be dropped with us at each drop zone, containing basic armaments and explosives. Any additional specialised equipment that we deemed necessary would be dropped later. That part of Mac's briefing was probably for the benefit of the intelligence section. After all of our extensive training, we certainly knew how to blow things up! The immediate enthusiasm gradually subsided as the cold light of reality illuminated the risks which came with this operation. We each departed with little else to say. I still felt bad about embarrassing Edward. As we left the hut, I wanted a word with him.

"I'm sorry about what I said, Edward. I didn't think; I didn't mean to embarrass you."

"Oh, don't be silly, you didn't embarrass me."

"That's a relief, I thought there might have been something going on between you and Lily!"

I just couldn't help myself. I climb out of one hole only to start digging another. Edward looked at me with a half-smile.

"You are insatiable, Dotty. As you know, Lily and I have a professional working relationship."

"That's a good word, I'll make a note of that. I must try not to be insatiable."

"I doubt you will manage."

We parted on good terms. He maintained his pretence while I continued with mine. It made me feel really happy that I shared such a friendly relationship with the man that my best friend loved. I did at least know better than to argue with Mac again about putting me with Osprey. If I couldn't be with Rob, then Lofty Cramer would have been my next choice. At six feet, he wasn't as tall as Rob, so I never really understood why we called him Lofty. Christened Henry, at some point he became Lofty, and it just stuck. Mac teamed Rob with James; neither had any complaints.

Those last few days before the operation seemed to drag by, with each day being much the same - constant training and language tuition. We studied maps of our designated areas until we could all draw the outlines from memory. Each day, I ran several miles. I climbed nets and ropes. I assembled explosives; I dismantled and reassembled every kind of weapon available. Live fire and unarmed combat were practised regularly if not every day. Lofty and I even blew up a bomb-damaged factory in Balham as an exercise. We were fully prepared. The mundane nature of the training left us all wanting to get on with it. Rob and I woke up next to each other on the morning of the 14th.

"This is it, Dot. How are the nerves?"

"Rock steady at the moment. You?"

"Yes, we've never been more ready, have we? Neither of us must take any unnecessary risk, but I want you to promise me something."

"I know, be careful and make sure I come back."

"Yes, but it's more than that. You can be reckless, Dot. When the odds are against us, you have no fear. Sometimes it pays to turn away and not be reckless. If you don't come back, Dotty, it would destroy me. I want you to think about that when the odds are against you, and I want you to promise me that you'll turn away if you can."

"Well, the same applies to you, Rob."

"Are you admitting it would destroy you if you lost me?"

"Of course it would. Don't make me say it, you already know it would."

"No, I'd like to hear it."

"I can't do without you, all right?"

For the first time in my life, I opened the door just a fraction and the light of our relationship shone through it. I saw it in Fiona's face, I heard it in Lily's voice. They both embraced it, but I feared it. That door had always been kicked in my face; it held nothing but terror for me. Nothing, not even Rob, could make me step through it - not yet!

Chapter Thirty-One
RAF Tempsford

We shared breakfast with the others in the canteen, enjoying the usual morning banter with Brenda. If any of us required a good reason to come back safely from Germany, then Brenda's egg and bacon provided all the motivation we needed. So far so ordinary, except it wasn't. We all laughed and joked but the silences were exactly that. The nerves were jangling; the apprehension started building. Nobody said anything; it would be poor form to admit such a thing, but we were all singing from the same hymn sheet.

The canisters to be dropped with us had been packed and repacked a dozen times. I couldn't think of a more futile gesture than repacking them one more time. But of course we did. The futility of our action was nothing to do with ensuring we overlooked nothing. Repetitious training is not merely about ensuring a spontaneous response to events, it's also about turning a stressful situation into a routine event.

My own Sten Gun went with me. It had the custom modification of the front pistol grip. They all joked that I treated it like a baby, and they were right, I did. I allowed no one else to touch it. That became my routine; I took it apart and checked every component, every day. Most importantly, I checked the magazines. They were not always new ones; we reloaded them regularly and here lay the danger. If the lead bevel into the chamber suffered the slightest damage, it might jam. It was well known that the Sten Gun could jam, but mine never did!

SOE were meticulous about local clothing. They either got the real thing or they were specially made. Even then, no chances were taken. French seamstresses were used, mostly. In our case, they were Polish. Original labels were used or exact copies. We hoped our documentation would pass any scrutiny, as would any nondescript items we carried in our pockets. In France, our French-speaking agents were indistinguishable from local inhabitants; unfortunately this would not apply to us in Germany. We obviously didn't intend to integrate ourselves into the local community. We wanted nothing to do with the locals, civilian or military, but we needed to dress accordingly as a precaution.

SOE operated in just about every country involved during the war, and in all cases fluent speakers were the priority. A handful of operations were conducted in Germany towards the end of the war. They were low key, often designed to enable rather than directly disrupt. "Operation Downend" in 1944 tried to create a sabotage organisation in the Ruhr and Frankfurt area. "Operation Fordwick" established a line of connection for agents between Germany and Denmark.

Direct action proved effective during "Operation Colan" in 1945, when the railway between Stuttgart and Heilbronn was effectively sabotaged. An unsuccessful attempt called "Operation Vivacious" failed in 1944-45 to sabotage the Bruno Hintze engineering works in Berlin, where they also made components for the V2. Our own Operation Cormorant would be the most audacious act of sabotage ever carried out in Germany. We were all aware that nothing like it had been attempted before, and we all knew why.

Our biggest problem if we were stopped would be the language. Our two language tutors were very good, but our command of both German and Polish rose only to the level of elementary. We concentrated on Polish because we would be working with them. Our cover would be that we were Polish workers. AK were going to provide us with passes and documentation for our places of work. With any luck, the Germans we might encounter at checkpoints would probably not be Polish speakers. These were the concerns we all wrestled with but the moment came when we needed to put those concerns behind us.

Mac fussed about us like an old mother hen. He wanted to be a part of the operation more than anything; he still had difficulty accepting that for him those days were over. My preparation was as good as it could be; there were no second thoughts, no last-minute worries. Rob said the same, we were both ready. I may not have worked directly with Lofty before but I had no doubts about him. He looked very calm and collected as he stood next to me.

"This is it then, Dot. Make sure you take good care of me."

"You look like you need taking care of, don't you!" I replied as I looked up at him.

I got on really well with Lofty. With his great sense of humour, he never failed to make me laugh. He and Rob lifted the canisters onto the lorry as if they contained straw. The rest of us followed them and took our places on either side. I was the last to climb aboard. We leaned back and rested our feet against the kit which sat between us. Each of us wore the same farm worker's overalls over our Polish clothing. We all looked the same, and no doubt we were all thinking the same. The lorry shuddered into life as the driver started the engine. Mac stood behind the tailgate dressed in his fatigues, hands on his hips, beige beret tilted to one side.

"Good luck, men. And you, Dotty. Remember, I want you all to report back here when it's over. Don't piss me off by not turning up. Okay?"

Our clandestine operation was exactly that, but that's not how it began. The lorry turned away from Hut 4 and towards the manor where it quickly became forced to stop. Everyone had assembled in front of the manor to wish us well. Mac obviously thought that it breached all protocols; I think he intended to say as much, but Patrick pre-empted him.

"Me Mammy sends you all a message. She says blow those fecking factories up and get your arses back here. The place is not the same without you."

"Perhaps your Mammy should come with us," I said.

"Oh, to be sure she would love to, but her opportunity for travel is limited these days."

"I also have a message," Edward said, "this is not from Patrick's Mammy; this came directly from the Cabinet War Rooms. It says, and I quote, 'You were asked to set Europe ablaze, and you did so magnificently. I now have to ask you to take that blaze and deposit it into the heart of Nazi Germany. If anyone can accomplish such an audacious undertaking, it is you, the outstanding people of Station M. When you succeed in your endeavours, as I know you will, you shall have saved the lives of countless people, you may even shorten the war. When that day comes, the people of this great nation will once again step into the light of freedom; and when they do, they will be standing on the shoulders of giants. Godspeed to you all. Winston Churchill'."

The silence that followed was utterly profound. I swear the wind dropped and the birds in the trees became mute. That was the first time I experienced the extent to which oratory can motivate people. To a person, we sat there with those words echoing in our minds, as we pulled our shoulders back and puffed up our chests. Some of us swallowed hard, and some found a piece of grit in their eyes. I looked at Lily and she looked like a rabbit caught in the headlamps. Edward left her side and stepped forward; I think he wanted to say what she couldn't. He reached up and took my hand.

"Good luck to all, and safe return."

I hardly knew what to say, so typically, I said something stupid. "I think the Prime Minister must be referring to Lofty and Rob when he called us giants."

"I think not, Dotty," Edward replied. "In fact, he quoted from a letter Sir Isaac Newton wrote to fellow scientist Robert Hooke in 1675 where he wrote, '*If I have seen further, it is by standing on the shoulders of giants.*' The Prime Minister wanted to symbolise the enormity of the debt the nation owes to its armed forces and to you."

"Well, I suppose we mustn't let the Prime Minister down then, must we?"

"I don't think there is any danger of that."

I looked at Lily and Fiona as the lorry pulled away; nothing more was said. We drove several miles out of the village before anyone spoke.

"That was something, wasn't it?" Ray said. "Something to tell the grandchildren."

"You're getting ahead of yourself, Ray," Alan replied. "You need a wife first, and who's going to marry you?"

"Don't you believe it; women fall over themselves to get to me."

"Are you sure about which direction they're falling?"

This is how it continued; we gently let off steam rather than admit the immense pride we each felt. Gradually the banter subsided, and as the journey continued, we each retreated into the comfort of our own thoughts. Little more was said; we looked up occasionally, we smiled, we nodded, but all the while Middlebourne became further and further away.

We arrived at RAF Tempsford in the late afternoon. Tempsford itself is just a sleepy rural hamlet, located a couple of miles northeast of Sandy, Bedfordshire. Mostly a farming community, the inhabitants knew nothing about the function of the airbase. We accessed the base via a little country lane, where a prominent sign said, 'This road is closed to the public'. Tempsford was the most secret RAF airfield in Britain, home to the Special Duty Squadrons 138 and 161.

Nearly all SOE airborne operations began from Tempsford. 138 Squadron flew the Handley Page Halifax II, specially modified for SOE operations. 161 Squadron flew the Lysander Mk 3. The SOE did indeed set Europe ablaze, but the match was lit at Tempsford. These pilots flew missions all over Germany and the occupied countries, delivering agents and supplies. And when agents had to be extracted, the Lysander with its unique capabilities needed only a small field to land.

From the moment we arrived, we became part of a well-oiled machine. Brief formalities over, our driver drove us the short distance to Gibraltar Farm on the eastern perimeter of the airfield. This ramshackle collection of one-time farm buildings was converted into a reception centre. This is where we carried out our pre-flight preparation. It also provided a secure home for SOE supplies. The RAF boys were brilliant; in every respect we worked as a team. We didn't have to explain anything about the operation; they were already briefed. They knew where and when, they would assume the nature of the operation from our number and equipment, but they were told nothing beyond that. We were about to embark on the most ambitious raid into Germany that they or SOE ever attempted, and they didn't ask a single question about it.

"If AK are as professional as this lot, we'll be okay," said Bill.

"Let's hope so!" I replied.

"You're right, Dotty," said Phillip. "We hear good things about them, so let's hope they're well organised."

"They're the unknown quantity," replied Rob. "As you say, let's hope."

"I'd like to be relying on a bit more than hope," said Raymond.

"You can be sure of one thing," I said, "any Pole working against the Nazis in the heart of Germany is a brave man."

"No one doubts their courage, Dot," replied Rob.

On that we all agreed. The Polish Resistance was the largest in Europe. They were an extremely effective force; their renowned courage was fuelled by their hatred of the Germans. The brutal occupation of Poland served to unite its people against the aggressor. This became their greatest strength; all were united against the enemy. You would be hard-pressed to find a Nazi sympathiser amongst the Polish ranks. I couldn't help but make the comparison with the French; a Polish collaborator was as rare as an autumn daffodil. That fact alone gave me confidence.

The ground crew prepared the two Halifax's, and they were rolled out ready for take-off. With our gear aboard, we just waited for the time. They gave us the safety drill, including everything we needed to understand about the Halifax. We then shared a meal with them in the Officers' Mess. Tempsford enjoyed a reputation for taking good care of its SOE agents, but I didn't realise that extended to the Officers' Mess. They served no alcohol, and that applied even to those officers who were not a part of the crew. They asked plenty of questions about us as an SOE special contingent, but never specific details about the operation. We all used our communication code names, and no one strayed from that. We were amidst some of the RAF's finest, and it showed.

At 23:00 hrs, we were kitted out in jump suits and parachutes before being marched off towards the two aeroplanes. They stood menacingly in the darkness side by side on the runway. As we approached, we combined into our two groups. Me in one, Rob in the other. I wanted to remain resolutely professional; I thought perhaps for the sake of appearance we might just wish each other good luck. Rob probably felt the same as me until we neared the aircraft. He broke ranks seconds before I did. We stood on the runway, locked in each other's arms. There were hoots and cheers from all around.

"Remember what I said, Dotty, don't take any chances. I can't live without you."

"I promise," was the only thing I managed to say.

We boarded our respective aircraft and immediately became occupied with procedure. Our last few minutes on British soil seemed to vanish unnoticed. The crew ensured we were secured and at 00.05 hrs the four Merlin 22 engines roared into life. With its light load and up-rated engines, the big aircraft took off surprisingly quickly. Alpha's One and

Two were airborne almost simultaneously. Viewed from the ground, we would have vanished into the night sky within a minute. Lofty and I had the longest flight in Alpha Two, but the RAF boys understood precisely what they were doing. They accumulated a lot of experience flying over Germany; they knew precisely which areas to avoid.

As we crossed the Channel, we were invited forward. I could see the moon's reflection on the water racing beneath us. The sea looked calm and peaceful. When we crossed into occupied Holland and then German territory, it all felt rather less peaceful. Being uninvited guests in your enemy's country is not the most reassuring feeling. We flew over some broken clouds and I caught occasional glimpses of Germany. Hardly any lights appeared, their night time blackout proved to be strictly enforced. The countdown to our first drop near Pinneberg began.

Phillip and Raymond had their chutes hooked up and their canister made ready. We shook hands and wished each other luck. We dropped down from our safe high altitude in search of the drop zone. The crew explained that they might have to make one or two approaches. There was no room for error. The navigator must have been spot-on because they detected the signal from the ground on their first approach. That alone was a considerable achievement. The aircraft approached at its slowest speed but it still left only split seconds for decisions. Phillip sat with his legs dangling in the wind while Raymond stood ready to go, waiting for the green light. An airman stood next to him with his hand on his shoulder.

We trained so hard for occasions like that, when the time came Phillip didn't hesitate, with Ray not two seconds behind him. The cylinder followed two seconds later. The Merlin engines roared back into full power and we climbed up through the cloud cover. So far, so good. The navigator came back to report a textbook drop. What happened on the ground only Raymond and Phillip knew, but the air crew executed their part perfectly. It gave me enormous confidence. The Halifax could fly at an altitude of 24,000 ft. At that height we were relatively safe, certainly from flak. The risk of German night fighters existed, but a lone aircraft presented an elusive target.

The danger came as we descended towards our drop zone southwest of Furth. They approached in a curved descent to avoid possible flak and also to disguise our true course. We were detected from the ground and flashes of exploding AA shells momentarily lit up the fuselage. The Halifax continued undisturbed. I guessed the German gunners were probing the sky rather than targeting us. We descended lower as we approached where the navigator plotted the drop zone. They hooked us up. Lofty stood immediately next to me, the crew stood ready with the cylinder.

I earned my wings during training but jumping out of aeroplanes did not come naturally to me. The wind pushed violently against my legs, as the noise of the wind combined with the engines to exclude all else. The material of my trousers thrashed against my legs and my strap ends flapped. I'm sure my heart must have been pounding, but I didn't notice it. Every sense I possessed prepared me to push off, when a crew member shouted abort! The engines roared back into full power and we climbed steeply above the clouds. I stepped back with something of a sigh of relief. With no sign of the signal, the navigator had to recalculate. This meant going around and risking the flak again in a slightly different approach.

They closed the "Joe hole", and we were left again with no sight of the outside world. Several minutes passed before I felt the aircraft start another descent. Again the flak lit up the inside of the fuselage but this time it shook the Halifax violently. One after another, exploding shells buffeted the aircraft. Each shock wave hit us like a mighty hand swatting a fly. A near hit would tear us apart. Not having experienced flak before, I found it quite terrifying. We were at the mercy of random chance, as Lady Luck rolled the dice and we waited to see if we won or lost. The crew remained very calm, which reassured me. Suddenly the hatch slid open again, and we took our places. The flak receded into the distance behind us, and the engines throttled back.

A crewman stood with his hand on my shoulder, shouting, "Get ready, it looks good."

Minutes felt like seconds and the seconds vanished. Once again the wind lashed at my legs and the noise isolated me from everything around me. The light went green and the hand on my shoulder pushed me. The sudden impact of the air resistance knocks the wind out of you. My stomach plunged in one direction only to be wrenched back in another when the chute opened. One moment the roar of the aircraft and the wind fills your senses, the next moment you are immersed in relative silence. Looking down, I just made out the outline of a field rapidly approaching me. Above, I saw Lofty safely following me. In the dark, the ground seemed to fly up towards me extraordinarily quickly, but I maintained a good line. I braced and landed perfectly towards the edge of the field. You hope desperately that you are in the right place, but still have to act as if you aren't.

I instantly gathered in my parachute and ran towards cover. Only then did I look for Lofty and the canister. He landed awkwardly in a depression; it was bad luck. The canister crashed into a hedgerow. With no sign of AK, I hid my chute in the hedgerow by pushing it deep into the undergrowth at the base. Lofty limped away towards me. His thumbs up came as a relief. Had he been injured at this stage it might have been a disaster. The next thing we saw was a flashlight and the sound of someone approaching.

We assumed it was AK, but there is that part of you that has to think it might not be! My Sten Gun hung safely around my body, I now prepared to use it. When I heard the password, "*gajowy*", which roughly translates to gamekeeper, I knew we had found them. They were as pleased to see us as we were to see them. There were four of them, three men and a woman. They spared no time for pleasantries, we obviously needed to get out of there as quickly as possible.

Chapter Thirty-Two
Welcome To Germany

Two of the men carried the canister, and the woman told us to follow them through a wooded area. Her tone of voice and their haste to leave all showed a sense of urgency. Lofty and I looked at each other, the imminent danger obviously concerning them now became our own imminent danger. They made full use of their local knowledge; they knew their way in the dark. Within minutes we reached a small open-backed lorry full of bales of straw. The bales concealed a hollow space in the middle where they hastily directed Lofty and me to follow the canister. They bundled us into the open space without ceremony. We both breathed heavily as they placed the bales over us. The dust instantly caught in my throat, and I started coughing.

One of them told me to be quiet; I understood what he said well enough! I desperately tried not to cough but the straw dust made it almost impossible. We pulled away and drove over an extremely rough track. They didn't avoid the ruts; we needed to get away from there in haste. We were thrown from one side to the other, one moment Lofty lay on top of me, the next moment I landed on top of him. All the while, the dust filled our eyes and lungs; we had difficulty breathing. When we found ourselves on a made-up road, it didn't come a moment too soon.

"We have to stop meeting like this, Dotty."

"There's nothing I would like more. Can you try to get off of me? You're pressing my Sten Gun into my chest. I can hardly breathe."

"Mac said we would work closely together."

"Yes, but not this bloody close, get off!"

Try as he may, Lofty struggled to get away from me. The bales collapsed around us and the canister now pressed against him. We had to make the best of a difficult situation. Lofty, gentleman that he is, took his weight on his elbows. Even in that awful position, he made me laugh. I doubt a situation existed that Lofty couldn't make a joke of it.

"Tell me when you get bored with this missionary position; we can try something more adventurous."

He joked, but we were in a nasty situation. Whatever the danger that caused us to flee the drop zone, we were trapped and helpless to respond. The journey seemed as if it took an age; in reality it probably took about half an hour. Half an hour where we remained exposed on an open road. With travel restricted and petrol rationed, a vehicle travelling in the dead of night would be extremely conspicuous. All of those thoughts and more filled our minds. I have never felt more helpless than I did under those bales of straw.

Nothing about operating in Germany compared to Occupied France. The notion of a safe house did not exist in the same context. The risk the Polish Resistance took on our behalf should never be underestimated. AK were enormously successful operating in their own country. So much so that German reprisals against them attained a level of barbarity difficult for us to comprehend. As a result, their activities had to be scaled back for periods. We had been extensively briefed about AK, but still didn't know what to expect.

As a nation, they suffered horribly at the hands of the Nazis when they invaded Poland. To compound their misery, the Polish nation then had to contend with the Russians advancing from the east who brought with them even more unspeakable horrors, the massacre of 4500 Polish officers in the Katyn forest being one example. Against that backdrop, the Poles were prepared to facilitate our operation in the heart of Germany. Here they did not have the option of disappearing into the community as they might in Poland. Whoever they were, the people helping us didn't lack courage.

The lorry stopped not a moment too soon. I felt as if I couldn't take another minute. We heard the banging of doors and voices. A dim light shone through the cracks in the bales. Those cracks became windows of light as they removed the bales entombing us. We must have looked a sorry sight, lying one on top of the other, covered in straw. Finally, we saw our new friends, as they gathered around us with the aid of an oil lamp. The woman offered me her hand with a welcoming smile.

"Welcome to Germany," she said in very good English. "I am Krystyna, this is Jan, Tomasz, and Stanislaw."

"My code name is Goshawk, and this is Osprey."

"Yes, but what are your names?"

I hesitated for a moment, but I didn't tell her. I knew they had work permits for us, and therefore we had names. In the alien world that we inhabited, I wondered if she had given us their real names. I intuitively thought she had. I guessed Krystyna to be about my age, late twenties, but she looked older. Her chestnut brown hair hung lank and unkempt. She probably had lovely eyes before the war; they were still there but sunken into her skull. It made her cheekbones appear even more prominent, and the hollow at the base of her neck sat in a dark shadow cast by the oil lamp.

The years of Nazi occupation hung on them like an old threadbare coat. Emaciated and dressed in whatever they managed to lay their hands on, they looked like the product of a broken nation. Broken, that is, until their indomitable spirit shone past the worst that the Nazis had done to them. I have met no one whose tired bodies concealed people of such stature.

Jan clearly had an attachment with Krystyna. Of a similar age, he had once been studying to be a doctor in Poland where he met Krystyna. With his blonde hair and blue eyes, I could easily imagine they would have made a beautiful couple in pre-war Poland. No doubt they envisaged a bright future. None of that remained; the Nazis took something beautiful and replaced it with emaciated war-weary bodies. He had a smattering of English, about as much as I had of Polish. I had so many questions for them, and they wanted to be told everything about ourselves and the progress of the war. My first question was, are we safe? Krystyna smiled and nodded.

We were sheltering in a rundown farm building on the outskirts of Furth. The farmer was German with a Polish wife. When I asked if they trusted him, Jan looked at me with a frown. Apparently the man had Jewish ancestry, which alone was more than enough to get him killed in Nazi Germany. When I asked how secure we were, they rubbed their hands along their weapons. They carried an assortment of guns, all of them stolen from the Germans.

I noticed immediately that they had an MP 38, and two MP 40 submachine guns. Tomasz carried an MP 35 made by Bergmann for use by the Waffen-SS. I recognised all these weapons from training and from Caen. They understood precisely what they were doing; all those weapons fired the same 9mm Parabellum ammunition. These were freedom fighters in the genuine sense of the word. They would fight their way out of any confrontation with the Germans, and I understood why.

In Occupied France, if an SOE agent found themselves apprehended, they would deny everything and maintain their false identity. The Poles were forced labour; they should never be anywhere other than their place of work or where they slept. For many, they worked and slept in the same place. Krystyna made it clear that if they were stopped and questioned, they would only have one reason for not being at work. Either they were going to or coming from their place of work. The same applied, therefore, to our false identities. So if we were stopped any distance from our place of work, or at any time of the day not consistent with that, we could potentially be shot on the spot.

They lived in a world where they were not just second-class citizens; their lives had no value. In Poland, a German might shoot a Jew or a Pole for the slightest infringement and it would have no more significance than swatting a fly. What that does to a person's spirit, I dared not imagine, but the result stood before me. Their humanity had been crushed almost out of existence. In its place, they had a steely determination to fight back. Courage built upon hatred for their oppressors. They were prepared to take enormous risks on our behalf.

The Germans made a fundamental mistake when they tried to subjugate the Poles. They thought by treating them as valueless second-class citizens, they would behave as such. It seems this is a mistake that tyrants have made throughout history; they fall prey to their own falsehoods. I saw it in my own people of the East End of London during the Blitz, and I saw it in those brave Poles. They turned their contempt and hatred into an unassailable courage.

All the while we spoke, nothing had been mentioned about the overpowering stink filling the building. I knew precisely where it came from, no one is more familiar with the smell of pig shit than me. When

I worked on Reg's farm, I cleaned out the pigs regularly; but this smell resulted from not cleaning them out. When I mentioned it, they all looked at each other with a knowing expression.

Stanislaw beckoned us into the pigpen; Lofty and I followed apprehensively. Tomasz picked up a large, long-handled scraper and cleared part of the floor while Stanislaw ushered the pigs away. A concealed trap door emerged. Closely fitting and barely visible, it had no obvious way to lift it. Jan produced a large turnkey. He slotted it into a small hole, a half turn and he lifted the heavy door. It revealed a wooden staircase leading down into an underground cellar.

It reminded me of one of the public underground shelters in London. There were bunk beds, tables, and chairs. The barn had no electricity or lighting, but to my amazement the cellar had an electric light. In pride of place, a German field radio sat on its own little table. It boasted some comforts of home, except for the smell. Lofty thought he would never get used to it but I assured him I had a lot of experience with pig shit, and in next to no time he wouldn't even notice it. Krystyna laughed and agreed.

I then suggested we unpack the canister. Lofty smiled at me as they dived into the contents. They opened it like the children of an orphanage might open a pillowcase full of Christmas presents. They had so little, and what they did have, had been hard won. The contents of the canister were manna from heaven. They touched and caressed the weapons. Each one carefully placed with reverence. Lofty removed the explosives and detonators to reveal an enormous pile of army food rations. That is the reason I suggested we open it. British army rations were nothing to write home about but when you have been undernourished for years, they represented a banquet.

Our rag-tag bunch of resistance fighters were but a minor cog in a much larger wheel. AK's web of connections might have been spread thin in Germany but nevertheless, every link in the chain led back to AK. Brave people like our group were the last link in our particular chain. Krystyna and Tomasz worked on the farm as forced labour. In other circumstances, their lives would have been far more intolerable.

Jan, despite his medical training, had been forced to drive an ambulance for the Germans. Stanislaw worked in an engineering factory because as a qualified engineer he had skills the Germans needed. Each one of them had been forcibly removed from Poland to work in Germany. If their lot in life sounds bleak, then you have to remember - they were the lucky ones. Thousands of Poles were worked to death as slaves, including those forced to work on the V1 and the V2 in the underground tunnels at Mittelwerk. Even closer to home, over 16,000 people were forced to work as slave labour in the Channel Islands, building fortifications - many of those came from Poland.

One of our first priorities was to notify Station M of our safe arrival. AK had long since established excellent communications with MI6 and Bletchley Park. They all knew how to use the radio transmitter, but Krystyna was the principal operator. Communications with Rolo at Station M had already been established. Krystyna sent a single word code, she repeated it three times only, and stopped transmitting. The Germans were not as actively trying to intercept radio signals in their own country as they did in Occupied France or Poland but she still took no chances, sending the briefest possible signal.

Every second that passed, I worried about Rob. I liked to delude myself that he really was invincible, but that only applied when we were together. Not being together, I worried like any other woman who had a man in the forces, except what Rob and I did was not like the other forces. Lofty and I had been the last drop so, failing disasters, we should have been the last to confirm our safe arrival. Every minute that elapsed provided another minute for me to conjure up a worst-case scenario. The second I heard the transmission my heart jumped. Krystyna wrote the letters down, it amounted to one code word sent three times. As she decoded the word, I had to admit the obvious to myself - the odds of four successful drops in an enemy country were not in our favour.

I watched as the letters spelt the word, "summer". We had four teams and four potential outcomes. Rolo chose a season for each one. Summer was what I wanted to hear. I punched the air with a cry of "yes". Lofty did exactly the same. Our Polish friends were only aware of our own operation so my reaction was ill-advised. They must have made some assumptions, but they said nothing. I couldn't help but think about Lily and everyone at Middlebourne. I pictured Susan in the communication hut with Rolo standing by her side. Everyone else would wait in Hut 3 desperate for our signal. At that precise moment, they would be celebrating the success of Phase One.

Jan and Stanislaw had to be leaving well before dawn and none of us had slept at all, so they decided to call it a day. Lofty and I had only known them for a short time, but we both felt an immediate connection and an implicit trust. We hugged each other like long established comrades. They told us to stay put in the cellar until one of them opened the door the next day. As the hatch closed, we became a little like an Egyptian pharaoh entombed for all time. I heard the pig muck being scraped back over the door. Our lives were now in their hands.

"What do you make of them, Dot?"

"I suspect there's far more to this group than we realise. They have access to the forgers who will provide us with work documents, and somehow they do all this while being forced labour. They have far-reaching connections."

"You're right, and you wouldn't want to tangle with them, would you?"

"They've got nerves of steel and more guts than a butcher's shop. They drive around carrying those weapons. If they're stopped, they don't intend to bluff their way out, do they?"

"They're people who have nothing left to lose."

"There's no one more dangerous than a person who has nothing to lose. I really admire them."

"Me too. I think this might work."

With that reassuring thought, we both turned toward our bunks.

"I need to go outside, Lofty, I need a wee."

"I think that's what the bucket is for."

"Have you lost your mind? I'm not having a wee in front of you!"

"Well, if you don't, I will."

I turned my back as he made that noise that only a man and a tin bucket can make. Unfortunately, he proved to be right about the bucket. Toilet arrangements for SOE agents are best glossed over.

Chapter Thirty-Three
Untermenschen

Neither of us slept well; our minds didn't rest. Both awake, we just waited for someone to knock on the hatch. When it came, we both breathed a sigh of relief in unison; two rapid knocks followed a moment later by another. I remembered it as the letter U in Morse Code – dot, dot, dash. We were greeted by Krystyna's gaunt but smiling face. She declared it safe for us to venture out into the fresh air, an offer we eagerly accepted. The contrast in light and air instantly lifted our spirits.

We welcomed our first glimpse of the surrounding area. I'm not sure what I expected but the countryside was beautiful. A gently undulating green landscape reminiscent of England disappeared into the distance. A patchwork quilt of fields with areas of forest disappearing towards the horizon. I even recognised some cattle; they were Aberdeen Angus. In a separate field in the distance I saw a breed of cattle I hadn't seen before, a lovely red brown colour. Krystyna told me they were Angeln cattle. Perhaps a part of me expected the evil of Nazi Germany to be reflected in its landscape. Needless to say, it wasn't. We fight over it, we often lay waste to it, but Mother Earth is only ever a spectator to the abuses of humankind.

The first priority was photographs of me and Lofty. Krystyna produced a Leica camera and understood precisely how to use it. She had obviously done this before, probably many times. The requirements for our forged work permits and passes were precise. Without them, we dare not go anywhere. When I asked how long they would take, she told us they were already complete, only our photographs had to be included. We would have our documents by the evening. This left us with what amounted to a day of rest. It all felt slightly surreal; we wandered about the farm with Krystyna and Tomasz keeping a constant eye on us. Once or twice, we had to make ourselves scarce as various people came and went, but by and large we just relaxed.

Come the evening, Jan and Stanislaw joined us and we sat together in the still evening air. Our brief holiday ended. They presented us with our documents, and I immediately realised just how connected these people were. First, we needed a *"Kennkarte"*, our basic identity document. This folded into a six-page document, and crucially for the Germans they were colour-coded for ethnicity, ours being grey for Polish. What you didn't want in Germany was a yellow one. That denoted you as a Jew or a Romany. A bold letter J made sure there was no mistake. Russians, Belarusians, Ukrainians, etc had a blue document, with an identifying letter for each region. I quickly realised the Nazis were obsessed with ethnicity.

The next and vital document was our work permit, *"Arbeitskarte"*. The local Employment Office issued these and crucially it contained the name of our designated workplace. We were both classified as *"Zivilarbeiter"* which meant civilian worker. They gave us both a cloth badge that had to be sewn onto our clothing. It proclaimed the letter P. I found that very disturbing. I immediately noticed that we had work permits for the foundry we were sent there to destroy, Hofmann and Kohler, Gmbh.

"What does it mean to be a *Zivilarbeiter*?" I asked.

"This is good," replied Krystyna. "This means you are an ethnic Pole from the German governed regions of Poland."

"Why is this good?" asked Lofty. "Does this give us some kind of privilege?"

"Oh, yes!" she replied. "It means you can be paid. The wage will be a fraction of that of a German worker, but at least it's something."

"Why do we need the badge?" I asked.

"That is so the Germans can treat you as *"Untermenschen"*, which means sub-human."

"Are you serious?" Lofty asked.

"Oh yes. You are not allowed on any kind of public transport. There are many public spaces where you may not go, and you certainly can't go somewhere like a library or restaurant. Our food ration is smaller, our working hours are longer, we have no holidays, and we work seven days a week. Anything of value is forbidden, we may not even possess a cigarette lighter. That camera this morning would have got me shot!"

"What would be worse than being a *Zivilarbeiter*?" I asked.

"Everything else is worse! *"Ostarbeitor"* means eastern worker. They are effectively slaves. They live in camps and that is where many of them die. Perhaps the worst of all is being a young woman. They are taken as sex-slaves to work in German military brothels for the amusement of the Third Reich. Even that kind of existence has to be seen as a privilege because we are Polish. The worst crime you can commit is to be born a Jew. The best they can hope for is to be worked to death."

"What do you mean, Krystyna?" I asked. "How can that be the best they can hope for?"

"That would give them a few more weeks or months of life; most of them are killed within an hour of reaching the camps. We will tell you everything you need to know about that; we want you to go back to England and tell them. For now, we have to concentrate on your operation."

If I hadn't seen it before, I could see it then - their hatred of the Nazis was so obvious. They were more than prepared to risk their lives to help us. For them, an act of sabotage which might shorten the war was worth dying for. It focused my attention I can tell you. I looked at our documents again. I had become Natalia Wozniak, Lofty went by the name of Jakub Kowalczyk. We both worked at Hofmann and Kohler. If we were seen outside of work, we needed a reason for being wherever we happened to be. We could not own a bicycle or use a bus, so we had to walk everywhere. The regulation banning us from public transport ensured the German people did not have to suffer the indignity of being near us.

Outside of the military and officials, only the well-to-do had access to a car. Petrol rationing made it even more difficult, even for the privileged few. One of those privileged few was Stanislaw! He possessed the gold-plated version of the *Arbeitskarte*. They classified Stanislaw as *"Gastarbeitnehmer"*, or guest worker. Older than the rest of them, Stanislaw was an aeronautical engineer. Highly qualified and well known in his native Poland, the Germans fast-tracked him into the design and development arm of Messerschmitt. His highly privileged position allowed him access to a motor vehicle. While we could not use public transport or own any valuable possessions, nothing in the regulations forbade us from riding in a car. Our Polish friends knew precisely what they were doing.

Stanislaw produced two of the privileges of his position, a freshly baked loaf of bread and a bottle of German wine. Krystyna unwrapped a piece of cheese, and Jan proudly produced a jar of pickled cabbage. Supplemented with some British army rations, what lay before us amounted to a banquet, a rare treat for them. Personally, I found the *sauerkraut* to be disgusting, but they eagerly devoured it. The scented air cooled as the setting sun slowly melted into the distant horizon taking the warmth of the evening with it. For a moment, our gathering felt like a group of friends enjoying a glimpse of normality. It might have been an illusion, but we enjoyed it all the more.

"To Natalia and Jakub," Krystyna said.

We raised our chipped earthenware mugs, each generously filled with Riesling, and proposed a toast to our operation. We established an instant bond with them. We each sat with the letter P sewn onto our clothes. It didn't single us out as *untermenschen,* it united us in strength. I wore it as a badge of honour. The Nazis created, encouraged, and ultimately exalted the racial and ethnic hatred which suffocated their minds and justified their actions. We six sat together united by our common purpose.

Lofty and I slept well that night. Our evening spent sharing simple pleasures had brought us all closer together. When Tomasz opened the hatch to our cellar in the morning, he did so as a friend. The morning rituals were performed as best we could, and breakfast, such as it was, didn't take long. Operation Cormorant had begun. Stanislaw would arrive at the farm soon after first light. He would be there to buy his generous ration of two eggs, with his ration book stamped accordingly.

He would then drive us the short distance into Furth, for us to join the throng of early morning workers outside the Hofmann Kohler works. The larger day shift would arrive, while the smaller night shift left. Lofty and I would mingle with the workers, keeping our mouths shut, finally wandering away as a part of the retiring night shift for Tomasz to pick us up in the small lorry on his way back from delivering eggs to the butcher's shop. They thought the possibility of us being stopped by local police or Gestapo to be very unlikely in that part of Bavaria. Should it happen, we would present our papers and say as little as possible. In all likelihood, the local policeman would not speak Polish.

Stanislaw arrived on time. Krystyna stamped his ration book as Tomasz placed his two eggs on the front seat wrapped in newspaper. A wave and we were on our way. Driving out of the farm onto the road, it quickly became apparent just how remote we were. We passed the village of Ritzmannshof, it amounted to nothing more than a few buildings. We left it behind almost immediately. Travelling southeast, the outskirts of Furth appeared little more than a few miles away. Lofty and I had studied maps of Furth until we saw them in our sleep. As soon as we orientated ourselves with our memory of the map, we realised how close we were to the foundry. Should it prove necessary, we could easily walk the seven miles.

Stanislaw dropped us off about a thousand yards away from the works on Lobitzweg Strasse. I thanked him in Polish and we made a point of innocently waving goodbye. We stood some distance from the centre of Furth with its monuments and fine architecture. Fingers of farmland gave way to residential areas containing relatively modest housing, small closely spaced houses with red-tiled roofs and little pockets of garden. One or two inhabitants looked up; most chose to look away. Ordinary working-class people, probably not a Nazi among them, but still they chose to look away.

Ahead of us lay the industrial area. Many of the buildings spoke of a time from another century. Blackened by decades of smoke and dust, some buildings had broken windows and were cluttered with discarded paraphernalia. Piles of scrap metal sat in racks, dressed in a blanket of rust. None of it looked like modern heavy industry; this relatively small collection of industrial buildings consisted largely of artisan and craft workshops. Some of the craft workshops appeared to belong to a bygone age. No doubt many of the artisans who once worked there were now fighting on the eastern front, unlikely to return, even if they survived the war.

Sheet metal fabrication, glass blowing, metal grinding and welding sat alongside jewellery manufacture and a silversmith. Some of the empty buildings had desecrated signs and graffiti that spoke of an abrupt end to long-established family businesses, the principal exception being the Hofmann Kohler works. By far the largest industrial building, its blackened walls sprawled over a third of the area like so much creeping bitumen.

Smoke from its tall chimney announced its presence long before we saw the building. The grey column of smoke snaked its way vertically into the air before eventually bowing to the soft breeze. As we walked closer, the number of workers walking in the same direction increased. Not everyone headed for the foundry, but they all had the same thing in common. Sunken eyes and prominent cheekbones accompanied by blank expressions. Every one of them walked with their head down, no one wanted to draw attention to themselves. They wore their cloth badges just like us. Many wore the letter P, but there were also Ukrainians and Belarussians. Those without a badge troubled us most.

Hardly anyone spoke. A word out-of-place might be overheard by the secret police. Not a single person made eye contact. A combination of fear, indoctrination, and fatigue fixed their gaze to the ground. We immediately adopted the same posture as our fellow workers, heads down with a shuffling gait. Anonymity came easily. Our principal interest was the security at Hofmann Kohler, but the movement of the workers from the other factories was also important. We watched carefully who went where.

As we approached the main entrance, we saw the workers being checked in by civilian-looking guards. Prominent among them, a man dressed in civilian clothes but wearing a swastika armband pushed the workers around as I might have separated Reg's pigs. Another stood at the large double doors, the entrance to the works. I noticed how the workers assiduously avoided looking in their direction. Another man not wearing an armband received a similar wide berth. The secret police had a presence, as we expected they would. We decided anyone not wearing a cloth badge had to be viewed with considerable suspicion.

Our eyes were everywhere, as far as we dared. Our training taught us to be especially observant. Little things that others would miss we noted. When the small night shift started to come out, I noticed they did not appear as a group. They came out in one's and two's, with a delay between them. I concluded there must be a security check as they left. Institutional mistrust was their daily gruel. They lived and breathed it; we recognised it in all of its guises. In an instant, the foundry security became apparent.

The workers in the foundry didn't know what they were producing. The castings would be familiar to them but they would not know what they were for. They probably produced many types of casings for engines, the V2 components would be just another casting. This and the absence of a uniformed presence told us precisely what we needed to know.

The waiting day shift amounted to about twenty-five workers, and so we concealed ourselves among a crowd of people. The moment the day shift started to go in, we had to mingle with the much smaller out-going shift. Lofty noticed the security looking at him. Try as we may, years of abuse and undernourishment results in an expression of fear that is hard to replicate. We had a coded signal that warned me.

I immediately turned my back towards the swastika armband and bent over double coughing loudly as if I had difficulty breathing. A sickly worker would only draw his attention for a few seconds, but it provided sufficient time for Lofty to move away. I made a miraculous recovery and joined him with three of the night shift. We said nothing, just walked away with our heads down. The three workers did exactly the same. They walked as if every laboured step might be their last. When I looked at them, they offered no recognition, they glanced at me, but they didn't see me. Whatever lay behind those dark sunken eyes didn't even have the strength to acknowledge a fellow human being.

The three of them entered a damaged building. A plume of soot rose above a broken window where flames once licked the brickwork. Other window panes were broken with long jagged cracks emanating from holes in the glass. The front door had splinters of wood where the lock had once been housed. Although partially removed, we saw the remains of a Star of David painted on the door. Furth had a large pre-war Jewish population.

We can only imagine the horrors which followed the desecration of that house. The Jewish occupants would have been forcibly removed and their home ransacked. Anything of value would have been stolen, anything useful destroyed. The same applied to the deserted factory buildings. As for the occupants themselves, they would no doubt have been transported to one of the death camps.

I looked at Lofty as the three emaciated people disappeared into what had once been someone else's life. That pattern of events would have been repeated all over Germany. It began on November 9th-10th

1938 when the Nazi leadership instigated a series of pogroms against the Jewish community in Germany. Known as *Kristallnacht,* it marked the moment when the Nazis crossed the divide. They embraced the fire and brimstone of the hell they created.

With their possessions looted or destroyed and their homes and business premises re-purposed, the Nazis then wanted to erase every trace of the Jews. The look in Lofty's eyes said it all. Two houses further along, the same thing had happened. The people may be gone but generations of families left a memory of themselves in the fabric of those buildings. The Nazis only saw the Utopia they'd created in their own image. They were oblivious to the sea of memories lapping at their feet. I looked at the buildings and heard children playing and parents laughing. I felt the horror they experienced as they confronted their persecutors.

Tomasz appeared not a moment too soon. Had I been confronted at that moment by one of those swastika-wearing Nazis, I would probably have killed him! Driving away, we noticed several more ransacked homes, each one equating to a shattered life. Tomasz had seen it so often it became that most dangerous of events - normal. We drove back, using a slightly different route to give us another perspective. This time, we passed some of the Allied bomb damage that had occurred. Furth had its own strategic targets like the aircraft assembly and repair works, but its greatest offence was to be next to the industrial city of Nuremberg.

Repeated Allied bombing raids destroyed numerous targets such as the Mann factory that built diesel engines for submarines and Panther tanks. The large Nuremberg motorcycle industry had been targeted as well as the marshalling yard. Even the old historic centre of Nuremberg was completely destroyed. The Bachmann von Blumenthal aeroplane factory in Furth where Stanislaw worked was bombed in April 1945. The bomb damage we saw only confirmed the indiscriminate nature of war. We assumed one of the industrial factories had been the target, but residential homes had suffered.

Our first reconnaissance operation had been brief but extremely useful. We returned that evening when the shift changed, and again the next day. Using different approaches to the foundry, we formed a complete picture of the layout and movement of people. Their security was deliberately low-key. Rather than draw attention to the foundry, the Nazis chose not to have a uniformed presence. That implied the

Sicherheitsdienst were involved. This is the intelligence agency of the SS. They would normally be dressed in uniform, so this had to be a significant departure from normal procedure. We had seen the swastika armbands and the obviously authoritative personnel who formed the security. They were about as inconspicuous as a bloody nose.

Lofty and I agreed; anything involved with the production of the V2 must have top level security. The precautions being taken at the Hofmann Kohler works appeared to us to be more concerned with internal security rather than an external threat. Why else would they meticulously search the workers before they left, and why would they not have a military guarded perimeter. Tomasz provided the answer.

"How can you trust someone you consider inferior and who you have to force to work for you? This is all a part of their obsession with controlling us. They create their own insecurity."

"I think you're right, Tomasz," replied Lofty. "This is their weakness."

"It appears the number of SD personnel is proportionate to the number of workers," I said. "This confirms where their priority lies. It also implies that the smaller night shift has less security."

"What we desperately need to know is just how many are there, and how can we identify them?" Lofty asked.

"We knew you would ask that question, Jakub," Krystyna said. "It is too risky for one of us to get inside the works, but we could try to recruit one of the workers."

"I've already thought of that," I said. "How risky would that be, Krystyna? Do you know any of them?"

"There is no social life away from work. So no, we don't know anyone, but many of them are Polish. The problem will be that they will not trust us, Natalia."

"I think you should try. But tell them nothing."

"The moment we ask anyone about security, they will realise. There is another thing. We decided not to tell you and Jakub, but perhaps you should know. If your operation is successful, there will be an inevitable outcome. As soon as the SD realises it is sabotage, they will interrogate all the workers."

"Oh, my God! They'll kill them, won't they?"

"The best we can hope for, Natalia, is that they confine the reprisals to the night workers."

My heart sank like a stone. Lofty and I had considered every eventuality, every outcome except for that. It should have occurred to me. I knew Lofty so well; he thought exactly the same thing I did. How could we live with ourselves knowing we had condemned those innocent people? We exchanged glances but no words. Our unspoken conversation said a thousand words that we could not bring ourselves to utter. Krystyna put her hand on my shoulder.

"This is why we didn't tell you. You are good people; you live by values the Nazis have abandoned; you value life. We have seen things you can't even imagine. We know where all those people go that the Germans consider *"Lebensunwertes Leben"*: life unworthy of life. They are killing thousands every day. When you have seen these horrors, it is no longer possible to place a value on each and every life. To try to do so would consume anyone in an instant. For us, death is our constant companion, as it is for those workers. We are all prepared to die, and so are they."

It was an impassioned speech. All four of them might have appeared to have lost their humanity along the way, but this is how they defended themselves from the world they lived in. Krystyna quickly wiped tears from her eyes, reverting to her hard exterior as if it were a suit of armour. A lot of my humanity had been left on the streets of Caen; I knew she was right. The lives of six people are neither here nor there unless, that is, they live in your consciousness.

We agreed they would try to get information from one of the workers. That essentially meant recruiting one of them because they would realise what the questions were for. It also meant one of them risking their life to ask that question. I didn't doubt we were taking an enormous risk, but the success of the operation depended upon inside information. Lofty and I were ready in all other respects. We had the layout of the foundry in our minds. We knew the movement of the workers and memorised the faces of each member of the night shift. The faces of the known SD had also been committed to memory.

The wait proved more difficult than the observation. If any of them were discovered, we would all be in danger. They avoided contact with us for a few days, only Krystyna opened the hatch night and morning. When they all appeared one evening, we realised they had something to say. Jan looked pleased with himself.

"I have what you want, Natalia," he said. "I chose my man carefully.

It took two days for him to trust me, but the moment he did, he agreed. There are two SD guards each night. There is no production at night but the furnaces have to be kept burning so the night shift are skilled maintenance people. The two security guards follow them around all night, watching their movements. I told him nothing, but he told me he would do everything he could. He provided me with a drawing of the interior layout of the foundry."

"Did you tell him not to say anything to his colleagues?"

"Of course. I impressed upon him to say nothing to anyone."

"Do you trust him?"

"He is Polish, so yes I trust him as much as it is possible."

"Okay!" I said. "Krystyna, send the ready signal."

Krystyna knew what to do but not why she was doing it. Operation Cormorant relied upon a simultaneous attack on all four production sites. Once one had been attacked, the Germans might put two and two together and assume their V2 program had been compromised. The ready signal meant exactly that. When all four teams had made ready, we could confirm the time. Another excruciating wait followed. Waiting for news is agony when you're desperate to receive it. We maintained reconnaissance every other day. The Germans despised the forced labourers so much they didn't exist in their eyes. They foolishly refused to see what hid in plain sight right in front of them. Once or twice they might look at one of us, but they didn't see us, they only saw an *Untermensch,* an inferior person.

We had one or two moments when we encountered German troops or police on our travels. On one occasion, we had to present our papers. Tomasz spoke in broken German and the German helpfully spoke no Polish. My heart was in my mouth. As I handed him my papers, my hand went to my .38 pistol. I had never been more pleased to be *Untermensch*; we were beneath their attention. Nevertheless, every day the operation became extended put us at greater risk. When the signal finally came through, I breathed a sigh of relief. The brief coded message brought the best possible news. All four teams were in place and ready, including Rob. The time to go was the night of September 23rd. The moon would be reasonably favourable, and the weather looked set fair. Krystyna sent back confirmation. We would go in two days' time!

Chapter Thirty-Four
Operation Cormorant

Operation Cormorant began on September 23rd, 1944 at 00:15 hrs. Even without communication between us, I knew all four operations had begun. Rob would be on his way. During those long hours trapped in our underground cellar, those four bare walls confining us left Lofty and me with little else to do but prepare our weapons and explosives. We mentally rehearsed every step we would follow until it became so familiar it felt like a recalled memory. We considered every eventuality; every element of the operation had a Plan B, and even a Plan C. Preparedness is always the key to success. It removes fear of the unknown and replaces it with confidence.

There is always the unexpected; the unforeseen event, the "what if" - those moments when the wind drops from your sails. With any luck, the unforeseen event would fall into one of our broad scenarios. If not, we'd have to fall back on our instincts. We confidently didn't expect that to happen. This was not Caen, where the unexpected waited around every corner.

The enemy made the not-altogether poor decision to conceal the manufacture of V2 components in plain sight. When you embark upon a secret deception, it should be foolproof. There in the heart of their homeland, the enemy had been complacent. Just like the stick insect, the slightest inconsistency, or a single mistake, can give the game away. Lofty and I chuckled between ourselves when we thought about how successfully we fooled the Germans into thinking the invasion would take place in Calais. Operation Fortitude had been flawless; individual operations like Operation Mincemeat, were meticulous.

The scale of Operation Fortitude had been enormous. Fake tanks and aeroplanes. Divisions of troops which didn't exist. In comparison, the Germans' attempt to conceal the production of aluminium castings proved to be a fiasco. They thought the V2 components were hidden in plain sight; instead, their fatal error hid in plain sight! They overlooked the obvious, that foundries always put their initials inside the castings!

Tomasz puffed up his cheeks as he loaded our heavy packs onto the lorry. As a precaution, we each wore our regular day clothes with our Polish badges. With our threadbare, ill-fitting garments we looked indistinguishable from the forced labourers. Our appearance had served us well. We were two more autumn leaves beneath the tree. The time had come to drop the charade. Armed and carrying heavy packs, we would stand out like a sore thumb. We had to transform from autumn leaves into snakes-in-the-grass.

The squealing pigs calmed down as we left the barn. We became nocturnal predators, the dead of night our natural domain. Tomasz drove with Krystyna sitting beside him. Lofty and I sat uncomfortably in the back. We each carried a Sten Gun and a belt of five magazines. A lorry travelling in the dead of night would instantly draw attention. Our documents were now replaced with sub-machine guns. With eyes already adjusted to the moonlight, we were ready for the challenge that lay ahead.

Light cotton-wool clouds shared a dance with the moon, each pirouetting in and out of prominence. One moment the moon defined the landscape in colourless light and dark. The next moment, the shadow and light merged to form the uniform grey of a sea mist. Without a word passing between us, the engine rumbled into life and we left the sanctuary of the farm. Travelling with no lights, we needed Lady Luck to light the way for us. During the day, we would have called it a patch of blue just large enough to mend a sailor's trousers. Now we called it our vision from God.

Lady Luck dealt us three aces that night. Only occasional clouds no thicker than cigarette smoke drifted over us. Tomasz knew every twist and turn in the road. He intuitively avoided the potholes and ruts without looking. We played to full advantage the hand Lady Luck had dealt us. The road remained completely empty. No one noticed us, nobody challenged us. Tomasz drove as near as he dared; just on the edge of the industrial area, there was a place where two small lorries always parked at night. Tomasz inconspicuously pulled in behind them and immediately switched off the motor. The old engine rumbled on for a second before shuddering abruptly into silence.

None of us moved. I was only aware of my heart beating. We just waited to be sure we remained unnoticed. What greeted us was the undisturbed still of the night, the only noise being the ticks and cracks coming from the cooling engine. Our plan had been rehearsed a hundred times. Nothing needed to be said. Krystyna and Tomasz would come with us part of the way inside the industrial area. Moving silently, we melted in and out of the shadows cast by the moon. A moth in search of the light would have been no more visible. Within moments, we came to an unused empty building. Once the home of a family jewellery business, it now provided secure cover for our friends. If the operation went hopelessly wrong and we had to beat a hasty retreat, they would be our backup.

"Good luck, Natalia, Jakub," said Krystyna. "Be sure to come back to us."

"It's Dorothy. And don't worry, we know what we're doing."

She hugged us both and Tomasz shook our hands.

We slipped out the door back into the night. Lady Luck looked down upon us again. She summoned a bank of clouds to roll across the moon's iridescent face. Like a snuffed-out candle, the moon retreated behind the cloud and the ambient light reduced almost to nothing. The old working buildings were tall, and the windows were too numerous to employ an effective blackout. Lights shone from nooks, crannies, and even whole windows. The way ahead could not have been better sign-posted. First, we needed to be sure where the night guards were. Our reconnaissance told us that two guards were patrolling around the factory buildings.

They posed a threat that we should either eliminate or avoid. If we avoided them, they remained a threat. If we eliminated them, we didn't know when they might be missed. Our decision became obvious when one of them walked towards us. He obligingly announced his presence with a torch. A convenient doorway provided us with the perfect ambush. Like a fly about to step onto a spider's web, there was only one outcome.

One pace beyond the doorway and Lofty stepped out behind him. The spider pounced, and the fly was no more.

Too late, we realised the guard didn't carry a firearm. Even out of uniform, the SD always carried a holstered pistol. The unfortunate man was a German civilian, a simple night watchman. With him gone, we had no option but to eliminate his associate. We went in search of the man like predators desperate for a kill. Neither of us felt remotely happy about the situation. I hadn't undergone all that intensive training in order to kill an unsuspecting civilian night watchman. Like it or not, we tracked him down with ruthless efficiency, as if we smelt the blood.

The deed might have fallen to either of us and I hoped it might not be me, but it did! I dispatched him quickly and efficiently. He silently crumpled to the ground with little more than a murmur. Remorse urged me to look at his face. A man in his fifties, he might have a wife expecting him home; he might have grandchildren.

Rather than approach the foundry from the front entrance, our route took us behind it. Completely invisible in the dark, we hugged the walls like ivy, circling around to the main entrance.

The smell of burning coke surrounded the building as the furnaces were maintained throughout the night. Inside, the industrial noises of the day were replaced with the constant hum of the fans supplying air through the furnaces. Light shone from around several blackout screens. I gave Lofty the thumbs up sign.

We deposited our heavy packs behind piles of aluminium ingots - big bars of bright shiny metal looking like railway sleepers. The large double doors were locked at night with a strong hasp and staple padlock. The fact that the lock was on the inside spoke volumes. The building retained various other smaller doors as it expanded over the decades. Our target door led to an internal store room; it appeared to be ideal for our purpose.

Upon closer inspection, we found it had a single mortice lock, but of course, it might also have a padlock on the inside. Rather than risk that, we planned in advance to cut away the hinges. Equipped with a brace and bit, a series of holes were silently drilled before breaking the hinges away with a crowbar. The decayed timber of the door surround made our job easier. We gained access with barely a sound. Not even an owl would have noticed us. Grabbing our backpacks, we stepped inside the pitch-black storeroom, replacing the door behind us. Our torches ensured we disturbed nothing. Beyond the next door, we intended to disturb everything.

Our inside man knew nothing except that resistance fighters were interested in the foundry. He was either intuitive or maybe just hopeful. He said he could be recognised by a red neckerchief. All operations have their weak points, their Achilles' heel, those areas where we cannot calculate with absolute certainty. Like the devil in the detail, this is where the "what if" lurks. When dealing with the imponderable, anything is possible. Our inside man was one such imponderable. The other uncertainty was that we didn't know where the SD guards would be, or how we would identify them. A swastika armband would be helpful, but we shouldn't rely on it.

Holding our Sten Guns at the ready, we opened the door to the storeroom just sufficient to let the light stream in. Both crouching low, we didn't move; we just observed. Racks of metals sat only yards in front of us. Remaining low, Lofty closed the door behind us and we took up a position behind the racks. You need a bit of luck in life, and in our business we probably needed it more than most. The racks of metal bars could have been made for our purpose. We peered through the spaces, taking our time to observe our surroundings.

The plans and drawings we'd studied gave us the layout but not the scale of the building. A huge open space full of equipment spread all around us. Great metal arches vaulted the ceiling, suspending chains and pulleys. A metal gallery spanned one end above the furnaces where giant cog wheels controlled chain hoists. Beneath them, rollers and stands. Overhead, huge crucibles hung in massive cast iron hooks. Underfoot, beads of shiny metal gathered in unswept corners, and everywhere the heat of the furnaces. The hot air hung heavy with the smell of coke and metal impurities mingled with sweat, oil, and grease. Decades of accumulated smoke grime blackened everything, so that it all looked the same. I visualised the place during the day with sparkling molten metal and dancing flames lighting up that cathedral of industry.

The floor space was like a maze laid out in a grid between sand pits and heavy pieces of equipment. The maze followed no recognisable plan. It obviously evolved around each new piece of equipment over decades. And like a maze, we had to beware the dead end. Lofty spotted him first, our inside man wearing his red neckerchief. I saw instantly why Jan had selected him to approach. A big man with broad shoulders, he carried his body with a hint of defiance. Unlike the others, he occasionally ventured to look up and straighten his back.

Just in time, I spotted one of the SD proudly wearing his armband. He turned a corner and walked in our direction. He might have taken either path towards us through the maze. Had he come to our side of the metals rack, we would have needed to move quickly. He didn't; he walked along the other side. Lofty positioned himself behind a solid pile of metal. I silently moved to an opening. The guard walked slowly, methodically inspecting everything he saw. He seemed to miss nothing. Had the workers stacked the metal bars neatly, had the floor been swept properly? A creature of habit, he looked towards his left for fifteen seconds before looking right for the same duration. His gaze always went from top to bottom.

Lofty repositioned himself. With a clear vantage point now behind the guard, he had my back. As the man approached the end of the rack, I readied myself. He looked left in my direction, first up and then down. The moment I saw his head predictably turn to the right, I silently stepped out behind him. With one hand over his mouth, I forcibly yanked his head back. With my knee in his back, his body arched backwards, placing him completely off balance. I simultaneously thrust my fighting knife through his throat.

I must have missed his carotid artery. A big strong man, he struggled more than I expected. Unable to make a verbal sound, he might nevertheless have made a noise. With the blade edges parallel to the ground, I pushed the knife violently back and forth. A few seconds passed before he became limp and I eased him to the ground. Lofty quickly came alongside me and we dragged him behind the racks. A trail of blood slithered in his wake. A few beads of shiny metal lined the edges like flotsam marking the extent of the red tide.

Rather than risk clearing the blood, we concealed ourselves again. The night workers seemed to be concentrated towards the furnaces. It didn't take long for us to spot another SD guard. The difference in gait between the oppressor and the oppressed was clear to see. We took our time; we had no reason to rush. Lofty, like Rob, is the man you want when you're confronted by the enemy. Six feet tall and built like a brick shithouse, you didn't want to be on the wrong side of him. However, his advantage of size and strength counted against him when it came to stealth. I said I would deal with the second guard.

This man didn't walk about. For the moment at least, he stood watching the workers doing some kind of maintenance. If we knew for certain there were just the two of them, I might have risked taking him in the open, but we didn't have that reassurance. In uniform or not, the SD always carried a firearm in a buttoned-down holster on their hip. What we didn't want was the sound of gunfire.

Between us, we took a calculated gamble. I had removed the armband from the other guard. I had to wait twenty minutes for our inside man to walk in my direction. The moment he did, I made myself visible to him. I held the swastika armband aloft on the end of my fighting knife. I couldn't think of a clearer signal to send him.

The man understandably took a moment to acknowledge me. His tired sunken eyes no doubt suffered failing vision. When he realised the significance of my signal, he raised his head. In that environment, a slight gesture is a tremendous act of defiance. The side of his mouth lifted into an attempted smile. A spontaneous reaction like that always comes from the heart. Our inside man was exactly what he purported to be. I gestured how many guards, and he raised two fingers. I shook my head, gesturing back with one finger. That the death of a human being should be met with a broad smile I found reassuring, if a bit unnerving.

I indicated with my fingers that I wanted him to go and talk to the remaining guard. I ran my knife across my throat and indicated that he should not look in my direction. Prior to that moment, his focus of attention had been concentrated on his shoes. Now he looked up defiantly and walked with purpose. I shadowed him while remaining concealed. He stood boldly in front of the guard, looking him straight in the eye. He would never have done such a thing before. The guard instantly recognised that as an act of rebellion. He immediately reached for the flap on his holster. I didn't know if he might have used it or not, but I didn't give him the chance.

It seems incredible to think now that I had a preferred method of silent killing. I preferred Gran's cake to any other. I preferred beer to whisky. Should I think of it in those same terms? And when does "preferred" become "favourite"? I approached the man intending to sever his carotid artery. But at the precise moment I reached out towards him, he raised his right hand to strike the worker.

Without thinking, I continued my left hand towards his mouth but my knife entered his back between the fourth and fifth ribs. Provided the knife doesn't bounce off a rib or come up against something beneath the victim's clothing, a knife through the heart is instantaneous death. The guard crumpled to his knees and fell forward. Our inside man kicked the body for good measure.

The other workers looked on in stunned silence. Our man with the red neckerchief raised his hands in the air and shouted something in Polish to his colleagues. A subdued cheer filled the air. They looked at each other in disbelief, but as the realisation dawned, one after another they looked towards one of their number. I heard the Polish word for informer. Like hounds on a fox, those broken people became incensed. They surged towards the man with obvious intent.

Lofty read the situation correctly and stepped forward. Confronted by his menacing frame, they backed off but kept shouting the word, collaborator. The accused man attempted to run, but he would never get past Lofty. Without giving him the chance to defend himself, Lofty did what he had to do. The man fell to the ground dead. The workers looked on with wide eyes, had retribution come at a price?

At the farm, we had privately discussed the fate of the workers at length. Krystyna told us they would be interrogated and probably killed by the Gestapo. To ensure the success of the mission, we should kill them all. Lofty said it and I agreed. We sat on our beds in the cellar and looked at each other. When interrogated, they would describe us to the Gestapo. I now looked at our man with the red neckerchief.

"Rope," I said in my broken Polish, "I need rope."

Eager to cooperate he ran off, seemingly ten years younger. Lofty's Polish was slightly better than mine. He tried to explain that we would ensure their safety, but first we had to tie them up. Unsure about us, they looked terribly frightened, but we gave them no option. They remained the oppressed, while we became the oppressors. Lofty secured them to heavy equipment. It had all taken longer than expected, but with everything in hand and the place secure, we had plenty of time to place our charges. With our backpacks retrieved from the storeroom, Lofty wasted no time laying out the RDX, detonators, and fuses.

The moment our captives saw the explosives they panicked thinking they would be killed along with the building. I cupped the face of the man with the red neckerchief in my hands. "No, no, we will release you." He had little reason to believe me, but as I realised, people cling to hope, regardless. Lofty and I stood looking at the structure of the building. A complicated cathedral of steel, we had to consider every detail. All buildings have structural stress points where maximum loads are transmitted to the foundation. Like any table, if you remove a leg it becomes unstable. Remove another and it will fall down.

The cathedral of steel columns proved to be no exception, except it was much harder to decipher. The massive hoists were supported by two huge girders that ran the length of the building. These in turn were supported by cast-iron pillars. The building had clearly evolved with time, the one constant being the central gantry. Everything else had been built around it. Except it wasn't! The designers worked with what they had, and they used the same pillars to support the roof.

We had options. If we destroyed the furnaces, that would be a severe setback for the foundry. If we destroyed everything, that would be a permanent setback. With time on our side, we elected for total destruction. It's never the size of the explosive which determines the effectiveness of the explosion. If we placed our charges in all the right places, the building would become a table with only two legs. If we placed charges at the base of the chimney in exactly the right place, it would obligingly fall into the remains of the building.

The gantry support pillars were the key to it. With much of the roof-load being transmitted to those same pillars, the place was a house of cards. We worked quickly, as we had practised so many times. The Polish workers were not sure about us but they watched silently in awe. It took us about forty-five minutes to place all the charges. As Lofty finished, I went in search of the moulds. They were everywhere! A gallery off of the main hall housed the mould-making room. This is the heart of a foundry; this is where it all begins.

My problem was knowing which ones were for the V2 turbo pump. The boys in Hut 3 showed me photographs of the turbo pump, but the moulds look completely different. The first pattern is made of wood and a variety of materials. From that, a sand casting is produced, probably in cast iron. This then forms the permanent mould for all future castings. If the moulds were not destroyed, it would be a relatively straightforward matter for the Germans to transfer production.

Much of the work done there involved sand castings. The boys told me to ignore those. A very high precision mass production mould would almost certainly be made of cast iron. These were heavy and required hoists to manoeuvre them, so I concentrated along the central gantry. Sure enough, I found several. I asked the workers which of them was in constant use, and they all pointed to the same one. It was the right size and shape; I had almost certainly found it.

Cast iron is a wonderful material. Immensely strong in compression, the foundry pillars would support many times their weight. As a mould material, it's impervious to damage from the liquid aluminium being poured into it. It does, however, have one disadvantage, it's brittle. Our strategically placed charges would shatter the pillars like eggshells, and the same applied to the moulds.

Lofty reported that all the charges were in place. I pointed towards the cast iron moulds. A handful of magnetic limpet mines would have solved the problem quickly, but we decided against them because of the weight. With plenty of C2, we simply attached blobs to each mould. As a final precaution, we placed a charge in the middle of the mould-making room. The time had come to arm the L-delay time fuses. An hour seemed about right. That would give us plenty of time to get completely away. The problem with an hour is that it's a long time for someone to potentially intervene. We had either one hour or thirty minutes. I stood looking at Lofty.

"Thirty minutes," he said.

"Thirty minutes, let's do it."

The race was on to arm the timers as quickly as possible. Once armed, there was no going back. I worked at one end, Lofty the other. We ran between timers. As Lofty activated the one in the mould-making room, I cut the ropes on the workers. I told them to follow us and do precisely what we did. As a group we ran from the foundry, keeping close to the buildings. Everywhere remained quiet, but we checked every open space before we crossed. Krystyna and Tomasz waited patiently in the old jewellery factory. Hearing us approach, they took up a defensive position but quickly realised it was us. They were startled to see the foundry workers.

"Tell them, Krystyna, they have less than twenty minutes to get away. They are on their own."

"I understand. Thank you for giving them a chance."

We reached the lorry slightly quicker than when we left it. The engine rattled into life and we were on our way. While Lady Luck had been with us every inch of the way, she now deserted us. The moon, now lower in the sky, had been consumed by thick clouds. We dared not risk the headlamps, certainly not anywhere near the built-up area. Tomasz proceeded at a snail's pace. An accident now would be a disaster. We each willed him to drive faster, knowing he couldn't.

I looked at my watch. One minute had elapsed from when I last looked. Lofty counted out each five-minute interval. Fifteen minutes and we were still in the residential area. Twenty minutes and the last of the houses came into view as one or two early morning lights came on. At twenty-five minutes we lost sight of the houses. We put the headlamps on and made a run for it.

Sat in the back, Lofty and I had the perfect view towards where the foundry was about to collapse. Those L-delay fuses were very accurate. I set my watch to the first one we armed, and to the very second we heard the muffled crump as it detonated. The others followed almost immediately. One after another they merged together. Within a few seconds the muffled crump had become an audible explosion.

What we heard next was music to our ears. Unlike an exploding bomb, a demolition charge is the start of events, not the conclusion. We heard the audible signature of fracturing steel as it groaned and creaked before finally collapsing like so many tubular bells. Finally, an almighty crash silenced the sound of steel on steel as the brick chimney fell into the tangled remains. A red glow filled the sky like an early morning sunrise as a fire took hold.

We slapped raised hands together. Job done! Tomasz now made up for lost time. We had no reason to think we would be seen, but that didn't allay our fears. When the lorry turned into the farm entrance, we all breathed a sigh of relief. The pigs welcomed us back very vocally. Thank heavens we were remote. We segregated them and made the cellar hatch ready; Krystyna immediately sent the mission accomplished signal. Only then did we stop and congratulate ourselves. Much backslapping and hugging followed.

"We nearly came in after you," Krystyna said. "You were longer than we expected. I thought you were in trouble."

"You remained disciplined, Krystyna, well done," said Lofty.

"There's nothing worse than waiting. Lofty's right, you and Tomasz both conducted yourselves like professionals."

"Lofty! Does this not mean tall in English, Dorothy?"

They laughed at me. One moment I'm telling Krystyna she behaved professionally and the next I'm giving away Lofty's name. I shouldn't have told her my name either. I had a misguided excuse; I trusted them with my life. If Mac knew, he would have torn me off a strip. We sat in the barn on bales of hay. Between us, the oil lamp lit up our faces to the exclusion of all else. We sent fading shadows reaching out to the extremities of the walls. With the operation a complete success, we allowed euphoria to sweep over us like the warm light of the lamp. For a moment, we were the centre of the universe. We drank wine and didn't stop talking.

"What do you think the workers will do?" Lofty asked.

Krystyna translated for Tomasz. His reply sent a chill down my spine. "If they stay, they will be killed. If they run, they are guilty. They will almost certainly be found, and an example made of them."

"Is there no chance for them?" I asked.

"At least it's a chance. However slender, you gave them that chance. They will be grateful for it."

"The man Jan chose, the one with the red neckerchief," I said. "I recognised a brave man. I'll never forget him."

"If he survives, Dorothy, he will not forget you!"

We made light of the subject. What else could we do? Life for us only comprised the raid. The adrenalin-filled euphoria which follows a successful operation excludes all else. It's a high with nowhere else to go. There is no possibility of sleep. Only the rising sun of another day can convince you that a new dawn has begun. Starting as an orange glow no brighter than the oil lamp, the new day found us still sitting together. The final act of blowing out the lamp consigned the operation to the past.

Once the Germans realised what happened, there would be hell to pay. Assuming success for the other operations, it might take them a while to connect the events. When that happened, we were assured of a major manhunt. The most dangerous part of Operation Cormorant had yet to begin. We all understood what the dangers were but brushed the thought aside. For now, we needed to sleep during the day, because the danger we tried to ignore would become a reality in the evening.

Chapter Thirty-Five
Arbeit Macht Frei

I slept fitfully, while Lofty snored. When I heard the pigs squealing, I hoped it was Krystyna or Tomasz. Lofty woke up and simultaneously reached for his Sten Gun. It hadn't occurred to us before that we might be discovered, but suddenly it did! We were relieved to hear the knocks on the hatch. They were all there to greet us. Jan described the reaction following the explosions. The foundry had been completely destroyed. Like a line of dominoes, everything collapsed. A fire still burned in the coke store. The Germans were understandably miffed! The place crawled first with SD and later Gestapo. Regular troops were being brought in.

"Any news about the workers?" I asked.

"The day shift has all been arrested and we believe one of the night shift has been found."

"Do we know his fate?"

"No, we don't."

I could guess; I knew all about the Gestapo. We were about to enter a perilous time for our friends. Everyone would be under suspicion. They needed to lie low now and do nothing out of the ordinary. Instead, they were all there to help us escape. I worked with a lot of brave people during the war. We were highly trained and very capable; our Polish friends were not trained professionals. They were ordinary people doing extraordinary things. There is no greater sacrifice a person can make than when they put their life on the line for you. For those of us who got to walk again in the light of freedom, we did so because of people like them. They were the giants whose shoulders we walked upon.

The plan had been discussed many times. RAF Tempsford already had the coordinates of the proposed landing strip. All we had to do was get there and radio the coded signal confirming our state of readiness. We chose the last of the daylight because with the Germans on maximum alert, a night time journey would look even more suspicious. The dangers were obvious. In the event of being stopped we could not reasonably account for our movements. With us and a radio on the lorry, they would not get past an inspection.

We relied upon our one advantage, their local knowledge. The requirements for a landing strip are very precise. The Lysander pilot is searching in the dark for a single blade of grass in a land of pasture. Every field looks like another. You need a distinctive identifying feature that will be seen from the air. There must be no power lines, no tall buildings. With a take-off distance of 300 yards to 50 feet, the height of trees had to be precisely known. The ground must be firm and reasonably flat. The local terrain has to provide cover. All of that had been done in advance, with alternatives just in case.

They chose the landing strip very well. It had three different approach routes, all remote country roads. The Germans could not block every minor road in Bavaria. The odds were on our side, although it didn't feel like it. We had additional weapons from the canister including Mills grenades. Between us, we were heavily armed and would be able to fight our way out of a difficult situation, but what would follow?

The engine rattled into life, but this time I felt more apprehensive. Once again Lofty and I were under the bales, but this time they were less hastily positioned. We each had our own space. Completely in their hands, we could only place our trust in them. I did that without hesitation. We were told the journey should take about half an hour. At the halfway point, we stopped. Krystyna came and sat on the bales to keep us informed. Tomasz, she said, had gone on foot across a field in order to reconnoitre the road beyond. At least we knew what was going on. I felt helpless just lying there.

"He's coming back. He's running, something must be wrong. Get ready."

I heard Tomasz shout, "Turn around, road block."

We hastily retreated the way we had come. After a detour, I assumed they were trying another approach. Considering they were not trained agents, their common sense fieldcraft was excellent. They did everything I would have done. We stopped again where they knew they would be able to see the adjoining road from a high vantage point. Once again, the Germans blocked our way. They tried every route but to no avail. The Germans were everywhere.

"We simply can't afford to be stopped in the lorry," Krystyna said. "Do you want to confront them or shall we try again tomorrow?"

"No, we need to rethink," Lofty replied.

At least our journey back remained clear. It was with some relief when we pulled into the farm. The RAF had insisted upon only two chances; the phase of the moon and weather all prevented a third try. Lofty and I were a cat with two lives, now reduced to one. The next time would be all or nothing. We quickly unpacked and hid everything away in the cellar. Reasonably safe, I thought perhaps we might relax with them until the following evening but that didn't happen.

We ate what they had and relaxed a little but all the while I remained aware of the leather satchel that didn't leave Krystyna's side. She saw me looking at it and drew it across her body, placing it on her lap. They looked at each other. The atmosphere became heavy.

"What's in the bag, Krystyna?" I asked.

"Hell," she replied.

I looked at Lofty and back towards her as she placed her hand inside the satchel. A handful of papers emerged. They were followed by some large photographs. Her expression completely changed. She had an indomitable spirit that despite everything always shone through her sunken eyes. It suddenly left her, extinguished like a snuffed-out candle. Whatever those papers contained, they had the power to drain the spirit.

"What is it, Krystyna, what is it that's so terrible?"

Slowly and with careful pronunciation she said just six words. I had not heard the words before but they were place names that came to haunt me forever more. Six places synonymous with hell. "Auschwitz, Belzec, Majdanek, Chelmno, Sobibor, and Treblinka."

"What are these places?"

"This is where the death trains go. These are the death camps in Poland. We have seen them; we have all the evidence."

"We've heard talk about death camps," Lofty said, "but it just doesn't sound credible."

Krystyna translated for the others. They looked at one another. "We have sent you information before but it is ignored. We can't understand why you have done nothing."

"The abandoned houses we saw in Furth, the Jewish homes; would those people have been sent to these places?" I asked.

"Almost certainly. They are most likely dead."

"But there must be hundreds of them. How can they be doing that to so many?"

"It's not hundreds, Dorothy. It's not even thousands. It's millions!"

I looked at Lofty in total disbelief. Surely this was not possible. It sounded almost absurd. Krystyna saw the incredulous expression on our faces. What she told us next changed my life. Right from the start of the German invasion, the Poles had been treated dreadfully. Nazi ideology had conditioned its forces into believing their Arian superiority meant that the Poles, and especially the Jews, were effectively sub-human. They committed unspeakable atrocities, simply rounding people up to shoot them. As the Occupation consolidated, the arbitrary killing became more organised. The Jews, especially, were rounded up and taken to execution sites, such as Babi Yar in Ukraine. Some were sealed in the back of lorries and gassed by the vehicle exhaust. They marched others into open trenches and shot them.

As the number of victims grew, the very scale of the barbarity reached practical limits. Local people become aware of the mass killings. Even the German execution squads became revolted by the hell they had created. This was when the Nazi regime signed its pact with the devil. They deemed the mobile killing units inefficient and not good for morale. It would be more efficient to concentrate the killing in centres specially equipped for the purpose. At that point I had to draw breath. What Krystyna implied sounded like a human abattoir. This was not possible!

"It sounds like you're telling us they built factories to process people. Surely that's not possible?"

"That is exactly what they have done. They have created extermination centres where they kill people and then cremate the bodies. Thousands of people a day can be killed. It's a processing factory for human beings."

I remained in a state of disbelief. It was what happened next that changed my life forever. It's one thing when someone describes the impossible. It's quite another when that impossible truth questions your entire existence as a human being. The contents of Krystyna's satchel proved to be incendiary. Auschwitz, Belzec, Majdanek, Chelmno, Sobibor, and Treblinka: AK had a file on each one, containing statements from many witnesses, with detailed drawings of the layout of the camps together with photographs.

There were photographs of the train station at Auschwitz-Birkenau. We could see endless lines of victims being herded away. Krystyna said AK estimated from their observations at the train station that many thousands of people were being killed each day. The trains kept coming, and every carriage left the station empty. Nobody ever left Auschwitz. It stunned us into silence. The photographs taken at the station were horribly compelling. The scale of the death camp was unimaginable.

As we looked through the paperwork, the cold, calculating horror of it became ever clearer. Upon arrival at Auschwitz, they sent fitter people in one direction to be used for slave labour. All others went directly into gas chambers. They considered those used for slave labour to be expendable, and the moment they became unable to work, they were condemned to the gas chamber. Majdanek was another slave labour camp. Treblinka, Belzec, and Sobibor were used for killing people.

I found two photographs especially disturbing. A queue of people being segregated at the entrance to Auschwitz was clear enough to see the people's faces. Wretched, broken, bedraggled people walking to their death. The photograph was just clear enough to see the humanity in their faces. Humanity that I knew was about to be extinguished. The photograph of smoke billowing from the crematoria chimney might have come from any of those people queuing in front of the wrought iron sign that hung suspended across the sixteen feet wide entrance. *"Arbeit Macht Frei"*. Work makes you free, it cynically proclaimed.

Finally, she handed me several small photographs taken from inside the camps. Grainy indistinct images that despite all their imperfection brought the death camps into sharp focus. I saw people, apparently prisoners themselves, forced to drag lifeless bodies from the gas chamber. A tangled mass of humanity reduced to its constituent parts minus the spark of life. I saw huge piles of glasses, and hair. They exploited the dead as a commodity. According to Dante, hell comprises nine concentric circles representing a gradual increase in wickedness. What I saw represented the last and final circle, the centre of the earth where mankind can descend no further.

"I'm speechless, Krystyna. This is incomprehensible, it's so much to absorb. Why are those people queuing in an orderly fashion? Don't they realise what lies on the other side of the gate?"

"That is precisely what the Nazis intended. Work makes you free; they want to believe it's true. They are just like you and Lofty, they have heard the rumours, but it's too incredible. We all believe what we want to believe. We've been told they are sent into a shower room where they believe they can finally clean themselves. Instead of water they are gassed. Right up to the last moment, they cling to the hope of life."

"The Nazis that physically do this day in, day out, how do they live with themselves?" asked Lofty.

"We don't know! You might say that Hitler or any of his immediate followers are deranged psychopaths. But can they all be? They are not just brutal savages; this is something far worse."

Krystyna was right, I couldn't comprehend the place where the Third Reich had descended. They considered the Poles and Jews to be sub-human. The terrifying reality was that they created their own interpretation of sub-human in their own image. They held up a mirror against those they despised, but what they saw was their own reflection.

I was terrified by what they had become, and the evil they committed horrified me. What they represented filled me with an anger so intense it frightened me. It terrified me to think I could be capable of such thoughts. I didn't want to inhabit any part of their hell, but at the same time I wanted them vanquished, I wanted them dead! Those terrible images filled me with irreconcilable contradictions and impossible questions. I have never been able to stop asking those questions of myself.

I finally understood the inner strength of our Polish friends. Like me, they too had irreconcilable contradictions and impossible questions. Those brave, determined people were motivated to defeat the Nazis because they understood their enemy better than anyone. They knew what the alternative was.

Chapter Thirty-Six
Krystyna

Following what we had been told and seen, attitudes changed abruptly. Jan and Stanislaw had to leave. The parting between Jan and Krystyna was painful to watch. I got the feeling they tried hard not to let their relationship affect their work. But try as they may, they could not conceal the love between them. Like Rob and I, they lived with the constant threat that their relationship hung in the balance. I dealt with that by never admitting that relationship to myself.

Perhaps Krystyna felt the same, a life of denial is maybe better than a life of fear. After everything that we had seen and discussed, the look of love in their eyes said much for the human spirit. I found it reassuring. Even after all that, something good still existed. It explained a lot about the personality which lay behind Krystyna's gaunt face. Even with her dark sunken eyes and prominent cheekbones, an expression of happiness lived in her face.

There seemed little else to be said. The photographs we had seen excluded all other thoughts from our minds. Lofty and I retreated to our cellar and the sound of the squealing pigs took on a new chilling significance. Neither of us slept very much. I even got up for a wee in the bucket without giving it a second thought. On my way back to bed, the beam of my torch picked out a spider surveying its territory in the corner of the cellar. Content in that dark world, it obviously had all it required for a successful life. I envied it.

The following day, we emerged back into the light. Like a pair of troglodytes, we grimaced under the intensity of the sun. We immediately discussed our plan for reaching the landing strip. We had all been thinking about it. Tomasz thought we needed a different approach, and I agreed. With us all on the lorry, we would never get past a German inspection. It was too risky. Tomasz's idea was that we should take Stanislaw's car and the lorry. Krystyna suggested she travel with me and Stanislaw in the car, while Lofty sat up front in the lorry with Jan and Tomasz.

When I suggested we load some pigs onto the lorry, they all agreed. The men would look credible as farm workers transporting pigs, while two women being driven in a car should not arouse undue suspicion. Like all hastily contrived plans, it was full of holes, the principal of which were our papers. Lofty and I were foundry workers. The foundry that we had destroyed! Hindsight is a truly wonderful thing. I would like to think if we had provided our own papers that we would have noticed such a fundamental error. But perhaps not.

"Is there time, Krystyna, to get more papers?" Lofty asked.

"I wouldn't think so, but we can try. We produce hundreds of work permits; we have a unit that produces them in Nuremberg."

"What could we plausibly be working as?" I asked.

"Stanislaw is an engineer, you two women could be secretaries or something, working with him," Lofty said. "You're travelling on important business."

"That's so bloody ridiculous, Lofty, it might just work! I suppose you're a pig farmer?"

"As happy as."

We talked as if it were possible, the triumph of hope over expectation. I didn't like any of it. The one thing we didn't want to happen, happened. The unexpected! None of us expected the Germans to stage such a big search effort. It seemed implausible that they had put a ring around Furth and Nuremberg. It seemed more likely they guessed we came from the west. That, of course, raised its own questions.

They might have suspected AK, but the roadblocks suggested otherwise. The operation had the signature of SOE plastered all over it; perhaps they were smart enough to realise that. Or perhaps the unfortunate Polish workers in custody told them about the two British agents. Either way, we were placing our friends at risk; I could no longer justify that. When I said as much Krystyna was deeply offended. When she translated to the others, they shared her indignation. The fire in her eyes when she answered me took my breath away.

"You have risked your lives to come here in order to strike a blow against the Nazis. You asked us to help you and we agreed to do whatever it takes to achieve your objective. We are the Polish Resistance Movement. We never turn away, Dorothy, we die before we surrender."

That put me in my place! They decided, however unlikely, getting new documents might be worth a try. She dispatched Tomasz in the lorry to contact Stanislaw. We hoped, however unlikely, that perhaps he might drive to Nuremberg. His *Gastarbeitnehmer* work permit provided the only possibility. Krystyna remained adamant - we would go ahead regardless. Our only other option would be to stay there until a new phase of the moon. That didn't fit with their plans. Although the two other workers on the farm were both Polish, they were not part of the resistance, and knew nothing of their activities. I understood why they didn't want to overstay their welcome.

Lofty and I had a very unsettled day. We tried unsuccessfully to get some sleep, at least we were out of sight in the cellar. The uncertainty played on my mind. I liked to be in complete control. All the advanced planning gave me that control; remove it, and I floundered. A large part of an SOE agent's life is spent waiting, but it got no easier. It proved to be a long day. Come the early evening, they were all there again except for Stanislaw. He had gone to Nuremberg in the hope of hastily getting more forged documents. Beyond that we knew nothing. I helped them load some pigs onto the lorry, a task far easier said than done. To their amazement, I understood more about pigs than they did. They concealed the radio in a false compartment in the bed of the lorry, beneath the pigs.

We were ready except for Stanislaw. With the likelihood of being checked on the road, we dare not travel in the dark. That gave us just a few more minutes to leave. Even I, as an eternal optimist, began to have doubts. Without documents, our weapons were the only alternative. Six well-armed people would easily overwhelm a lightly manned checkpoint. What might happen next concerned me much more. With only an hour of light left, we had no alternative; we all climbed aboard the lorry.

Once again, the semblance of a plan had fallen apart. Driving out of the farm a decidedly uneasy feeling extended up from my stomach. My hand didn't leave my Sten Gun. Five minutes into our journey, I noticed a car rapidly gaining on us. At first it raised concern, but as it drew closer, we saw Stanislaw's smiling face. Somehow, and against all the odds the forgers produced new documents for us. Stanislaw doubted they would pass a close inspection, but they offered us a chance. Krystyna and I quickly joined him in the car. The boys would follow. If they drove a few minutes behind us, they would still arrive at a checkpoint in good time to support us if it went wrong, but we would not appear to be together.

We had a plan! It might have more holes than a trawl net, but a plan, nevertheless. In the circumstances it boosted my confidence. With only a couple more miles behind us, the first checkpoint appeared in the distance. In the middle of nowhere on a small country lane the Germans were leaving no stone unturned. The decision had been made to bluff our way rather than detour. As we slowly approached, I studied every detail of what lay ahead of us - a military vehicle parked at the side of the road, while four Wehrmacht soldiers blocked the way through. Each armed with a submachine gun, they appeared to be alert.

Stanislaw stopped as requested and the soldier came to the window demanding to inspect our papers. Stanislaw had reasonably good German and complained about the interference. Despite his privileged guest status, he remained a Pole in the eyes of the soldier. Stanislaw's papers were genuine. The soldier studied them before handing them back, seemingly satisfied. He asked where we were going. Stanislaw told him he had an important meeting; we were late and were in a hurry. For a moment I thought the conversation between them sounded reassuring, but the German still demanded to see my papers.

Krystyna spoke in Polish, while I remained silent. The soldier didn't speak Polish, that offered me hope. I handed him my forged documents through the window. Perhaps they didn't look authentic; either way, the soldier appeared unconvinced. He asked me to step out of the car. With my Sten Gun under my knees, I had two options. Shoot or bluff. If I decided to bluff, then only I should get out of the car, leaving Krystyna on the non-driver's side of the car to cover me. It was vital she stayed in the car with our weapons.

Before I managed to say anything Krystyna stepped out, having decided her documents were better than mine and might still work. With a gun pointed at me, I had no option but to follow. Krystyna had covered her Sten Gun with a coat on the back seat. We obviously could not allow them to search the car but now we were both separated from our weapons. That situation should never have happened. I looked at Stanislaw, willing him to stay in the car. We were reduced to only one armed person, and on the wrong side of the car.

Another of the holes in our plan was our clothes. I wore filthy brown trousers with shiny pockets and a well-worn leather belt. My white blouse was grey and mostly covered with a green V-neck woolly. Threads dangled from holes and part of the hem hung loose. We looked exactly like foundry or farm workers. We didn't look like a pair of assistants to the eminent Stanislaw. If I had to speak, that would instantly raise more suspicion. As a trained and experienced agent, you develop an intuitive instinct for danger. Like a deer hearing the snap of a twig, my eyes widened and I could hear an ant move.

When things start to go wrong, it's often the beginning of an escalating process, it's rarely the end. The soldier shouted something in German. I saw a shiny shoe appear from the cab of the parked vehicle. The shoe was followed by a non-uniformed man who I guessed was a Gestapo officer. I desperately wanted Lofty and the others to pull in behind us. For some reason they were nowhere to be seen. The Gestapo officer walked up to me with a swagger befitting the master race. His black leather greatcoat was unbuttoned, it flayed out behind him as he strode towards me. He sent a chill down my spine.

A man in his forties, he wore round gold-rimmed glasses which accentuated the fact that his cold dead eyes were close together. It was like looking into the breach of a double-barrelled shotgun. He didn't bother to look at my papers. With a sinister leer, he demanded I raise my hands. As I did so, the straight line that formed his mouth curled up at one end. He ran his hands over my body under the pretence of searching me. I had my fighting knife concealed in a scabbard attached to my bra strap. I knew full well where his hands were going, he would obviously find more than he bargained for.

Memories of Caen came flooding back. My heart raced. Images of Auschwitz flashed before my eyes. A crisis is only a crisis if you allow it to become one. Those are precisely the moments when a level head and cool mind are called for. For me, that ghastly monster became the personification of all that was evil about the Third Reich. I saw red, I completely lost it! I misdirected him with a smile and a turn of the head. With no thought for the consequences, I withdrew the knife and thrust it into his chest. I didn't do it once or even twice; I thrust the knife repeatedly.

For the first time as an SOE agent, I completely lost control. I placed everyone in danger, including myself. Only one thing saved me from being shot by the other soldiers. Stanislaw stepped out of the car and opened fire with my Sten Gun. There was a brief exchange of fire. Had Stanislaw not reacted so quickly, and had the soldiers not been standing together, it would certainly have been a different outcome for me.

All four soldiers fell to the ground while I remained standing. At that point, the lorry pulled in behind us. The boys ran towards us, guns raised, but the crisis was over. I stood there with the cold light of reality re-entering my body like a penetrating frost. I had become so incensed that nothing else existed for me. As I stepped back into myself, I looked down at the Gestapo officer lying at my feet. Four soldiers lay motionless on the road. I saw some bullet holes in the car's windscreen. Then I saw Krystyna lying on the ground.

The shock hit me everywhere at once, like falling into iced water. I wanted to gasp but struggled to draw breath. Jan joined me seconds later. We both fell to our knees next to her. Blood seeped out over her chest, already the size of a dinner plate and spreading. Jan froze in horror. I ripped open her clothes to reveal a hole in the top of her left breast. It pulsed bright red blood. Then I noticed blood spreading from beneath her. Her eyes slowly moved and met with Jan's. He held her hand and for a brief moment she clenched her fingers. I pressed hard against the entry wound to staunch the flow of blood, but I knew it would give her only seconds more.

When you live with the sight of death you realise that, given the opportunity, people cling to life until the last second. When that last second comes, people seem to know, they submit to it. Krystyna smiled at Jan. The happiness that lived in her face remained until that final second. The smile relaxed and her head fell softly to one side. Death beckoned with a cold hand and Krystyna followed. Jan remained motionless, clutching her hand. He didn't breathe as reality fought against acceptance. When it finally came, it was horrible to witness. A huge intake of breath resulted in the primordial cry of those that love leaves behind. "No, no, no."

As for me, I'd seen it all before. For many, I was the bringer of death. After Caen, I began to wonder if I would ever feel the warm touch of life again. I stood up, trying to remain detached and dispassionate. We needed to reassess the situation, to regroup. We needed to act quickly. Lofty came and put his arms around me. He said nothing that his face hadn't already told me.

"What are you doing, Lofty?"

"She's gone, Dot."

"I know she's bloody gone. Why are you putting your arms around me?"

"I'm putting my arms around you because you're shaking. You've got tears rolling down your face."

It took Lofty to tell me - I *did* have a heart, and it was broken. He hugged me and I realised I needed it more than anything else. Stanislaw and Tomasz knelt next to Jan; their grief was palpable. Time stopped, no one moved. The entire world became frozen in time. For a very brave and wonderful woman, time now only existed in that last second. For us it started afresh, time without Krystyna. The rest of the world remained unaware that time had stopped.

I looked towards the young soldiers lying on the road. We didn't mourn their passing. For their family and loved ones, life continued as it did before, but I realised it was only a matter of time before the stultifying fog of grief would descend upon them. As for the Gestapo officer, I felt nothing. Certainly not pleasure, but not regret. I felt very little at that moment. The world was too painful to inhabit.

"You've got to pull yourself together, Dotty. We must get out of here immediately."

"Sorry, Lofty. What did you say?"

"Pull yourself together, Dot, we have to go."

I stepped out of that ice cold water and drew a deep breath. "Sorry, Lofty, I don't understand what came over me. It won't happen again. You and Tomasz get Krystyna's body in the lorry, we can't leave her. Jan, I know it's hard, but we have to go now."

The imminent danger focused our minds; we had to see through the fog of grief. Lofty dragged the German bodies behind their vehicle to make them less obvious. We had to continue on our route as before, Lofty in the lorry, me with Stanislaw. Krystyna lay in the back of the lorry wrapped in a tarpaulin. In open countryside, the sound of gunfire travels a long distance; we had no way of knowing if other German patrols had heard the sound or not.

Chapter Thirty-Seven

Do Widzenia (Goodbye)

Within another two miles, we discovered they had heard. I grabbed my binoculars and watched an open-topped troop carrier racing along the adjoining road. It would reach the intersection before we could. I watched them closely as we both approached the intersection. We didn't have the option of retreating; we would have to confront them.

"What I do?" shouted Stanislaw.

"Stop short of the junction and let them confront us."

"We not turn around?"

"No, Stanislaw! They will only come after us. So we stop, and we let them."

"There are too many."

"Did you count them?"

"No."

"I did, there are only twelve of them. Apart from one officer, they look like fresh recruits, no more than young boys. They are only armed with rifles. We can deal with this, Stanislaw."

He did as I asked and we stopped about 150 yards away from the junction. Lofty and the others pulled up alongside us, completely blocking the road. Lofty knew what to do; we each got out of the vehicles and took cover behind them. The German soldiers stopped at the junction. They appeared hesitant, not knowing what to do.

The troops in the back of the vehicle jumped down and crouched low. They fired several shots at us. I told everyone to return fire with single shots only. They were indeed raw recruits; their shots were random and from 150 yards they were wide of the mark. With only ineffective occasional fire from us, they started to approach using the ditch on either side of the road as cover.

"Lofty, I'm going to break away and double back. We need them to think we are making a run for it. We need them to come at us. When they do, we charge them head on."

"Should we not stay behind cover?" asked Jan

"No. If we fire from behind cover they will do the same. They have the better position in those ditches, we will end up with a prolonged fire fight. There may be more of them but when we run at them, they will panic. They will think they see more of us than we are, and they will turn tail."

"How can you be sure?"

"Trust me, they will panic. We are in control here, not them."

I stood up and ran, just wide of the car so they would see me. Crouching low, I stepped out of their line of sight behind the lorry and doubled back.

"Here they come," shouted Lofty.

We waited a few seconds before opening fire. The Sten Gun is not particularly accurate, but it can fire 500 rounds per minute, effective up to about 100 yards. The reality was that raw recruits armed with rifles, standing in the open, didn't stand a chance. Faced with five sub-machine guns running towards them, they either froze or turned and ran. It was neither brave nor courageous; it was none of those things. We slaughtered them as the rules of war demanded. At least three of them appeared to be no more than fifteen years old. Lofty checked each one. Two of them, although mortally wounded, were still alive. Lofty shot them.

"We didn't sign up to do this, did we, Lofty?"

"They would have killed us given the chance."

"I know. Try telling their mothers."

"Let's be on our way, it's almost dark."

In the rush to get away from the area, the lorry couldn't avoid driving over one of the bodies. It moved as if still alive. Following in the car, I saw it happen. We avoided them but it didn't feel right. The sun that had witnessed events descended into darkness as if our world was no longer fit to receive its life-giving force. The orange orb clung to the western horizon for a final second before turning its back on us. With only a few miles left to go, Tomasz put on the headlamps. Having announced our presence for all to see, we made a dash for it. The pigs squealed as the lorry heaved around corners. Krystyna's body rolled across the bed. Stanislaw looked at me but we said nothing. Finally, Tomasz stopped at a tiny road junction and turned off the lights.

"Are we there?" I asked Stanislaw.

"Nearly. Road ahead go to nowhere. You call it dead end."

"I understand; we'll wait to see if it's safe to proceed."

"We do."

The darkness became our friend. It drew a veil over us. Like specs of dust in a shaft of light, the moment the light was gone, so were we. We sat silently for two hours. Stanislaw and I had so much to say and plenty of time to say it in. Instead, we said very little. Krystyna looked at us both. No longer pale and gaunt, she smiled a beautiful smile. The happiness that lived in her face now shone from her lips and her bright eyes. Stanislaw saw her as did I. She haunted me then, she haunts me still.

"Your man, Dorothy, he waits for you?"

"He's here in Germany."

"He's here like you?"

"Yes, he is."

"You love him, you afraid?"

"I can't love him because I can't be afraid all the time."

"This work for you?"

"No, not really, but we survive." There was a long silence. "It's my fault Krystyna is dead, Stanislaw."

"No, no. Not your fault."

"It is, I lost control, I placed you all in danger."

Our stilted conversation had much further to go but Tomasz started the lorry. With no sign of anyone, the decision had been taken to proceed to our destination. Stanislaw started the car and once again we were on our way. Branches and undergrowth brushed the sides of the lorry as it bounced along the track. It dived in and out of ruts that were almost too much for the car. They chose the site well; a more deserted and featureless area I couldn't imagine.

The moment we stopped, they retrieved the radio and set up the aerial. A long wire dipped between the branches as they pulled it through the trees. Powered by the lorry battery, the radio crackled into life. The dials glowed faintly in the dark and the valves hummed. Krystyna had been the usual radio operator but Jan understood how to use it. He sent the prearranged single word code. He then sent it again, and moments later a third time. Then we waited for the acknowledgement. Communication was always a nervous time. Even a very brief coded signal might alert the enemy. Then there was the waiting, the interminable waiting. It felt like an age but finally it came. Tempsford received our signal. Now we had to wait about two and a half hours for the pilot to arrive.

While the landing site appeared featureless on the ground, that was not the case from the air. Krystyna had shown me on the map. A large pond lay exactly in the line of approach about a thousand yards away. The field edges wandered about, searching for their boundary except for one straight edge lined with trees. The pond reflected the moonlight like a beacon, while the treeline marked the final approach.

The usual signal to mark the landing strip was to form an inverted L with torches. First a coded signal, followed by the landing lights. Our friends understood precisely what they were doing. The Polish Resistance did not have the extensive training of the SOE; they mostly learned on the job. But like poachers turned gamekeeper, they were experts at their craft. Outside of SOE, I have never worked with more capable people and certainly none braver.

Content that we had not been discovered, they made ready with the torches. We were each aware where we should be at the allotted hour. Once again, Lady Luck had an important role to play. The pilot needed at least some moonlight; navigation alone would not be sufficient. Now we had to wait - more time to contemplate and reflect. I didn't want to do any of those things. I didn't like what I saw in my reflection. Krystyna filled my mind, every detail, every painful moment.

I had never lost control like that; it seemed inexplicable. What else could I have done, I told myself. It might have been true, I had to kill him. Or did I? When he found my knife, what would he have done? He might have taken me prisoner, that would have given the others time to react. Then again, he might have shot me on the spot. No, he would have taken me for interrogation. I got Krystyna killed! If only she had stayed in the car, why did she have to get out? These thoughts and others raced through my mind. I realised I had made my lower lip sore. Lofty came and sat close to me.

"Don't blame yourself, Dotty. We all run the same risk. That shot could have gone anywhere."

"No, you didn't see, Lofty. I lost it. I stabbed him about ten times. If I had let him take me prisoner, Krystyna might not have been shot."

"You don't know that, Dot. They might just as easily have shot all three of you. In fact, after what we did at the foundry I think that's more likely. You might just as well say it was my fault for not getting there a minute sooner."

"This has got to be my last operation. I can't live with the memories I have now, let alone any more. I've let my comrades down, Lofty."

"That's bollocks! I'm proud to serve with you, Dotty. More than that, it's been an honour. I would serve with you again any time."

"That's a nice thing to say, Lofty, but this has broken me."

"Is this the Dotty that the Gestapo couldn't break? Is this the same Dotty who fought off half the German army in Caen and has been put forward for the George Cross? You've just witnessed the death of someone we had both become very close to. How do you think you're supposed to react! You don't really believe this crap about the lipstick assassin. You're no more a heartless assassin than I am. We've become what we need to be, but it's not who we *are*, Dotty."

"Bloody hell, Lofty! You're a dark horse. I thought none of this affected you."

"Of course it does, how can it not?"

"How do you deal with it, then?"

"Before the war, I was just like anyone else, the same as you. Nobody was more surprised when they singled me out in training. It's not much of a career is it, Dot? There's no place for us in peacetime. I didn't choose this; I'm not proud that I'm good at it. Our country needs us and we do what we have to do, but it's not me. I keep it separate."

"I know that, Lofty. It's what Mac keeps telling me. I'm just having difficulty doing it."

"Can I give you an opinion, Dot, without causing offence?"

"We've peed in the same bucket, Lofty; you won't cause me offence."

"Well, I hesitate to say it, but I'll give it a go. I can separate it because

I know it's not me. Maybe deep down you think it *is* you. You react to situations spontaneously. Everything you do seems to be intuitive, like a predator. You're the best of us, Dotty, we all recognise that. I think perhaps it's such a large part of you that you believe it's who you are. Well, I can tell you I don't believe that."

"Fucking hell, Lofty! That was below the belt."

"You mean close to the truth?"

"Well, it's a big thing for me to admit, especially to you, but yes!"

"You've got a heart and trust me it's not made of ice. You're just bloody good at pretending it is. Don't allow this to become who you are, Dotty. Don't lose sight of the other woman I can see. She's funny, warm, and caring. She's also feminine and attractive; in fact in a good light I'd say you're bloody gorgeous. I think Rob is the luckiest bloke I know."

Talk about a sail with the wind removed. I didn't know if I should burst into tears or kiss him. In the end, I did both. Neither the tears nor the kiss were advisable, but that's what happened. I realised Lofty held a candle for me, you can tell, can't you. But I also knew he was as professional as they come, and a proper gentleman. I never expected him to say such a thing! Certainly not while we sat in a field in Germany, wondering if we were going to escape alive.

"What do you mean, in a good light?"

"Yes, I'm sorry about that. It's been a bit of a day, hasn't it?"

"You're a lovely man, Lofty. I mean it, you're a really lovely man."

"Well, I have my moments and I reckon that was one."

We laughed! A kind of nervous but genuine laugh. Many people had died that day, and yet still we managed a few seconds of happiness. Five seconds of all that's good about humanity in a world where it was largely absent. Life normally consists of significant moments connected by the everyday experience of making it through the day. During the war, everything seemed to be significant. The fog of time gradually erodes those memories, but that conversation with Lofty will always remain with me. If you had told me then that Lofty and I would remain close friends for the rest of our lives, I don't think it would have surprised me.

Normally, waiting was a kind of psychological torture. Those hours spent sitting in the dark in a German field went by so quickly I didn't notice them go. Jan had to tell me it was time. We each took up our positions with torches and stood silently listening for the distinctive sound of the approaching Lysander. Only minutes later, I heard the distant sound. We raised our torches up to the sky. I hoped beyond hope the pilot would make a successful landing. Then I realised there was so much left unsaid between us and our Polish fiends. Without Krystyna to interpret, it was difficult to really express how we felt.

The aircraft came in on a good line. Lady Luck lifted the thin veil of clouds it held over the moon. The reflection in the pond guided him in perfectly. The pilots of 138 Squadron were the best of the best at what they called moon landings. He descended so slowly I worried he would stall and drop out of the sky. This is why the Lysander was the aircraft of choice. It could approach a landing as slow as 55 mph without stalling. The wheels touched down, and it bounced to a halt well within our signal lights.

The Polish boys manhandled the aircraft around to face the other way. It all happened so quickly; I had no time to consider what to say. We gathered around the Lysander with the pilot telling us to climb aboard immediately. The RAF thought in terms of a three-minute turnaround. That was when it hit me, we were about to leave our friends behind. Almost certainly we would not meet again. After all that we had been through, and Krystyna, it was an intensely emotional moment. I left a tear on each of their cheeks.

"I'm so sorry, Jan. I will never forget you and Krystyna, any of you. Thank you. It has been an honour. I will make sure the right people see the evidence you've given me. Krystyna did not die in vain, Jan. Her spirit will live on forever. You will see the liberation of your county because of people like her. Like all of you."

"Do widzenia! Goodbye my friends. Godspeed," Jan replied.

With Krystyna's satchel around my neck, we climbed into the cramped confines of the rear seat. Being tall, Lofty struggled. Even I struggled, at five feet ten. The Bristol Mercury engine revved to full power, and we bumped and then bounced along the field. As the aircraft gained speed, I worried we would be shaken to pieces. Rapidly the lift from the wings reduced the contact with the field below until suddenly like a bird, we took to the sky. Lofty put his hand over my shoulder. I grasped it in an awkward handshake. We were on our way home but a part of me remained in Germany, on an isolated country road.

Chapter Thirty-Eight
Return To Blighty

Our emotions were the same, Lofty didn't let go of my hand for a couple of minutes. We gained height above the broken clouds, and the moon, now low in the sky, cast sharp shadows across the cockpit. With only the stars to look down on us, our place in the universe felt very fragile. Below those same stars, Jan would be sending the successful extraction signal to Station M. Neither of us felt the slightest elation that we were on our way. My mind raced with mixed emotions. The horrors existing in the death camps, the death and destruction that we left behind - Krystyna.

One thought rose above all others - the anguish I had suppressed successfully for so long. Did Rob make it home? Was he looking at the stars at that same moment? The second I allowed those concerns to enter my mind, my heart skipped a beat. I thought of Krystyna and Jan, how they denied their love. Did that make it any less real? Was I capable of loving Rob? Lack of communication left us completely in the dark. We didn't know if the other operations had succeeded or not, with no idea if any of them made it home. There had been no time to ask our pilot if he knew anything, but now as we levelled off at 21,000 feet I noticed he visibly relaxed.

"Did anyone get back yesterday?" I asked.

"No, I'm afraid not."

"Did you hear any reports of the other operations?"

"Only one other plane took off tonight."

"Do you know why there were only two?"

"No, but one was called off at the last moment."

Lofty placed his hand on my shoulder. He understood as well as I did what that meant. The Dusseldorf team were making their way home through Holland. That meant one of the three remaining operations failed to get to the extraction point. At best, it implied they were stuck in Germany and couldn't get away. Alternatively, it might be far worse. A prospect like that is so bad, you try to exclude it from your mind. You try to be rational, to remain positive. You command each wave of thoughts to ebb away, but the tide rises above your head, regardless.

The flight in a Lysander was uncomfortable to say the least. They were renowned for the cramped conditions endured by agents. They were also renowned for their outstanding record in Occupied France and Germany. Thousands of flights involving SOE agents were successfully flown in and out of enemy country by the "Moon Squadrons". Incredibly, less than three percent of the Lysanders were lost during pickups, with the loss of six pilots. With all my other fears, it didn't occur to me that we were in any danger at all. With every minute that passed we left danger further behind.

The sunrise from 21,000 feet was spectacular. The eastern sky heralded a new day long before the sun greeted us. At first the distant clouds were the colour of a sad wedding before a pallet of colours gently touched them from below. As we flew over the English countryside, the ghostly light suddenly contained colour. Shafts of light separated the clouds guiding us home. We were unable to look at anything else. A new dawn, a new day, a new beginning. Approaching RAF Tempsford, we descended through some wispy clouds and the patchwork of the English countryside beckoned us home. We landed like a bird returning to the nest. For us, Operation Cormorant was over.

They were so used to returning agents, they understood better than us we needed help to get out of the aeroplane. Our legs seemed set in one position. Half frozen, I struggled to move. Once on the ground, we stretched and groaned, but it was good to feel the grass beneath our feet. We knew where to go and I realised news of one kind or another awaited us. We shook the pilot's hand, and I thanked him. I probably effused more than I should have done, but we owed so much to the skill and bravery of those pilots. We walked toward the reception centre with a nagging dread consuming us.

We were immediately confronted by an RAF coordination officer who should have been pleased to see us return safely. SOE was a tight-knit community, so when disaster struck we all felt it. Tempsford was effectively an SOE station, the officer couldn't hide his grief. I just knew it was Rob!

Unable to ask, I stood motionless, an envelope without a letter.

"You're the last in, I'm afraid," he said, "I'm sorry to tell you one of your teams didn't make it back."

"Which one?" Lofty asked.

"Pinneberg! AK sent the compromised signal, but it was too late to abort the other flights."

It took a moment to digest the news - "compromised" was the worst possible code word. It meant our agents had been captured, and so the entire operation might become compromised. Obviously it hadn't because we were safely home. I remained numb with the cold, unable to move or think. Only then did I hear Lofty say, "It's not Rob!" Rob's operation was Frankenthal. He rushed forward and grabbed me.

"Are you all right, Dotty?"

"Of course, it's just a bit of cramp."

"I suppose you're too weak to find Rob and Jim?"

"No, I can manage."

The moment we opened the door to the inner reception area, there was Rob. Occupied with his debrief, he hadn't noticed we'd landed. He jumped to his feet, his chair falling to the floor with a crash. We met in the middle of the room and melted into one. Our actions were not in strict accord with SOE protocol, but nobody saw fit to intervene. Eventually the coordination officer stood next to us.

"I take it you two know each other?"

"I've never seen this woman before in my life," Rob replied.

Actually, he hadn't! I left that woman behind in Germany. Krystyna had taught me a valuable lesson. Love denied can easily become love denied forever. I held on to Rob, never intending to let him go. The atmosphere in the room changed. Rob and I might have had something to do with that, but so were Lofty and Jim. We hugged each other, torn between grief and celebration. We all realised what captured and interrogated meant. Two of our number had suffered a terrible fate; Phillip and Raymond would not be coming back to us.

The other side of the devil's coin was that our operations had been a success. The coordination officer knew nothing about Dusseldorf, but he confirmed that the three other targets were destroyed. The Pinneberg team were captured trying to get to the extraction point. Operation Cormorant sounded like an incredible success and failure in equal measure. Our adrenaline-fuelled bodies soared to heights where few dare to venture, and then they plummeted to depths few would want to go.

It is the cruelty of war that combatants have to live with the deaths of comrades. If you were to survive the war, you had to somehow detach yourself. You couldn't erase the meaning of the lives lost, but you had to decrease the significance. As hard as it seems, celebration always had to take precedence over commiseration. The realisation that we had succeeded and survived to tell the tale took precedence, whether or not we wanted it to. Our spirits soared like an eagle, albeit one with a damaged wing. We agreed I should telephone Station M, having no doubt Lily and the others would be beside themselves with worry. I dialled the direct number to the communications hut. Susan answered.

"Susan, it's Dotty."

"Oh, thank God! Are you at Tempsford, are you safe?"

"Yes, I'm with Rob, Jim, and Lofty."

"Oh, Dotty, we can breathe again. They've been up all night in Hut 3; you must put them out of their misery. I'll put you through."

"Is that you, Lily?"

"Dotty, you're safe!"

"Of course I'm bloody safe! You didn't think I was going to stay over there, did you?"

"Is Rob all right?"

"Rob's fine. It's bad news about the Pinneberg boys, I wonder what happened?"

"We don't have any information yet, it's terrible news. Did you get away with no problem?"

"I wouldn't say no problem, but let's just say it was a bigger problem for the Germans."

"What about the targets?"

"I've been talking to the others. It sounds like all that extra training paid off. The foundry we had to deal with seemed to be a really old building. It looked like a gust of wind would blow the roof off. You should have seen it, Lily, talk about a gust of wind, the whole bloody thing came down!"

"I know you too well, Dotty, what are you not telling me?"

"No, it went like clockwork."

"Dotty!"

"Don't ask me Lily, not now. Put the kettle on, we're coming home."

oo0oo

The four of us rattled about in the back of the lorry like so many rag dolls, each of us so exhausted, our limbs had a mind of their own. Never had the sight of Middlebourne been so welcome. We climbed out of the back of that lorry like potatoes spilling out of a bag. They were all there to greet us. If only Gran had been there as well, for me they were family. Lily and Fiona ran towards me, arms open. We stood, the three of us, in each other's arms. Tears rolled down Lily's face as always. She laughed with us when Fi and I stood back to look at her.

"I'm sorry, I just can't help it. I've been so worried, Dotty."

Edward hugged me, Patrick kissed me, Rolo didn't know what to do, but he was pleased to see me. They were desperate to be told everything, but most of the day had already gone and we hadn't slept since I couldn't remember. We welcomed a cup of tea in the canteen, but I hardly had the strength to chew a bacon sandwich. They were desperate for answers but they might as well be having a conversation with one of Reg's sheep.

We made our excuses, we really had to sleep. They were too polite to say but Lofty and I had lived in a cellar beneath a pig pen for days on end. The nearest we had come to a bathroom was a bucket. We looked like vagrants and no doubt smelled much worse. I needed a shower like roses need rain. They understood; tomorrow would be another day. The four of us walked towards the accommodation block. With such weary legs, we were too tired to walk straight.

"Thank you for taking care of her, Lofty," Rob said.

"She took care of me, Rob."

"We made a good team, didn't we, Lofty? Did you know Lofty's a bit of a philosopher, Rob?"

"Really?"

"No one would accuse Rob of philosophising," Jim said. "Mind you, he probably saved my life, so that's worth thinking about."

"Seriously, Lofty, thank you. I owe you one."

"Nonsense."

"No, it's not nonsense, it's a big thing." I put my arms around him.

"Looks like you did something right, Lofty," Jim said.

Jim was right; what Lofty told me about myself really got through to me. We had grown close during that operation. The candle he held for me flickered and went out as we parted but a waft of smoke from that candle followed him towards his room. I breathed it in and took it with me. Rob looked at me quizzically; I understood what he wanted to ask, but I also knew he wouldn't ask it.

"No, nothing like that happened. He's just a lovely bloke. I'm not sure I realised before just what a lovely bloke he is. Don't worry, you don't have a rival, but I think I've got a true friend."

"That's good enough for me."

We both showered, thinking about each other. I rubbed, scrubbed, and soaped until my skin was practically raw. Only then did I see the bruises on my body. We walked to Rob's bedroom looking at each other as we went in. He fell into bed with a sigh that filled the room. I slipped my dressing gown off, letting it fall to the floor. Rob held the sheet open, and I melted into his arms. We fell asleep almost immediately. We slept for ten hours; I only woke when the sun shone through a gap in the curtains and Rob kissed me.

"Did we make passionate love last night?" he asked.

"If we did, I missed it," I replied.

"That's a relief, not the kind of thing I'd like to forget."

"What's the time? How long do we have?"

"Long enough!"

Chapter Thirty-Nine
Krystyna's Satchel

We arrived at Hut 3 for our debrief to find everyone waiting for us. They wanted every detail from both operations. I sat listening to Rob's account for the first time. Everything had gone well for them. Rob and Jim described the building, the guards, how they approached and how they left. He didn't elaborate upon the guards, but we realised what "dealt with them" meant. They destroyed all the essential equipment, including the offices where any plans and drawings would have been held. They also destroyed a stock of finished parts.

Typical for Rob, the operation had been flawless. He later confided in me that they had one or two difficult moments. A difficult moment for Rob would be a perilous situation for someone else. Above all, like me and Lofty, they were impressed by the Polish Resistance. Rob sang their praises. Lofty and I told our story in as much detail as possible. Mac made copious notes and constantly asked questions. When it came to light that we had demolished the entire building, Mac raised his eyebrows.

"You weren't supposed to endanger yourself beyond the essential equipment," he said sternly.

"We didn't endanger ourselves, Mac, we endangered the building."

"You know what I mean!" retorted a slightly annoyed Mac. "It took extra time and put you both in additional danger of being discovered."

"We understood exactly what dangers we faced, Mac. They only had two night-watchmen patrolling the place, not German soldiers, just civilians. We took care of them. Inside, they had less than a dozen night workers who kept the furnaces fired up; they were guarded by two SD. We also took care of both of them. Apart from the two night-watchmen, their security turned out to be virtually absent. We assessed our situation carefully. We had no reason to believe we aroused any suspicion, and so we demolished the building. Don't think for a second that we made a spur-of-the-moment decision, Mac. It was the right call!"

"Dotty's right, Mac, we made the right decision," Lofty said.

"What did you do with the night workers?" Mac asked, changing the subject.

"When we left the building, we let them go," replied Lofty.

"They might have derailed the entire operation," said Mac.

"You weren't there, Mac. They were Polish forced labour; no way were we going to kill them. Sorry, but that's how it is."

"You took a risk."

"We did," replied Lofty "If you had seen them, Mac, and worked with the resistance - well, I can tell you, you'd make the same decision."

I told them about our Polish friends, how they took care of us, the risks they took. When I told them about our encounters with the roadblocks, they responded with a sharp intake of breath. I thought better about telling them how I lost control of the situation; I wanted to talk to Mac privately. I did, however, make it clear that Stanislaw saved my life. They began to understand why Lofty and I held them in such high regard. Lofty described our battle with the twelve Wehrmacht soldiers. Except for Mac, none of them had directly faced the enemy. They thought we acted heroically.

"No, that's not how it was. They were fresh recruits, most of them teenagers. Some of them looked about fifteen years old. They were only armed with rifles, and I expect some of them hadn't even fired them before. We lured them into a trap and in the space of fifteen seconds, we slaughtered them. There's nothing else to be said about it."

Rob looked at me and nodded his head. Only the slightest movement, an insignificant gesture to anyone else, no more than a kiss on a baby's forehead. He understood. The mood in the room changed. Despite our casualties, the almost total success of Operation Cormorant had lifted everyone's spirits. We still awaited the debrief from the Dusseldorf boys, but the RAF reported the target destroyed. I didn't doubt that without our casualties, it would have been a party celebration. Rob and Jim were not in a celebratory mood, and neither were we. Lofty and I were about to pour ice cold water over the gathering.

Even more than Lofty, I found myself in a dark place. They all sensed it, but if they imagined they would rise above it, they had another think coming. Lily noticed the leather satchel I carried around my neck; she didn't ask, but she wasn't alone in wondering why it never left my side. When we concluded the debrief, the time had come for me to reveal the contents. My stomach knotted and my heart rate increased at the mere prospect.

It wasn't only the contents of the satchel. It had been Krystyna's mission to get those documents and photographs to England. She entrusted me to complete her mission. I felt obliged to stand up. With my hand on the contents, I looked towards the back of the room. Krystyna stood there smiling at me. I saw her so clearly. Still wearing the face which years of undernourishment had given her, but now free of the burden of life, her smile filled the room.

"I need to show you the contents of this satchel, but first I want to tell you about the woman who gave it to me. Her name was Krystyna. A bit older than me, if you saw her you would say she looked frail. Like her resistance comrades, she was Polish forced labour. You have no idea how the Germans treat the Poles. Those who are not killed or worked to death have no life of their own. Krystyna was the product of five years of German occupation. Every year lived in her face. Most of the workers we saw dared not look up; they only existed - their spirits broken. This did not apply to Krystyna. Her spirit could never be broken. It was as if she alone carried the will of the entire Polish nation. There's a terrible wrong contained in this satchel. Somehow we must right that wrong, for Krystyna."

"What happened to her, Dotty?" Patrick asked.

"She died in front of me with my hand on her heart. She's gone but her spirit will never die. This is her satchel; this is the evidence she gathered. We've all heard the rumours about death camps, how the Nazis want to eliminate the Jews. I didn't doubt that thousands have been killed, but I couldn't believe some of the stories we've heard. This is what Krystyna wanted us to know.

The Nazis haven't killed thousands of Jews, they've killed millions. They continue to kill thousands every day. And they do not confine themselves to the Jews. They kill anyone against whom they are prejudiced. Homosexuals, disabled people, Roma, Poles, Black people, and anyone who is mentally disturbed. This is the evidence of the death camps in Poland."

I opened the satchel and laid out the documents and photographs. Touching them seemed to release something evil. As they looked at the evidence, the evil spread its tendrils throughout the room. Initially they asked questions. The photographs of Auschwitz-Birkenau were inconceivable, impossible, unthinkable. The questions slowly diminished. Each answer met with increasing silence. They were confronted by the single worst crime against humanity the world has ever seen. Gradually, the inconceivable became an awful reality.

Auschwitz, Belzec, Majdanek, Chelmno, Sobibor, and Treblinka. Those names are synonymous with evil, but there is something else. Those names terrify me. The Nazis sank to a level of monstrous barbarity that we can only adequately describe as evil. I like to think that evil is confined to those places, to those people, but it isn't. War has taught me one thing above all else. Evil resides in each of us! We don't close the door to prevent the devil from coming in. We open the door to let it out. There are no sides in the battle between good and evil - only good and evil outcomes.

Life changed for them that day as it had for me. We couldn't undo what had been done; all we might do was to bring justice to those victims. I wasn't even sure it wouldn't happen again. Perhaps we will never see evil on that scale again, but when does it begin? Is it with one death, or a hundred. Perhaps a thousand, or a hundred thousand. I didn't dream that I would ever consider such things, but events had turned my thoughts inwards.

"Are you all right, Dotty?" Lilly asked. "This has affected you badly, hasn't it?"

"It has. I'm not sure I can do this any more."

"Do you mean us here, talking about it?"

"No, I mean working as an agent."

"Get it off your chest, Dot, tell us what you're thinking."

"It's these photographs, it's Krystyna; I suppose it's just the war. It's all getting a bit on top of me. When we drove into the German checkpoint, I did something terrible. I completely lost control, I placed everyone in danger."

"What did you do?" asked Mac.

"I did the opposite of what I've been trained to do. All I could see was the images of the death camps and the man in front of me was a Gestapo officer. I saw red, I didn't warn the others, I acted alone. He intended to search me, and he would find my knife. So I stabbed him! I lost control, I must have stabbed him ten times. The other soldiers would have shot me had it not been for Stanislaw in the car. He acted quickly enough to shoot them before they had time to react. Those shots alerted nearby troops, and we were really lucky to get away with it. I placed everyone's life in danger. But worst of all, they shot Krystyna."

Mac understood and so did Rob and Jim. Lofty had already tried to change my mind, now Rob tried.

"When we rescued you in Caen," he said, "the moment I saw what they'd done to you, my anger took over. I didn't only want to kill them, I wanted to tear them limb from limb. I lost control, Dotty, and you were the one who told me to calm down."

"I did, didn't I?"

"After what we witnessed in Germany, what kind of person would not loathe and despise them? That unfortunate Gestapo officer represented everything that's evil about Hitler's Third Reich. You overreacted because you despise what he represented. The difference is that we have a moral compass to guide us, so in the cold light of day, you regret your action."

They all nodded in unanimous agreement. "Well said, Rob," replied Woody.

I attempted a half smile. "Thanks everyone, you're not a bad lot, do you know that?"

They were all well-intentioned, but I had experienced too much. I don't know which event pushed me over the edge, perhaps they all did. My flashbacks continued, I rarely slept well. I tried to keep it to myself but those panic attacks surfaced every so often. I carried on training with Mac and the boys; the exercise seemed to help. Had another operation come along, I think I would have refused to go. But as the war advanced in Europe, new SOE operations were being scaled back. I was not alone, we all felt it. Station M with the wind in its sails had contributed out of all proportion to its size. With our sheets becalmed, we remained a stately galleon but the Operations Section now sat in the doldrums.

Chapter Forty
Know Your Demons

Rob struggled to understand me, probably because I didn't confide in him. Of all the people in my life, only Lily came close to really knowing me. She watched over me like an old mother hen, kept saying she worried about me. I always believed I should watch out for Lily, not the other way around. One evening as I left Hut 4, I found Lily standing waiting for me. Wearing one of her usual dress suits she looked so confident, so self-assured. A smile greeted me, fresh lipstick and makeup catching the last of the autumn sun. I smiled back, but in my case no lipstick, no makeup, only me in my fatigues.

"We're going down the pub, Dot."

Are we, I didn't know."

"I've just decided. We need to talk, the two of us."

"That sounds ominous! I'll need to wash and change out of these fatigues."

"There's no need. This is the Dotty I need to talk to."

"That sounds even more ominous."

"Come on, just for an hour."

I did as I was told, you kind of did that when the Chief of Staff told you to jump to. We walked together toward the barrier, the late afternoon sun still visible through the trees. When we saw Corporal Harris standing on duty, both of us found we were wearing a smile. He stood with an enormous grin on his face. Brian simply couldn't help himself; we braced ourselves for one of his inevitable cheeky comments.

"What a sight for sore eyes, my two favourite women in the entire world."

"You need to get out more, Brian."

"Well, I keep asking, Dotty."

"No one could accuse you of not being persistent. What would your Sergeant say if he knew you regularly propositioned the Chief of Staff?"

"Firing squad, I expect."

"Now there's a thought," replied Lily.

"Sounds to me that this war hasn't got long to go now. My chances of being put before the firing squad are diminishing by the day. This might be our last New Year's Eve together, Mrs Heywood."

"Do you know what, Corporal, I might actually miss you."

"That sounds suspiciously like an inappropriate comment, Mrs Heywood."

"Good heavens, you may be right, Corporal. I don't know what came over me. Imagine me missing you!"

"I imagine it all the time, Mrs Heywood."

Lily walked right into that one. I often wonder what Brian would have done if either of us had taken him up on one of his many proposals. I imagine if Lily had accepted, it would have scared him to death. She was right about one thing, though. We would indeed miss him after the war. Brian had one of those special personalities, he simply made you feel good. I didn't admit it, but if I hadn't met Rob, well, I just might have taken him up on it.

Lily and I walked on towards The Forge, arm in arm. We caught the attention of several villagers, obviously thinking what an incongruous pair we looked. With my short hair and army fatigues, I could be mistaken for a man, a squaddie. Don't get me wrong, it wasn't intentional, it's just how it was. Lily, on the other hand, could be mistaken for nothing else. Those tailored suits of hers simply exuded style, not to mention expense. Add to that, her great shock of red hair and Lily certainly made an impression. Villagers also knew she was some kind of a big shot at the manor who would be seen occasionally with His Lordship. No wonder we looked like the odd couple!

There were very few people in the pub that evening, we were early. Roger, the barman, greeted us warmly as he always did, pulling us a couple of pints even before I reached the bar. Lily sat straight down, discouraging the usual banter with Roger. As I walked towards the table with our two pints, I had the distinct feeling I was walking into something. Lily can be quite forthright - she calls a spade a spade. When she gets a bee in her bonnet, she doesn't stop to take prisoners. I heard the bees buzzing as I approached.

"What was Brian on about when he mentioned New Year's Eve?" I asked.

"Oh, do you remember the other year when we were all celebrating here? Well, I'd had far too much to drink and when the clock struck twelve, everyone was hugging and kissing one another. I didn't even notice who I was kissing until I found myself in Corporal Harris's arms. He kissed me all right, I mean he *really* kissed me. And me being drunk, I kissed him back."

"I'm amazed you lived that down. I bet Brian had a field day. He's actually kissed the Chief of Staff!"

"Yes, it was a bit embarrassing afterwards. I had to deflate his ego by saying I was so drunk I thought he was someone else!"

"I wonder if that was before or after I kissed him?"

"Between you and me, Dot, I quite enjoyed it. He's a lovely bloke, isn't he."

"What's all this about then, Lily, why all the rush to get me here?"

"It's about you, Dotty, I'm worried about you. Nobody can do or see the things you've endured without being affected by it. I understand that, but you've changed. You always shone a light in my life. I can't sit by and watch that light go out."

"I'm okay, really, I just need a bit of time."

"Nonsense! You might convince your mates in Hut 4, but you can't convince me. We're two branches on the same tree, Dot. The East End taught us to stick together, to take care of each other. Neither of us came into this world with any advantage. And yet look at you, look at what you've achieved. You're nominated for the George Cross, Dotty. That puts you amongst the most remarkable people in the history of this country. I'm not about to let you throw that away."

"That's not how I see myself; there's nothing remarkable about me."

"Really, you think you're not remarkable! Do you remember the first time we met? I stood in our bedroom at Gran's wondering who I would have to share with. Fi's clothes were all neatly folded and put away. On the other side of the room, your clothes lay everywhere, and I thought, oh dear, who is this untidy woman? Then I heard your footsteps coming up the stairs.

I couldn't believe what burst in through the door. It was as if I'd opened the window and allowed a storm to blow into the room. You stood in your farm overalls covered in pig shit with the biggest eyes and the biggest smile I'd ever seen. The first thing you said was, 'Cor blimey, look at you.' You instantly lit up my life and I never want that light to go out."

Lily uses words like I used a knife. Deliberate and well-aimed, she cut me in two. I could defend myself against anyone, except her. Perhaps we are two branches on the same tree, we seem to understand each other without a word passing between us. For my part, I regarded Lily as a role model. Completely unlike any East Ender I'd ever met she showed the world just what an East End girl is capable of. She was my hero. When that same woman described what I brought into her life, she left me feeling exposed and vulnerable.

"I don't want that light to go out either, Lily. I see it too."

"Then fight your demons, Dot, don't let them take it away from us."

"How do I do that?"

"I know all about demons! They live in those dark recesses of your mind waiting for an opportunity to torment you. All they require is a careless word from someone, or the return of a painful memory. One thing is always the same, they live in the dark. They can't exist in the cold light of day. Bring them into the open and they twist reality, they trick and deceive you, they will do anything to return to the dark. Don't let them, Dot, you're a giant compared to them, force them to stare at the sun."

First she cut me in two, then she dissected the pieces. Her piercing eyes penetrated through everything. If ever I wondered what propelled Lily to the top, I need look no further. She's a force of nature, a spirit with no bounds. To feel that spirit is to be lifted and motivated by it. I didn't imagine my darkest thoughts as demons; I saw them as the real me. Lily was so clever, she realised if I saw those thoughts as demons, as the enemy, then I knew exactly how to fight them.

"I have dreams, Lily. I see them time and again."

"Who, who do you see?"

"It's the faces, I look into their eyes. They are alive and then they're not."

"Are these people you have served with, people like Krystyna, or is it everyone?"

"It's everyone. It's the people I've killed. It's Krystyna and Henri. The prisoners I saw killed in Caen Prison."

"I've not heard you mention Henri."

"He was the man who saved me from the sea when we landed in Normandy. It was his wife Renée who, at enormous risk, took care of me that night. Henri was such a brave and courageous man; he was also a lovely man. I went back for him when he was wounded. As I lifted him in my arms, he was hit with a hail of bullets. His head exploded in front of my face."

"Oh my God! Oh, Dotty, no wonder you're traumatised. no one should have to see what you've seen."

"Will they ever go away?"

"No, I don't think such horrors can ever go away. I pray you will control those thoughts rather than them controlling you. You will remember Henri in life, not in death."

"I hope you're right, Lily, I can't bear it. Krystyna is even worse because it's my fault."

"You're wrong! I spoke to Mac about it, and that's not how he sees it. He says you had no option but to kill the Gestapo officer. When he found your knife, Mac is convinced he would have shot you on the spot. Krystyna was killed in the crossfire."

"Maybe, but I'll always have that doubt. I can't forgive myself."

"That is the one thing you must do. You didn't ask to be in that position, you didn't start this war. You're one of the many who have tried to put an end to it. You mustn't blame yourself."

"I always will."

"When we were in Hut 3, you told me something quite profound. You said, 'We don't close the door to prevent the devil from coming in. We open the door to let it out.' I realise what you meant now. You believe evil doesn't only come from monsters like Hitler, it comes from within each of us. You think that because you've been forced to do horrible things, you must be an evil person. That's why you can't forgive yourself, isn't it?"

"Of course. Not everyone is capable of doing what I did. So what does that make me?"

"That makes you the bravest person I have ever known. That's why you're nominated for the George Cross. There's more though, isn't there - you've always had a poor opinion of yourself. What happened to you as a child, Dotty? What is it you will never talk about? Did your father do something to you?"

It seems I could hide nothing from Lily. These are things I didn't admit to myself, and certainly not to anyone else. Even the prospect of thinking about it made my heart race. I had a Mills grenade in my head and Lily pulled the pin. Her eyes widened, and she moved slightly away from me in anticipation of my reaction. If anyone else asked such a question, I would dismiss it out of hand. But when Lily asked it, she already knew the answer. I had never been so exposed in my entire life. Not since my father abused me. To actually admit it required more courage than anyone could imagine.

"He did."

"Can you tell me?"

"No, but you can guess."

"I don't want to guess. I'm so sorry, Dot. This explains a lot. Oh, I'm so sorry."

"Yes, well, it's always been there."

"Are you alright? You look bad! Can I do anything?"

"No, not really. I'm having one of my funny turns. Doc Harrington said I… need to control… my breathing."

"Then slow down, take a deep breath. Now let it out slowly."

Only Rob knew about my funny turns, I didn't want anyone else to know. But now Lily knew everything. A dandelion seed had more control over its destiny than I did. My feelings were obvious to see. I wore embarrassment, guilt, and shame like a bright red coat. Lily looked at me like a mother looks at her sickly child. She didn't see those things; she only saw me in pain. I put my head on her shoulder and sobbed my heart out.

"Tell me you don't feel better for that," she said finally. "A good cry works wonders, doesn't it? I do it all the time."

"It's never worked for me before, but maybe you're right."

"Of course I'm right. You've just exposed your demon to the light. It didn't like it, did it! You can't change those horrors from your past, but it's your past now; you can do with it as you like. Put it behind you, Dot, that's where the past belongs. It will continue to haunt you, but now you know where it belongs."

Lily never ceased to amaze me. It's an uncanny feeling when someone can see through you like a pane of glass. We all possess some little defence mechanisms, little secrets which define us. I lost all of my secrets that day. Lily dissected me into fragments so small, I had nothing left to hide. Nothing that even I knew about. I doubt I could live with the pain of other people knowing what I had told Lily, but with her it was different. Anything between us, remained between us. The limbs of a tree share everything in silence.

"There's just that last thing."

"What's that?"

"The guilt you carry with you. That all comes from this thing with your father, doesn't it?"

Lily seemed to realise that buried in the deepest recesses of my mind another demon resided. A Russian doll with so many layers not even I knew what festered at its heart. At first I didn't understand what she meant. Lily looked at me, her eyes seeing what I was searching for.

"I think it was my fault. I must have encouraged him. I should have done more to stop it."

"Of course it wasn't your fault, don't be ridiculous. You're going back as an adult and asking questions of a child. How could a child possibly understand what was happening? Isn't it bad enough that your father did these things when you were a child; don't let him torment you again as an adult. There's only one guilty person, and it certainly isn't you."

"I haven't thought about it like that."

"Maybe it's time you did. It's not only my life where you shine a light. This must also come between you and Rob. Leave it all in the past where it belongs; we need you back, Dotty."

"That's easy to say."

"I know. After what you've been through, it's going to take a long time. But all journeys start with a single step. Even one step gives you room to see what lies ahead, as well as what you leave behind."

"I always said you were the cleverest person I know."

"And you're the bravest person I know. So between us we can work this out."

We drank some more beer and our hour in the pub became two hours.

Everything Lily said had been correct. Somehow she understood me better than I did myself. Her indomitable spirit helped to build Station M; you could feel it in every room. Now I felt it personally, it gave me the confidence to believe. I trusted her completely; if Lily said I could put the past behind me, then I knew it to be true. The battle lying ahead of me was to be one of the hardest I ever fought. But that evening in the pub, I glimpsed the possibility.

"Tell me, Lily. How come you can understand me so well, and yet you still cling to your impossible dream about Edward?"

"Maybe it's not impossible."

"You must know his future is preordained. The Ninth Earl can't marry a woman from the East End, even if he wanted to. Why do you torment yourself so?"

"I can do nothing else, I love him, Dot. I can't imagine a life without him. The thing is, he loves me too, I know he does. He can never show it, he will never say it, but he can't hide it, not from me. We belong together. Fi says we're like two halves of the same person."

"I know you love him, and I'm sure you're right about Edward, he says as much every time he looks at you. But do you realise how bad it's going to be if it doesn't go as you hope it will? You know he's supposed to marry Lady Beatrice."

"You're right, I should think the unthinkable. I should be prepared; I should have a contingency plan. The truth is, Dot, I've done none of those things, I can't! I'm like the gambler at the Monte Carlo roulette wheel who closes her eyes when the wheel spins. Except I haven't just bet the farm, I've bet my life!"

"Well, I can't accuse you of not knowing how reckless you're being."

"You're right, but I'll never lose hope."

"Then neither will I. It's what I hope for as well. It's mad but Fi's right, you are like two halves of the same person."

"What about you and Rob, any more talk of marriage?"

"No, to be honest it's been a bit strained of late."

"I can guess why."

"That's right. I don't understand why he puts up with me."

"I think you do! You owe it to Rob to tell him what you told me."

"I know. Maybe I'll try. Rob's the only one I've ever allowed to get close to me. This relationship thing is all new to me."

"Can you not admit that you secretly love the relationship thing? In fact, can you not admit you love Rob, because you do."

"I'm trying, and I'm going to try harder. Do you think we're right for each other? We've been through so much together. He has his problems like I do. Does that bring us together, or does it keep us apart?"

"Only you two can answer that. My advice comes from a woman who plays the roulette wheel with both her eyes closed, so I would take it with a pinch of salt. But I think you need each other like flowers need rain. Without each other, you would both be the tide without land to rise against. Give each other time, heal yourselves, let it grow."

"Oh, Lily. Will you always be there for me?"

"Always, just like you're there for me. The three of us, you, me, and Fiona."

We drank a toast to ourselves, a toast we have upheld to this day.

Chapter Forty-One
Operation Bernhard

From the day she travelled to Middlebourne in 1941, Lily has influenced my life. That night in the pub was a new beginning for me, and I owe it to Lily. I didn't make a dramatic recovery, far from it, but initial baby steps became strides away from the past. I didn't know where those steps were taking me, but I knew it was the future. With the panic attacks gone, I just took it a day at a time. When I explained some of it to Rob he agreed, we needed time. I didn't have to promise to work on the relationship thing; he understood better than me, I had already set out on that road.

The intelligence section of Station M continued to gather information about the V1 and the V2. It seems Operation Cormorant had been highly successful. The Dusseldorf boys finally arrived back safely via Holland. In contrast to Furth, they described their target factory as being extremely well guarded. Their decision not to sabotage but to "light up" proved to be the right one. The RAF destroyed the facility, as well as some surrounding factories. There was a price to pay, however. Two RAF crews were lost.

The number of V2's falling on Britain, and to a lesser extent on Belgium and France, declined steadily. Without our operation, they were destined to increase. The boys in Hut 3 estimated that we probably saved the lives of many thousands of people. For Lofty and me, the memories would remain bitter, but it didn't prevent us from sharing the sense of pride that became all-pervasive at Station M. The Operations Section remained on alert. What we were being alert for, we didn't know. And so we entered a strange phase of the war. As the Allies fought their way across Europe and finally into Germany itself, we just remained on alert.

The final chapter of my wartime involvement proved to be the most unexpected. The only predictable thing is that it started with a phone call from Lily. She had been away for a couple of days, and it all remained very hush-hush. That suddenly changed when Edward rushed into Hut 4 asking for me. He appeared quite agitated; I had to drop what I was doing and follow him to his office. With no explanation, I felt it must be a reprimand in front of the headmaster.

"Sit down, Dotty."

"Have I done something wrong, Edward?"

"Of course not, Lily needs you."

"Where is she? I'll go immediately."

"No, let me explain."

What he told me was a story so unlikely it had to be true. It seems the Germans, even at that late stage of the war, were determined to debase the British currency. The Germans called their plan "Operation Bernhard". It all started in 1942 as a creation of the *Sicherheitsdienst,* the SS intelligence agency. The forgeries were really good; they even produced a similar rag paper to the British notes. It seemed, from what our intelligence gathered, that there were internal frictions within the SD because they shut the unit down. They later revived it, but rather than the SD producing the forgeries, prisoners were selected from various concentration camps. Presumably they were all known forgers, and they sent them on to Sachsenhausen concentration camp.

We knew little about the camp inmates or their methods of production, but the results were extremely good. The forgeries continued to improve although there were problems duplicating the rag paper precisely. Bank of England experts could tell them apart by using ultraviolet light. But by 1943, even that problem had been overcome, and a larger printing press allowed four notes to be printed from each sheet of paper.

The Germans initially intended to use the currency to finance their intelligence operations. Our own latest intelligence showed that production had now been dramatically increased. It seemed that the German plan had gone back to its original intention of debasing our British currency. MI6 had agents on the ground trying to get information about the

German operation but it proved to be extremely difficult; Sachsenhausen concentration camp is just north of Berlin.

They spent many months developing a contact within the camp, only for that contact to be lost. However, the latest information indicated that production of British five-pound notes had been stepped up to unprecedented levels. Large quantities were being packed into crates and being transported. Another piece of information from a source with access to Berlin Tempelhof Airport told us of a warehouse within the airport perimeter receiving and storing sealed crates. The source believed those sealed crates come from Sachsenhausen concentration camp.

My head spun with detail, but there was more. MI6 also had a report from the Norwegian Resistance. They reported suspicious activity in and around Harstad Airport. Security had been stepped up, and troop numbers were increased. Our last piece of information came from Ultra intercepts. A very sharp analyst at Bletchley Park found a pattern with some recent transmissions. He noticed an Enigma-coded message from Narvik port authority. It amounted to a routine German security check. The sharp-eyed analyst recognised it as an Enigma message. There had never been one before from Narvik. The other factor is that an Enigma machine indicates a military presence.

Suspicions alerted, the analyst checked to see if he could find any other coded radio traffic mentioning Narvik. It seems there had been coded communication with both Harstad Airport and the railway depot, both of which are in Narvik. They initially saw none of this as a priority because the messages referred to what we might interpret as normal activity.

However, the latest intercepts from Narvik port authority were particularly interesting. A message from Berlin asked about sea-time. In response, the reply referred to five days sea-time to London for a "*Massengutfrachter*". That had been translated as a bulk carrier. The latest intercepts confirmed the analyst's suspicion, each message coming under the code word heading of *"Untergraben"* or subvert.

It seems that Lily and Edward had been summoned before the Prime Minister, no less. They attended a meeting in the Cabinet War Rooms. Sir David Petrie the head of MI5 somehow knew Lily had managed a shipping agency and because of her high clearance level, she was nominated to the position of merchant shipping advisor to the War Cabinet. Edward talked so rapidly I had trouble keeping up, but suddenly the reason for Lily's involvement became clear. Intelligence reports hinted at the forged five-pound notes coming to London on a ship from Narvik.

This would be very unusual as there were no ships registered to come from Narvik to London because Narvik was in German occupied Norway. Now I understood; they wanted to understand how the Germans might smuggle the forgeries from Narvik into Britain via the shipping system. And who better to ask than someone who had worked in the shipping industry for many years! Edward finally stopped to draw breath.

"You understand this is designated as most-secret, Dotty."

"Of course. But how can I help Lily? I don't know anything about ships or smuggling."

"Lily has alighted upon the idea of undertaking what she calls background research. I would call it undercover surveillance. She visited a very dubious public house in Dockland. Using her past connections, she has entered into conversation with what she called 'old mates'! I do not understand this concept; she is referring to highly undesirable nefarious individuals who work within the industry."

"You mean dockers?"

"Yes, I believe that is the correct term. Well, Lily has confirmed my initial assessment. The information she obtained indicates that local mobsters are involved. An undesirable called Jack Comer."

"Not Jack 'Spot' Comer! He's a proper hard case."

"Does that equate to undesirable?"

"Yes, Edward, that equates to 'extremely undesirable'."

"As I thought. Lily has arranged to meet this, er, said undesirable, in the same public house which is obviously a place of ill repute."

"Do you know which pub?"

"Yes, it's called The Pelican."

"Oh my God! The Pelican is in the Isle of Dogs."

"Is it a place of ill repute?"

"Edward, this is the worst shit-hole for miles around…sorry!"

"Not at all, I appreciate your frankness."

"Jack Comer is precisely that big word you used…what was it, nefarious. He breaks people's legs, Edward, and probably far worse. If Lily's meeting him, she's in massive trouble. Now I understand."

"Lily needs a bodyguard, she needs you, Dotty."

"Of course, just give me the details."

"Can you guarantee her safety? I have to be sure she will come to no harm."

"You talk as if you're in love with her, Edward."

He smiled, one of his "only you can get away with saying that" looks. Which, of course, is how I got away with it! We had an understanding, we both loved Lily. In a way, I kind of loved him as well, and as unlikely as it seemed, he had a soft spot for me.

"Don't worry, Edward, you can rest assured if Jack Comer wants to get to Lily, he has to go through me first."

"And what if there are several of them?"

"In that case, they all have to go through me. Please don't worry, I'll be armed, Edward. I promise you - I will kill them all before they harm Lily. You have my word."

Poor Edward, he remained quite lost for words. The Ninth Earl hugged me, alone in his office, and me without a chaperone! I had never seen him frightened. We were close, and I didn't like seeing it. He had reason to be concerned; Lily had obviously put herself in a very difficult situation. I offered all the reassurance I could. So we had a plan - Lily would telephone me in the office the following day at lunch time. I should prepare to take the afternoon train. We would stay with Lily's parents.

First thing the following morning, I spoke to Mac. I didn't tell him about the fivers, but I told him the rest of it. I wanted a .38 to take with me. He shook his head.

"What I would take is a Ballester-Molina 45 calibre semi-automatic handgun."

"Why not my .38?"

"This doesn't sound like a shoot-out situation. These are hoodlums, not trained soldiers. You might only need to frighten them, and the Ballester-Molina is a big and very noisy gun."

"Good advice, Mac, I'll take it."

Not knowing what to expect, I packed various clothes options in a holdall. I obviously needed to look feminine, in fact I probably needed to look provocative. That's always a good cover as far as men are concerned. Standing alongside Lily, I would also need to look a bit up-market. I needed a jacket to conceal my knife so I included two of those. Both tweeds, one was a red and brown mix and the other a black and white dog tooth check. Plain blouses looked best with the jackets, I had both white and cream. I chose a couple of skirts that were tight around the bum. They didn't do much for my big thighs but I had a shapely backside in those days. I finished it off with some high heels.

I left for Lily's office with my fighting knife under my jacket and the .45 in a handbag. Fiona looked as worried as Edward. I felt relaxed about it. I agreed with Mac, I wouldn't be facing trained soldiers, but they didn't understand that. Just as Edward started to comment on how attractive I was looking, Lily telephoned.

"Has Edward told you everything, Dotty?"

"Yes, I've been fully briefed. What's the plan?"

"We're going to the pub tonight where I previously met some dockers I used to see around the Docks. We need to get them talking. They know something about this man, Jack Comer, I'm sure he's involved."

"You do know who Comer is, don't you?"

"Yes, that's why I need you, Dotty."

"So will you meet me at the station?"

"Yes, I've got an MI5 driver but don't expect much conversation from him."

"I'll be there; bye, Lily."

"Bye, Dot."

"You were interrupted, Edward, you were about to say how nice I look."

"Well, yes indeed, you look very attractive."

"You might say it with a bit more meaning, Edward."

"Actually I'm a little preoccupied with Lily's safety. With both of you."

"I told you, Edward, there's not the slightest thing to worry about. It is important, however, that I look attractive."

"I don't see that this is a concern, Dotty. You look attractive whatever you wear."

"Now that's much more like it!"

The pair of them almost managed to laugh. At least I left Edward and Fi with a smile. As I crossed the Great Hall, Mr Jennings appeared to be waiting for me.

"Might I have a quick word, Miss Archer?"

"Only if it's quick, Mr Jennings, I have a train to catch."

"It's not my place to raise such matters, but His Lordship mentioned something about Mrs Heywood being in danger. Would I be assuming correctly that your trip to London is in some way connected to this?"

"What you mean, Mr Jennings, is that you overheard His Lordship speaking to Mrs Heywood on the telephone, and you're worried about her."

"Actually yes, that sums up the situation rather well, Miss Archer."

"In that case, yes, I am going to be by her side. So there's no need for you to worry."

"Oh good. That puts my mind at rest."

"I'm pleased you have such confidence in me, Mr Jennings."

"My confidence in you is boundless, Miss Archer, and for good reason."

I left him with a spring in my step only to be confronted by William at the door. He was dressed up in his chauffeur's livery.

"Your car awaits, Dotty."

"What, have you been told to take me to the station?"

"Of course, His Lordship was most insistent."

I followed him outside to find the Rolls Royce sitting in front of the Grand Entrance, its two-tone paintwork gleaming in the sunshine. William opened the back door for me and dealt with my holdall. I'd never sat inside a Rolls Royce before. I really felt like Lady Muck. It occurred to me I had entered Lily's new world. The difference, of course, being that Lily inhabited that world seamlessly, while I was the upstart interloper. Thankfully, William didn't ask me to take good care of Lily. I would have liked someone to tell me to take care of myself.

I arrived at Tunbridge Wells West as if I were the Lady of the Manor. William carried my holdall onto the platform. I doubt an SOE agent had ever started an operation in such impressive style. But, as I thought about it, another interesting thing crossed my mind. I wasn't acting as an SOE agent; I had been recruited by MI5! When William placed my holdall on the train, my fellow passengers showed me a reverence I hadn't experienced before. I confess I quite enjoyed it. When we arrived at Charing Cross, I was almost sorry to leave the carriage.

Lily stood outside the station waiting for me. She omitted to tell me she would be dressed as a Customs Officer. Then she told me her name was Hawkins, Mrs Hawkins. The look on her face said it all. Lily was out of her depth, she really needed me for moral support, if nothing else.

"Who's the chap in the car?"

"He's the one I told you about, Collins."

I walked over to the car. "Hello Colin, I'm Dotty."

"No, he's not Colin, he's Collins," Lily said.

"That's not a proper Christian name, why do you call yourself that, then?"

"If you prefer, Miss Archer, you may call me Mr Collins."

"No, don't be daft, what's your name?"

"Collins will be fine," he said.

"Well, all right, bloody silly name if you ask me. So where is this pub, Collins? Where are you taking me?"

"We shall be going to The Pelican public house. A less than salubrious establishment in the Isle of Dogs."

"Yes, I've been there."

I wasn't sure what to make of Collins. Lily described him as just a driver; I thought he was an MI5 agent. We were obviously wasting no time and set off immediately to drive towards Poplar. Having poked a bit of fun at Collins and joked with Lily, the time had come to take the situation seriously. I asked Lily how she wanted to approach the dockers. Her basic idea had merit; she was posing as a bent Customs Officer. Unfortunately, she had no idea how to go about it. I gave her chapter and verse, first how to approach the men, and second how to remain safe. I would control the dockers in all respects. They would be encouraged to drink as much as possible, while Lily asked the questions.

"I am informed, Miss Archer, that you are SOE," Collins said. "May I ask to which level you have been trained?"

"All of it. I finished up at Arisaig with Sykes and Fairbairn."

"Really? That is impressive! Are you carrying any weapons, Miss Archer?" he asked nonchalantly, as if asking about my lipstick!

"Why do you need to know, Collins?"

"I'm charged with watching over Mrs Hawkins. If you are to carry out the same function, I need to be sure how competent and well-equipped you are."

"You don't have a very high opinion of SOE, do you, Collins?"

"Perhaps not, MI5 is a professional organisation. I'm not used to dealing with irregulars."

"We may be irregulars in your view, Collins, but don't make the mistake of thinking we're any less professional."

"For everyone's sake, let's hope you are. I am assuming you are armed, Miss Archer."

"Of course. I have a fighting knife concealed inside my jacket, and a 45 calibre semi-automatic handgun in my handbag.

"That's an extremely noisy handgun," he said.

"Exactly, frightens the shit out of anyone who hears it."

"What is it?"

"Ballester-Molina, one of those South American things."

"Good, a sensible precaution," Collins said. "Organised crime frequents this pub. You should not underestimate the danger. I would remind you that these people are not German soldiers, so you come under civil law here. I suggest you try to avoid discharging your weapon. I shall observe from a distance and will only intervene if it is absolutely necessary."

Collins cautiously parked the car well away from the pub leaving us to walk the remaining distance. Lily looked nervous despite me telling her to smile and look cheerful. I remembered The Pelican; it sat right in the middle of the Isle of Dogs. Never a nice place to go to but it did at least provide the beating heart of Dockland. Now it stood as one of the few buildings to survive the Blitz, in the middle of a landscape of destruction. Lily entered as confidently as she could manage.

The locals would call it a good old-fashioned spit and sawdust pub. I regarded it as nothing of the kind. The Pelican remained an awful dive, it stank of beer and had all the charm and character of a bomb site. Lily knew one man in particular, a docker called Freddy. When she saw him, he beckoned us over.

Chapter Forty-Two

A Drink With The Dockers

They were all dockers, some were rough diamonds, some were just rough. I flashed my eyes and showed them plenty of cleavage. Even before we sat down, they'd taken the bait. I smiled at those who smiled at me and pouted my lips at those who didn't. They lined up to buy us drinks but I needed to take control of that.

"Let me see what they have behind this bar. My friend here is paying, so I might as well enjoy it."

I went to the quiet end of the bar well away from them and beckoned the barman. "A quiet word in your shell-like, barman. Have you heard of a cocktail called a passion-flower?"

"No, I can't say as I have. Not much call for that kind of thing around here."

"It's made with two-thirds lemonade and one third Ribena, and you put it in a fancy glass."

"Don't you mean gin as well?"

"No, that's the point. Now, here's the thing, I don't want to hear any mention about what goes into it, not to anyone. I'm prepared to pay for the gin even though it's not there. Do you understand?"

"I'm not sure I do, but I think we have an arrangement."

"Good. We'll have pints all round and two passion-flowers, please. My friend over there is paying."

The boys didn't expect a woman to be buying them pints. It boosted my favour and gave the impression that Lily had plenty of money to splash about. The moment their glasses were empty, I gestured to the barman for some more. They paid for some and Lily stepped in when they didn't. Our passion-flower cocktails were not questioned. They only saw us drinking glass for glass with them, and seemingly becoming just as drunk as they were. Within an hour, I whispered to Lily.

"Your dockers are ripe for picking."

"I had a nice earner a couple of weeks ago, Freddy," she said. "There were some crates of sugar where the paperwork had got mixed up. You know how easy that can happen. Well, naturally I agreed it had to be a simple mix-up. Provided I got the going rate for one of those crates, well, it was something we might overlook."

"Well done, Lily, you always had a good eye for these things," Freddy replied.

"Yes, I was pleased with that. It would probably surprise you what a crate of sugar fetches these days. You got anything on the go, Freddy?"

"Only small stuff. Between you and me, Lily, there are some big players getting their nose into the Docks these days. You probably know that."

"Yes, Jack Comer's becoming a bit of a problem. Comes to something when a hard-working docker can't get the odd little perk."

"Didn't I tell you, fellas? Lily's all right!"

"Are you boys losing much to Jack?"

"Well, I can't say too much," said Freddy. "You do a bit of work for Jack, don't you Thumper."

"Thumper? How the hell did you get a name like that?" I asked.

"How do you think?" said Freddy.

"Do you do much for Jack, Thumper?" Lily asked.

"I do the occasional little errand, you know, there's sometimes one or two down the Dock I need to have a little word with."

"Any other of Jack's boys here tonight?"

"No, they've all clammed up, something big's going on, if you ask me," said Thumper.

"Well, it's a shame you don't know what it is, I could do with the heads-up. Last thing I want in my job is getting involved with a lot of paperwork. If I was told where, I'd steer well clear."

"You're all right, Lily. Word is it might not be the Docks."

"Thank heavens for that! I only want a quiet life."

Lily orchestrated the conversation brilliantly. She might have looked like a porcelain doll but scratch beneath the surface and the East End girl from Dockland lay just beneath the surface. While she spoke with them, I sat quietly fending off my admirers. I gained several of them; the trick is to tantalise them but keep them at arm's length. One in particular thought this was his day, his hands began wandering. I did my best to control him. Maybe I'd led him on just a little too much. He didn't represent a danger, but I didn't want a docker's filthy hand down my blouse. Lily made the mistake of believing we were in trouble and she decided to put an end to it.

"I tell you what," she said, "we'll see you lot again; tomorrow might be a good night for us."

"You'll probably meet some of Jack's boys tomorrow," Freddy replied.

My admirer had no intention of letting me out of his sight. Convinced that Christmas had arrived, he wanted to open his present. I had to deal with him.

"You don't have much style, do yer?" I said. "Not in front of this lot; what are you thinking? Outside, come on, I'll give you a treat."

We left with the rest of them shouting and jeering. I led him to the side of the pub where we were completely out of sight. I manoeuvred him into the right position so that he faced the wall, then a simple trip with my hand behind his neck and his head hit the wall with a dull thud. He fell to his knees with his head bleeding. Dazed and disorientated, the combination of alcohol and concussion rendered him almost unconscious. I carried him back into the pub with his arm over my shoulder. I told them the silly sod had drunk so much he fell over and banged his head. The unfortunate man became the subject of derision rather than concern. I left them smiling.

Lily stood as if she'd woken up from a sleep walk. She'd scratched deep to find the East End girl she had just played; it left her exhausted. Walking amid the rubble of what was left of the Isle of Dogs felt invigorating compared to The Pelican. Even Dockland air tasted fresh after the beer and fags. Content that we were not being followed, we made our way to the meeting place with Collins.

"May I say you handled that situation admirably, Miss Archer, extremely professional."

"I'm glad you approve, Collins."

"Now, the thing is, did you get any information, or is that man suffering a concussion for no reason?"

"Not for nothing, no. I think we have a significant piece of information," Lily said. "The feeling among the dockers is that something big is happening, but it may not be in the Docks."

"Not in the Docks!"

"I just heard an echo, Lily," I said.

"It's interesting, isn't it, Collins," Lily said. "Perhaps you need to ask the powers-that-be how confident they are with their intelligence."

"This is indeed an interesting development," he said. "If not the Docks, then why is it known to the dockers?"

"I've already thought about that, Collins," Lily replied. "If it was something being parachuted into the wilds of Kent, then why on earth would the dockers have wind of it. I suspect your intel may be right about it coming by ship, but perhaps you're wrong about the London Docks and the cargo. Maybe it's being unloaded somewhere else, and somehow one or several of the London dockers are involved."

"That sounds like a sensible hypothesis, Mrs Hawkins."

"That's a good word, Collins, I must make a note of that," I replied.

"Is there any way you can follow up on this?" he asked.

"We could go back to the pub tomorrow when they said some of Jack Comer's gang will be there."

"I take my hat off to you ladies; you've done remarkably well. It was well worth that unfortunate man's concussion."

"I thought so, Collins," I said. "Not bad for a pair of irregulars!"

We set off towards Stockwell and Lily's parents. At least we had a comfortable bed for the night.

"I think we should involve the boys in Hut 3," Lily whispered.

"Why not, we have some of the best brains in Britain at our disposal. Why not use them."

Collins stopped at a telephone box so that Lily could speak to Edward. When she returned, we discussed our plans for the next day. Her original plan had been to go around the various shipping agents near the Docks under the pretence of checking their paperwork. Disguised as a Customs Officer, she wouldn't draw too much attention, and her experience completed the picture. The possibility of finding documents relating to the hypothesised iron ore from Narvik had always been a long shot. Having already visited most of them, Lily intended to see the last handful the next morning.

Collins dropped us off and even watched us until Pam answered the door. What a gentleman! They were so pleased to see us. I regarded Lily's mum and dad as family and they seemed to treat me the same. I loved it because it gave me another example of what people called a nice family. They smiled at my wide-eyed appreciation of it all. Jack welcomed me with open arms.

A warm hug from a father-figure provided me with another new experience. A hug from my father was neither warm nor inviting, but how could they know that? We sat at a table sharing a meal together. How should they know I didn't experience that as a child? I'd picked up leftovers with my fingers; I scavenged like a rat. And like a rat, I hid in the crevices when the cat appeared.

We had a brief but lovely evening with them. I really enjoyed being a part of it. They asked questions, most of which we couldn't answer. It only compounded their curiosity when the next morning Lily appeared wearing her Customs uniform. Pam and Jack didn't know what to make of it.

"I understand you can't tell us about it," Jack said, "but I want the pair of you to promise to be careful."

"Don't you worry, Jack, I'll take care of Lily."

"Who's going to take care of you, then?"

"You don't need to worry about me, Jack; the Government has spent ages training me to take care of myself."

Lily gave me one of her looks. Jack noticed it and seemed to understand the implication. I had said too much. He smiled at me. When Collins arrived, we said our goodbyes to Pam and Jack and set off once again. Lily went in to each of the remaining agents while I sat with Collins. He didn't try to disguise his apparent contempt for us irregulars. Once or twice, he entered into conversation before thinking twice about it. He obviously felt we were not made of the right stuff. I made a wild guess that MI5 contained no one like me!

A man in his late thirties, he wore a cheap suit, and a rather crumpled fedora hat. He actually had a pleasant face when he smiled, which wasn't very often. His gold-rimmed reading glasses were either a source of comfort or embarrassment to him, I couldn't be sure which. He would put them on and off to read, and then fiddle with them in his pocket.

"I suppose you think I look like a bank clerk with my reading glasses on?"

"Collins, you look like a bank clerk without them."

Lily came back from the last of her calls looking perplexed. "This doesn't seem right to me, Collins," she said. "It's possible it might be a shipping agent from somewhere else, but shipowners tend to use agents local to the dock. I haven't picked up even a hint of anything suspicious. If it's possible, I'd like to go back to St James' Street and discuss the whole thing again."

"I'm afraid you can't just demand a top-level meeting, Mrs Hawkins."

"I thought you regarded this as an extremely grave matter of national security. At a meeting in the Cabinet War Rooms, the Prime Minister himself was fully behind it."

"You attended a meeting with the Prime Minister?"

"Yes, I did."

"I didn't realise you were so well connected, Mrs Hawkins."

"What have they told you about me, Collins?"

"They only informed me you were SOE, and therefore an irregular."

"Did they tell you I have considerable experience as a shipping agent?"

"Yes, that's all I've been told."

"We're all on the same side, Collins, this departmental mistrust is absurd. I think you need to telephone them and tell them we're coming in for a high-level meeting. I expect you'll find them cooperative."

I smiled to myself as I listened to their exchange. One moment Collins regarded us as something akin to contemptible, the next moment Lily had him eating out of the palm of her hand. It didn't surprise me but I expect Collins wondered what happened to him. He meekly pottered off to the nearest telephone box. It also came as no surprise when he returned saying MI5 had agreed to a top-level meeting. Only Collins looked baffled.

We drove to St James' Street, to a completely nondescript building with a "To Let" sign outside. Now it was my turn to appear baffled. We entered an empty room and then walked through another door to be met by a receptionist who prompted us to continue through. I found myself in a large room devoid of any embellishments, looking at a line of terribly important looking men sitting behind a long desk. Needless to say I had no idea who they were. I soon found out they were the combined heads of MI5 and MI6, Sir Stuart Menzies, and Sir David Petrie. They sat with another three high-ranking men. I noticed Collins had vanished. Lily asked why he wasn't there.

"I would assume he doesn't have high enough clearance," replied Petrie.

"This is rather silly, Sir David," Lily said, "Collins knows everything about our activities."

"Yes, of course," he said. "Someone fetch Collins back here."

Collins appeared looking completely overwhelmed by all the top brass. As he entered the room, the poor man seemed to diminish with each stride. He stood awkwardly fiddling with his glasses. I had the advantage of not knowing who they were or I might have reacted the same. Then it occurred to me, if Collins didn't have high enough clearance - why was I there?

"Gentlemen, this is my colleague, Miss Dorothy Archer," Lily said.

"We know all about you, Miss Archer, it is a pleasure to meet you," said Menzies who introduced himself.

I was taken aback. "You say you know all about me, sir, that sounds rather ominous."

"I am sufficiently well informed, Miss Archer, to know that you have been put forward by Lord Middlebourne for the George Cross, and with the highest possible recommendation. It is an honour to meet you."

They each shook my hand; I didn't know what to say. Collins appeared equally dumbstruck.

Menzies continued. "I spoke with Lord Middlebourne this morning. He was insistent that you should be told everything, Mrs Heywood. Having discussed this matter with him, we agree."

"Good," she said. "I've failed to uncover anything even slightly suspicious among the shipping agents. I know these people; I understand exactly how they work and I am confident that there isn't an iron ore shipment coming into London during the next two weeks. So the question is - how reliable is your information?"

"This is always the question, Mrs Heywood. There continue to be Enigma coded messages being sent from German military headquarters at Narvik, to and from the airport, and the railway. They are all connected by the code name, *untergraben*. It looks increasingly likely that they have flown the forgeries from Berlin to Narvik. What the connection is with the railway, we are only speculating. Our analysts confirmed your idea, Mrs Heywood, that the cargo is most likely to be iron ore."

"I'm afraid iron ore is now looking rather unlikely," Lily said. "If we're sure the vessel is a bulk carrier, then it would be sensible to consider alternatives."

They obviously knew the forged five-pound notes were coming our way but their intelligence remained inconclusive. Everything pointed towards the port of Narvik. Only then did I fully appreciate the possible significance of that snippet of information we had gleaned the night before.

"It might be hearsay, but the feeling among some dockers is that something big is happening," Lily said. "The important information is that whatever it is, it may not be happening inside the London docks. It also sounds likely that Jack Comer is involved."

"That would make sense," said Petrie. "Comer has control of a lot of the race tracks, the ideal place to distribute the counterfeit money."

"We're going back to the same pub tonight," she said. "We're told some of Comer's gang will be there. I am also assuming there must be a German agent involved. I can't imagine Comer having direct contact with Germany."

"Yes, I agree, he is already under surveillance," Petrie said. "We have been very successful in rounding up and turning some German agents with our "Operation Double Cross" but I agree, there must be one we have missed. This is not without danger, Mrs Heywood. You had better go with them, Collins, but keep yourself separate."

"Yes, sir," was all Collins said.

"Thank you for doing this, Mrs Heywood, and you, Miss Archer," said Menzies. "My gut feeling is that we are on the right track. I would ask you to take great care this evening, Mrs Heywood, but you could not be in more capable hands."

Petrie shook my hand and handed me a card. "Have you considered what you might do after the war, Miss Archer?"

"No, not really, sir."

"You are one of SOE's most outstanding agents, Miss Archer. I think it would be a terrible waste if you did not continue to serve your country. Would you consider a career in MI5?"

"I really don't know, sir. I've no idea what would be involved."

"Please think about it. Perhaps at the appropriate time, you might arrange to see me again and we could discuss it."

I left with my head buzzing. We walked back to the car in complete silence.

"It seems I owe both of you ladies an apology," said Collins.

"What have you done?" I queried.

"I assumed they had given me a job with a couple of amateur irregulars. The way the top brass received you - well, that's not the case, is it? I simply didn't know who I was dealing with; you must think I'm a complete fool."

Needless to say I milked the situation for all it was worth. Collins took it all in good heart. Having driven all the way back to Poplar from St James' Street, we finally parked some distance from The Pelican. We sat discussing our plan. Lily and I would go in early, probably before the dockers arrived. Collins would follow us about an hour later. He would sit at the bar and remain inconspicuous. I thought he would be good at that.

"I would like you both to be careful. If it gets at all unpleasant, just leave. That would be much better than using your firearm, Miss Archer."

"For goodness' sake, call me Dotty, like everyone else."

"I didn't like to presume. It's Raymond, friends call me Ray."

"You've got friends?" I replied.

"Not many!"

As we opened the door to the pub, the rank smell of stale beer greeted us. As did the inevitable Guinness Pelican poster where the bird's bill is full of bottles, and another poster for Bisto Gravy. I've been in some dumps in my time but the Pelican took the biscuit. We sat at the largest table in anticipation of the dockers joining us. Above us a bare light bulb hung from the ceiling. Beneath us the uneven floorboards harboured a hundred years of dried beer. Fortunately, the same barman stood behind the bar. When he said, "Same again ladies?" he did so with a large if greedy smile. When Lily asked if I wanted any food I looked at her as if she'd lost her mind.

Chapter Forty-Three
An Evening With Jack Comer

One by one the dockers came in and sat with us. One of them had a nasty bruise on his forehead. He remained content to say very little. Next, Ray came in and sat at the bar. He didn't look at us once. It all started well enough; they seemed to accept us East End girls without question. The atmosphere changed abruptly when some new arrivals appeared. First of all, four henchmen came in wearing long dark overcoats and black hats. They were followed by a much smarter man wearing a suit and tie beneath his tan coloured overcoat. He didn't lift his hat and show his face until he stood in front of us. It was Jack 'Spot' Comer.

He said nothing but conveyed a sinister message to the unfortunate man sitting next to Lily. Without hesitation, the man vacated his seat and Comer sat in his place. Another of his gorillas sat on the other side of her. Lily looked extremely uncomfortable. I sat opposite them with one of them next to me. Jack was in his thirties then and clearly enjoyed his position as the self-proclaimed king of the East End. His power over people lay solely in his use of violence, intimidation being the currency he traded in. I watched him look around the table. Anyone who didn't look submissive would have incurred his displeasure.

"Freddy tells me you work for the Customs, Lily, is that right?"

"Yes, that's right, Jack."

"Freddy says you're a good girl, you know which side your bread's buttered."

"I don't understand what you mean, Jack."

"He says you were married to one of his mates; says he's known you a lot of years."

"Yes, we go back quite a few years."

"He says you can be trusted, but how do I know if that's true?"

"You don't need to know, so I shouldn't worry."

"What if I needed to know, Lily? What if I needed something you could do for me?"

"I'm not sure I understand what you mean, Jack."

"Would you be interested in knowing what kind of thing you could do for me?"

"That depends; if I like the sound of it, maybe."

"I could use a tame Customs Officer; could that be you, Lily?"

"It might be, depends what's in it for me."

"Do you get any say in where you're assigned?"

"In theory no, but in practice yes. I can usually wangle myself into where I'd like to be. I assume you'd like me to turn a blind eye, Jack. Perhaps you might like me to give you a nod about some interesting consignments. Is that the kind of thing you've got in mind?"

"That's right, Lily. All you need to do is look the other way, easy money."

"How much easy money?"

"Depends, could be as much as a 'monkey'."

"For five hundred quid, Jack, I can't see a bloody thing."

Everyone laughed. Lily spoke with a broad East End accent; she completely convinced me. I don't know how she did it. I sat in amazement.

"Freddy said you were all right. What about this friend of yours, what's your name, luv?"

"You can call me Lorraine; friends call me Lolly."

"Can I now? Do you come with a reference, like Lily here?"

"No, you take me as you find me, Jack."

"If I need to come looking for you, darlin', I'll find you all right."

"So Lily's got a blind eye and I've got a deaf ear?"

"That's right, is that going to be a problem?"

"What did you say? I'm deaf!"

"You're a bit too clever for my liking."

Amazing how the big tough Jack Comer felt threatened by the likes of me, but I had shown dissent. He made an imperceptible movement with his finger and the gorilla to my right took to his feet. His big hands reached out and grabbed me by the lapels. As he pulled me up, I raised my knee into his groin. I doubt anyone else saw what happened. The man groaned and bent double, whereupon I pushed him back in his seat. I noticed Ray looking extremely agitated, Lily looking horrified. I stood with one hand inside my jacket and the other close to my handbag. If I didn't see it coming, one good punch from men like that could put me down. If the situation escalated, I wasn't about to risk anything like that happening. That meant it might be fatal for one of them.

"You need to teach your gorilla some manners, Jack."

Initially Comer looked furious. But I didn't look down, I just looked straight at him. His eyes turned to narrow slits as he frowned. Had I been a man, there would have been bloodshed. Nobody challenged Comer, certainly not a man, but he didn't know how to deal with me. In his twisted world of violence, he felt a grudging respect. Slowly the eyes widened and the corner of his mouth lifted.

"If you want me to do you the odd little favour, Jack," Lily said, "upsetting my friend is not the way to go about it."

"Do you trust her, Lily?" he asked.

"Of course I bloody do; she's got me out of quite a few scrapes, she takes care of me."

"How do I contact you, then? Where do you live?" he asked.

"I was in Stepney, but I'm just moving to a place in East Ham. I won't have a phone, but if there's a monkey in it for me, I'll damn well get one. In the meantime, you can always leave a message here at The Pelican."

"Good girl, if you get a phone, give the number to Freddy or Thumper."

"I will, Jack. Have you got anything for me now?"

"No, not right now."

"Oh, that's a shame. Times a bit lean on the river, are they, Jack?"

"You've got some nerve, like this friend of yours, I admire that. As it happens, I do have something on the go, and the beauty of it is that it doesn't involve Customs."

"No Customs, ah, that's convenient. How do you arrange that on the river, then?"

"You don't need to know that Lily; your opportunity will come."

"You be sure and ask for me, Jack, next time you've got a job on the river."

"I will, Lily."

I have no idea how Lily did it. She appeared calm, but beneath the surface I knew she was terrified. It took a lot of courage to overcome her fear like that. I gave her a reassuring smile. I thought we were doing rather well but Lily had obviously had enough. She looked at her watch and announced that we had to leave. The moment she did, I realised it had been a mistake. I blamed myself, I should have seen it before. She continued to wear the watch Edward gave her for Christmas. Decidedly not the kind of watch a Customs Officer would wear.

"That's a very expensive watch, Lily, what's a girl like you doing with a Patek Philippe?"

"What do you mean, a girl like me? That's a bit of an insult, Jack. It didn't fall off the back of a lorry if that's what you're thinking. It didn't get as far as the lorry!"

There was laughter around the table but it didn't distract Comer. He took what he wanted in life. Now he wanted Lily's watch.

"I'm very attached to it, Jack, you can take your eyes off it."

"You're a piece of work, you are, Lily," he said.

He nodded to the gorilla sitting on the other side of her. My heart sank, what a stupid way for us to lose control of the situation. The man grabbed Lily's arm intending to remove the watch. I couldn't allow that to happen, it was a present from Edward. I hurried around the table.

"It's not polite to take a lady's watch," I said. "I would leave it if I were you."

He ignored me with a cynical look and violently pulled Lily's arm towards him. I instantly hit him in the throat with an open hand and he crumpled back into his chair gasping. Such a blow can kill someone, he was lucky to be gasping! The other men stood up, intent upon retribution. I hesitated to draw my gun conscious of what Ray had told me, but it looked like the only way we would leave there in one piece. I thought a single shot in the air would probably solve the problem. Mac was right, the .45 made a lot of noise. As I reached into my handbag, to my profound amazement, Lily intervened.

"I told you, Jack, my friend Lolly takes good care of me! I can't afford to take chances, I've got a nice little earner going on around the Docks, and I can't risk it being ruined by idiots like this bloke of yours. Now, the reason I'm looking at my expensive watch is because I need to go. But there's no reason for you to be broken-hearted, Jack, I'll be back. Now you know me, and you know how I operate. I can get the job done, Jack. You also realise now that Lolly can take care of me. So the thing is, Jack, if you want what I can offer, then Lolly comes with me."

Once again I had no idea where Lily found that. She was so frightened, she had trouble saying the words, but say them she did. She presented a simple choice to Comer. If he wanted what he imagined she could offer, he had to accept the situation. This was unfamiliar territory for him. Accept a small degree of humiliation and gain the use of Lily. Or give in to his usual response to violence and lose her. He opted for the former.

"You really are a piece of work. Both of you. Where did you learn to do that, Lolly?"

"East Ham, Jack; would you like me to show you another little trick?"

He almost smiled, anything more would have been backing down for him. The dockers sat with wide eyes, while Comer's gorillas were enraged. Backing down did not exist in their limited vocabulary. The man I struck sat holding his throat still struggling to breathe. Their honour depended upon vengeance. With my hand gripping the .45 in my handbag, I remained prepared for whatever happened next.

"Sit down, you idiot," said Comer. "Lily's right, this can be a nice little arrangement."

"Good," Lily replied. "As long as your gorilla doesn't upset my friend again, I think we're going to get on just fine, Jack. I'll see you all in here again soon, then."

I saw Lily edging towards the door. The colour had drained from her face, her eyes were like saucers. Her instinct was to run. Ray sat at the bar, looking extremely tense. I assumed he had a firearm, and so I assumed he had my back. Between us, we had the situation completely under control. I just needed to convince Lily of that. We needed to leave in an orderly fashion so I stood between Lily and the door.

"I'm looking forward to working with you, Jack," I said. "Sorry about your man there, I'll be kinder next time."

"I hope he'll be more polite next time."

"Do you suppose he's bright enough to learn from his experience?"

"You've got more front than Selfridges, you have. Where did you learn to do that?"

"The army! I hoped it might come in useful one day. See you then, fellas."

With my hand on the concealed .45, and with Ray sat close by, I had all the confidence and bravado in the world. The psychology of violence is all about intimidation. I projected an aura of invincibility. They didn't need to understand where my confidence came from; they just needed to realise I had it. I opened the door slowly and allowed Lily to step through. They stood there in their long overcoats like a bunch of emperor penguins huddled together against a storm. Not one of them wanted to step into that storm. I gave Comer a nod as I left.

"Just walk slowly and talk normally," I said. "One of them might follow us."

Lily desperately wanted to run but I doubt she had the breath to do it. She gasped for air as if she had just been saved from drowning. We strolled to the next sideroad where I pulled her by the arm to follow me. We waited out of sight.

"What are we doing?" she asked.

"It's only been two minutes; we wait for another two just to make sure nobody follows us."

"Why? Do you think they will?"

"Probably not, it's just standard precaution."

I half expected Comer to send one of them after us, but he didn't. When I was sure we were safe, we went on to the rendezvous point and waited for Ray. Lily said very little as if recovering from running a marathon. Reliably the car pulled up, and we hurriedly stepped into the back. Lily puffed up her cheeks and let out an enormous breath of air.

"Thank goodness that's over; I'm never going back to that pub again, Collins, that's it!"

"I've really got to hand it to the pair of you," he replied. "You were brilliant."

"Really? I worried he would see through me at any moment."

"No, Ray's right, Lily, you were amazing, especially when he saw your watch. Where on earth did that come from? I had my hand in my handbag."

"I saw you do that, and when you hit that man I was terrified; I was sure you were going to shoot him."

"I was!"

"Well, thank heavens that didn't happen," said Ray, "that would have been a disaster at this stage. So tell me, did you get any information?"

"I think we almost got the Crown Jewels, Collins," Lily said. "Comer admitted he has a job coming up, and he more or less admitted that it was a job on the river. Best of all, he said he didn't need me as a Customs Officer; he didn't need one at all."

"So when you say he more or less admitted it was a job on the river, he didn't actually confirm it was an inbound ship. He also didn't say where or when."

"That's right, but this is the impression I got; didn't you, Dotty?"

"Yes, I would say it's definitely somewhere on the river. So it must be a ship."

We discussed every word that had been said as we drove to Stockwell. We analysed every little nuance looking for clues. By the time we reached Stockwell, the only conclusion we agreed upon was that Lily would not under any circumstances go back to The Pelican. On that, we all agreed.

"I suggest you take us to St James' Street in the morning and they can debrief us," Lily said. "We can catch a train to Tunbridge just as soon as everyone is satisfied."

I looked at Ray, and we exchanged a quick smile. Lily couldn't wait to get the hell out of there! I didn't blame her in the slightest, but what she accomplished that evening was really amazing. Lily went on ahead of me towards her parents' front door. Ray touched my arm, making me turn back.

"That was an education tonight, Dotty. You played them like a violin. Would you have shot that man if it came to it?"

"It wouldn't have come to that, but had he drawn a knife or a gun on me, then yes, I would have shot him. What about you Ray? If it came to it and I was in trouble, would you use your gun?"

"I've never shot anyone before, but I suppose so."

"That's the difference, Ray! While you were thinking about it, I would have shot him!"

"As I say, it's been an education."

"See you in the morning, Ray."

Pam and Jack realised something had been going on but as always with these things we couldn't say a word. Lily did at least say that whatever we had been doing was now over. We would go back to Middlebourne the next day. They were relieved but not half as much as Lily! For all that she is the most accomplished woman I know, Lily would never make a field agent. Our minds were full of the day's events, we thought of little else. It made for a difficult conversation with Pam and Jack. They didn't admit as much, but I had the feeling they understood far more about their daughter's activities than they let on.

The following morning, Ray sat outside, as punctual as ever. I realised by now that families clung to their time together during the war. Parting from Lily was painful for them. The opposite had been true for me, parting from my own family proved to be where joy began. Such a simple everyday experience, should I grieve for its absence or revel in its late arrival? I enjoyed my hug goodbye. They wouldn't understand, why should they?

They welcomed us like returning heroes in St James' Street. It seems our information, as scant as it was, provided one of the few solid clues they had. Sir David Petrie was there, as well as an assortment of other people. We were sitting in front of a row of them. All of them were intelligence officers. They asked searching questions about our conversations in The Pelican. They searched for the last remaining stone, determined to turn it over.

I might have been guilty of thinking about the forged fivers in terms of financial gain. Sir David made it abundantly clear just how seriously they regarded the possibility that our currency might be debased. With the war hopefully nearing its conclusion, the next big battle would be the financial rehabilitation of our economy. Suddenly I saw the bigger picture and the reason for all the effort they were putting into the operation. They had Comer and his henchmen under surveillance. They would have people in the London Docks, as well as a man in The Pelican pub.

They considered the threat from the forgeries to be so serious that RAF Coastal Command was flying reconnaissance missions over the North Sea and the Western Approaches. They had at least two Sunderland's in the air during daylight hours, seven days a week. Bletchley Park remained on high alert for any Ultra intercepts that showed heightened German activity.

Our part in the operation had concluded, but the search continued. With our job done, they each thanked us for our contribution. One moment I was involved in something important, the next I felt as if I had stepped into an empty box. I had the strangest feeling that my war was over! Sir David took me to one side.

"Have you given any consideration to what I said, Miss Archer?"

"No, I'm sorry we've been rather busy, but I will think about it."

"Good. MI5 desperately needs people of your calibre. This war might be nearly over but the next war will soon begin. It will not be fought with ships and aeroplanes; it will be fought with secret intelligence. Your country continues to need you, Miss Archer."

"That's a persuasive argument, Sir David, I'll give it serious consideration."

We left with my head spinning. Ray had been waiting for us to appear. We found him walking alongside us.

"It's been a pleasure to work with you both," he said, shaking our hands. "If all of SOE are like you, well, perhaps you're not a bunch of amateurs after all."

"My, my, Raymond, steady on now, that sounds like a compliment!"

"It does, doesn't it! May I give you both a ride to the station?"

"That would be kind of you, thank you," Lily said.

He drove us to Charing Cross, passing all the reminders of the war that had raged for the past five years. The bigger picture that Sir David planted in my mind expanded to encompass Europe and now Russia. I began to see the war in its long-drawn-out entirety. For the first time, I saw it as something with not only a beginning but eventually there would also be an end. When we arrived at the station, Ray shook our hands once again.

"Goodbye, it has been an unexpected pleasure. Actually, it has been an honour. Good luck to you both."

Without further ado, he stepped back into the car and drove away. We watched as he mingled with the traffic and seamlessly disappeared. It seemed appropriate that an MI5 agent should simply vanish. Lily and I looked at each other. Our adventure had come to an end, or at least we assumed it had. We sat quietly in the train, both secluded in our own thoughts. Sir David Petrie's suggestion that I might join MI5 played on my mind. It was just a suggestion, nothing more, but I found myself returning to the idea. Could this be another of those events that mark one of life's crossroads?

ooOoo

We were greeted at Middlebourne with enormous enthusiasm. I enjoyed my moment in the sun, but I wasn't the hero. What Lily achieved was infinitely more important than my contribution. Her experience of the shipping industry had been invaluable to both MI5 and MI6. What neither of us realised was just how valuable we were about to be. Edward greeted us both with open arms but all the while he didn't conceal his excitement.

"What are you not telling us, Edward?" asked Lily.

"I confess I have been desperate for your return. We have an interesting hypothesis to put before you."

"That's a good word, Edward, hypothesis," I said. "What does it mean?"

"I'm not falling for that any more, Dotty! You know full well what it means. Let's go straight to Hut 3 and we shall disclose all."

Intrigued, we followed Edward, his excitement becoming ever more intoxicating. Whatever it was, he couldn't wait to tell us. As we entered Hut 3, the boys looked as if they each had a present to open. They'd been briefed each day by Edward who passed on all the information Lily had given him. They had no more to go on than we did but I had the distinct feeling they were about to give us a master class in logic.

"Who's going to tell us, then?" asked Lily.

"Would you like to start, Patrick?" said a smiling Edward.

"Well, you see, me Mammy said, 'when you go to buy a hat, you have to try them all on before you find the one that fits, the one that sits just right'."

"So what does your Mammy say about these fivers?" Lily asked.

"She said fivers are the same as hats!"

"Is there anyone here who can tell me what the hell Patrick's Mammy is talking about?" I asked.

"We've put ourselves into the shoes of the Germans," said Corky, "or should I say their hat."

"Don't tell me, we're now looking for hats?" Lily said.

"Well, in a way, yes," replied Edward. "We worked out what the perfect hat is from the German perspective."

"That's right," said Rolo. "We worked out every plausible scenario, from the sublime to the ridiculous. Then we had to wait for you to tell us which one is likely to be correct."

"Have I told you, then?" replied Lily.

"Probably!" said Rolo. "You said Comer didn't have to worry about Customs, and you just confirmed what the Norwegian Resistance says is being loaded at Narvik. If a shipment of iron ore is looking increasingly unlikely, we should look at the other possibilities that we know are being loaded. When we do, it makes one of our scenarios statistically highly probable."

"You've lost me, Rolo."

"Do try to keep up, ladies," teased Patrick.

"What's the best way to avoid a Customs check?" asked Rolo.

"Well, there might be several ways, but all highly risky," Lily replied.

"Precisely," said Edward, "so why risk it when there's a class of consignment that requires no Customs? Answer - a ship leaves one British port destined for another British port - no Customs required."

"What is the one cargo that routinely leaves a British port in a bulk carrier destined for another British port?" asked Corky.

"I can't think, so which one of you 'clever clogs' is going to tell us?" I asked.

"According to Norwegian intelligence," replied Edward, "the magic ingredient was contained in the last list of goods being moved through the rail depot. It's coal!"

"This is how it works," explained Woody. "They load the ship with coal and fake fivers at Narvik. It sets sail at night when the North Sea is blanketed in fog. It steers directly towards Newcastle before heading south along the coast towards the Thames estuary."

"The last part is the best bit," said Rolo. "Your dockers hinted at the job not being in the Docks, and why would it be? The Docks are full of officials and Customs people, not to mention the gangers who would recognise if something didn't look right. A bulk carrier is a big ship and needs to go somewhere away from the glare of the Port of London. It also needs to go to a place where it would be inconspicuous. So why not take the ship to where most bulk carriers go? The obvious place is Beckton Gas Works! It's in Gallions Reach, just west of Barking Creek, and the gasworks are the only thing for miles around. This is the largest gasworks in Europe, bulk carriers full of coal routinely dock there, a lot of them bringing coal from Newcastle."

"It's perfect," Lily said. "You are a clever lot!"

"It's also the perfect time," said Edward, "because there is a thick fog forecast for several days."

"I must telephone Sir David immediately. It's only a best-guess scenario, but it's really compelling."

"We don't *guess*, Lily," retorted an extremely indignant Rolo. "We base our scenario upon statistical probability."

"However, you do it, it's brilliant! I'll tell them."

I would love to have been a fly on the wall when Sir David received that phone call. The belief that SOE were a bunch of amateurs persisted in the security services for much of the war. It had everything to do with interservice rivalry and nothing to do with reality. The contribution that Station M collectively made went far beyond what the intelligence people achieved. The statistical probability that the destination would be Beckton Gas Works proved correct.

At 10:45 am on November the 22nd, a bulk carrier seemingly from Newcastle docked alongside Beckton Gas Works with a cargo of coal. They unloaded five crates of forged five-pound notes into a lorry before being intercepted by MI5. Petrie remained convinced that Jack Comer had been involved, but they didn't find evidence to connect him. There was also no evidence pointing to the suspected German agent who he was sure must have acted as the go-between. In the end, only a handful of people were charged. Those included the Captain and crew of the ship, and four London dockers, one of whom was Freddy.

Chapter Forty-Four
Battle Of The Bulge

If the truth be told, the fake fivers were little more than a diversion for Station M. Not that we didn't enjoy our triumph - Lily dined out on it for years to come. I didn't realise at the time but it marked the end of my active war service. We stood ready as a unit in case another special operation became necessary, but it didn't. Hut 3 continued to track the V2 launches, and they concluded that Operation Cormorant had greatly reduced the Germans' capacity to produce more rockets. The fact that we saved countless lives was a great comfort to us all. Nothing would bring our fallen comrades back, but we tried to console ourselves that they did not die in vain.

The measure of our success had to be set against the carnage that the V1 and V2 continued to rain down on Britain. On the 25th of November 1944 at twenty-six minutes past twelve in the afternoon, we had yet another graphic example of the devastating effect of the V2. One of them fell directly into the Woolworths department store in New Cross. The store had been full of people and the rocket exploded among them with devastating effect. 168 people were caught directly in the blast and a further 123 people were injured. This was the single most deadly V2 attack which took place during the war.

A tram just happened to be passing, and they found all the passengers dead in their seats. Bodies lay everywhere, and they discovered remains far and wide. The store had been especially crowded. It was a Saturday, and Woolworths had obtained a supply of saucepans. It seems almost incomprehensible now that something as mundane as a saucepan would attract a larger crowd of people than usual. So many people died just because they needed a new saucepan.

The British public steadfastly maintained morale but for a war-weary nation, the carnage at New Cross struck a devastating psychological blow. Casualties in Normandy continued to mount while progress remained faltering. With the aid of hindsight, the end of November and beginning of December 1944 proved to be the lowest point. But not knowing that, it simply remained a terrible time. Some of my colleagues were desperate to be doing something; it's difficult for trained agents to be bystanders. Rob and I felt differently; we both left a large part of ourselves in France and Germany.

We were effectively on standby but neither of us was really fit for active duty. I admitted it, but Rob remained in denial. They called it battle fatigue in those days and it often had a name tag attached to it. Other people attached that name, it varied from malingerer to coward. There was no psychotherapy or real understanding of what we now call post-traumatic stress disorder. Only another traumatised person can understand. The consequence was that we had to suffer in silence. Men like Rob didn't even admit it to themselves. I began to think it would never go away.

One single event above all others lifted our spirits during November. Florence gave birth to baby George. We were all reminded that in amongst death new life offers fresh hope. The sight of Gran holding the baby rendered me completely silent. Had anyone spoken to me at that moment, I might have burst into tears. The image of a previous generation holding the future generation in her arms really touched me. Gran would take all of her collective experience of life to the grave with her, while baby George stepped into the future empty-handed.

Every new month comes with expectation attached to it. Baby George entered his first new month without a care in the world. For those of us less innocent, the shortest days of the year reflected our outlook. Johnny still flew regular flights over Occupied France gathering intelligence about the V1 and V2 launches. On the ground, activity now fell largely to F Section, but we also had some of our agents involved in minor roles. Mac didn't once suggest Rob or I should go, and we didn't suggest otherwise. The notion that we were observers of the war rather than participants didn't rest easy with us.

Despite the Allied advance in Europe, our apprehension prevailed because it had long been assumed that the Germans would at some point launch a decisive counterattack. The fear on everyone's mind was that such a counteroffensive might reverse the course of the war. When I realised the boys in Hut 3 were seriously considering that scenario, it sent a chill down my spine. After five long years of war, could we really face even more years?

The long-awaited German counteroffensive began on the 16th of December in the Ardennes Forest. Thirty German divisions, containing 200,000 men and 1000 tanks, launched a ferocious attack. They achieved almost complete surprise. The consequence was that the Germans took the American Forces totally unexpectedly, immediately pushing them back. American losses were huge. The area of land conceded to the German advance formed a defensive line on the map which resembled a gigantic bulge. This became known as the Battle of the Bulge.

Lily and I spent time in Hut 3 every day. They had every aspect of the battle illustrated on an enormous map pinned to the wall. We were as well informed as anyone. Our daily diet of stressful news came as a thin gruel that proved hard to swallow. It only added to the anxiety which seemed to be consuming me. I realised that Rob and I were drifting apart and yet felt powerless to do anything about it. It was against this background that Lily sprung a surprise on me.

"We need to think about Christmas, Dot, it's so close now and we have no plans."

"I can't think about Christmas. Why don't we just forget it?"

"That's what I said, but Edward made a really good point. If we ignore our time-honoured traditions, then what have we been fighting for? Edward says it's tantamount to giving in."

"I hadn't looked at it like that."

"Edward asked me if I would spend Christmas day with them, and I said I couldn't spend Christmas without my family. He understood completely and suggested we all spend Christmas at the manor."

"I'll just stay at home with Gran."

"When I said my family, I meant all of my family - everyone."

"Do you mean literally everyone going to the manor, including Gran?"

"I mean Gran, Mavis, Mildred, Jim, and especially you and Rob. The only family who can't be there will be Fiona. She has to spend Christmas with Johnny's parents."

"Have you thought this through? I can just see the three sisters at the manor! They'll be like fish out of water! And I'm not family."

"Of course you're family! But you're right about the sisters. I said as much to Edward and Lady Caroline. None of them can hear, so conversation is difficult. They won't know what to do, they'll do and say all the wrong things. Everyone will be embarrassed for them and for me. It has all the ingredients for being a complete fiasco!"

"So why even consider it, Lily?"

"Because they are my family and I love them. I think they're wonderful; if other people can't see that, then shame on them."

"This is a big step for Edward as well, isn't it?"

"It is. If he's prepared to accept my family in the full glare of his social circle, then yes, it's an enormous step for him."

What option did I have? When I told Rob, he echoed what I'd said about the sisters, except he meant us. I didn't disagree; what on earth did I have in common with Lords and Ladies? He didn't want to go, and I understood why, but it had become more than just Christmas at the manor. This was about me and Rob. I sensed if we didn't spend that Christmas together, then we would never spend another with each other.

"Please, Rob. This is really important to Lily. I don't want to let her down."

"Well, you can go without me, can't you?"

"No, I couldn't."

"It looks like a choice between me or Lily, then."

"Please don't force me to make a choice like that; it would break my heart."

"Yes, because you would choose Lily."

"No, because I would choose you."

Rob didn't answer, perhaps he was lost for words. We were like two actors trying to perform our part but never quite inhabiting the characters we played. He eventually agreed, but it didn't bode well for Christmas Day. Then Lily told me that Lady Beatrice would be there with her parents, Lord and Lady Stratton. That really threw the cat among the pigeons. Both families assumed Beatrice and Edward would combine their two families in marriage. Lily regarded her as the arch enemy, but there was nothing she could do or say about it. My vision of Christmas was a line of troops entering a minefield, except it was us lot!

Chapter Forty-Five
Christmas 1944

The sense of foreboding I carried into the manor on Christmas Day had been exacerbated by events in the Ardennes. The weather remained freezing, with snow and fog continuing to ground the Allied air power. So much depended upon the weather, but the forecasters were predicting clear skies on Christmas Day, of all days. This would mean we could finally bring our superior Allied air power to bear. The possibility that the Allied counter offensive might begin on Christmas Day was greeted with mixed emotions. We had overwhelming air superiority so, given the right conditions, Christmas Day was likely to be an important turning point in the battle.

Edward greeted Rob and me so warmly, it made quite an impression on both of us. Lily said later that it's because I gave him no option, but that's not really true. I did put my arms around him and plant lipstick on his cheek, but his response was completely genuine. Lord and Lady Stratton arrived moments after us. They were lifelong family friends, which for Edward means their families had known each other for hundreds of years. His show of affection towards me crossed a social divide which would have been unheard of just a couple of years previously. Lord Stratton, in particular, looked on in astonishment.

Rob and I tried to keep a low profile; I reasoned that a fish out of water is best not to draw attention to itself. We chatted with Lily's parents Pam and Jack. Somehow, Lord Stratton latched onto the fact that Jack served in the last war, as indeed he had. Jack served as a sergeant while

His Lordship had been a general. You can imagine the conversation, can't you. Their area of mutual understanding was shall we say, restricted. Jack spoke about the horrendous casualties and the general spoke about the inevitability of those casualties. He hinted at what was considered to be the accepted rate of casualties. My blood boiled at the prospect that any death is acceptable. I obviously should have kept my mouth shut like Rob, but he always had more sense than me.

"I'm sorry, My Lord, I can't agree with you. Let's call it what it is. You're referring to the wholesale slaughter of men, women, and children. In modern industrialised war, such slaughter is inevitable I agree, but that's wholly different from calling it acceptable."

He looked at me seemingly in a state of shock. I wore a lovely red dress that hugged my figure. I might not have a silhouette like Lady Elizabeth, but I thought I made quite an impression. The general obviously thought so as well except, for him, it was the wrong impression.

"Probably best to leave such discussion to those of us who have the experience, my dear," he spoke in the most sanctimonious tone of voice.

Rob appeared alarmed; he might have seen the steam coming out of my ears! I drew a deep breath to prepare for the verbal broadside I was about to unleash. Edward, who'd been standing only yards away, also appeared alarmed. He stepped forward just as I opened my mouth.

"Actually, Douglas," he said, "I feel duty bound to correct you on this issue. Both Miss Archer and Mr Bartlett have served this country with such distinction that I have personally put their names forward for the George Cross."

Lord Stratton wilted like a tulip in the desert. As he turned his eyes away from Edward and towards me, his entire demeanour changed.

"Oh my goodness!" he said. "I've put my foot in it. Please accept my abject apology, Miss Archer. Appearances can be deceptive, and I have allowed myself to be deceived. The George Cross! There is no higher civilian honour. That tells me a lot, Miss Archer. I understand now what your role has been. Ignore my ill-considered comments, Miss Archer, Mr Bartlett; it is an honour to meet you both."

He left me lost for words. Fortunately, Lily stepped forward and said what I was thinking.

"May I say, Lord Stratton, I've seldom seen a tactical retreat carried out with such dignity and aplomb. I congratulate you."

"Thank you, Mrs Heywood. Regrettably the ignominy of defeat can only be erased by retaking the high ground. In this case, I am outgunned by the highest honour this country can award. I have no option but to regroup!"

"I too should apologise, Lord Stratton," I said. "This is not the time for such a discussion."

"Be that as it may, my dear, you have taught me a valuable lesson. The nature of your nomination tells me a great deal. As a civilian award, I believe I can assume what your role has been. Would you be able to tell me anything about the operation?"

"I'm afraid not, I'm sure you understand."

"Miss Archer is quite right, Douglas," said Edward. "I can, however, tell you that the work we have been involved with has changed the course of the war."

"I am delighted to hear it, Edward. I've long since made assumptions about what goes on here at Middlebourne. Perhaps one day you will be able to tell me. In the meantime, I congratulate you; all of you."

From that moment on, attitudes changed dramatically. Jack looked at me knowingly. He realised that what Edward said also applied to Lily. He understood he shouldn't ask questions, but he gave me a proud smile. For Lord Stratton, the fact that we were nominated for the George Cross transformed his opinion of us. The social divide previously sitting between us like a gaping chasm, now no longer existed. He chatted with Rob and me as if we were old friends. The same applied with Jack; they each reminisced about their experiences in the First War. It even came to light that Lady Stratton served as a nurse during the battle of Passchendaele where Jack was wounded. They speculated she might even have tended him.

I observed from a distance as Lily negotiated her way around the social obstacles spread all around her. She rose above it all, as only Lily can. As the evening progressed, Lady Stratton even insisted Lily should call her Cynthia. The three sisters committed all manner of social blunders in their confusion, just as we assumed they would. None of it seemed to matter; they shared 266 years between them. When the other guests made allowances for that, their cumulative experience became a treasure trove that we were privileged to explore. The only problem Lily was unable to overcome was Lady Beatrice. That they were arch rivals as far as Edward was concerned had always been put to one side but this happy state of pretence ended abruptly that evening.

Lily's champion would have seemed unlikely a few months previously, but I noticed how Lily and Elizabeth had come closer together. Elizabeth stepped in just as tensions were becoming embarrassing.

"Bee is concerned, Lily, that you are taking over the household and turning Edward away from her."

"I didn't say it like that, Elizabeth," Beatrice replied, looking embarrassed.

"Maybe not, but that's what you mean, isn't it?" Elizabeth said. "You're both my best friends and I don't want to fall out with either of you."

"That's very diplomatic of you, Elizabeth," Lily said, "and I would rather we didn't fall out over this, Beatrice."

"I'm doing my best, Lily, but this is an intolerable situation."

"You're right, it is," said Elizabeth, "but I don't see malice in either of you. My brother will have to choose one of you, and that is not an enviable position for him either."

I listened with interest, knowing how important that conversation would be for Lily. It obviously had much further to run but Edward returned from a quick visit to his office with what was the first piece of welcome news we had received since the whole counteroffensive began. A high-pressure weather pattern had set in over France. The ground was frozen hard, tank tracks would now bite into it and make progress. Best of all, the high atmospheric pressure meant clear skies for the first time during the battle; Allied aeroplanes could take to the sky. Even for those among us that day who didn't fully understand the situation in the Ardennes, the news that progress in the war had turned back into our favour provided enormous relief.

Christmas 1944 proved to be memorable for many reasons. Rob and I were fish out of water, but we were out of place during the most wonderful occasion. For the first time, Rob and I received recognition for our wartime achievements without grimacing. I will even admit to a moment of pride, which was an unfamiliar experience for me. There I was, an East End 'toe-rag', sitting among Lords and Ladies yet being treated with respect and affection. I realised Edward had a lot to do with that, but it showed me a side of myself I'd never seen before. The news coming from the Ardennes obviously contributed. I left there that night feeling considerably taller.

Chapter Forty-Six
VE-Day

By the end of January, the German counteroffensive had fatally failed in its objective. The Battle of the Bulge had been a hugely significant conflict, marking the last major German counteroffensive. It was the beginning of the end for the Third Reich and remains the bloodiest battle for U.S. forces in World War Two. When Woody gave us the figures, it became one of those sobering moments we greeted with silence. The Americans suffered casualties of 75,000 which included 8,400 killed, 46,000 wounded, and 21,000 missing. German losses were even higher.

We couldn't be certain at the time that the Battle of the Bulge would be the last German counteroffensive, but of course we now know it was. From that moment, the fate of the Third Reich had been sealed. Not that anyone on the ground would have noticed - the war continued for another four bloody months. Events moved apace. The Yalta agreement was signed. The Russians advanced from the east while the Allies advanced from the west. Many German cities like Dresden were completely destroyed. One by one the concentration and death camps were liberated to the absolute horror of the advancing Russian and Allied forces. The V1 and V2 production site at Mittelwerk was captured by the Allies, where yet again unspeakable horrors were discovered.

On the 30th of April 1945, an event took place which, had it been widely known, would have resulted in most of the world rejoicing. Adolf Hitler killed himself; the monster had been vanquished. The all-consuming enormity of the Second World War is impossible to convey. The full extent of human suffering is too vast to comprehend. It's estimated that about seventy-five million people lost their lives. The number of broken and grief-stricken families, wives, husbands, mothers, fathers, brothers, and sisters who were left stranded in its wake is incalculable. The infrastructure, and the historic and cultural heritage of most of Europe lay in ruins.

None of that could be undone, just as the evil endeavours of a lone dictator could not be reversed. The burden of all that had happened crushed us as a nation. You cannot even begin to imagine the collective reaction of a nation when such an aberration comes to an end. Not just the British people, but our great American Allies, the Canadians, and members of the British Empire and Commonwealth. In fact, every free nation on earth became swept up in the greatest outpouring of human emotion the world has ever seen.

For us, it started on May 7th when the BBC announced that the Prime Minister would address the nation at three o'clock the following afternoon. We all knew what that meant, but nevertheless, the people of Great Britain waited to hear Winston Churchill address the nation. Every single person at Station M waited with mixed emotions. For us, Victory in Europe Day marked more than just the end of the war in Europe. For all of those directly involved, the end of the war meant the beginning of peace. After six years of knowing nothing else, peace felt like a step into the unknown.

Lily and Edward were in London; we were all hoping they would return in time for the announcement. She telephoned Fiona in the office to say that they had been caught unawares by the announcement, and they didn't want to risk missing the Prime Minister's address by travelling on the train. They were staying at the Savoy and would return the following day. We were disappointed; I thought a celebration without them would be like a pub with no beer, but I underestimated the pent-up emotion already simmering in Middlebourne.

Without thinking about it, we spontaneously gathered in the Great Hall of the manor. We were all there - the military guard, the household staff, the gardeners, the canteen ladies, and every member of Station M. We represented a microcosm of every gathering in the country. There were no rich or poor, no class structure, not even authority figures; we were all simply people who had survived the war.

Mr Jennings placed the big Drawing Room wireless set in the Great Hall and one by one we gathered around it. The sense of anticipation and occasion built with every minute. I stood looking at Rob, knowing where his thoughts were taking him. At precisely three o'clock, the unmistakable voice of Winston Churchill filled the ears of every single person in the British Isles. He told us that yesterday at 2:41 pm the German High Command had signed the Act of Unconditional Surrender. He continued with much of the technical detail of the surrender. We absorbed and savoured every word in silence. His concluding remarks are burnt into my memory.

"The German war is, therefore, at an end. After years of intense preparation, Germany hurled herself on Poland at the beginning of September, 1939; and, in pursuance of our guarantee to Poland and in agreement with the French Republic, Great Britain, the British Empire and Commonwealth of Nations, declared war upon this foul aggression.

After gallant France had been struck down, we from this Island and from our united Empire, maintained the struggle single-handed for a whole year until we were joined by the military might of Soviet Russia, and later by the overwhelming power and resources of the United States of America. Finally almost the whole world was combined against the evildoers, who are now prostrate before us. Our gratitude to our splendid Allies goes forth from all our hearts in this Island and throughout the British Empire.

We may allow ourselves a brief period of rejoicing; but let us not forget for a moment, the toil and efforts that lie ahead. Japan, with all her treachery and greed, remains unsubdued. The injury she has inflicted on Great Britain, the United States, and other countries, and her detestable cruelties, call for justice and retribution. We must now devote all our strength and resources to the completion of our task, both at home and abroad.

Advance, Britannia! Long live the cause of freedom! God save the King!"

The delay-fuse had run its course. The detonator cap fired and the largest explosion of human emotion in history erupted across the British Isles and in every village, town, and city of the Free World. I didn't expect it to be like that, no one could have imagined the outpouring which followed. Like everyone else, I completely lost it! We cheered, we shouted, we threw our arms in the air one moment and then we threw them around whoever stood close to us. Nearly everyone was in tears. People sobbed in the arms of complete strangers. Like everyone, I felt compelled to hug and kiss everyone in the Great Hall. We must have said things to each other but the cacophony of sound made it impossible to hear yourself think.

Mr Jennings singled me out, and we stood in each other's arms for an age. Neither of us spoke. Brian Harris didn't even use the opportunity to kiss me on the lips; he just stood with his head in my neck. Greg Norton kissed me on the lips, I remember enjoying that. Cheeky young Alfie found me and enjoyed his moment. I searched for Fiona and we finally saw each other through the crowd. We ran into each other's arms and just stood there with the world celebrating around us. Fiona, especially, cried tears of joy. Johnny had flown reconnaissance flights almost up to the end. Poor Fi lived in fear every day he was in the air. She would take months to recover from that.

Celebrations continued for an age but then a kind of national contagion spread to every corner of the country. We all felt the need to share our joy with more people. Mr Jennings had organised drinks in the Hall but with no consultation, we found ourselves leaving the manor and heading towards the village green. Wherever people normally gather, they did so that day. All the village was there. The more people there were, the better. The national contagion drove us to seek out fellow revellers. We were intoxicated with joy and patriotism, and like intoxicated people, we behaved completely irrationally.

Not until well into the evening when our initial fervour subsided, did we consider how to properly celebrate. In places like London, that moment never came, people simply sang and danced their way through London into the night. At Middlebourne, we hastily assembled rows of tables on the green. Food appeared, bottles of beer and spirits appeared. When we mixed the intoxication of alcohol with the euphoria of the day, we ended up with the biggest party of all time. I never experienced anything like it before, and will experience nothing like it again.

The war left a legacy of death and destruction on a scale hitherto unseen. The price we paid for that carnage took the form of a burden so heavy, it required an entire nation to bear it. It took an event of seismic proportions to lift the weight of that burden from our shoulders. That seismic event was VE-Day!

Edward and Lily returned the next day, to see all of Middlebourne continuing to celebrate. They described how they stood in front of Buckingham Palace and saw the Royal Family together with Winston Churchill. Lily said when Mr Churchill stepped onto the balcony, she thought her heart would burst. The reaction from the enormous crowd dwarfed anything that had gone before. The patriotic outpouring from the masses in front of Buckingham Palace was the nation's homage to its greatest ever wartime leader.

VE-Day was an unforgettable experience, but even something as wonderful as that is transitory. We gradually climbed down from the high peaks of euphoria to find ourselves in the same place, but in a different time. Station M had no function in peacetime Britain. Rob and I had no function either. For those who had homes and relationships to return to, like Fiona, it must have been the most wonderful reunion. Some would return to their previous lives and pick up where destiny had so brutally removed them. For those whose loved ones would not return, they were suddenly confronted with a new and empty life. An existence with all its meaning removed.

The entire country entered a state of flux. People everywhere started to think about picking up the pieces, rebuilding their lost and shattered lives. For Rob and me, and for many like us, we had nothing to return to. We only existed in a state of war. We had nothing to rebuild; there were no pieces to pick up. When the inevitable discussion started about how we were going to decommission Station M, I suddenly realised what a frightening place the future had become. Three days after VE-Day, Rob and I sat in the pub looking at each other while the party atmosphere continued around us.

"What are we going to do, Dot?"

"I don't have the faintest idea. They didn't train us for this, did they?"

"I'm going to admit something. Something I've never said before. For the first time in my life, I'm frightened."

"Big tough Rob Bartlett, frightened! What on earth are you frightened about, Rob?"

"I'm frightened I'm about to lose you. The war held us together; what are we without it?"

He completely took my breath away. I should have realised immediately that I stood at another of those crossroads. Rob always wanted commitment and I was never able to give it, but I didn't expect him to confront me with it in such stark terms, and certainly not then. If I could sneak up on my demon, it would never trouble me again. But those shadows from my past always saw me coming, they tormented and played with me. I found myself offering feeble suggestions like, why not just wait and see, and give it time. It even sounded feeble to me as I said it.

"At least you've got Gran you can live with," he said. "I've got to find somewhere to live, and I've got to get back into the building game. In other words, I'll have to start a whole new life. I want you in that life, Dot, but even if you're not going to be a part of it, I still have to do it."

Why is it you so often recognise those important crossroads in life only when it's too late? This was one of those occasions. I continued with my plea for more time, and let's-wait-and-see. What I completely failed to see was that we were running out of time to wait. I walked to the cliff edge, and I stepped off without even looking down. I made the biggest mistake of my life! Rob watched our relationship crash to earth with very little visible emotion. I wanted his reaction to mean we still had time, so I clung to what I wanted to believe.

During the course of the following week, the members of Station M gradually departed. We were all so close, every goodbye brought with it another moment filled with sadness. The first to go was Woody, he returned to his professorship at Oxford and his wife. Rolo went home to his mother but the Government never lost sight of him. He ended up at another top-secret establishment at Cheltenham. Corky returned to Geology - his old post at York University remained open. Patrick and Maggie decided their respective lives were a mess. For an analytical mind like Patrick's, the solution was a no-brainer! They would each walk away from the past and build a new future together. Rob, Lofty, and Jim were the next to leave together.

Lofty's parents ran a small family hardware business in Chelmsford. Lofty had often said he wanted nothing to do with it, but the war gave us all a different perspective. He now saw a future where he hadn't seen one before. Neither Jim nor Rob had a place to call home. They both had to find somewhere to live but with trades to fall back on, they simply wanted to get back to London. Mac drove us all to Tunbridge Wells West Station.

All five of us had been through so much together, we'd become inseparable, united around our common purpose. Remove that purpose, dress us in civvies, and what did we have left? I realised we had lost our identity. We needed time to adjust to each other as people, time we didn't have. Frivolous things were said, such as, we must keep in touch, all the best, send me your new address. I hugged and kissed Jim and Lofty, and only at the last second did we say anything meaningful to each other. They boarded the train leaving me to say goodbye to Rob. It was all terribly awkward with Mac standing on the platform and the boys at the carriage window.

I desperately didn't want him to go. The yawning gap between foresight and hindsight is where all of life's triumphs and disasters lie. Isn't it absurd how you can engineer your own downfall even while you know it's a mistake. Both of us accepted the situation as if it had been cast in stone, when in reality it could have been changed with a word. With seconds to spare, we hastily kissed before Rob had to board the train. We did exactly what I said we should do; we waited to see. What I saw was Rob walking away from me. As the train pulled out of the station, the moment dawned when denial gave way to reality. I realised I had just kissed goodbye to the only proper relationship I'd ever had. I didn't even know where he would be.

I closed my eyes and wanted to scream as the roar of the engine engulfed me in steam. It was only when the train moved out of sight that Mac put his arm around my shoulder. He didn't need to say anything, his expression said it all. What had been obvious to him as a bystander was obvious to me now. Lessons from the past take time to become obvious. It's usually only when we view the past within the context of the future that our past experience comes to bear. Those lessons were there all along if only I had the eyes to see. My future fell apart while I watched the past disappear into the distance. I stood alone, consumed by my own mistakes.

Chapter Forty-Seven
Maggie and Patrick's Wedding

One by one, the personnel of Station M drifted away; Mac and I were the last two to go. I reasoned that we both had the most to lose and the least to gain. For all of us, but especially for Edward and Lily, it proved to be a terribly sad day. We all felt the hand of history on our shoulders. I said goodbye to Hut 4 as if it were an old friend. Poor Lily stood in floods of tears; she also stood at one of life's crossroads. I consoled myself knowing that Fiona, Lily, and I would remain lifelong friends, and Middlebourne would remain my home.

Gran made a good recovery from her stroke. Of course she didn't regain the full use of her left arm, but her speech returned almost to normal. Considering her advanced years, she remained a tower of strength. The house echoed to the sound of four generations as baby George embraced his new world, a world at peace. As for me, it took an awfully long time to put the war behind me. In fact, it never really left me, it remains just a memory away. Maybe that's why I didn't contact Sir David Petrie at MI5. I kept his card in my top drawer; I picked it up on several occasions, I even carried the card as far as the telephone box on one occasion.

I made lots of excuses, one of them being that Reg needed me. Even that didn't last; things changed rapidly after the war. The attitude was that the army of women who worked in the fields and the factories should now give way to the returning men. I eventually found myself a job in Tunbridge Wells as a PE instructor. All the training SOE gave me and the only thing I used in civilian life turned out to be my physical fitness. That may not sound much to you, but I remained part of a nice family, and I had a job. Compared to my life before the war, I'd gone up in the world!

In every respect I had a new life, but not a complete life. How could it be when a large part of me remained in the past? Memories of the war filled my daily existence. I decided that without it, I didn't amount to anything. It would be fair to say I found myself in a dark place. I look back now in disbelief. Why on earth did I not see the reason for that gaping void in my life? I blamed the war, and in a way it was, because for me, the war was Rob! Perhaps I had been so stupid that I didn't even want to admit the truth to myself.

I did nothing to contact Rob; I didn't even know where he lived. When you stand at the bottom of a deep hole and look up, you only see a small patch of sky. I wanted my life to change, but I lost the will to make it happen. Fortunately for me, my friends saw what I didn't. They decided fortune should smile at me, and needless to say, I didn't see it coming!

It all started with some news from Maggie and Patrick. Her divorce came through quicker than anyone expected. Maggie's husband, far from being distraught, had reason to welcome the prospect of a divorce. Much to everyone's delight they parted amicably. All that remained to be settled was the wedding. Patrick's extended family lived in Ireland, while Maggie's family lived in Hampshire. This presented something of a dilemma, because Patrick insisted his Mammy should have the final word on the subject. The marriage ceremony had to be in Ireland! Maggie pointed out that this would inconvenience all of their other family and friends far more than Patrick's Mammy. They then had to contend with different religions and the fact that Maggie was a divorced woman. A church wedding would be out of the question.

The solution of course was obvious! When Maggie telephoned Lily, they settled everything in five minutes. We all felt the same after the war; Middlebourne was such an enormous part of our lives; it remained our spiritual home. The prospect of a Station M reunion lifted everyone's spirits. Edward immediately offered them the Great Hall for their reception. Where else could it be for two of our own. Patrick's family ties to Ireland are strong, but his connection to Middlebourne is even stronger. I was delighted for the happy couple, and I confess the prospect of Station M getting back together really lifted my spirits.

We all became caught up in the excitement. Despite the ceremony being at the registry office in Tunbridge Wells, Maggie wanted things to be done properly, so I had to have another posh frock made the same as Lily and Fiona. Lily and I were the bridesmaids, Fiona was the Matron of Honour. When the big day arrived, I found myself excited at the prospect. This would be a huge step forward for me; I found little to get excited about, standing in that deep hole I dug for myself. I really looked forward to being with the others again, but the more you surround yourself with happy people, the more the contrast with your own life seems to be shoved in your face.

We filled the registry office to capacity; Patrick's Mammy was there if only in spirit. If Maggie had been disappointed not to be married in church, she didn't show it. They left as Mr and Mrs O'Sullivan, and a more radiant bride I couldn't imagine. As we drove back to Middlebourne, I suspect we all shared the same anticipation. The reunion aspect of the day had only just begun. As I walked into the Great Hall, my mouth gaped open, the sight that confronted me took my breath away.

The Hall was filled with tables and chairs. The top table looked resplendent with beautiful floral bouquets of white flowers; the green foliage was made more prominent by the white linen tablecloths. Vases of flowers stood all around the Hall. The Great Hall looked magnificent; the staff had performed wonders. Mr Jennings stood in all his sartorial elegance, positively beaming. The Hall seemed to buzz with excitement.

Mac came with his new lady friend, Amanda, who later became his wife. Woody's wife, Helen, was absolutely charming, while Corky surprised us all when he revealed his incredibly beautiful wife, Beth, many years his junior. Our wartime spirit remained alive and well, it lived in each and every one of us; we didn't have to reignite it. This is where Maggie and Patrick met, and where their romance blossomed. What better place could there possibly be for their reception.

I remained a part of it every second I mixed with people, but the moment I stood on my own, I felt really alone. There is a particular loneliness you feel among a crowd. Did everyone look at me, feeling sorry that I had no one to be with? Of course not, but I couldn't convince myself of that. Everyone had a partner except for Rolo and Elizabeth; I remained the last of us to make the big commitment. Everything served to remind me about Rob and my constant torment.

We would soon take our places at one of the many tables so I wandered off by myself to find my place. I looked down at the place names on my table and saw I had been seated next to Mac. Maggie obviously gave the seating a lot of thought, Mac and I enjoyed a unique relationship. He was my commanding officer, but apart from Rob, he understood me better than any other man I knew. That made us really close. I stood looking for him and his lady friend when I glanced to see who would sit next to me on the other side. I had the shock of my life; only a conscious effort stopped me from gasping out loud. I could not believe the name on the card. When I glanced up at Lily she stood smiling at me, obviously anticipating my reaction. My eyes flashed around the room almost in panic, trying to see if he was there. Then I saw him walking towards me. Dressed in a wonderful suit, it took me a second to recognise such an elegant figure. My heart skipped several beats as our eyes met.

"Rob! This is wonderful. I didn't realise Maggie had invited you."

"I hoped you wouldn't mind."

"Mind, why should I mind?"

"Well, you know. You look fabulous, by the way."

"So do you, Rob. Everyone has kept this very quiet."

Lily, Fiona, and Maggie were each looking at me with very satisfied smiles. Rob and I had obviously been the subject of one of their plans, but they assumed a lot, putting us two together. I always hoped I'd meet Rob again at some point; but I didn't expect my reaction. It appears that my friends understood me better than I understood myself; they knew how I would react. Nothing could have prepared me for meeting Rob again. A part of me had tried to convince myself that our parting was for the best. I didn't need a man in my life; I didn't make that kind of commitment. And yet here I was, feeling as if I were a badly shaken bottle of champagne from which Rob removed the cork.

I didn't see any of this coming, and I certainly didn't expect to feel like that. For the first time in my life, I admitted what had always been obvious. I looked at Rob, knowing he was the only man I had ever loved. We ate, and we drank, and all the while Rob and I didn't stop talking; we only paused for the speeches. I had so much to say, so many questions to ask, but we both consciously avoided asking anything requiring a serious answer. Eventually, I plucked up the courage to ask the question to which I dreaded the answer.

"Can I ask, Rob, are you with anyone?"

"You mean is there another woman in my life?"

"Yes, but you don't have to answer that. I mean, it's none of my business."

"Would you be upset if I answered yes?"

I hesitated. Pride made me evade the question. "It's not for me to comment, is it?"

We sat in silence for a moment, the first silence there had been between us. This is when I recognised I stood in that yawning gap between foresight and hindsight. I realised in an instant - this was how I lost Rob in the first place. All manner of obstacles stood in my way, and they all existed inside my head. Being with Rob again opened that door. It was like when you recognise a smiling face in a passing cloud that didn't exist the moment before. You look, but it isn't there, then the next moment it appears with perfect clarity. That's when you realise it must have been there all along, if only you had the eyes to see it.

Second chances in life rarely come along. I made what for me was an extraordinary decision. It's no small thing confronting your greatest fear. For the first time in my life, I realised I needed to reach out. It didn't matter that I would expose my innermost frailty; I had to open my heart without fear of the consequences. I did as the SOE trained me. I made a decision and I acted upon it!

"If you have found another relationship, Rob, I wouldn't blame you for a moment, but I would be absolutely heartbroken."

"Well, there is no one else. But you were the one who let me go, remember."

"I know I did, can you forgive me? That was the biggest mistake of my life. I've been so miserable without you, Rob."

"I've been miserable without you. But we can't go back to how it used to be; you have to be prepared to make a commitment, Dot."

"All right, I will! All these months apart, Rob, have been awful. I've done nothing but ask questions of myself. I thought the war came between us, but it wasn't just the war, was it? It was me! My childhood was horrible, I'm going to tell you everything about it. It left me unable to trust anyone ever again. I've never been able to commit to anything because I could trust no one. That's been a terrible fear, Rob, and it never goes away. It's taken my entire life to realise that I can conquer that fear because you've given me something even more powerful. You say I have to make a commitment, well I'm ready. So, how's this for a commitment? I love you Robert Bartlett, I have always loved you, I love you so much, I want to spend the rest of my life with you. I want you to marry me, I want it all."

The expression on Rob's face filled me with a joy I didn't even realise existed. I left myself completely exposed and defenceless, only to become twice as secure. We put our arms around each other and kissed passionately in front of everyone. Fiona had obviously been watching us because she rushed over and put her arms around us; Lily quickly followed.

"Does this mean you two are back together?" Fiona asked.

"You both planned this, didn't you?" I replied. "Well, thank you. Yes, we're together and I'm not letting him go!"

The rest of that afternoon seems like a haze to me now. I have never been so happy in my entire life. We laughed and cried; we sang, and we danced. Maggie danced with every man in the room. Except for a dance with Patrick and one with Edward, I didn't leave Rob's side. Had there been a passing cloud, I would have seen it as a smiling face. I looked at Maggie and Patrick; I recognised the spark which united them. Fiona and Johnny were inseparable, their marital bliss was always plain to see, but now I understood. I watched as Lily caught Edward's attention across the hall; they made love to each other with their eyes.

"I've realised something today, Rob. For the first time, I realise love is what I've been afraid of all along. I chose denial rather than risk being hurt by it. I love you, Rob, and it's the most wonderful feeling I have ever known, I'm no longer afraid. Love really does conquer all, doesn't it."

"Is this Dorothy Archer I'm speaking to?"

"It is. I'm sorry, we haven't met before."

"No, I don't believe we have! But hang on a moment, didn't you just ask me to marry you?"

"That's right I did! That's because I'm audacious, and I love you."

"That's okay then, because I love you being audacious."

"If you two lovebirds can tear yourself apart for a second," said Lily. "We're preparing a send-off for the bride and groom."

What a day that proved to be. Maggie and Patrick's day could not have been more perfect, and mine certainly was. Those life-changing moments have a habit of sneaking up on you. Sometimes you may not even realise your life has changed until after the event. I didn't see it coming that day, but the moment it did, I realised nothing would ever be the same again. We both shared a past that we carried with us into the future, but I learnt something important that day. You look back at the past from your place in the future. For the first time, I knew where my life was headed, and it was leaving the past behind.

oo0oo

Events moved at pace after the war, it was a time of great social upheaval. Countless thousands died for this bright new future, and thousands of men returned home from Europe wanting a new and better life. But what they found instead was a physically and financially broken country. For vast numbers of people, the bright new future comprised a shattered past and little else. The homeless struggled with the prospect of starting again. Thousands of homes echoed to the silence of lost loved ones.

The war united us with a common purpose; we would suffer any amount of deprivation for the sake of our country. With peace came the opportunity to reflect, people wanted a better life, a break from the old order. The great fear was that we would descend into the mass unemployment of the 1930s. Mr Churchill's wartime coalition, for all that it had steered us through the war, was viewed as the old order. When Mr Churchill was defeated in the 1945 general election, we were amazed. The nation voted for a Labour government led by Mr Clement Attlee, who promised the great social reform that the people demanded.

Rob and I were the lucky ones, we had nothing to lose and everything to gain. The bright new future was ours to build upon. We remained undecided about so many things but every possibility offered us hope and excitement. Gran didn't approve of Rob and I sharing a room before we were properly married; I had to persuade her to turn a blind eye to our temporary arrangement. It was during that period when fate once again intervened. Another of those life-changing events dropped through the letterbox. Gran picked up two envelopes with a quizzical expression on her face.

I thought her expression reflected the fact that one envelope was addressed to Rob. She handed us both our envelopes as we sat at the breakfast table. We looked at each other and then at Gran. The envelopes were clearly marked "House of Commons"! Rob and I smiled at each other, we both made the same assumption, this had to be the notification of our awards.

"What is it?" asked Gran.

"I think we can guess what this is, Gran. We were not allowed to say before, but Rob and I have both been nominated for an award. This is probably it."

"What kind of award?" asked Gran.

"Well, it's quite a big award actually, Gran," replied Rob.

"It's the George Cross, Gran."

"But that's the highest civilian honour there is! What did you do to receive such an honour?"

"I'm still not sure what we are allowed to say, but it's something we did on D-Day."

"I knew what you were doing must be important," she said.

Gran became quite emotional, saying how proud she was and how we would meet the King. We all got a bit carried away for a moment. I opened my envelope to find it signed by Winston Churchill. Just seeing his name took my breath away. The letter only said that we were invited to attend his offices in the Houses of Parliament. The letter politely asked if the date suggested would be convenient. Rob's letter was exactly the same.

"Well, of course it's convenient!" exclaimed Rob.

"*Bloody hell!* Sorry Gran! We have to meet Winston *bloody* Churchill."

"I think we can overlook that word, Dotty," replied Gran.

We replied with a letter confirming the date the following week. Every day I grew more nervous. I'm not sure if it was fear or excitement. Rob pretended to take it all in his stride but he was as excited as me. There I was, a "toe-rag" from the East End and I was going to meet Mr Winston Churchill. I couldn't believe it, and they were going to give me an award as well. When we boarded the train for Euston, my heart was already racing. When the taxi pulled up right outside the Houses of Parliament, I needed to take a deep breath.

The Palace of Westminster had been badly damaged during the Blitz. Building work now became an everyday occurrence. Edward forewarned us and told us where to go. We showed our letters to the appropriate person who raised an eyebrow when he read them. He directed us to a seat in what Edward called the Members' Lobby. An enormous space enveloped us; despite the building work we sat in a space designed to impress. The Members' Lobby made the Grand Hall at Middlebourne Manor look like a scout hut! The grandeur of that magnificent building simply filled me with pride. It had been bombed fourteen times by Hitler's Luftwaffe, but here it stood as a symbol of British defiance. I could have sat there for hours just looking at all the comings and goings but a smartly dressed civil servant requested we follow him.

Having walked along numerous corridors we finally stood outside a door. I looked at my future husband like a rabbit caught in the headlamps. The man knocked tentatively on the door. When I heard his distinctive voice answer, I nearly fainted. The civil servant opened the door and there behind a desk, sat Mr Churchill. He stood up holding a cigar in one hand and walked around the desk towards us. He was so much shorter than I imagined, no more than five feet six inches tall. We both towered over him but we looked up at a giant. He offered us his hand. I literally felt my knees knocking.

"Miss Archer and Mr Bartlett, it is my great pleasure to meet you both. Your reputation goes before you."

"It's an honour, sir," Rob answered, as I remained unable to speak.

"Please sit down, both of you. I requested this private audience with you because it concerns your nomination for the George Cross. You have the right to an explanation, an explanation that only I can give you. I had the honour to speak to the magnificent people of Station M in 1942. I had to tell them the plain truth, that their undertaking was so secret, all references of their existence had to be erased. I also told them they would receive no recognition, there would be no medals pinned to their chests. However, come the great day of celebration, I assured them that none would stand taller than those who stood before me that day.

I have read the report of your conspicuous gallantry, both before and after D-Day. If the British nation knew of these events, you would rightly be honoured. You would take your place amongst the pantheon of legendary heroes in the hallowed halls of British history. Instead, it falls to me, on behalf of the British Nation, to pay homage to your great valour. I am a poor substitute for the recognition which you so justly deserve, but I deem it a great honour to shake you both by the hand."

"What you have given us, sir, is a far greater honour," replied Rob.

"That is kind of you to say; however, denying you your rightful place in history weighs heavily upon me. The history of war is written by the victors, and your achievements have contributed towards that victory. General Eisenhower commented that the contribution of SOE in Occupied France was like having two extra battalions of troops. We must also remember that the success of Operation Overlord depended upon our elaborate deception which convinced the Nazis that Calais was the focus of our intention. Our Secret Intelligence Services have excelled in every area. Our ability to collect, decipher, and disseminate intelligence is without parallel. It might surprise you to know that nearly 10,000 people contributed towards that effort at Bletchley Park alone.

Without our clandestine forces, we would not be writing the history of this war. Without their ongoing guardianship of these British Isles, we would lay ourselves open to the next aggressor who seeks to prevail over us. The war is over, there is a new map of Europe, but within those geopolitical changes lie the seeds of the next war. It will come not from Central Europe this time, but from further east. It is, therefore, imperative we maintain and further develop our clandestine forces. We cannot afford to lose the expertise that our Secret Services are built upon."

"Do you seriously think it could all happen again, sir?" asked Rob.

"It is not a question of if, it is a case of when. Wherever the good sense of the people is usurped by the whim of a dictatorial regime, there lies the danger. The seeds of discontent have already been planted in the Soviet Union."

"Are we prepared?" I dared to ask.

"We are dismantling our armed forces as we speak, and our Secret Services are being diminished in size. It is therefore imperative that we retain our collective experience. You are a part of the collective experience to which I refer. The extent of your training, combined with your contribution in the field, has been outstanding. I cannot expose you or your expertise to the scrutiny of history. What you represent is far too important! *You* are too important!

The next conflict will be fought less with guns and more with science. The wars of the future will be waged with new and terrifying technologies. But you must never be in doubt; the lessons of the past will continue to inform the future. Your unique experience of conflict dies with your generation. You know what the next generation can never know. Your country needs you, Miss Archer, Mr Bartlett. Your country asked that question of you in 1939, and now I am asking you that same question again, today."

I looked at Rob, completely unable to speak. We both sat mesmerised in a state akin to shock. In front of us sat a giant of world history. His presence in that room crackled from floor to ceiling as if he generated an enormous static charge with every word he spoke. For all that he struck fear into us, a reassuring kindness sparkled through his eyes. He wasn't just our greatest wartime leader; he was a man of flesh and blood. A visionary who placed the love of his country above all else. In 1935 he was a lone voice when he warned of the gathering storm in Nazi Germany. Now he warned us again that threats continue to exist beyond our borders.

He made me realise that humankind's greatest tragedy is that the wisdom of the ages dies with each generation. Without that wisdom, the next generation is destined to repeat the same complacent mistakes. Rob and I, and people like us, stand as a bridge between the past and the future. We alone understand why it must never happen again. When our country asked us to serve we didn't hesitate, we stepped forward. And now, Winston Churchill asked us to step forward again.

What would *your* answer be?

The Final Word

In book one, "None Stood Taller", Lily recalls her story from the Blitz in 1941 up to and including D-Day. In book two, Lily continues her extraordinary story from D-Day to VE-Day. Dotty's son Charlie is of another generation. His story is told in "Autumn Daffodils – Charlie's Story".

It is my greatest wish that this book, and indeed the series, have enlightened and inspired you as much as they have me. As a self-published author without the marketing reach of a publishing house, the success of these three books has been entirely due to the support of readers. Together the "None Stood Taller" series have fully occupied my life for three years. So please spare two minutes of yours and place a review on my Amazon or Goodreads page. We cannot exist without your support. Share your thoughts and comments with me, either through my website or email me directly. Now it's time for me to move on to another adventure.

Come with me!

https://www.peterturnhamauthor.com
peterturnham.author@gmail.com

Principal Characters

Dorothy Archer (Dotty) later Bartlett - Narrator

Lily Heywood - Dotty's great friend

Fiona Robinson (Fi) later Albright - Dotty's great friend

Edward, Lord Middlebourne - The Ninth Earl of Middlebourne

Caroline, Countess Middlebourne - Edward's mother

Lady Elizabeth - Edward's sister

Jack - Lily's father

Pam - Lily's mother

Jim Smedley - Lily's cousin

Gran (Mrs Margaret Taylor) - Lily's maternal grandmother

Spencer Tracy - Gran's dog

Mavis - Gran's sister, Lily's aunt

Mildred - Gran's sister, Lily's aunt

Reg - Farmer

Ruth - New Land Army girl

John (Johnny) Albright - Wing Commander Albright (Fiona's husband)

Corporal Harris (Brian) - Corporal of the guard

Private Thomson - Private, soldier of the guard

Alfie - Apprentice gardener at the manor

Greg Norton - Estate manager

Mrs Morgan (Elsie) - Middlebourne housekeeper

Jennings (Charles) - Middlebourne butler

Florence - Lady's maid, Lily's great friend

Mary - Housemaid/trainee estate manager/estate manager

William Evans - Footman/chauffeur

Albert Reynolds - Footman (later butler)

Mac - Major McBride, Head of Operations, Station M

Maggie - Photo reconnaissance analyst

Rolo - Boffin

Corky - Boffin

Woody - Boffin

Patrick - Boffin

Susan - Radio operator

Brenda - Canteen lady

Roger - Pub landlord

Rob Bartlett (Goldfinch) - SOE agent/Dotty's husband - Charlie's father

Charlie Bartlett - Dotty's son - Lily's godson

Eliane (Gabrielle) - SOE agent

Marcel (Harry) - SOE agent

Gaston (Joe) - SOE agent

Pierre (Donald) - SOE agent

James Hollingworth - SOE agent

Isabel - SOE agent

Neil - SOE agent

Bertrand/Bertie - SOE agent

Nigel - SOE agent

Phillip - SOE agent

Raymond - SOE agent

Henri - French Resistance

Renée - Wife of Henri

André - French Resistance

Michêl - French Resistance

Albert - French Resistance

Krystyna - Polish Resistance (AK)

Jan - Polish Resistance (AK)

Tomasz - Polish Resistance (AK)

Stanislaw - Polish Resistance (AK)

Collins, Ray - MI5 driver/agent

Freddy - Docker

Thumper - Docker

Lady Stratton (Cynthia) - Friend of Edward's family

Lord Stratton (Douglas) - Friend of Edward's family

Lady Beatrice (Stratton) - Lily's marriage rival

Prominent historical figures

These characters are dramatised to add context to the period portrayed in this book

* **Winston Churchill**. Sir Winston Leonard Spencer-Churchill, KG, OM, CH, TD, DL, FRS, RA. Prime Minister of the United Kingdom 1940-1945, and 1951- 1955. Popularly accepted as Britain's greatest ever leader, and the most inspirational voice of World War Two.

* This book contains Parliamentary information licensed under the Open Parliament Licence v3.0.

Vera Atkins CBE. Recruited by British intelligence in her home country of Romania. A part of the team that evacuated the Polish Enigma codebreakers together with an Enigma machine. Joined SOE in 1941 and quickly became assistant to Colonel Maurice Buckmaster, head of SOE French section. After the war ended, she embarked on a remarkable mission, attempting to account for all the agents who died in her service, succeeding in almost every case.

General Sir Colin McVean Gubbins. KCMG. DSO. MC. Seconded to SOE November 1940, Gubbins became Head of SOE September 1943 when he replaced Sir Charles Hambro. He helped to transform SOE into a highly effective organisation.

Colonel Maurice James Buckmaster, OBE. In September 1941 Major Buckmaster assumed command of F-Section, which recruited agents from among those Frenchmen who had not chosen to directly ally themselves with General Charles de Gaulle. His task was to build an organisation which could carry out sabotage and collect information about the enemy and provide money and equipment for the French resistance.

Buckmaster worked closely with his assistant Vera Atkins, who was also the Section's intelligence officer and a spy mistress. During the war, the F Section handled more than 400 undercover agents, many of whom went missing.

At the end of the war Allied commander General Dwight D. Eisenhower said the section had helped shorten the war by six months. "It was the equivalent of 15 divisions," he said.

Noor Inayat Khan (Madeleine) SOE agent killed in Dachau, 1944.

Odette Sansom (Lise) SOE agent. Later:-Odette Hallowes, survived Ravensbruck, awarded the George Cross.

Sir David Petrie. KCMG, CIE, CVO, CBE, KPM. Director General of MI5 from 1941-1946.

Major General Sir Stewart Graham Menzies. KCMG; DSO; MC: Chief of MI6 1939-1952.

Eric Sykes. Englishman, best known for his work with William Fairburn. Expert in close quarter unarmed combat, recruited by SOE to train its agents. Developed the infamous Fairburn-Sykes fighting knife with Fairburn.

William Fairburn. British Royal Marine and policeman. Taught martial arts to the Shanghai police force. Later trained SOE agents in unarmed combat and pistol shooting techniques.

Jack 'Spot' Comer. Son of Polish immigrants, born in Whitechapel. Notorious East End gangster.

Harold Heyns. Head of the Gestapo, Caen.

Constance Babington Smith. Served with the Central Interpretation Unit (CIU) at RAF Medmenham, Buckinghamshire, reaching the rank of Flight Officer.

Working on the interpretation of aerial reconnaissance photographs, Constance was credited with the discovery of the V1 at Peenemunde, Germany. In 1942, Babington Smith was Mentioned in Dispatches for her work and she was awarded the MBE in 1945. She was portrayed in the 1965 film 'Operation Crossbow' by Sylvia Sims.

Printed in Poland
by Amazon Fulfillment
Poland Sp. z o.o., Wrocław
24 January 2023

e6a01416-c46a-44fa-b75c-02e2e2462cbdR01